"I love her. I hate her. Ever feel that way about some-one?" Catherine asked.

"She's your mother," Diana said, firmly. "You're a grown woman, almost. She's your past, not your future. You'll be gone from here, soon enough. It only seems like a big deal right now, but it won't once you're on your own."

Catherine held her breath. She closed her eyes tightly.

"On my own . . . " Catherine whispered. Then, in a clear voice, she said, "Have you ever wanted to kill someone?"

Diana didn't answer. She felt a chill creep up her spine.

"I mean *really* kill someone?"

"That's mad, Catherine."

"Being held prisoner is mad. Is wanting to escape as mad as all that?"

"You're angry and upset," Diana said, trying to calm herself every bit as much as she was trying to calm Catherine.

Catherine was silent for a long time. But then, just as Diana was about to fall asleep, she heard Catherine whisper, "It would be so easy."

*St. Martin's Paperbacks Titles
by Brian Rieselman*

WHERE DARKNESS SLEEPS
DREAM GIRL

DREAM GIRL

BRIAN RIESELMAN

St. Martin's Paperbacks

DREAM GIRL

Copyright © 1997 by Brian Rieselman.

ISBN: 0-312-96091-3

Printed in the United States of America

St. Martin's Paperbacks edition/January 1997

10 9 8 7 6 5 4 3 2 1

To John Peyton Cooke

and

To Dana Edwin Isaacson

Chapter One

On the rare occasions when a new person was admitted to the Albion Clinic for Sleep Disorders, the handful of other patients in residence were all but locked away in their upstairs rooms, like mad relations.

It wasn't as if brute force were used against the patients; the shelter was too genteel for anything of the kind, and the wealthy patients much too used to being pampered.

Patients were instead gently, politely (maybe just a bit firmly) *shooed* away from the white marble-plated foyer and leaded glass entryway, and banished to rooms with fireplaces and jet-powered baths and other fancy modern amenities, like the gothic-inspired skylights that almost always drew an appreciative swoon from a new arrival.

When new patients came to the clinic, they had reasons for not wanting to be seen. A state of bug-eyed insomnia (as in the case of Mrs. Bennett Kearney), nattering anxiety (poor, manic Miss Lynndale), or free-floating dread (Richmond Garfield to a tee) didn't put one at his social best. Sometimes the symptoms of a patient's sleep disorder were manifested in nasty nervous facial tics, or even (in extreme cases) a kind of palsy in which one's face freezes in a toothy, gaping grimace, an unmovable rictus. (Annette and Ginger Montgomery, twin sisters of a certain age, had both come down with this frightful condition simultaneously.)

A few cases arrived mute, borderline catatonic.

Even the less extreme cases—patients with whom absolutely nothing was wrong, those classic monied hypochondriacs who only pretended to have bad dreams because what they really craved was sympathy, drama, and a doctor's care—demanded and received utmost privacy.

Privacy (some might say secrecy) was the prime reason why most of these patients came so far north, so deep into these dark woodlands of Blackburn County. These sufferers wanted to be alone, and they wanted the comforts of isolation. Or maybe they'd already burned out on all of the legitimate headshrinker spas and health-haunts of the world and needed a new luxury retreat in which to cool their brains for a while, a different head trip.

The Albion Clinic was a place where they had to listen to your dreams, because you were paying for the privilege.

One longtime live-in patient, Catherine Price, was the exception to all the arcane rules and expectations that had attached themselves to the clinic in its first decade of existence, not only because the clinic had been built expressly for her by her mother, Theda Price, the illustrious state representative, and not only because Catherine was seventeen.

Rules were for other people, not for Catherine Price. Catherine Price was not like other people.

Catherine peered out her open bedroom door and listened. She looked up and down the empty hallway. Her long blond hair, parted in the center, fell past her shoulders and over a soft cream-color sweater she favored. Her baggy faded blue jeans had a way of flowing perfectly over her long slim legs and curving slender hips. Her large eyes, the irises of which reminded at least one of her boyfriends of crushed blue bottle glass glowing in a white furnace, gleamed in the dim hallway light of a low-burning lamp.

She produced a small smile, eyes askance. Her sidelong glances always put those who knew her on alert. It was as if she were suddenly aware of some blinding, mischievous truth no one else had quite yet perceived, and she had to look away from it.

She knew much about the arrival of the new patient—even more than she was expected to know on this unseasonably cold October night, when Diana Adams was brought here from Chicago. It was as though the air itself buzzed with a current of expectation and mischievous, elusive truths. This was no ordinary patient, this new girl. Catherine sensed Diana's presence in the house. She could not have heard, in these upper-eves suites and through the solid floors and walls, the commotion that heralded the new patient's arrival. This was something she could only *feel inside* and it was making her giddy, as a good fright often did to her.

Catherine crept out of the third-floor room and walked on light socked feet down the gray-carpeted hallway. Overhead was the glass skylight dome, one of the elegant features of the Albion, which her mother had insisted upon when she oversaw the construction of this building ten years ago. The high concave glass, ribbed with raw steel, was beaded with raindrops that glistened beneath the glowing white storm clouds of a late October night. Rows of tall potted plants lined the walls, moist tropic-green leaves fanning upward like jungle thicket. The light here was soft and golden, muted by the watery shadows of pooling rain on the skylight, shadows that played over the carpet and walls. The shadows of the tropic leaves, too, slithered along the floor and walls in this eerie shifting light, so that the hallway at the top of the stairs seemed weirdly alive with movement, yet as silent as a cave ceiling gorged with restless, ranging black snakes.

The arrival of Diana Adams, age seventeen, on a cold October night, when winds howled out of the north and the lashing rain slicked the highways with black ice, was not to be missed—not when Catherine could hide in the shadows on the stairs and take it all in unseen.

Down she went, two stories, until she could crouch at the balustrade and take in her first frightening glimpse of the strange young woman, seated on one of the imported Edwardian slipper chairs in the foyer, every inch of her drenched with cold rain.

Diana stared blankly ahead. The lids of her dark eyes were droopy, probably from a sedative. Her hands were folded together in her lap, and Catherine saw that Diana's wrists were bound with a fuzzy blue band. Diana wore a drab dark coat that fell almost to her ankles. A flap of the coat had fallen partway open. She wore black jeans, but, oddly, no shirt whatsoever; she was naked above the waist and the line of a pale white breast was clearly visible. A puddle of rain had pooled at her feet on the white marble floor, and her leather shoes were stained black with rain. Her dark hair, flattened to her skull, gleamed in the light of the crystal chandelier. It looked as if someone had recently hacked most of it off, violently, for it hung in lopsided hanks with blunt, angled ends.

Hovering high above on the shadowy stairway, Catherine's heart pounded. She strained to listen to the conversation of the harried adults, who stood with their backs to Diana. Catherine was nothing if not an expert eavesdropper.

"... nearly went off the goddamn road ..." the man was saying.

He was tall. Diana's father. No, her *step*father; Catherine remembered the crucial distinction. Wore a long London Fog-type coat, spotted with rain. His immaculate executive haircut was beaded with raindrops that glistened under the chandelier. His wet brow was furrowed angrily.

"Fuckin' Blackburn County," he said, turning from his stepdaughter. "October, and the roads are sheets of ice. Shoulda known if I came up here I'd get this kind of welcome."

"Surely you can't blame us for the rain, sir, or for the unexpected drop in the temperature," Dr. Sterling said, a trace of annoyance in his voice, despite his smile and a nervous, fake laugh. "We can work a lot of wonders here, but we can't have the weather made to order."

Dr. Konrad Sterling was the director of the Albion Clinic, and his easygoing understanding of the capricious nature of Wisconsin weather might have made him sound less controlling and less of a perfectionist than he in fact was. Catherine knew better. A large man, Sterling wore a dark jacket and tie, and stood with his hand on the back of Diana's chair. He was a sixty-year-old physician and his hair was more salt than pepper, bushy and combed at the moment, but with a tendency to wildness.

Catherine exhaled through her nose, looking askance. The begging tone in Sterling's false-friendly voice had always annoyed her, and she'd known him since she was seven. She knew that behind his rather whiny diplomacy was an ego that matched inch for inch the grandeur of this very house, both epics of style and gentility that masked their true purpose. Hidden just beyond the rose-scented air and the collected antiques and the dramatic floor-to-ceiling windows was an ultra-modern facility, a sleek paean to the outer limits of scientific inquiry. Whatever their external appearances, the house and the man were one, a precise arrow aimed at a dark summit.

Sterling was as tall as this virile businessman, but somehow managed to shrink himself.

"Get me a towel," he snapped at his assistant, Harriet Evans, fifty-ish and matronly. She pushed her glasses back up her nose and walked briskly from the room, heels clacking on the marble.

The stepfather bent down to write a check on the top of a glass table. He ripped the check from the book and stuffed it into Sterling's hand. Catherine caught a trace of Sterling's burnt tobacco scent, a spiciness that seemed to intensify and sharpen whenever the scientist was made to hold his tongue.

Sterling stood looking at the check. His eyes rose doglike. "But, Mr. Adams, I thought that we had discussed—"

"I've got the other part right here," Adams said, and pulled from his coat pocket a brown envelope. He withdrew from the perspiration-stained envelope a thick wad of bills, the most cash Catherine had ever seen. The bills were folded over and held together with a red rubber band. "It's all there," Adams said.

Still unseen, Catherine nodded with the self-assurance of a seasoned con artist. The check established a paper trail for the IRS, the cops, any other snoop who might come looking, tomorrow or a hundred years down the road. But cash was strictly anonymous. She'd learned that much, and so much more, from the people who had raised her.

"Thank you, Mr. Adams," Sterling said, accepting the money with a shit-eating smile Catherine had seen a thousand times before. "Diana will be well cared for, I assure—"

"Shut up," Adams said. He wasn't looking at Sterling. He was staring at his stepdaughter. His mouth was closed, and his jaw twitched. She must have looked to her stepfather like a veritable zombie, because that's what she looked like to Catherine. Harriet Evans returned, holding out a thick white folded towel. But she stopped, heels silent, when she saw Mr. Adams's stern, sad eyes fixed on the young woman. Harriet held the soft towel to her breast, and heaved a silent trembling breath.

"Diana," Adams said softly. "Diana, can you hear me?"

"Really, Mr. Adams," Sterling began. "With the sedative, it is doubtful she can—"

"You can make her sleep, can't you?" Adams said, still looking at Diana, who seemed to be looking right through him.

"Well, of course, but it is her *dreams* that we—"

"She hasn't slept since the day the boy fell from the school rooftop," Adams said softly. "Fell to his death, you understand."

"Yes, a terrible trauma," Sterling said.

"But she's always had . . . bad dreams," Adams said. "Ever since I came around."

Sterling, in his flattering way, in that vile and condescending tone of voice with its occasional traces of a German accent, started to say, "Mr. Adams, it is not for you to blame your*self* that the girl suffers nightmares and—"

"And hallucinations," Adams whispered. "Voices . . ."

Adams bent close to Diana's face.

"Yes," Sterling said. "*Hallucinations.*"

"Good-bye, Diana," Adams said to his stepdaughter.

Diana's head trembled. A small light came suddenly into her dark, liquid eyes, as if they were focussing on something for the first time. Her chin rose up slightly, and her lips pursed together. Her eyebrows slashed downward in an expression of anguish.

Through her lips she spat out a tiny forceful spray of saliva at her stepfather, covering his face with a misting of droplets as white as sea foam. Then she gasped and closed her eyes.

He blinked and jerked backwards.

"Goddamn you," he hissed at her, wiping his forearm over his face.

"Diana!" Sterling cried. Adams was headed toward the door, and was soon out of it, running down the drive toward his car, a dark sedan. "Mr. Adams!"

The headlights were still on, white beams swarming with rain. Adams had left the car running.

Sterling stood in the entryway, his glasses beading up with raindrops. The cool smell of rain filled the foyer, up to where Catherine sat riveted in the shadows of the stairway, watching Diana, with whom she would soon be sharing a room here at the Albion Clinic.

Catherine closed her eyes, reading what she could out of that poor girl's frazzled mind. But she found herself scooping up only the bad reception of a sedative-deadened wave. A soggy wet, gray channel.

Impossible.

"Mr. Adams!" Sterling cried through the open door. "We will help Diana! We will help her!" Catherine heard the car door slam and the sound of tires on wet gravel.

Harriet was drying Diana's hair gently with the white towel when Sterling closed the door. Catherine watched, her hand around one of the curving white posts of the balustrade, relying on merely physical senses. For now. Diana's face was calm again, blank, as if unseeing and uncomprehending. And mysterious as the face of an old, old statue.

The face of newborn winter, of cold, insolent rain and strings of stark, dark days, appeared like a deepening stain upon old Blackburn County, making October—a normally temperate and even placid month in Wisconsin—a cold hell.

A damp chill permeated every domicile inhabited by northern creatures of the land and air, every fox den and sparrow's nest, and every room in the houses and rectories and farmsteads of Blackburn County.

Work went undone, sleepers preferring to remain in the warmth of their beds. School children woke stubbornly and were late for their school buses; bus drivers were more cross and harried than usual; divorces were filed, but judges and lawyers failed to show up in court on time, and prisoners in the county jail were made to wait extra long for unsatisfactory breakfasts.

Even the dead were left unburied as the freshly dug graves were left to drain. No one in Blackburn County wanted to put a clean coffin into mud and see it covered with a foot of murky rainwater. Everything and every deed was left to wait.

Every molecule, every atom, seemed to say . . . *sleep*.

One cold, late morning, in deepest woods, in a strange building and an unfamiliar bed, a sleeper stirred.

She didn't know what time it was, what day it was, or even where she was; only that she was coming awake after a long sleep.

Diana Adams groaned as she tried to blink her eyes into focus. She pulled the pillow over her head with arms weak from sleep, and let her head fall back again into the warmth and comfort of the pillow. Her head throbbed from the residue of a strong sedative.

She blinked her eyes. Weak daylight coming through the skylight above her bed cast the shadows of thin, high, bare tree branches over the white sheets, across her puffy face, and over the polished wood floor with its sleek gray carpet. The branches and their shadows waved in the wind that rushed around outside this room, this building, and rustled through the creaking treetops, and through the chinks and passageways of the house, making a dull harmonious whistle.

She was aware of being somewhere high up. Some attic-like place. A place that was in fact one of the high rooms of the clinic.

"Are you gonna throw up?" someone said to her in a voice unmistakably young and feminine.

Diana blinked sleep-crusted eyes. An involuntary yawn clenched her body, and she stretched and turned. Eyes unfocussed.

"Do you want the wastebasket?" came the voice again. Diana heard the tap of a finger against a plastic basket, and the crinkle of the bag that must have been inside it. "I've got the basket here, ready," the stranger said. "Or do you think you could make it over to the toilet?"

Diana wearily pushed herself up and saw, coming into hazy focus, a young woman. She was sitting on a neatly made bed just a few feet away from the bed Diana was now waking in. A small round gray plastic dustbin stood beside her. Diana blinked her eyes again.

The girl, Diana's age, was dressed smartly in a soft cream sweater and tapering green slacks, and her long blond hair, parted in the center, was combed stylishly to fall upon her sweater-clad shoulders. Her bare neck was long and well formed, and she held up her face and chin in a way certain self-conscious young people did when they knew they were being looked at or appraised by a new set of eyes.

This girl *was* pretty, and her penetrating blue-steel eyes shone in the cloud-muted October sunlight, coming in from the large bedroom windows.

The light hurt Diana's eyes. This strange room resembled a greenhouse, with windows angling overhead to where the high ceiling peaked.

"Oh, God," Diana groaned and lowered her head, eyes closing. "I feel like I'm coming back from the dead."

The girl moved off her bed, and springs creaked.

"Here," she said, and placed the basket beside Diana's bed. Diana looked up.

"I'm not going to throw up," Diana said. Her voice cracked a little.

The girl turned her head and squinted her eyes.

"Sure?"

"Yes, I'm sorry to disappoint you."

This produced a small giggle from the girl.

"Well, Dr. Sterling told me it was possible," she said. "The sedative they gave you makes some people sick. Sooo . . . precautions, you know." She thrummed her fingers on the basket.

Diana cleared her throat, trying to remember her dream —or had it been a nightmare again? She couldn't remember a thing.

"Anyway, I'm very pleased to meet you," the girl said. "I'm Catherine. I already know who you are, and that your name is Diana. Don't get up or anything! You've been asleep for almost two days, ever since they brought you here."

Here.

"Where?" Diana asked.

"The Albion Clinic," Catherine answered.

The Albion Clinic. A swank, live-in laboratory for the study of night terrors, deep in the Wisconsin countryside. How could she have forgotten? Hadn't her stepfather dragged her up here from Chicago? Hadn't she been in a state of panic, fighting and screaming? And barely human.

A feeling of shame and embarrassment—and a twinge of pure rage—flushed her cheeks red.

She touched her head and felt with a spasm of shock the bristles of her newly shorn hair. They had cut most of it off! The once lovely and silken mass of red-tinged dark hair had grown into a wild tangle over the past several weeks, making her look like a kind of madwoman. She'd refused to brush it, she now remembered, or change her clothes.

Or sleep.

"Are you all right?" Catherine asked.

Diana didn't answer. She closed her eyes, feeling hot tears pushing through to her face. She remembered it now: Ted Lenox, falling from the roof of the school—her school, Rawson. Falling just as the dark, faceless figure in her nightmares had fallen. She put her head down.

No, she thought. Not all right. She trembled. And she felt consciousness slipping away again. Felt herself giving in to the gravity-like pull of sleep.

Catherine said, in a voice that seemed distant, echoing as if from deep inside a dark cave, "Hey, can you hear me? Diana . . . ?"

It would be hours before Diana woke again.

Now it was night. The room was dark, blue squares of light from the skylights angled across the beds and, Diana now saw, blinking her eyes, the small fireplace. Black marble picked up glints of cloud-muted moonlight.

The room was large, opening up to the niches where the beds were positioned under angled walls and sloping windows. Bookshelves lined the walls. A large print of Edward Hopper's *Nighthawks* was framed in glass, and hung on one of the interior walls. The door to the large bathroom stood open. A faint night-light glowed from within.

Diana turned from her stomach onto her back. She sat upright, pushing, and saw across the room the breathing shape of the other girl, beneath bedcovers.

Diana's heart pounded. Pushing off her blankets, she rose unsteadily, bare feet touching the carpeted floor. The room was warm, but Diana sensed the coldness of the wild country beyond the windows. She had a strange sort of nightgown on, a soft white filmy thing that swirled at her bare ankles.

She went to the window closest to her bed, and looked down three stories through the murk of night. She saw the dark, landscaped grounds below, the white-paved paths, and the dark silhouettes of the tall, old trees. Old-fashioned gaslight lamp posts stood along the paths. A white haze shimmered at the horizon. Diana felt the loneliness of a country place.

It must be morning, Diana thought, judging by the faint colorless sunlight. The house was too quiet for it to be early evening. It had that settled, sleeping air. The window pane radiated cold and now her breath made a patch of fog appear there. She squeaked her finger through the cold foggy film. And now she had this eerie feeling of being watched.

Diana turned and saw Catherine's blue eyes gleaming through the night. Catherine's bed was caged in a grid of deep blue shadow, angling down from the skylight. A shadow moved across the moon, like a dark cover seeping up from the foot of Catherine's bed, until just her eyes glowed.

"You're awake," Catherine said softly, propping her head up on her hand.

From some far corner of the house came the faint soft sound of a bell ringing, a small bell, judging by the delicate crystalline sound of it.

So soft it might not have been real, Diana thought. She might have imagined it. Or maybe it was only someone's alarm clock.

The sound, whatever it was, frightened Diana. She rushed back to her bed and climbed in. The bed squeaked. She trembled, pulling the covers up to her neck, and turning her back to the young woman whose eyes she could feel upon her.

"You don't have to talk to me if you don't want to," Catherine said.

Diana closed her eyes and swallowed. "Thank you for giving me permission, then."

The girl was a long time in answering. The strange sounds of a sleeping house played like needle pricks on Diana's skin; distant sounds of water running through pipes hidden in the floors and ceilings, the sigh of a settling foundation, probably contracting in the cold. An invisible internal plume of grit spilled downward within the wall. As if ghosts were stirring there.

Catherine said at last, "I was only trying to—"

"Don't try," Diana said.

Diana remained awake for a long time, listening to the other girl breathing. Staring at the wall beside her bed. At the crossed shadows of the window muntin.

It seemed like a half hour later when Catherine said, "Aren't you even slightly curious?"

Diana didn't answer for a time. Then she said in a thick voice, "Curious about *what*?"

"About me? Don't you wonder what I'm doing here? It might have occurred to you that you're not the only person with a problem."

Diana didn't reply.

After a while, Catherine said, "Have you ever heard of noninsane automatism?"

Diana took in a long breath. Her heart pounded again, and she was very annoyed. She hated this hour of the morning. This was what poets sometimes called the *hour of the wolf*, she knew. Couldn't remember where she'd heard of it, but never forgot it. It was the hour when old men died in their sleep of heart attacks. An hour of darkness after the moon set and before the sun came up. A time when death stalked. She hated this hour.

"Insane, what . . . ?" she said.

"*Non*insane," Catherine answered matter-of-factly, as if it were *noon* or something. "Noninsane automatism. Like sleepwalking, only you do things to other people. Like," Catherine laughed into her pillow, "like throw them out of windows. But you're *asleep* when you do it so you don't really know what you're doing, you're not really responsible."

Diana felt herself fully, sickeningly awake now. She could hear something else coming from Catherine's side of the room. The snap of gum being chewed. Catherine was actually lying there nonchalantly chewing a piece of gum.

"You woke me up to tell me that?" Diana said.

Catherine guffawed. "You were awake, don't gimmie that. Please."

"I'd like to try and get some—"

"No, nah," Catherine said. "Better try another one. You don't want to go to sleep. I know all about it."

"I really don't want to hear about *insane* whatever it is."

"*Non*insane. Non. Well, it's a real thing and I might have it, or—correction—I *used* to have it. Now I just have nightmares."

Diana thought, they put me in a room with someone with noninsane automatism?

Diana felt herself suddenly seized by a wave of panic. It was awful. She remembered her nightmare—a dream that had been slowly building heat and light in her slumbering mind for two days. A dark faceless being. Chasing her.

Mixed into this cold, dark dream were actual memories she'd tried to keep at bay. Ted Lenox's scream as he fell from the rooftop of the Rawson School. It had been a bright September day. He was wearing a red jacket. A yellow shirt. She and some of her friends saw the whole thing, standing outside on the sprawling Rawson School grounds. Now he was lying there dead on the concrete drive. Brown wavy hair moving in a light breeze. She remembered it now, remembered it clearly. Confetti from the parade, earlier that morning, on the ground all around his bleeding head.

"What?" Catherine said. "What is it?"

Plunged back into the reality of this dark room, Diana rolled over onto her stomach and punched her pillow, hard.

Diana lifted her head. She whispered, frantically, "Please stop talking. Could you please be quiet? And please be quiet with your gum, too!"

After a while Diana heard a squeak of bedsprings followed by the small dull *thup* of Catherine's gum landing in the trash can all the way across the room.

Then a whisper, "G'night."

When she awoke again, later, Diana felt better. The grogginess of the sedative had finally worn off completely. The room was bright. Looking up, she saw blue sky and bare tree branches through the skylight. Now she could see everything in this room, which was dappled with sunlight and the shadows of the last leaves that remained on the trees.

Diana struggled out of bed, throwing a large wool blanket, blue-and-gray plaid, to the floor in the process. She saw in broad daylight the long white gown she'd been dressed in.

Now she saw Catherine clearly, too. She was seated at a desk, hunched over a drawing, her back to Diana. She was darkening a line with a pencil and didn't bother to turn around; Diana couldn't see the drawing very clearly.

"Is that door locked?" Diana asked, pointing to what she hoped was the exit.

"Of course not," Catherine answered without turning to look. On top of the desk beside her was a stack of fashion magazines, and beside that a large half-empty bottle of soda.

The room was decorated with modern blond wood furniture of Scandinavian design—two sleek dressers, an armoire, two padded overstuffed chairs, and a single desk, now occupied. The furniture corresponded with the slim blond molding and woodwork and door, and with that of the polished headboards of the twin beds, pushed into separate niches beside walls painted terra cotta. The ceiling was high and white, brightened by the peaked skylights.

Diana turned around, taking it all in.

The large French windows looked out from a height of at least three stories to a wood and a leaf-strewn path. In late October most of the trees stood bare of leaves. Diana walked to the windows and thrust open one of them, the one closest to her bed.

A wood-scented gust of cold air blew in, along with several bright blood-red leaves. Despite the sunshine and the clear blue sky, the chill of the north, and of Blackburn County in particular, was palpable. The gushing air was loud.

Close the window.

Diana turned around quickly and looked at Catherine, who was smiling rather wickedly at her, a pencil in her hand. She saw now that the portrait was of a dark, short-haired girl. Rather crudely done. Diana thought, Is that supposed to be me?

"Did you say something?" Diana asked.

Catherine laughed. "No, but I guess you knew what I was thinking."

Diana pulled the window shut. Affixed to the window was a leering cartoon jack-o'-lantern, the kind sold in dime stores. It looked so insipid, smiling like that. Diana was tempted to pull it off the window and tear it in half.

"Thank you," Catherine said, "for not freezing us to death."

Catherine took a thick fashion magazine that was open on her lap and abruptly dropped it on the floor, where it landed with a slap. It was open to the face of a young model, with short dark hair. Diana felt somewhat relieved, as Catherine's portrait was clearly based on this anonymous model and not on Diana. Catherine kicked the magazine under her bed.

Still smiling, Catherine rose to her sock-covered feet. She bent and picked up the maple leaves that had blown in the window and fallen to the floor.

Diana watched her carefully.

Catherine held the leaves up to her eyes and turned them

over, examining them. Drops of water glittered on their shiny veined surfaces, and ran like drops of mercury down the burgundy-hued midribs and onto Catherine's fingertips. The russet tones of the leaves, blotted here and there with fiery orange and a seepage of deepest green at the jagged edges, were remarkably beautiful in her long fingers.

She turned the leaves over like playing cards and traced a painted nail (a burgundy shade) over one of them. A strange trail of ugly brown bumps dotted the powdery dull side of one of the leaves.

"Eggs," she said, absently. "How disgustingly gross."

She went to the window, opened it, and tossed the rejected leaves to the winds. The gust blew her hair around her well-made face. She slammed the window shut, walked to her dresser, and picked up a heavy, hardbound book. It was old and jacketless, cloth, a time-worn brown. Diana could see the title from where she stood: *Complete Works of William Shakespeare*. Catherine opened the book and turned a few pages.

Without once looking at Diana she deposited a single red maple leaf between two pages of the book, and then closed it. At last she looked up.

"Well, roomie, I guess it's time you took a shower and did something with your hair." She replaced the book on her dresser-top.

Diana looked away.

"Roomies, huh?" Diana sat slowly down on her bed, unsmiling, gathering up a pillow on her lap. She held it tight. "Isn't that just the coziest."

Catherine smiled again. "I can't blame you for being a little . . . tense. They said you hadn't slept in over a week when they brought you here. My mother told me you looked like a real freak—unbathed, hair a knotted mess, practically psycho . . ."

Catherine stopped, seeming to read the thoughts behind Diana's glare.

Diana simmered inside. It was all coming back to her. Her stepfather had driven her up here from Chicago. Had taken her out of school, taken her against her wishes. The school had recommended she be removed, even though this was her second-to-last semester of high school. Diana's physician had also recommended some kind of institutionalized treatment. She wasn't crazy, he'd told her family; she was merely suffering from a kind of self-imposed insomnia, brought on by something called posttraumatic stress disorder.

Other students had responded well to counseling after Ted Lenox's fatal fall, but not Diana. She kept herself awake at night, every night, because, she had told them, told everyone, she didn't want to dream.

Didn't want *those* dreams.

Dreams that had grown steadily worse.

Terrible nightmares that seemed to come true—like Ted Lenox's fall. And sometimes . . . sometimes she could seem to *hear* what people were *thinking*. Even though she could barely believe it. Even though she pretended like it wasn't real. Ignored it, or chalked it up to some kind of intuition. It was like a feeling of déjà vu—brought on by being tired. Déjà vu was an illusion, it was a sensation of remembering something as if it had happened before, when in fact it hadn't. It was your brain crossing signals, one of her teachers had told her.

Yet sometimes it felt so real. Like she *knew* things were going to happen. Things that nobody could know. Things she would make herself forget. Even when they came true.

Maybe that thing in everyone's brain that gave people the occasional feeling of déjà vu was just overdeveloped in her, she speculated. Like having an overlarge thyroid or something. A physiological aberration.

Whatever it was, it was weird, and it scared her. And she doubted whether it could ever be fixed.

Diana bit down on her lip, trying to fight that awful sinking feeling. She'd only wanted to be just like everybody else—just *normal*. She didn't want to know what other people were thinking (awful things, *crazy* things!) but sometimes she did, and maybe she always had.

Or *seemed* to. She just honestly didn't know for sure, and now she was feeling defeated again.

They'd finally sent her away. Just like she always thought they would. She really was a nut, after all. She looked at Catherine, who simply stared at her.

Diana looked at the floor. At the ceiling. Yep, this is the loony bin all right, she thought to herself. She sighed.

Diana stood up again, and this time she went to the full-length mirror, beside the bathroom door.

More bad news. The black rings around her eyes had faded, and some color had returned to her skin, but her hair was awful, like a mess worn by some freak backwoods hillbilly girl. A thatch hung down over her forehead. The sides and back stood out from her head at crazy angles.

"Oh!" Diana cried and rushed once more back to her bed. She picked the blanket up off the floor and wrapped it around her shoulders.

"It's not that bad, Diana," Catherine said.

Diana looked at Catherine through tears. "That's easy for you to say. You look like a friggin' walking shampoo commercial!"

Catherine self-consciously ran her fingers through her own silken hair. "Come *on* now. I'll help you make it into a cute new style."

"Like hell you will."

Catherine clucked her tongue. "To tell you the truth, you look a lot better now than when they brought you in here. From what I hear, anyway."

"Those bastards didn't have to cut my hair!"

"Yes they did. Oh, yes. It was a rat's nest."

Diana pulled the blanket up over her head, like Little Red Riding Hood. "To hell with this place," she muttered. Then she whispered, "And to hell with you!"

"Oh, really? Well, I might agree with you about the former. As for the latter . . . it's too late. I'm already in hell."

"What's that supposed to mean?" Diana said, peering through the opening in her blanket, like a prairie dog peeping out of its hole.

"I already told you. I'm here for the same reason you are. Nightmares. Night *terrors*."

Diana was breathing hard through her nostrils. She watched Catherine get up and light a stick of incense. Streamers of scented smoke curled across the room, carrying a pleasant odor of sandalwood. Catherine picked up a magazine from the stack of them on the floor and flopped down on her bed, on her belly.

"Might as well make the best of a bad situation, Diana. That's what my mother always says, anyway."

"You don't know what you're talking about. You're a spoiled little . . ."

Don't say it.

Catherine was looking at her. Unsmiling.

Diana didn't finish her sentence. It was as though she'd read Catherine's mind again. She looked at Catherine's face, and at her shining eyes, which were now boring through her like icy blue beams. But soon a smile crept across Catherine's lips.

"You know, Diana," Catherine said now. "My mother always says, if life gives you lemons, make lemonade."

Diana pulled the blanket around her shoulders. She laughed bitterly. "Oh, yeah," she said. "And what if life gives you *shit*? What are you supposed to make—*shit-*ade?"

Catherine closed her magazine. She came over to Diana's bed and sat down next to Diana, still bundled up in her blanket. She put her arm around Diana's shoulder.

"Why don't you go take a shower?" Catherine said, pointing to the bathroom door. "You'll feel better. Refreshed."

"Nothing could make me feel better," Diana said. She looked like a refugee.

"Come on," Catherine said. "Don't be a pill. Haven't you ever been sent away before? To boarding school? Or to some fancy headshrinker camp? Or even to a bogus sleep clinic for rich darlings, like this one? You strike me as a misfit from a snooty family with dough."

Diana thought, I'm *not* a pill. She looked away from Catherine for a second, then back. Catherine smiled now.

"Of course you're not really a pill," Catherine said, eyes twinkling knowingly.

Diana opened her mouth to say something, but nothing came out.

"I know what you've been through," Catherine said. "My mother says—"

"Why do you keep talking about your mother? Do you have some sort of mother hang-up?"

Catherine looked a bit stung. "Well, my mother built this clinic," Catherine said. "But of course she couldn't have built it except for she's a state representative."

"A politician?"

"Yes, do you know what a state representative is?" Catherine seemed to be reciting now. "She's a person who gets elected every two years to the state assembly and votes on laws at the State Capitol, down in Madison. She's part of the state legislature. You see, there's the state senate, and the state assembly, which mother is a part of, and—"

"Politics bore me silly," Diana said.

Catherine closed her mouth, as if such a sentiment had never occurred to her before.

"Your mother's a big shot," Diana said. "I get it."

A dark cloud seemed to pass over Catherine's pretty face. It was as though she wanted to say more, but stopped herself.

Diana stood up and saluted, suddenly feeling she wanted to make this stranger smile again. The blanket fell to the floor.

"Prisoner X reporting . . . I'll take that shower now," Diana said.

Catherine snapped out of her reverie and smiled.

"Oh, wait! Don't forget your dream journal." Catherine pointed to the nightstand next to Diana's bed. Upon it was a notebook and pens. "We're supposed to record our dreams as soon as we wake up in the morning, and then take the notebooks with us to our therapy sessions with Dr. Sterling."

Diana looked over at the new notebook. She'd kept a diary for a couple years now and liked to write, so the labor of keeping a dream journal wouldn't be too awful, she decided. Yet the last thing she wanted to do was recall a bad nightmare. She shrugged.

"For once, I didn't dream," Diana said. But she knew that wasn't true, even as she said it.

"Everyone dreams, but some people don't remember their dreams," Catherine said. "Dr. Sterling is bound to be disappointed."

"Really?" Diana said, over her shoulder. "Well, screw him." She went into the bathroom and closed the door.

Catherine said, looking askance, "That job's already taken." She stuck out her tongue like she'd tasted something awful.

Diana took a long hot shower. The bathroom was large and featured yet another skylight that let in lots of golden October light. Whoever designed this place—Catherine's mother, or her architect?—was mad for glass. Windows everywhere. The ceramic tiles in the shower were all deep blue and the faucets were bulbous and made of old-fashioned porcelain and shiny brass. As the hot water beat down upon Diana's head she couldn't help but remember her recurring dream.

Falling. The tinkling, tiny sound of a bell, like the one she'd heard last night, or thought she'd heard. A race through dark hallways, and the sound of tiny claws behind the heavy plaster walls . . .

She opened her eyes. She was still weak and had to hold a hand out against the tiled wall of the shower to keep her balance.

She thought of her leafy neighborhood in Chicago, the distant wall of skyscrapers you could see from the school rooftop on clear days. Had she really gone crazy? In safe, leafy suburbia?

The school she went to was a private, exclusive one, supposedly safe from the hazards of urban life, and life in general. But as all the students at Rawson knew, that aspect of safety was an illusion their parents paid for. Diana's stepfather, a lawyer with a successful firm dealing in high finance ventures, never failed to point out to Diana that the Rawson School was not only one of the best private college prep schools in the state, but also one of the most expensive. He'd wanted to send to her off to Switzerland, but her mother had insisted Diana be close to home. Because of the nightmares.

When Ted Lenox got too high and fell from the roof of the school, Diana's trauma began. Not that she and Ted had any kind of special friendship. They barely knew one another. And not because foul play was suspected. The police blamed the fatal fall on the air freshener Ted liked to inhale, something called English Country Garden. The problem was, for weeks before the incident, Diana had dreamt about it. Not about Ted, but about someone falling, a dark, shadowy figure.

But Diana had dismissed the dreams, because, as her therapist told her, the falling figure was just a stand-in for her burgeoning sexual desires.

The dream was also an exaggeration of her well-established fear of heights.

Diana snorted now, thinking of that comment about sexual desires, and squirted a blue glob of perfumed shampoo into her hand. Shrinks always related every dream to sex. There wasn't much her shrink didn't relate to sex. Even the office building where she had her appointments was, according to Dr. Linden, a big phallic symbol created in the architect's subconscious mind.

Ted Lenox was not someone Diana would have chosen to dream about, if the dream really *was* about a crush. She knew that now, in retrospect. But back then, even before Ted fell, she didn't believe her dream was about a boy, or even about sex. She'd told Dr. Linden that. Diana thought the dream was maybe just about falling and being crushed to death by gravity and by the weight of your own body.

"How sexual!" Dr. Linden had nearly screamed.

Diana didn't quite buy it. It wasn't like she was some sort of sex maniac, dwelling on the subject of sex all the time. And she resented it when Linden suggested that she was repressed. Diana had nothing against sex, so why would she repress it? She'd made out with a couple boys, and she liked to read sexy romance novels. But sex was not her number one priority like it was for some people. There wasn't even one single boy at Rawson she particularly was in love with.

Dr. Linden had said, during one of their therapy sessions, "Of course in matters of sexuality our desires preclude our will." Linden never stopped scribbling notes into her file book.

Diana had then blurted out, "Are you speaking of the package delivery man?"

Linden's jaw dropped open. Her clunky blue-framed plastic glasses slid down her nose half an inch. Diana hadn't until that moment had a clue about the package delivery man. But a sudden fleeting image floated in and out of her brain: the young strapping Italian with the curly cap of black hair, who after delivering a package the week prior had come into Linden's office and made love to her on the couch. Diana had felt as though she could feel the body heat in the brown leather couch, even though the incident had happened days before.

"How did you know about that?" Linden said, lips pursing. She coughed into her bunched fist, catching herself. "Or, to rephrase, how did you come to assume what it is you think you know, hmm?"

Diana blushed. How did she know any of these strange bits of information that had filtered into her brain most of her life, and sent her scuttling off to therapist after therapist, each one more expensive than the previous one?

"I . . . don't know," Diana had answered. "But it's true, isn't it?"

"Someone saw him come in here? One of your student friends? And then the extrapolation, jumping to conclusions about me, an older authority figure?"

Diana said, "I don't remember anybody gossiping about you. I don't even remember ever seeing the delivery man come in here."

"Diana, stop this foolishness. You are only lashing out at me because you're angry with yourself."

"But it happened, didn't it? Why don't you try and tell me why I know these things—feel these things? Am I just a good guesser? Is that it? And why can't you explain a dream I have almost every night? A terrifying dream! I'll tell you why. Because it can't be explained! They don't teach about people like me in psychology school."

Linden closed her eyes and set down her file book. Her face was red. She took a calming breath. "I think we've accomplished all we can here today, and now we're just going around in circles.'' She looked at Diana.

''But if you really wanted to help me—''

''You wish to talk about drivel and impossibility, of lies passed off as some sort of magic intuition . . .'' she stopped talking, tried to compose herself. ''Really, that is all for today, Diana. Please go now.''

Diana could feel the rage in Linden's mind. She could fairly hear the unspoken thoughts and curses:

How did this goddamn little snip know?

She couldn't have seen inside my office.

Couldn't have seen that guy, seen me go down on him.

Nobody saw. Nobody knows.

How could they? Impossible.

. . . and yet . . .

The next week, Ted Lenox fell off the roof of the Rawson School, broke his neck, and was pronounced dead on the scene.

Diana's disintegration had begun. The ''coincidence'' of her dream (as Linden called it, before ''canceling'' Diana as a patient) only added to the ''posttraumatic stress disorder'' Diana was now experiencing.

So she stopped sleeping. She stopped bathing and stopped combing her hair, and she wore the same clothes day after day. She went nuts, people said. Lost her marbles. They had to take her away, people said. How sad. Who'd have thought it? Such a pretty girl, so intelligent—and it was all over at seventeen.

After her shower, Diana dressed in a black sweater and faded black jeans. Catherine watched her as she combed what was left of her hair in the mirror.

Diana sighed with frustration. They might as well have shaved her head bald. Catherine came over and took the comb from her.

''It's really not that bad,'' Catherine said. ''May I?''

Diana looked at herself in the mirror, not at Catherine.

''What have I got to lose? Make lemonade.''

She watched as Catherine combed the longest length of dark wet forelock across her forehead. There was something amusing about the look of determination on Catherine's face. This was serious business. Catherine ran over to her desk and came back with her scissors, snipping at the air.

"Mind if I get rid of a few strays?" she said.

"Do you know what you're doing?" Diana said. Touching her hair she said, "Guess you couldn't make it look any worse."

Licking out her tongue above her lip, Catherine made a few snips.

Then Catherine squirted out a glob of clear hair gel and rubbed it together in her hands, and smoothed it out over the shorter hair on the sides and back of Diana's head. At last Catherine stood back.

Diana looked at herself. Despite everything, she felt a rush of pleasure. "It's not half bad."

"It's sort of Beatle-esque mod, wouldn't you say?" Catherine offered.

Her resemblance to Paul McCartney, circa 1964, was striking, she had to admit. She exaggerated the somberness of her dark eyes, and let her lips protrude with photo-model petulance. "I like it," Diana said. "It's a new me." She batted her dark eyelashes.

Catherine laughed and reached out and started fooling around with the hairdo again. "We can pooch this top part up, give it that mod sixties retro look."

"Okay, that's enough," Diana said, laughing. "I'm starved. When's breakfast?"

Catherine smiled.

"Well, now you're talking," Catherine said.

Dr. Konrad Sterling was a large man with big facial features. Heavy eyebrows, broad nose, and salt-and-pepper hair that stood up brush-like and bushy. He wore dark-framed glasses and a white lab coat over a tweed jacket, and a dark tie. His shoes, Diana noticed, were old oxfords like her stepfather wore, black, the outsoles of which were battle-scarred and crater-pocked.

Diana felt there was something distracted about him. She stood in the doorway of his windowless office-laboratory on the ground floor of the Albion Clinic. She felt full from lunch.

"Please come in and close the door behind you," he said.

Diana pulled the door shut. The large chamber was so dark she could barely see. Her eyes slowly adjusted to the gloom. Now she could see the banks of electronic equipment, video monitors and winking lights, like the instrumentation panels in a 747 cockpit.

The dark walls curved around a wide central black column, where Sterling stood. The ceiling was high, almost invisible. The large room seemed to disappear at the edges, where hazy light had been directed. Sterling sat down on a small stool next to a large black leather sofa, a kind of oversize chaise longue, richly padded.

"Welcome to the dream chamber," he said, and smiled.

He seemed at first oafish and stupid in appearance, sort of a nutty professor (too single-minded to have developed any social skills). But there was another side of him that she found scary—an intelligence in him, strength and power. His hands were at least twice as large as her stepfather's hands. In his solid forearms and legs were a kind of horse or elephantine power.

Diana saw for the first time the large aquariums built into the curving walls and the central column—five big tanks with thick curving glass that ran flush with the dark walls. The tanks were brightly illumined within, where large hot yellow and orange and red pieces of coral glowed like pop art sculptures. Tropical fish with neon stripes trolled the tanks. The soft whir of the filtration system created a dreamy sort of white noise.

"You changed your hair," Sterling said.

"No," she said, perhaps too quickly, looking away from the fish. "You changed it. You or one of your assistants clipped it off while I was sleeping."

His eyebrows crawled up a notch. The reflection of a metallic blue fish swam across his eyeglass lenses. "Yes, of course. I remember. You were in pretty sad shape when you arrived, Diana. It was necessary to free your head from your tangle of hair. Your stepfather approved it, and your mother had specifically requested it, when I talked to her on the telephone. I hadn't given it a thought that underneath that mass of tangles was a pretty young girl.''

Diana bristled.

''Won't you please lie down here?'' he said, gesturing to the long black sofa. In this strange office laboratory, pinpoint lights hung from the dark black ceiling on long thin wires. More strange white noise hummed through the room, which Diana saw now in greater detail. The walls were indeed rounded, concave here, convex there—no corners anywhere. A dark blue-black carpet covered the floor, giving an insulated, sound-absorbing quality to the room. A pleasant faint scent of violets was in the air. The windowless place looked every bit the high-tech dream lab, Diana decided. She sat down on the couch, next to which was a round table, and several large black electronic machines resembling VCRs, into which were fed continuous slow-moving scrolls of paper. Still farther back into the gloom were coils of wires, and cabinets, and a large stainless steel sink. Everything neat, orderly, sleek.

''Please lie down,'' Dr. Sterling said. ''Would you like a blanket?''

''No. It's warm in here.''

''Warm, and very safe, Diana.''

She looked up to the ceiling, which she now saw was painted deep blue, nearly black. A pattern of glittering stars, of swirling galaxies, had been painted over the blackness.

''Are you comfortable?'' he asked.

''No.'' She smiled a little.

''Would you like something to drink? A soda, perhaps?''

''I'd like a juice, kiwi and orange if you have it,'' she said.

Sterling picked up a slim portable phone and murmured into it.

He scooted his chair up closer to her. For a few moments he merely looked at her.

''You are not happy,'' he said. ''No, of course not, but we are going to help you.''

She sighed. Swallowed nervously. He continued.

''You are very frightened, in fact,'' Sterling said.

"Something has been scaring you out of your wits lately, and keeping you from the sleep you desperately need. I could give you some mild tranquilizers, and we could induce sleep in you again. But the point here isn't that you can't sleep, it's that you won't. You don't suffer from insomnia, you suffer from a complex phobia. In short, you are frightened of your own dreams."

Diana felt something catch in her throat. She didn't want to cry. "I'm not crazy," she said.

"I wasn't suggesting—"

"My family suggested it for you," she blurted. "Everyone thinks it. Well, to hell with them."

"Diana, your family loves you and wants to help you."

"Sure, and so do you."

"And so does Catherine."

She looked at him. "I want my own room. I don't want to share with Catherine or anyone else."

"That's out of the question, I'm afraid. And besides, having a friend here will help you along. You will like Catherine, I promise, she is a delightful girl. Now, shall we proceed with the therapy?"

Diana sighed.

"Yes, I suppose so," Diana said.

He cleared his throat. "Yes, then. You reported in your dreams a sensation of falling, of being pursued, of being pushed to the edge. And then over it. You also have a feeling of clairvoyance in these dreams, undoubtedly enhanced by coincidence."

"Undoubtedly." Diana rolled her eyes upward. The door opened and Harriet Evans came in with a bottle of juice and a glass filled with ice, carried on a small tray. She put it on the table next to Dr. Sterling and silently left, closing the door firmly behind her.

"A-hem. . . . What I want to do, Diana, is to record your dreams, meaning I want an account of your dreams in each of our regular therapy sessions. But also, once you begin to sleep regularly I will monitor you with an EEG, an electroencephalographic mapping of your dreamscapes. This process measures in microvolts your brain activity during REM sleep."

"REM?"

"Rapid Eye Movement. When you are asleep, your brain produces ninety-minute cycles of slow wave sleep, with occasional episodes of REM sleep, in which your most intense dreaming occurs. I am very interested in imaging your brain, and in viewing, as it were, your cerebral cortex, which is the surface area of your brain where sensory data are processed."

"Hmmm," Diana said, taking a sip of the juice. Her stomach made one of those funny whirly noises, and she felt embarrassed.

"Ah, and did you know," he said with a soft smile, "that you are also producing brain wave activity here?" He pointed at her stomach.

She shook her head.

"Yes, the enteric nervous system, or the gut-brain. Here, too, are neurons and neurotransmitters sending messages and learning, remembering, just as is done in the brain inside your skull, but independent of that brain."

"Weird."

He smiled. "This, too, we shall study."

Diana listened intently. But as often seemed to happen with her, a sudden sense of hopelessness seemed to rise in her blood. She turned her head away from Dr. Sterling. She doubted if there was really a scientific answer to her nightmares. It was not as if an imbalance of brain chemicals could make you dream things that had actually happened—to other people. Or make you read their thoughts when you weren't even trying.

She swallowed hard. Everything she had tried to deny during the day, during her waking hours, flooded back in at night, when she was asleep. When she lost control to her sleeping self. To her untrustworthy mind.

"One of the things I will do for you," Sterling said, pouring more juice into her glass, "is to help you sleep without drugs. To foster a natural sleep, as it were."

Diana raised her head. "But how?" She really doubted he could make her sleep.

He smiled. "I plan to use physical exhaustion, for starters."

"What?"

"Exercise and diet. Hard physical labor. Oh, it works very well for many of our patients. Especially those who are fighting sleep, rather than pursuing it." He looked at his watch. "It's about time for you to go and change into your sweat suit. You're due outside on the track in about twenty minutes."

"The track? Wait a minute—"

He reached out and touched her hand, silencing her. His touch was cool and dry.

"Diana, look at me. Listen to me. Do you want our help? No, perhaps you do not. But do you want to solve your . . . *problem*? I think you know the answer to that."

She turned her head away from him. Again she was filled with panic and doubt. She turned back to him, her chin pointed out defiantly.

"No one can really help me."

"But I intend to try," he said. "Please give my therapy a chance, Diana. You might surprise yourself."

She took a sip of the tart juice.

She thought, like I need more surprises.

The pine wood air outside was cool and clear. A few fat clouds stood still on the blue horizon, and a mild breeze moved over the hilltop, sending leaves spiralling into the air. Diana could see her breath as she walked from the clinic down to the cinder track where Catherine stood, wearing the same nondescript gray sweat suit as Diana. A young man stood next to Catherine.

Diana had to stop when she saw him. She wasn't expecting to see a boy, especially a nice looking guy like this. She touched her hair, feeling self-conscious.

The dark-haired guy, who Diana guessed must have been eighteen or nineteen, wore navy blue nylon shorts and a ripped white sweatshirt. He was tossing a football up a few feet and catching it, talking to Catherine. Diana cleared her throat and walked toward them. Catherine watched her.

"Hi," Diana said.

The boy didn't smile, but instead picked up his clipboard,

not even looking at her. Short dark hair blowing slightly on his forehead in the breeze.

But at last he looked up, and he looked into Diana's eyes for a long moment. Large dark eyes, deepset, drinking her in.

"Uh . . ." he said.

Then he didn't say anything for the longest time.

Diana was standing next to him now, an old elm towering above, its bare branches spread majestically beneath the autumn sky.

She couldn't tell what he was thinking—she was suddenly feeling far too self-conscious to even have made an educated guess. She was absolutely sure of what *she* was feeling, no mistaking *that* feeling. The attraction made her speechless, too.

Catherine managed to cough against her fingers. "Excuse me, I'm here, too," she said.

"You're late," the guy said softly to Diana.

"Only by a minute or two," Diana stammered. "Sorry."

"Five minutes, actually," he said, looking at his watch, then back into her eyes. "But, I guess it's okay, since this is your first day out here." He cleared his throat. "Let's not waste any more time," he said firmly.

"Oh, David, stop with the army drill sergeant routine," Catherine said. "Don't you want to me to introduce you to Diana?"

"Pleased to meet you," Diana said. She stuck her hand out.

"Catherine, please," he said, annoyed. "I'm supposed to be in charge here."

"Yes, I know," she said. "And you're supposed to be merciless with us, grind us to dust." She batted her eyelashes.

Diana took her hand back, held it behind her, where it met her other hand. She squeezed them together.

He sniffed and spat into the brown grass at the side of the track. "I know your name already," he said to Diana. "You can call me David. We're going to warm up with five laps," he said, and he looked at Catherine. "Let's cut the bullshit and start out with some stretching."

He turned his back. Diana, a bit ruffled, looked at Catherine. Catherine shrugged.

David demonstrated some leg stretches. Diana watched him. She noticed that he was solidly built, though his hair was kind of greasy and his chin was unshaven. His brown eyes had flecks of gold in them, or maybe it was just the autumnal light that caused them to twinkle like that. It was as if she'd never really looked at anyone's eyes before. Never noticed. He held onto one of his white running shoes and stretched his leg, and he grunted.

He was being very careful not to look at Diana. Being very serious.

"Okay," David said, while Diana and Catherine were still on the ground, "let's get moving." He made a notation on the clipboard and then tossed it into the grass. He started to run.

Catherine yawned at Diana. Diana started to run. Soon they were both running side by side at a slow pace, shoes crunching cinders beneath them.

"What's his story?" Diana said.

"He's kind of cute, isn't he?" Catherine said.

"He's kind of serious."

David was moving out far ahead of them.

"Don't let him scare you. He's just a local boy. I've known him for years. He went off to college for a couple years and turned into a big athlete. But before that he was just a skinny nerd type. His mother works here as a housekeeper and cook. Have you met Shirley? And now David works here full-time as a handyman maintenance guy, with the added title of physical fitness trainer recently thrown in."

"A job he takes quite seriously."

"Oh, he's a serious-minded guy all right. It's gone to his head. Frankly, I don't know what you see in him."

"Who says I see something in him?" Diana started to run faster, a little bit ahead of Catherine.

"You don't have to *say* anything. It shows."

Diana and Catherine turned their heads to see David rushing up behind them, and then passing them.

"Come on," he called out between breaths, running

backwards for a moment. "Get the lead out of your asses!"

"Oh, my God, he's mean!" Diana said.

"Welcome to Blackburn County," Catherine said. "It's mean man country!"

Diana felt winded by now, and a side-ache was coming on. Catherine seemed to have more stamina.

"I think I'm going to have to stop," Diana said.

"That's not an option," Catherine said. "I know, I've been out here with David every morning this week."

Diana looked at the rolling hills, and then at the Albion Clinic, perched on a gentle slope. It was an impressive modern building, solid. It resembled a mountain chalet, but instead of the frills and fringes of a cuckoo clock, its three stories featured clean lines, tall windows, a sloping, guttered copper roof, oxidized an antique green. The exterior was painted white. In the windows were the reflections of the trees, birch and ash and black maples and sycamores, most of them leafless and dormant. Pines and evergreens, too, were reflected in the clinic's windows.

David ran up to where Diana was crouching with her side-ache.

"You okay?" he said, puffing.

She looked at his face, shining with sweat now. She felt stronger, all of a sudden. The sun made the fall day as immaculate as she could have hoped for.

"Fine, fine," Diana said between breaths. Truth was, she felt quite out of shape.

"Ready for some cross country?" he said, almost managing a smile.

"Let's go," Diana answered.

David smiled at her now, for real. "Good," he said. He ran off the track, toward the woods, where a trail opened up. Catherine took hold of Diana's arm, pulling her up, and together they started to run.

They ran at an even, brisk pace along the wooded trail, where pine needles made a carpet. Through the gray blur of leafless trees were flashes of white birch and the green of the tall pines, the lush evergreens.

For a moment Diana wondered if there could still be bears up here in this forest country of the north, or timber wolves. It didn't matter—she felt she could outrun them now. She felt kind of fearless with Catherine and David, who was a good distance up ahead.

She heard the river before she saw it. She could smell its mossy essence.

The three ran along the banks, beside the dark water. Douglas firs and blue spruce lined the banks along the trail, their green spires piercing the sky. In the distance Diana could see the magnificent rock bluffs and towering rock formations, high overhead. Suddenly David stopped. It was all Catherine and Diana could do to keep from slamming into him.

He pointed, and Diana looked over at a patchy red sandbar, thick with leafless gray brush. From the brush a huge white bird rose to the air, awesome in its size, its long, bent wings beating slowly. Diana felt her heart thumping, partly from the exertion of running, and partly from seeing this great animal take to the sky. Its shadow passed over a rock that stood out into the river next to a grove of oaks.

"Sandhill crane," David said.

"Cool," Catherine whispered.

Diana was sweating like mad. Droplets ran down her face and she had to squeeze her eyes shut.

"There are raccoons and opossums and foxes, and lots of other animals. I see them out here when I go running," David said. "Deer, too."

"Whew," Diana said, and dropped to the grass. She was so tired now.

David turned and looked at her. "We're only getting started."

Diana groaned, leaning back on her elbows.

"Maybe we should give her a break, David," Catherine said, pulling her blond hair back and fiddling with a band. "She's a rookie."

Diana took a deep breath, stood up, and said, "I'll race you both back," and, grinning, she gave Catherine a light push, just enough to make her lose her footing. Catherine let out a mock-outraged cry and would have stepped right into the shallow river-edge had David not caught her—as Diana somehow expected he would.

While David and Catherine embarrassedly pulled themselves together, Diana ran back to the trail as fast as her aching legs could carry her.

"This is an obstacle course," David said. Diana looked at the tires, lined up in rows, and at the strange high wood barricade, with rope netting, a muddy patch beneath it.

The sun was beginning to set in late afternoon. A rosy hue shone on their faces. "Where did this obstacle course come from, anyway?" Diana asked.

"I built it myself," David said proudly.

Catherine stood with her hands on her hips. She had a streak of mud on her face. She watched David intently.

"Now wouldn't it be boring if the only way I could physically exhaust you would be to make you run up and down a flight of stairs all day? Or run yourselves dizzy around a track? That would be mind-numbingly unproductive. Here we have a problem, something that will take some hand-eye coordination, and something that involves a little bit of risk. Who wants to go first?"

Catherine smiled. "I told you the first time you showed me this thing that I didn't want any part of it," Catherine said.

"Yeah, well, now it's part of my mandatory program for all grunts."

"Grunts?"

"Step up, Catherine, or step aside."

Catherine looked at Diana.

"How about a demonstration?" Diana said.

David smiled. He looked at his towering invention, up through the netting at blue sky and pink-tinted clouds. "No problem."

The two girls looked at one another. They simultaneously crossed their arms over their chests and smiled at David.

"I've done it a million times," David said.

At exactly the same time, the girls said, "Do it now." They both laughed, but David grimaced.

"No fair ganging up on me," he said.

"Like you haven't been kicking the crap out of *us* all day," Catherine said.

David wiped the sweat from his palms onto the front of his sweat shirt. He spat into the grass. Then he ran at the obstacle.

He jumped onto the rope webbing, which swung with his weight beneath the wood frame structure. The thing creaked and some of the smaller crossbeams trembled. The top of the structure, over which a "grunt" would have to hurdle, was about twelve feet from the muddy ground. David crawled and scrambled up, struggling to get a foothold in the net. The trouble was, Diana observed, that the net was hanging too loosely from the structure. Parts of it were giving way under the stress of David's weight and the vigor with which he attacked the netting.

All at once the top of the net broke free of the structure. There was a kind of ripping sound. Then the unattached part of the net started to whip over the top beam.

"Whoa!" David cried, as he and the portion of the net he was hanging onto started to slide, and fall.

Once he started to fall, still hanging on to the net, he fell quickly.

David and a good portion of the net fell in an instant to the muddy ground. The remainder of the net and several loose ropes coursed over the top of the structure, and followed down in a heap on top of David.

Diana screamed, "Oh, my God!" but couldn't fight her laughter. Catherine laughed even harder. They hurried over to help free David from the piles of rope netting on top of him.

"Are you all right?" Diana cried.

"Get this thing off of me," David said, trying to stand, but unable to because of the weight of the net.

They pulled most of the net off him, and at last he rolled free of it, muddy and red in the face.

They helped him up.

"How about we call it a day, huh, coach?" Catherine said, and snorted.

Diana only smiled at him. If she could have, she would have willed him just then to smile back. She liked him. She felt he liked her. But something held him back. He didn't smile. He didn't seem to think the accident was funny, though he was standing up and didn't look hurt.

Catherine stepped between Diana and David, a little closer to him. She touched his arm. She looked very concerned. Somehow, it didn't look genuine on her pretty face. But then, Diana recognized her own budding feelings of jealousy—silly feelings.

"You're sure you're okay?" Catherine asked.

He just shook his head and turned his back, stooping down where the pile of net lay.

"Never mind," he said, wearily. "We have to put this thing back together. You're both going over it, even if we're out here past dark. Now c'mon and give me a hand."

"What?" Catherine yelped. "You gotta be kidding me! I'm tired!"

"You heard me," he said.

Diana looked down at her shoes, covered in mud. She felt herself smiling, and tried to hide the smile from Catherine. The sun was setting. Twilight made a gauzy blue film in the air between them, darkened the hills, deepened the woods around them. The lights in the clinic windows, up the hill, glowed golden against the misty blue of near-night. Earlier in the day, Diana felt she'd already had enough of this place. Now, oddly, she felt she wanted to stay. She felt tired, her arms and legs aching. But she felt relaxed, too. She took in a big breath of cool country air.

Without a word, Catherine and Diana began to gather up the rope netting with David.

The fiasco with the obstacle course was observed from a high window of the clinic. Up here, Theda Price, state assemblywoman of the district which comprised all of Blackburn County, watched unobserved her daughter and the recently arrived new patient. The only other person in the room with her was Dr. Sterling, who sat on a low, stylish gray sofa and fiddled with a pencil.

Theda let go of the length of muslin curtain she'd been holding in her hand.

Theda, in her early fifties, but looking younger, was dressed in an expensive dark raincoat. Her fire-bomb red hair was set in a conservative style, and looked almost as though it was sculpted in some shiny acrylic material, each strand molded like the banded grooves in an old-fashioned LP record. The light moved over her shiny hair and face as she turned from the window. Her face had once been pretty, as pretty as Catherine's was now. It was soft, somewhat childlike, and her deep hazel eyes retained a youthful gleam. Her mouth was small and full, lipsticked red. Her voice was soft.

"We seem to be making some sort of progress out there, Kon," she said. "Maybe we'll actually get somewhere this time." She lit a cigarette and dragged on it. "Anyway, the bills are still coming due on this white elephant." She blew smoke clear across the room at him.

"I assure you, Theda, that this time it's for real," he said, watching the cloud of smoke climbing up the tube lampshade. "This is the culmina—"

"The culmination of your life's work," Theda said, mockingly. "Yadda, yadda-da-da." She looked for the hurt in his eyes and found it.

He sighed and said, "Your investment will pay off. Why, in pure scientific terms . . ."

"Isn't that what you told the boys back east? Before they ran you out of town?"

Sterling frowned. It wasn't like Theda to bring up the wretched events of the past in so cavalier a fashion as this. Something was setting her on edge.

Yet if she'd meant to hit a nerve, she'd succeeded. Yes, his unorthodox studies into the paranormal aspects of dream research and psychic mind control had managed to get him banned from the world of respectable scientific research. It had taken a woman of power and influence—and a desperate need—just to get him back to the place he'd reached ten years ago; a woman whom he had loved for ten years. She had saved him, yet she could also bring him to the brink of violence with a few choice words. He took a slow calming breath. Counted to ten, thinking, remember priorities, Sterling, old boy.

Remember Catherine. Theda's gifted, but troubled, daughter.

His research into her dreams and subconscious mind had

justified the creation of this sleep clinic. Others had been brought here for treatment, to be sure. But the clinic existed for the purpose of exploring the gifts of a single extraordinary patient—until now.

Now Diana was here.

"Very cruel of you, Theda," he said at last. "We mustn't in our impatience lose our heads and start to mention . . . certain things."

She looked at him sharply. But her cold look soon faded. She was, after all, a consummate politician, repeatedly re-elected since the time of her husband's death. He'd been the incumbent office holder, her mentor, the father of her only child and the owner of the vast livestock concern from which she derived her considerable income.

Theda smiled. "Certain *things*?"

But he knew that *she* knew what he was talking about. It was a game they played all too frequently. He might have called it "find the soft underbelly"—find it and rip into it.

"So many to choose from," he said. Knowing he should stop while he was ahead. But not stopping—plunging in. "How's the ethics probe coming along in Madison?"

"The ethics probe is bullshit," Theda said. "It's a damned nuisance."

"So I read in the papers."

"Do you really think I'm worried about it?" She laughed sort of bitterly. Yet, for all her bluff, she was damned worried about it, he knew. "I'll be completely vindicated," she said, lighting a new cigarette with the glowing butt of the one she'd only just finished.

He didn't say anything.

She came around to the sofa. "In the meantime, my business is going to hell," she said. "Not even the lobbyists are talking to me, Kon. You can't go much lower than that."

"You know your business, I know mine."

Her eyes narrowed as she smiled. "All I've ever wanted was the very best for Catherine. That's your business. The thought of bringing even an ounce of shame upon her . . . but that isn't going to happen."

"There's talk of a recall," Sterling said. "It's that Nessie Jasper—"

"Please don't mention that name in my presence. She's an alcoholic miscreant, a veritable backwoods hillbilly."

"The papers say she's a populist and she's going to oppose you in the next election, even if there isn't a recall because of the lobbying scandal—"

"And you claim no interest in the local scandal, Kon. You sound like a fishwife with a load of backfence scoop."

"The talk of your precarious position as an elected official has gone considerably further than the back fence, Theda. Why the editorial page of *The Milwaukee Listener* just today opined that—"

Theda held up her hand, the cigarette smoldering between her fingers. "As you said, I know my business. You stick to yours."

Diana walked back to the room alone after the gruelling workout. David had promised today's drill was just for starters. Also on the program was wood chopping, digging, and a host of gardening chores, such as a mulching project, already well underway in preparation for winter. If that weren't enough, Diana and Catherine were also given additional "problems" to solve, such as devising a weight/mass ratio for spreading sheep shit over square acreage.

Catherine had volunteered to help David bring a couple of trail bikes out of the shed and pump their tires with air, and Diana was sent back to the house.

Now Diana felt left out. Did Catherine have a sudden interest in David now, too? It was maddening.

Diana entered the clinic, feeling the warmth as she passed through the large kitchen where a stout woman busily prepared supper. David's mom, Shirley. Stirring vegetables in a skillet, her dark hair going limp in the steam. Diana felt hungry. She also felt slightly worried. Catherine had an uncanny ability to intuit almost everything Diana was thinking, and even what she was *feeling*.

Diana passed the small book-lined room where two of the live-in patients of the sleep clinic sat playing cards, the Montgomery sisters, Annette and Ginger. White-haired old

ladies. She wondered why they didn't have to run around
in the mud. Maybe they were too old for it or maybe they
did their exercises in the morning. Diana didn't want to
ask; she was not inclined to get too friendly with any of
the Albion Clinic patients. Luckily, people tended to keep
to themselves here. The clinic was large enough to afford
a lot of privacy.

In fact, the clinic had the pleasant atmosphere of a kind
of resort. It could have passed for an expensive European
fat farm. Light, airy, clean, and modern, it was solidly built,
sturdy and rich. Splendid antiques contrasted nicely with
the sleek modern design, the floor-to-ceiling windows. It
was sort of funny then, she thought, to see cheap Halloween
decorations pasted up on the walls. Here, too, was an an-
nouncement for the upcoming Halloween party, just days
off now.

A comic skull leered at her, bloody eyeballs bulging
from green sockets. COME ONE, COME ALL, the skull beckoned in a balloon caption. A witch astride her broomstick
stared with wide golden eyes. Hours ago Diana wouldn't
have had the least desire to attend such a party. But now
she found herself wondering, would David be there?

She went to the cloakroom and opened the stiff wooden
door. It took her only a moment to find her coat, and to
rummage through the big pockets. She found her diary.

She kept a dream diary, which she would be expected to
share with Dr. Sterling. But this was her personal diary.
For her eyes only. Out of the same pocket she fished a
ballpoint, the cap missing, tooth marks impressed upon it.

She went back into the kitchen and sat down at the pine
table. Shirley was gone. No one else around at this presup-
per hour of early evening. A large pot simmered on the
stove, whispering into the room the rich smell of beef
spiced with garlic and rosemary. Diana was starved. She
wrote in her diary:

Getting used to this place at last, sort of . . . am I? . . .
well, not really. But telling myself so. Making
friends! and—oh—Catherine! She's exasperating!!!
My roommate. Very spoiled and rich, and never stops

talking about her mother, who is a politician and a big shot around here. Know the type? Know the type's *kid*? Catherine is soooo perfect, you see. And a little bossy. Used to getting her way . . . But, even so, even so . . . i like her. She's funny. *Sense of humor!* she's sort of cynical. No, make that very cynical. Considering where she lives . . .

Diana looked out the window. She took a green apple from the shallow blue bowl on the table. She rubbed the apple on her shirt, then took a bite. Tart and juicy. She wrote more: -

Like for example, Catherine says this isn't even a real clinic! Call 9-1-1 . . . She says it's a quack clinic set up for rich crazies. (Like me?) And it's also a place where rich parents can take their insane daughters for some R&R. (Hello . . . ! It's me again!) On the other hand, Dr. Sterling is kind of fascinating (and weird) and i am trying to cooperate with him. My nightmares seem to have calmed down. Can't remember them too well and don't want to, and anyway not sleeping much as usual. Oh help

David . . . met a guy named David . . . David . . . *help*

Last night had *foie gras*. Yuck. am i homesick? parents . . . they have no idea about this place, none. face it: Mother is a prescription drug addict and an alcoholic—*hate* her? (love her). My stepfather is *not* my father. Not his fault, I suppose. But he brought me here. He's to blame. For *that*, at least. thank you thank you thank you for ruining my life this way— that's all for today.

Diana closed her diary. She tossed her apple core into the sink and climbed the stairs. For a moment, she felt weary. She put her hand on the smooth wooden railing to steady herself, and climbed up the wide carpeted staircase. It was then that she heard the strange sound from within the wall. A sound that stopped her dead on the stairs. A soft scurrying, a scrape of claws, it seemed, accompanied by the drizzle of sand falling within the wall. She craned her neck to listen. But now she heard nothing. It must have been either her imagination, or maybe the place was infested with squirrels, she decided. Then came another sound. The ringing of a bell. Soft, clear, a tiny high note . . . it chilled her to the bone.

It's only a dinner bell, silly, she told herself. Yet it sounded so much like the strange bell from her dreams. She closed her eyes and shook her head. No, she thought. No, it's not possible. Don't let your mind play tricks on you.

Very late that night, Diana fought against the heavy sense of sleepiness that seemed to descend upon her and pull, like a river's undertow. She lay there in the dark of the room, staring up through the skylight at the scant clouds in the night sky, black, their outlines silverlit with moonlight.

"You really ought to try and get some sleep," Catherine said, from across the room.

Diana turned to see her, but the room was too dark. "Looks like I'm not alone in being awake." She could imagine Catherine as she'd looked, some hours ago, upon going to bed: dressed in a white nightgown (as compared to Diana's oversize T-shirt), hair tied back, a moisturizing cream still gleaming on her face.

"We seem to think alike," Catherine said.

Diana doubted that. She hoped her wariness about Catherine was not as easy to read as so many of her other feelings.

"We're very different," Diana said.

"But we have a kind of connection. You must feel it, too. It's like we can see into each other's thoughts."

Diana smiled slightly. "I don't know that I want anyone reading my thoughts . . . not even you."

"Let's try an experiment," Catherine said. "Ever play that guessing game where one person thinks of an object in the room, and the other tries to guess what it is?"

A typical sleep-over kind of game, Diana thought. She sighed.

Catherine's bed squeaked. She was "looking" around in the dark, picking out an object.

"I'm thinking of something in the room," Catherine said, the excitement in her voice barely suppressed. "Something red."

Diana smiled, thinking *this is stupid.* But then she had this feeling. A weird warm feeling inside her head. She closed her eyes.

Then she saw it. It just appeared in her mind. She had the answer.

"What am I thinking of?" Catherine asked again.

It was strange, but before Diana could even resist this game, she knew the thing Catherine was thinking about was the red maple leaf, secreted inside the book.

That red leaf just seemed to bleed into Diana's mind, like a color photograph on a velvety black background.

Diana laughed.

"Weird, isn't it?" Catherine said. "You got it, didn't you?"

"God, like I needed more *weird* in my life right now."

"Say it, then," Catherine said, her forceful self emerging. "What am I thinking of?"

It was funny, Diana thought now, but sometimes you can sense yourself giving over something to a strong personality, to a person you might even disapprove of, but whom you rather like for having a kind of power or strength that is perhaps lacking in yourself.

Simultaneously, Diana and Catherine said, "The red maple leaf."

They both burst out laughing. Catherine scrambled out from under her blankets and came over to sit on the edge of Diana's bed.

"Weird," Diana said.

"It doesn't have to be *bad* weird," Catherine said, smiling, looking radiant in the scant light of the moon. "Like your dreams."

Diana let her head fall back on her pillow. Catherine leaned against the wall at the end of the bed, and pulled her knees up to her chest. She wrapped her long arms around them and folded her hands together.

"What was your worst dream?" Diana said.

Catherine sighed. Diana felt a distancing, like a chilly vapor rising up between them now. "I don't know what my worst dream is," Catherine said. "But I had an awful one the other night."

"Tell me."

"Sure you want to hear it?"

"I said I did, didn't I?"

"Okay," Catherine said. "I'm a surgeon."

"You're a surgeon?"

"Yeah," Catherine said with a nervous laugh. "I don't know if I can tell this."

Diana was silent.

"Okay. In my dream I'm a surgeon," Catherine said. "I'm wearing a surgical mask, and I'm surrounded by a surgical team, nurses, machines humming, and a heart monitor blipping, and we're all lit up brightly under a lamp. But something is wrong. I'm not standing, I'm sort of reclining, on my back, with my upper body elevated . . . and I have these surgical tools in my gloved white hands . . ."

"Yeah," Diana said, feeling her heart flutter.

"Well, you see, I'm operating on *myself*. On my open lower gut."

Diana held her breath.

"I'm cut open, *clamped* open, and I can see my internal organs swimming there, wet and gleaming under the light, my intestines and dark red liver and . . . I'm performing surgery on myself!"

After a few moments of silence Diana said, "That's horrible."

"Yeah, I know. But I've always had bad dreams. Vivid bad dreams."

Diana sighed. "I'm not going to get any sleep tonight."

Catherine sprang up from the bed, making it quake.

"I'm starving!" Catherine announced. "Let's go down to the kitchen and raid the fridge."

"Your story wasn't exactly appetizing. Are we allowed in the kitchen at this hour?"

"Oh, who cares? Honestly, Diana. Don't be such a mouse."

Diana threw off the bedcovers and reached for her robe.

In the kitchen, the two friends feasted on ice cream and cold pizza, and cold lasagna—a real pig-out. They also found some cupcakes that had been made for the upcoming Halloween party. White cupcakes with orange pumpkins on them. They ate in the light from the open refrigerator.

Between bites they giggled and talked.

"Don't you miss being at a regular high school?" Diana asked Catherine. "This would be your senior year, right?"

"I don't miss it much. The only thing I really miss is the boys. Do you have a serious boyfriend?"

"Serious?" Diana burped lightly. "I don't even have a silly one." She giggled and Catherine laughed, too. Then Catherine burped deeply and massively.

They tried to stifle their laughter, but that only made it all the more explosive.

"Won't the staff hear us?" Diana asked. She put her hand on her belly, imagining that she could actually feel the skin stretching.

"The cook isn't due in for hours." Catherine looked up at the big clock above the stainless steel range. It was close to three A.M. "David and his mom, Shirley, live right here on the grounds of this place, in one of the condos Sterling and my mother built."

"Your mother again."

Catherine grimaced, nodding her head. "Her fingerprints are all over this place."

"She must be like a god up here in Blackburn County."

Catherine laughed so hard she nearly choked on a piece of cupcake.

"She's no god or goddess. I'll tell you how she came to power. My father was the state representative for years . . . I wasn't even born yet when he was first elected. He was a lot older than Mom. Anyway, he died when I was very little, and my mom took over as state rep. She's been re-elected ever since."

"Wow, she's really been in power for a long time."

"Like, forever." Catherine stood up. "Come on."

Back in their room they sat on their respective beds and talked. The gray light of dawn made the windows glow silver. Diana could see white mist hanging just below the distant treetops on the horizon. Color was slowly seeping into the grassy hills.

Diana felt sleepy, but she knew she'd triumphed. No nightmares tonight.

Diana thought with a sigh, it's true you can get used to anything—even a gilded cage. She didn't hate this place so much now. Didn't miss her mother as much.

According to Catherine, it was easy to play along with the games devised by Dr. Sterling. Soon enough they'd even be free to come and go from the clinic at will. That was more freedom than Diana had ever known. Her parents had been somewhat restrictive.

Her parents. Of course they were not allowed to visit during these first crucial weeks. And the parting had been so acrimonious. Diana let her head fall, so that her chin touched her chest.

"Oh, don't tell me you're nodding off," Catherine said.

Diana smiled. "No chance." She ran her hand through her close-cropped hair.

"We'll get out of here soon and take a trip to the village. Wait till you meet Randy and Jon," Catherine said. "God, my mother would kill me if she knew I was still hanging out with those guys. She positively hates them. The only thing she cares about is avoiding scandal. She's totally fucking paranoid." Catherine shook her head wearily. "Truth is, I hate her."

Diana lay down on her bed. "How can you say that? You talk about her all the time. And look what she's done for you—built you your own private nightmare retreat."

"She's getting something out of it, don't kid yourself," Catherine said. She frowned, and nervously rubbed her hands together. "Like I told you, this place is not a real clinic at all, just a cozy place for rich old fools to hide out for a while. And a place where Mom can keep an eye on me. She tries to control me."

"So do most moms—till you're eighteen, anyway."

"You don't know what it's like."

Diana concentrated hard. For a moment, she tried to *feel* what it was like.

"No," Catherine said, "don't go there now."

"But I—"

"Don't even think about me right now."

"God, Catherine, paranoia must run in your family."

Catherine lay back against the wall, a strange smile on her lips. "If you think I'm weird when I'm awake, you should see my dreams."

Diana felt a shudder pass through her. She knew she was very, very tired. It was as though her normal thought processes were disengaged. Replaced with the absurd logic of a dream. It's only a game, she told herself. All this stuff about reading thoughts—imagination mixed with a dash of coincidence, old-fashioned intuition, and a potent dose of sleep deprivation.

Staying up even one night could have a bad effect on a person's health, Diana knew. But in her case, sleeping seemed to pose a greater hazard: dreaming.

In the kitchen, later that day, Catherine and David removed Halloween decorations from boxes. David's mother, the cook, Shirley, was helping them. Shirley had her medium-length brown hair tied back loosely with a pink ribbon. She held up an enormous red rubber spider, and grinned.

Catherine was smiling, but her smile faded when she saw Diana walk in, yawning.

David looked up now, too, a skull candle in his hand.

"Man, you really look like hell," David said. Diana ignored them, her head fairly buzzing from lack of sleep. She had a heavy purple plaid sweater in her arms, and she pulled it over her head. Her hair was still wet from her shower. She'd had a bowl of breakfast cereal, but she still felt a little faint.

"Need some air," she said, heading to the back door.

She walked out into the morning light. The strong sunshine felt good. She took a deep breath and she smelled the clean, wood scent of autumn. She walked from the sloping hill and heard, behind her, the back door open. Catherine and David followed after her.

"Come and help us set up for the party," Catherine called. "It's tonight. Don't you know what today is? It's Halloween!"

Diana just felt like, who cares? But when she turned and saw Catherine so close to David, she found she did indeed care. They caught up with her, and the three of them took a walk along the wooded trail.

Diana was too tired to talk much, but Catherine had no problem keeping a conversation going. She gossiped about the other patients. David remained quiet.

Once in a while, Diana's eyes would meet his.

By the time they got back to the house, Diana was starving again. Shirley made her a big sandwich—roast beef, Swiss cheese, lettuce and tomato, and great dollops of mayonnaise. Diana wondered if she would put on weight, eating so much. It didn't seem possible with the workouts. The food gave her energy. She went for a long run with Catherine after lunch.

After a workout Diana spent the afternoon helping decorate the big dining room with fake cobwebs and hanging paper skeletons, and ghosts made out of bedsheets stuffed with newspaper. Catherine brought in from outside an armful of dry light branches, which she hung from the ceiling with fish-line. Diana shook up the cobweb spray and pressed the nozzle. Cobwebs hung from the branches. David moved the ladder around, wherever they needed it. He brought in a couple of bales of hay, too, and a moldy scarecrow.

Once, while Diana was up the ladder, she looked down at David, who was holding the ladder steady. He looked away, embarrassed. He'd been checking her out, obviously. Diana looked at Catherine, who turned her head to stifle a giggle. Diana wiped some of the cobweb liquid that had gobbed up on her fingers onto her jeans, and went back to work—cobwebbing a high corner.

But when David was up the ladder, she checked him out, too. Catherine silently elbowed her in the ribs.

"Nice butt," she whispered. Catherine might have

laughed, too, if Diana hadn't clamped a hand over her mouth.

Later, all three of them carved pumpkins on the kitchen floor, where they'd spread out some newspapers.

They placed the jack-o'-lanterns on card tables set up in the decorated dining room. David brought in a box filled with paper lanterns. He climbed the stepladder again and strung the orange and yellow lanterns high above the tables. Then they stepped back to look at their work.

It would be dark soon. Candlelight would help the transformation from dining room to magic haunted house. Diana felt proud of the work they'd done together.

David and Catherine gazed upon the room in silence.

Despite this nice warm feeling, Diana still felt very tired. And she had yet to figure out what to wear for a costume. She knew that she could be a fairy princess or a witch, but when she looked through the box of old clothes and costumes brought down from the clinic's attic, she didn't find anything that would really work. At last she discovered an old black eyepatch. If she could find a piece of string, it could be put to use.

Back upstairs, in the bathroom she shared with Catherine, she tied a red scarf on her head, put a big gold earring in her left ear, painted on a black moustache and beard with grease paint. She put on a striped red-and-white shirt of Catherine's that left her midriff bare. White slacks that came to the middle of her calves completed the costume. What about shoes? She decided to wear black flats. Not exactly up to pirate code, perhaps, but effective in a pinch. She looked in the mirror.

She was a pirate, and now all she needed was a sword.

Diana came out of the bathroom and sat down upon her bed and closed her eyes. Her eyes burned from lack of sleep. Her legs ached from running. Even her back hurt from decorating the dining room. Not exactly in a party mood.

"You look great!" Catherine said. "Now it's my turn." Catherine went into the bathroom and closed the door behind her.

Diana felt she needed to rest. She was thinking about her

parents. It was true they would not be allowed to visit under the terms agreed upon with the clinic. But what about phone calls? She wondered why they hadn't called. Maybe they were as sick of her as she was sick of them. But that didn't seem likely. She knew she'd hear from them soon—at least before Thanksgiving. Certainly by Christmas. And she had no doubt she'd be home by January 1st, which would be the absolute last possible day she could stay here. Her stepfather wouldn't pay for these costly digs forever.

As she leaned back on her bed, Diana felt herself once again drifting to sleep. Maybe she could risk it, she thought; maybe she could doze for a few seconds without a nightmare reaching out to her.

And hopefully she wouldn't smudge her black beard off.

Just as Diana felt herself drifting off to sleep, she was awakened by Catherine. The bathroom door opened, and out came Catherine, dressed as a ballerina. She wore a white leotard, and a skirt made of some limp white flowing material, filmy. Her hair was pulled up and tied in a braided mound atop her head, and she wore huge false eyelashes and lots of blue eye makeup, the kind with glitter in it.

"What d'you think?" she said, snapping her gum and turning around.

"Very nice," Diana said, wearily rising from the bed. She reached out and smoothed the elastic band along Catherine's collar.

"Thanks," Catherine said. "Are you ready?"

Diana nodded. "Sure."

Diana blinked her burning eyes several times.

The dining room glowed in the light of the flickering jack-o'-lanterns, grinning from their posts. The paper lanterns were strung festively from the cobwebby ceiling, so the floor below took on a magical garden quality, like something nostalgic. The floor-to-ceiling windows were black with night, and reflected the colored lights of the room. Diana recognized many of the other costumed guests, though she barely knew the staff and the other patients out of costume. But she was looking past most of the other guests, looking for someone.

She saw him across the room, standing at a table where punch bowls were filled with orange and pink mixtures, and colored rings of ice that bobbed as party-goers served themselves.

He was dressed as a beatnik, wearing black boots, dark slacks, and a ripped black turtleneck T-shirt. On his head was a cocked beret, and with black makeup he'd painted on his face a moustache and goatee.

David looked wonderful.

He filled up his glass with punch. At last he looked across the room and saw her. Did he recognize her? He didn't seem to. Took his punch and turned away.

Catherine was busy talking to the old Montgomery twins, dressed as two country farm girls. Red checked dresses and blond wigs tied into Pippy Longstocking braids, painted red freckles on their noses and cheeks. One of them smiled, a few of her teeth blacked out.

And there was Mrs. Kearney, dressed as an airline stewardess, dark navy blue suit and a small airplane brooch on her lapel.

"Ahoy, matey!" Richmond Garfield called. She recognized the eccentric middle-aged hypochondriac, even in his cowboy duds—chaps and a ten-gallon hat.

"Howdy," Diana said.

Richmond pulled a toy pistol out of his holster. "You forgot your sword, podner," he said. "Person shouldn't be without her weapon in these here parts."

Mrs. Kearney swept in. "Excuse me," she said. "But may I have this dance with Mr. Garfield?"

Sterling had just turned up the volume on the CD player—Elvis was singing "Jailhouse Rock."

Diana smiled as the cowboy and stewardess took to the center of the room, doing some kind of twist.

Diana looked at Catherine, now chatting with Sally, the young head nurse, dressed as a bum with a bundle on the end of a stick, and with David's mother, Shirley, done up as an opera singer, horns coming out of her hat. More blond braids.

Diana walked across the festive room toward David, who sat in the bay window drinking punch.

Catherine had described David, whom she'd known growing up, as a geek. Or maybe he was a frog who had recently grown into a kind of prince. Whatever the case, Catherine said she had herself been lately reassessing David—maybe he was worth a second look after all these years.

Was Catherine interested in David now just because Diana so obviously was? It was possible. A budding sisterly rivalry.

On the other hand, Diana thought, she might be jumping to conclusions. Diana regarded her presence here at the clinic as a temporary thing, so maybe she shouldn't take either David or Catherine too seriously.

If she did, she thought, she probably wouldn't be boldly approaching David right now.

"Hi," she said sitting next to David in the bay window.

He looked at her for a second. "Hi, Diana," he said, smiling shyly. He sipped his punch. "Are you gonna make me walk the plank?"

"Only if you read me some bad poetry," she said. "I probably *should* make you walk, after the workouts you've been giving me." She looked around, smiling. "The party turned out great, everybody seems to be having fun."

He drained his cup. "Considering where we are and who everybody is, that's a triumph."

She looked down at her black shoes. It was obvious he wasn't having fun. He probably felt like he was at work—like he *had* to be here, she thought. And with these *patients* . . . his mother here, too.

Diana could feel Catherine's presence before she looked up to see her standing there, smiling, looking radiant. Catherine took a few steps on tiptoe, and bowed.

"Cozy spot for a pirate and a beatnik," Catherine said with a laugh. She clucked her tongue. "People will talk, you know," she sang.

"Oh, let them talk," Diana said. "I'll run them through."

"But you don't have a sword," Catherine said, smiling. Diana laughed.

David got up from the window seat, holding his empty

cup. "Excuse me," he said. "Refill." He turned and walked away.

"Oops," said Catherine, looking at Diana.

"No, that's okay," Diana answered. "He's not in the best mood, I guess."

"Appropriate for a beatnik," Catherine said. "On the other hand, would you want to spend your Halloween night here if you didn't have to?"

"Is he forced to be here with us?"

"I wouldn't doubt it."

Diana shook her head. Then she smiled at Catherine. "Well, I'm going to make the best of it," she said. "The decorations look fabulous. Come on, let's check out the food."

Diana and Catherine walked to the table where the treats were arranged—pumpkin-shaped cookies and brownies and bowls of candy corn. Music blared from the stereo. Retro disco from the 70s and 80s pulsed through the room. Diana tried a cookie and found it a bit dry.

Again she felt her head throb.

She really felt exhausted. She ate the rest of the cookie in one big mouthful. Then Catherine pulled her out on the dance floor, and they danced.

Sterling must have had one of those disco hits compilations. Diana smiled. Even though she'd been feeling tired, she was enjoying the exertion.

"You're thinking about David," Catherine said, loud, above the music. No one could hear them, though; the music was cranked. Richmond Garfield was shimmying with both Montgomery sisters now. Others danced around them. David was nowhere to be seen.

Diana said, with a smile, "Get out of my head, Catherine."

Catherine smiled. "It's not that easy."

Diana closed her eyes and danced, listening to the old ABBA song, "Knowing Me, Knowing You."

At the end of the dance Diana felt warm. She was perspiring. She left Catherine with the Montgomery twins, back by the punch bowl, and walked to the side exit door, off the dining room entryway. A small chandelier burned low, making peachy light. Diana stepped out into the chilly night, not bothering to put a coat on. It felt good, bracing.

In the darkness, the orange tip of a cigarette glowed. The smoker saw her approach and pitched the cigarette away. David turned from the tree to stand before her.

"Oh, it's you," Diana said, cheerfully.

David didn't smile.

"Not enjoying the party?" she asked.

He rushed up to her, took her in his arms and kissed her on the mouth. The branches of the tree stirred in a light breeze. A filmy cloud obscured the moon.

She blinked at him in astonishment. But the kiss had felt wonderful.

They looked at one another. Diana wanted to smile. She actually felt dizzy. But thrilled.

They kissed again. In the shadow of the tree they held each other close.

"Stealing a kiss from a pirate on Halloween night," she said to him. "You seem to have gotten over your shyness."

"Not a word of this, or they'll have my job—and my mother's job, too," he said, his warm hands on her bare arms. "I can attend parties with the patients, but I cannot under any circumstances kiss them."

He kissed her again.

Diana smiled. "Your secret is safe with me." She noticed him staring at her face. "What is it?"

"It's my beard. Most of it came off on you." He laughed. "Some of it's on your nose."

Diana touched her nose. Black makeup came off on her fingers. A breeze blew up, scattering leaves around them. The cloud drifted off the not-quite-full moon, and the yard was filled with pale light. They were no longer standing in a shadow.

"Is my moustache smeared?" she said.

"It's a little uneven, yes," he said. He looked around. "I'd better be going. Someone could come out here and see you like this." He gently pulled the scarf from her head and wiped away the beard and moustache and most of the smudges from her face. He looked at her.

He handed her the scarf.

"Sorry . . . I . . ." David did not finish what he was trying to say. He turned to go.

"David, wait!"

He walked away, toward the house.

When she went back inside, Diana didn't see David at the
party, which seemed to go on and on. Wherever David had
gone, he wasn't to return to the party tonight. And even
though Diana danced and laughed and stayed to help Catherine and Shirley clean up the dining room under bright
lights, she felt terribly wistful.

And so very, very sleepy.

When Diana finally looked at her watch her eyes were
so bleary she could barely make out the time—nearly 1:30
in the morning. The floor of the dining room was littered
with napkins and streamers. Halloween was over.

A while later, Diana drowsed upon her bed. It had been
a struggle to climb the stairs. Now she was fighting sleep.
The light under the bathroom door went out and the door
opened. Catherine, looking grave, came into the room, and
set her brush down on her dresser. She must have been
exhausted, too, Diana thought.

"I'm so tired," Diana groaned, looking up through the
dark room at Catherine.

"Then lay your head down and close your eyes." Catherine was standing before the window, her back to Diana.
Her black silhouette shone with a gleaming silver aura, cast
by the moonlight.

Diana felt so weary. She didn't want to put her head
down on the soft pillow, but gravity willed it so.

As her head touched the pillow and sank deeply against
the cotton pillowcase and the springy fibrous substance
within it, the moon slipped from behind a cloud. A square
of blue light shone down through the skylight to the bed
where Diana fell fast asleep, at last.

Diana didn't hear Catherine step over to her bed.

"Diana?" she whispered.

Catherine clutched Diana's shoulder and gently shook
her.

"Diana?" Catherine said aloud now, in a normal speaking voice.

When Catherine was satisfied that Diana was indeed in a deep sleep she tiptoed back into the bathroom and took the slim black phone from the pocket of her robe. Glancing around to see Diana's chest rising and falling in the rhythm of sleep, Catherine punched the number. Catherine yawned deeply as the phone droned in her ear. She was dead tired herself.

Sterling answered.

"She's out," Catherine said.

"Completely?"

"Like a hibernating bear," Catherine said. Even as she said this, she sensed in her new friend a rush of memory and babble, voices at the whirling entrance to a borderland of dreams.

Dr. Konrad Sterling affixed to Diana's sleeping head the last electrode. Diana, sound asleep, was strapped to a gurney in the dream chamber, which was darkened as usual. The soft purring air-jets of the aquariums made the only sound. The wires attached to Diana's skull streamed to various machines, where dials throbbed and lights pulsed, and needles bled a continuous mountain range of black ink.

Diana's right arm slid from her side and dangled. Sterling gently replaced it to her side. He looked at the girl. Pale eyelids fluttering. Harriet affixed an electrode to Diana's bare ankle, then handed the oximeter to Sterling. He attached to her finger the small device that measured pulse and oxygen levels.

Next he placed the thermocouple beneath Diana's nose, a strip with sensors on it which would measure her breathing. The other breathing monitors were like belts, white, which went around her chest, fastened with Velcro.

Diana took a deep breath and stirred, then swallowed. Her sleeping countenance struck Sterling as oddly beautiful, and he watched her with fascination. She looked troubled, he thought, as if her subconscious mind were deeply involved in working out some terrible problem. Knitting and weaving, turning over and over, ceaselessly swimming forward like a shark that never sleeps, and can never stop moving.

He turned and walked past the banks of illumined aquariums and into a dark shadow of the oval-shaped room. He followed the lengths of black cable that led from where Diana slept. On the other side of the wide black central column, a dim light rose where yet another bank of instruments flashed, attached to these cables.

Upon another gurney, wires streaming from her head, was Catherine, sound asleep.

Chapter Two

The frostwork on the bedroom window reminded Diana of a strange piece of glass she had seen once at the Art Institute in Chicago. Like the artist's glasswork, the bedroom window seemed to contain an elaborate storybook etching, the thicker dimensions taking on a milky diamond whiteness, the finer aspects clear and delicate as a Christmas tree ornament. The result seemed a whorled enchanted forest.

She scratched at the frost, feeling the fuzzy ice packing up coldly beneath her fingernail. Outside, not a flake of snow had fallen. Morning fog was suspended close to the ground, ragged wisps draped to match the gray November sky. The faded brown grass of the hills surrounding the clinic was stiff with glittering frost.

Catherine tossed a sweater across the room to Diana, who turned to catch it as it was sliding down her back. A thick dark green sweater.

"You'll need something warm for the hike," Catherine said, head emerging from the neck-opening of her own heavy navy blue sweater. Catherine smoothed the sweater down to her hips. Diana smiled but looked back at the glass and the strange frostwork. It looked menacing, jagged lines forming a treacherous landscape.

Diana had slept through the previous night. In fact, she'd slept through the last three nights in a row. The change of scenery, the vigorous physical workouts, and perhaps even the strange sessions with Dr. Sterling, had helped her regain the confidence to sleep again.

The odd thing was, she couldn't quite recall her dreams. She was supposed to write down any dream—any shred she could recall—in her dream diary, kept at her bedside. But each morning she woke up with only the vaguest memory of her night fantasies, so vague they escaped from her grasp like smoke. That was good, she decided, even though Sterling claimed to be disappointed. Considering how awful her nightmares usually were, she thought maybe it was better she couldn't remember them.

Diana was almost feeling her old self again, with more energy than she'd felt in weeks. Yet these mornings she'd awakened with a strange humming inside her head. Sort of a musical note, but soft and airy. Something she was barely conscious of, unless she was dwelling on it. She tried not to. Occasionally she felt a dull headache, too. Not too much pain; more a sense of fullness, or swelling, like her scalp was being stretched slightly.

But of course she was used to feeling strange. So she tried to ignore the weird pressure that seemed to be building up in her head. Today she and Catherine could do whatever they wanted—no workouts, no therapy sessions, and Catherine decided they would grab a quick breakfast in the kitchen and take a hike around the grounds, and beyond them to the river trails.

Diana was hungry, as usual. "Will this sweater be warm enough?" she asked, slipping it over her head. She looked at herself in the long mirror on the back of the door. Her hair was growing out nicely, and she kind of liked the thick bangs that she could now brush over to one side.

"It might be too warm," Catherine answered. "We're going to climb Ice Rock, and it's pretty steep."

Diana frowned. "Ice Rock? I thought we were going to take it easy today," she said.

Catherine opened the bedroom door and Diana followed her through it. "Ice Rock is on top of a bluff with an incredible view of Blackburn County. Once we get up there, you'll be glad I brought you."

"What's up there?"

"A place to meditate," Catherine said. "A spectacular view, the highest point in the county. You'll love it. Trust me."

Catherine wore black jeans and tan hiking boots. Diana wore her regular tennis shoes. It hadn't snowed, so she figured she didn't need special boots. Blackburn County was pretty far north, and northern Wisconsin winters came early, Diana knew. It was unusual that not even a flake of snow had fallen.

At the second-floor landing, Catherine stopped dead. There, in the TV lounge, was Mrs. Bennett Kearney, the wealthy lady who had been a frequent patient at the clinic over the years, though she didn't seem to have any sleeping or dream disorders. What she had was a lot of disposable income and a habit of hopping from one quasi-medical recovery spa to another, all over the world. She sat in one of the heavy padded brown club chairs and watched a soap opera.

Diana could *feel* Catherine's dislike for Mrs. Kearney.

"Come on," Catherine whispered, pulling at Diana's sleeve. "We're going to try something."

"What?"

Catherine gave Diana a gentle push toward Mrs. Kearney, who now looked up. The TV lounge was dark. Arts and Crafts Movement designs were on the wallpaper and on the curtains pulled over the window.

Mrs. Kearney was in her fifties, had obviously dyed black hair (it contrasted rather hideously with her pale skin, even under all that makeup, Diana thought). She raised a hand to her throat, and the emeralds on her fingers gleamed in the morning light that came through a crack in the curtains. Catherine, meanwhile, had disappeared around a corner, just outside the lounge, where Mrs. Kearney couldn't see her. Voices murmured softly from the TV.

"Hello," the older woman said, extending her bejewelled hand. "I think we met at the Halloween party, but not formally. I'm Mrs. Kearney, and you are?"

Diana stole a quick glance at Catherine, who waved her off.

We haven't been properly introduced, but I know your daughter.

Diana swallowed hard. Where had this voice come from? Oh, God, it was Catherine's voice, but Catherine hadn't spoken. It was coming directly into Diana's head, clear as a radio signal. Diana wasn't imagining it this time.

Had they done something to her in her sleep? Buried a transmitter inside her head? She touched her fingers to her temple, then ran her fingers through her hair. Beads of sweat bloomed on her forehead.

Diana closed her eyes. No, she thought; this was too weird. She knew she should never have allowed herself to fall asleep.

I know your daughter Kit.

"My name is Diana," Diana said, shaking the woman's hand, noting how cool it felt compared to her own, which was sweaty all of a sudden.

Kit! Kit, Kit, Kit!

Diana stammered, "Uh, I'm a friend of Kit's."

Mrs. Kearney's face fairly fell. Her eyes narrowed.

"You knew . . . Kit?"

Diana said, "No!" She was going to have to ignore this, whatever it was that was happening. "I didn't *know* her exactly."

Stay cool, girl.

Diana looked up, as if the voice were coming from a hidden speaker in the ceiling. It wasn't. Only Diana could hear it.

Mrs. Kearney's eyes followed Diana's gaze, then narrowed. Her teeth—perfect, white—flashed. "But you just *said* you were a friend of my daughter."

Diana's heart raced. "What I mean is . . ." She was really grasping, trying now to "receive" another message. If she hadn't known better, she would have sworn that Catherine was over in the corner in hysterics, laughing out loud. But of course Catherine·wasn't laughing out loud. She was laughing inside. And Diana could *feel* it.

This was almost worse than having the dream about Ted Lenox falling off the roof of the Rawson School.

"What I meant to say is," Diana said, swallowing, "Kit

and I were just acquaintances."

"Acquaintances where?"

We were at the same nose job clinic.

"Nose job," Diana said. She absently placed her hand over her nose. Ran a finger along the bridge. "We had the same doctor."

"You were at Parkway-Somers? Two years ago, over the Independence Day weekend, with Kit?" Mrs. Kearney's words were coming out as a kind of shriek.

Diana shrugged. "Yeah. How's Kit doing?"

"You don't know? About the tragedy?"

Diana opened her mouth. "The tragedy?"

Mrs. Kearney rose from her chair. "You mean to tell me you hadn't heard that Kit never came out of anesthetic shock? She's still in a coma! Has been for two years. Two years!"

Diana gasped.

"You honestly didn't know?" Mrs. Kearney demanded. "No, I swear."

Mrs. Kearney roughly took hold of Diana's face with her icy fingers and turned it from side to side. "Excellent job," she said, bitterly, examining Diana's nose with narrowed eyes. "I'd never have guessed. Such a coincidence, your ending up here." Mrs. Kearney walked stiffly through the door. Catherine barely had time to duck behind a railing, and remained unseen.

When Mrs. Kearney was gone Catherine came out from her hiding place, giggling. She entered the TV lounge.

"God, I told you she was a bitch," Catherine said, laughing.

"Oh, very funny," Diana said. "That was incredibly cruel. And you really put me on the spot." Diana crossed her shaking arms over her chest. Her hands felt cold. "What in the hell is going on?"

"Just relax, Diana. Don't you see? We have a great thing going on between us. I just proved it to you."

Diana went to the window and roughly pulled the curtains open. She saw David outside. He was stuffing piles of leaves into a plastic garbage bag. A light breeze blew the leaves around his head. She wanted to go outside, to be with him. Instead she wilted into a chair.

Catherine sat down on the arm of the chair. She said, following Diana's gaze, "I honestly don't know what you see in him."

Diana thought,

No, but you're trying to!

"Now who's being cruel?" Catherine said with a laugh.

Diana swallowed hard. She hadn't intended Catherine to "hear" that. "What you just did was a mean trick, Catherine," Diana said. "I don't know how you did it, but I don't like games like that."

"Why? Because that old hypochondriac yelled at you?"

"Not only that. I don't want you inside my head."

Catherine looked a little crestfallen. "Maybe that wasn't the best way to play it. But I wanted to *show* you."

"Show me what? That your mad doctor planted some kind of radio device inside our brains?" Diana closed her eyes. She kept touching her scalp, feeling for an incision. But then she remembered with a sudden shock that some operations were performed through the eyes. Microsurgery. Or maybe a tiny transmitter had been deposited up her nose, or hidden in her ear. She ground her teeth together.

"Diana . . . Diana," Catherine said. "When are you going to stop freaking out about it?"

Diana looked up into Catherine's face. "About what?"

"About your *nature*."

Diana exhaled through her nostrils. After everything that had happened to her, it was a miracle she wasn't insane. She wondered to herself why this latest episode in her life should be any different from the weird events that had led up to it. She wasn't like other people. And maybe she never would be.

Just then, an ad came on the TV screen. A cheesy special effect, psychedelic colors and glittering letters fading into a galaxy of stars.

Letters faded onto the screen, forming *Psychic Pals Connection.*

A woman singer Diana recognized came on the screen. Someone who hadn't had a hit in a few years. "Wouldn't it be great to have a special friend who knew your past, your present and also your future?''

A toll-free 800 number appeared on the screen.

Catherine laughed out loud. "Can you believe this?" she said.

"Imagine," the singer said. "A real psychic to advise you, and to guide you—anytime, twenty-four hours a day. A friend you can always count on."

Diana jumped up from her chair and fled the room.

Catherine casually grabbed an apple from a carved wooden bowl on the pine table next to the TV. She bit into it. Then she stood up and followed Diana downstairs and into the kitchen. When Diana saw Catherine, she opened the kitchen door and ran outside.

"Hey, wait up," Catherine said with a mouthful of apple.

"Leave me alone, Catherine," Diana called, without turning to look at her.

"It's my nature, too," Catherine said, catching up with her, taking big strides. "Together . . . who knows what we could do? It could be a blast."

"A blast," Diana huffed. "We could go to work for Psychic Pals Connection! What could be more fun?" She walked faster, putting her back to Catherine.

Diana thought about that "nature" of hers. About how, when she was a kid, she would have these mild convulsions that really embarrassed her parents.

She knew what these *spells* were, even back when she was only six or seven. Visions, prophecies, psychic connections—there were lots of terms for the strange powers she seemed unable to control. Sometimes she could "hear" another person's thoughts. And sometimes Diana could seek out her mother's whereabouts, and locate her anywhere in the house, even while Diana was upstairs in bed, supposedly taking a nap.

A curse was what it was, Diana thought.

Diana had long tried to suppress this knowledge, this ability. To ignore what Catherine was now calling her "nature."

. She looked at Catherine now. Shook her head as she marched along, feeling this incredible anger—anger that she somehow understood opened her mind up to Catherine all the more. The frosty grass crunched beneath their feet.

What had they done to her? Were they trying to take control of her—to drive her mad, even?

That was it: This was all a big hoax, and Catherine was in on it. Paranoia raged through Diana's mind. She wasn't quite ready to dismiss the idea of a tiny transmitter planted in her brain.

Yet she had to admit to herself, this "nature" had been a facet of her life long before she ever met Catherine or heard of the Albion Clinic.

Once, when Diana was six, she'd been at her small cousin's birthday party in Oak Park. It was summertime. Everyone was in the backyard. She'd started having a frightening vision. A terrifying vision. Something no one else could see. White blood cells growing, reproducing, swimming through her cousin Jerry's bloodstream. His hair falling out. She could see his neatly combed wig and his white face, eyes closed as if sleeping in the strange, small carved box, with flowers all around him. Diana had been on her knees when the convulsions started. Her hands were clenched into tight fists that shook at her sides. Her eyes rolled back, so that only slits of white were visible as she started to babble, and moan, and foam at the mouth.

Her stepfather had rather roughly picked her up, so that her dress came up and the other kids could see her underwear, and laugh. And he hauled her stiff, shaking body out of the party, as she foamed at the mouth and her eyelashes fluttered. He took her to the car until she calmed down. The family doctor had told them there was nothing wrong with her physically—it wasn't epilepsy or a strange allergic reaction. It was probably an emotional problem. An embarrassment for all concerned.

Seven months later Jerry was diagnosed with a disorder of the blood. It turned out to be a fatal cancer. Diana's parents did not take Diana along with them to the funeral.

Now Catherine said, "I've had the same things happen to me."

Diana stopped dead now. She saw David, up ahead by the elm grove.

"When you're upset, you're easier to read," Catherine said. "It's like the border patrol takes a long rest."

Diana's head pounded now with a headache. Was there a transmitter melting down inside her brain?

"David!" she called.

David now set the rake against the big elm, whose leaves had all fallen. The sharp wood smell of a fall day was in the cool, bracing air, and it was intoxicating.

Diana came up to him, and reached out her hand. But he stepped back, away from her.

Diana had thought a lot about the kiss she'd shared with David at the Halloween party. Of course it could have cost him his job, had anyone found out about it. But wouldn't the staff at the clinic have assumed that an attractive guy like David would be noticed by a lonely young woman, who was far away from her family, and who, like everybody else, needed love?

"What's wrong?" he said.

Diana opened her mouth. It dawned on her just then that she couldn't tell him, couldn't really even talk about it. He probably already assumed she was crazy; telling him about this would assure him of that notion. She didn't really know what was happening to her, and couldn't define it. She only knew that it terrified her.

This was a craziness that existed between her and Catherine, she realized. No one else would ever be able to understand it. She didn't have a right to burden him with her weird problems.

Act normal, she told herself. Take that transmitter stuff and file it away for now. Look away. Do it now, or you're gonna lose him.

Catherine came up and smiled as if nothing at all had happened.

"We're going on a hike," Catherine said. "Come with us."

He looked at her with something close to contempt. "You think you're the boss around here?" he said.

Catherine opened her mouth, smiling, blinking her eyes. "Well, no, I just—"

"You're not the boss," David said. "I happen to have

a shitload of work to do. So have your hike by yourselves.''

Diana was stunned by his coldness. But she understood he had to keep his distance. And maybe he really did resent his job. She and Catherine were, compared to him, free. Free to take hikes, and have therapy sessions, and sit around discussing their dreams while he hauled trash and bagged leaves and raked the cinder track.

''What a grouch,'' Catherine said, pulling on Diana's sleeve. ''I'm really getting fed up with the attitude I'm getting here today, people.'' She pulled Diana's arm. ''Come on.''

David picked up the rake and walked away. He twirled the rake on his shoulder.

Catherine pulled at Diana's arm again, ''I told you he was a weirdo.''

Diana sighed deeply.

''Are you going to spend the rest of the day freaking out, or are you going to have some fun for a change?'' Catherine said. ''My mother always says, don't be like a mighty rigid oak tree, cracking apart in the winds of the storm; instead bend like the tiny supple reed, and survive. It's called the path of least resistance. Ever hear of it?''

Diana shook her head. ''Your mother again.'' She felt stunned. She didn't want to fight with Catherine, or with anyone. And especially not with David.

''Let's go to Ice Rock,'' Catherine said.

Reluctantly, her head swimming, and the faintest memory of last night's dream just starting to impress itself into her consciousness, Diana followed Catherine. They headed for the river trail that led to Ice Rock.

David put the last of the garbage bags on the back of the green Chevy pickup. He climbed into the cab and sat down on the vinyl seat, which was ripped and dusty. He ground the truck engine to a start, revved up, and put the truck into gear.

The lecture he'd received from Sterling, with his mother present in the room, lingered in his mind. It had been a bitter and embarrassing exchange. Had someone seen him kissing Diana? He couldn't look at his mother when she'd said, "Son, look at me. You have a solemn responsibility here. Perhaps it is natural that you would find some of the young women here attractive. But you must know that they are ill, and that they are very vulnerable, and that yours is a sacred duty."

He hit the steering wheel with his fist. He was driving too fast, but he didn't much care. What did his mother think he was, a priest? Or a rapist?

And as for those girls, he hadn't really up until now believed there was anything really wrong with them. A few nightmares? Who didn't have nightmares? He knew as well as his mother did that the Albion Clinic had been built by Theda Price for one reason: to make money off rich neurotics. And also to provide Theda with an excuse for her spoiled daughter's weird behavior, David thought bitterly.

Shirley had reached for his hand, and pressed it before she left Sterling's office. Then when she was gone, Sterling gave him the ultimatum.

"If you want to keep your job here," Sterling said, "then you had better keep your hands—and the rest of your anatomy—away from Diana."

It had been really humiliating. Like he'd committed some kind of crime. What bullshit. He reached into the glove compartment and rooted around until he found the packet with the multi-vitamin complex inside. He ripped open the packet and swallowed the vitamins dry. They left a bitter taste in his mouth.

If anyone could help Diana—really help her—it was him, and not Sterling.

He thought of Diana. Pretty much abandoned by her family. Troubled and abused. You could see it all over her, from the minute you set eyes on her, that what she needed was love. His feelings for her grew more intense the more he thought of her suffering.

But now he was supposed to forget about all those feelings. Forget them if he wanted to keep his good-paying job, a job that he hoped would help him to afford to go back to school in a year or two.

He recounted to himself his many virtues: a good strong body that he pushed with hard, regular workouts. He'd never touched a drop of alcohol, and drugs were unthinkable, despite the temptations. Even the assistant track coach, who'd done so much for him his senior year in high school, had once offered him a hit off a joint. That had been a shattering experience, and it ruined a great friendship. Because of course David said ''no,'' and pretty much ran home, turning down the coach's repeated offerings for a ride. Coach Randolph was so cool, it was disappointing to see this hypocritical side of him. He'd often used his special keys to the workout room just to let David inside after school hours, and many times they swam together in the school pool, late at night, when no one else was around. Just them. It had made David feel special.

And it was to Coach Randolph whom David had confided his secret desire to be a dancer.

But even Coach Randolph turned out to be two-faced.

And now this! Sterling was making out like David was some kind of filthy pervert. David, who did two hundred sit-ups every morning, and one hundred push-ups before bed. All he had done was kiss Diana.

All he wanted now was to kiss her again. Kiss her and make love to her. He couldn't help wondering what it would be like with her.

When David arrived at the dump he saw the mass of swooping blackbirds that hovered above it, thronging like gulls over a giant fishing boat.

He pitched the garbage bags onto the heap, and looked at the mass of refuse with a feeling of disgust. A dirty boot stuck out from the pile of rotting garbage and paper.

He was all alone, just like last time. And as usual, he thought about last year, when he'd left his dorm room and gone to a school dance recital, all by himself. His friends would never have understood. He remembered the music: Prokofiev's *Cinderella Suite*. He'd even bought the recording. He didn't need it now, because he remembered it by heart.

He looked around, humming, closing his eyes, seized with a kind of panic and desire.

He bowed deeply before the pile of garbage. Then he spread wide his arms and turned his head, in a classical dance pose. He leapt onto the garbage pile, and sank to his knees in muck.

It had to be up there, he told himself; who else would climb a garbage heap to find it? With any luck it would still be there, where he'd gotten rid of it. For good, he'd thought.

He fought his way up and through the mountain of stinking refuse. He needed to get all the way to the top, but of course the garbage was shifting all around him, so it wasn't easy. No telling what was left up there after all the rains. His goal was simply to reach the top. If he reached the top, he told himself, he would *win*. He would get it back.

He played a little game. If he made it all the way to the top, he thought, lunging, feeling his sweat coming down his face now, then he would stop thinking about Diana the way he had been thinking about her. God would put her out of his mind, as was right and proper.

He pushed past coffee cans and indistinguishable blobs of brown moist rot, past rusted bedsprings, and tires and naked dolls without arms, with eyes missing; swam and clawed upward past the discarded rags and brown blood-stained bandages, wigs and bifocals and teeth and eggshells, and bones—endless bones.

And at last he reached the top, breathing hard, nearly heaving from the stench of ripe decay in his nostrils and mouth.

And there it was.

He'd thought he didn't want that thing around anymore. Thought he'd discarded it the way a kid throws off his security blanket finally, or his teddy bear. He knew it was dangerous to have around, not to mention probably illegal.

He wrapped his fingers around the barrel, which protruded from a morass of—what?—coffee grounds and broken clumps of plaster, the stiff remains of a magazine, a beautiful cover model's face watermarked, defiled, smiling at him. He hoisted the rifle out of the sucking, damp refuse.

It looked a little worse for being outside on a garbage heap. The front sight was caked with some kind of yellow goo, and a few strands of spaghetti had hardened onto the breechblock. He broke them off with his thumb. The rifle would need a good cleaning, that was for sure.

Now David started back down the heap, sliding on his butt through the papery crud, the rifle held close to his body.

But even before he slipped on the last black banana peel and sprawled over the hard-packed dirt of the ground he knew he was in a losing battle. He felt even worse now. The weapon he'd vowed to get rid of was tight in his hands again, which were now almost black with the stinking smear of decay.

The fog was clearing off, and the sunshine felt warm on Diana's face. The hike might do her some good, she thought, and take her mind off the bad connections, at least for a while.

"I won't think about that today," she told herself, in a fluttery Scarlett O'Hara accent, "I'll think about that to-morrow."

No mean trick, taking your mind off the weirdness. The transmitter that might have been buried in her head. The Psychic Pals, leering out of the TV set.

And David. Another complication.

Good thing Diana had a lot of experience in the fine art of denial. Maybe not as much as Scarlett had.

Catherine marched beside her, silently, her face as contented as a cat's—or as Vivien Leigh's, in a devil-woman role.

Catherine let out a big, ravished sigh.

"You should see the flowers that bloom around here in the spring and summer," Catherine said. "The dogtooth violet, rue anemone, and let's see," she counted on her fingers. "Hepatica, bloodroot—look, there's some big blue stem." She pointed.

Diana tried to stay calm. If she stayed calm, Catherine couldn't "read" her. That's what she'd said anyway. Best to think of something else, distract the mind.

Looking over at the weeds Catherine pointed at, Diana tried again to remember last night's dream. Not that this would calm her. Luckily nothing came to her, no creepy nightmare residue. According to Dr. Sterling, you could dream at any point during sleep. But the most intense dreaming came with REM sleep. If someone woke you up during REM sleep, you could probably recall most of your dream.

Sterling had been trying to get her to "guide" her dreams, to take that voice or additional point of view—that awareness of dreaming when you tell yourself, "it's only a dream"—and then make the dream into a kind of movie. You're the director and the star, with two points of view. It was like you had two personalities, the character in the dream, and the character watching the dream. Both of them were you, the observer and the observed.

"Then if you can turn around and confront a demon, or make yourself get up and open a closed door, to see what's behind it, then *you* have the dream instead of the dream having you," Sterling had said.

There were lots of things Diana could think about, if she wanted to get her mind off . . . her mind.

Catherine and Diana walked side by side for a while, silently. When they reached a place where the trail led steeply upward, where stands of birch and sycamore and black maple lined the path, Catherine stopped and smiled sadly at Diana. She put her hand on her friend's shoulder.

"Are you still pissed at me?" Catherine asked.

"Pissed?" Diana said. "You scare me."

"Afraid you see yourself in me?"

Diana stammered, "That's not what I had in mind."

"What you *have in mind* if you'd only realize it is a rare gift. Don't fight it. Feel the power of it."

Diana said, "How long have you known about this . . . power?"

"Always."

"Does Sterling know about this?"

Catherine frowned. "Why would I tell him? All he cares about are my nightmares."

Diana kept walking. "I just don't think I can deal with this."

Catherine followed close behind her, Catherine, who—it seemed—could signal on a wave that travelled directly into Diana's brain.

Catherine, who suffered debilitating night terrors.

Catherine was so much like her, it was scary.

"Look," Catherine said. "We don't have to deal with this right now if you don't want to. I mean, we *could* have some fun with it, telegraphing messages—but only if we both wanted to. We would have to agree, okay?"

"But I didn't agree to that little stunt back there with Mrs. Kearney," Diana protested. "You have a hell of a lot more control over this . . . telegraphing thing, or whatever you call it, than I do."

"We could make money with it!" Catherine cried, as if she'd just discovered electricity. "We could prosper. I mean, we could make a fortune, the two of us. A killing with this thing!"

Diana looked up the steep trail, where a carved wooden sign announced ICE ROCK.

"How can you be so cool about it?"

"I'm just trying to see the positive side," Catherine said.

"Making lemonade out of lemons again, huh?" Diana managed a weak smile. "We could go on TV, be Psychic Pals and tell people which lottery numbers to choose. Join that army of happy-go-lucky psychics who dole out advice in their spare time. God, if they only knew what it was really like."

Catherine said glumly, "I really hate that word, psychic."

"What would you call it?"

"How about PWR—Person With Radar." She laughed.

"How about bananacakes?" Diana said. "How about Looney Tunes?"

Diana still wasn't entirely convinced the whole thing wasn't a bizarre sham, that in her sleep a radio transmitter hadn't been planted inside her head somewhere. But for what purpose? She hadn't a clue. Or maybe it really was true, what Catherine was saying. Diana didn't want to believe any of it. She wanted to pretend everything was actually fine, normal, run-of-the-mill.

Her ex-shrink Dr. Linden had once called her Cleopatra, Queen of Denial.

Diana felt that if you ignore something long enough, it

will go away. Even your dreams and your (stolen) thoughts.

"Okay, okay," Catherine said. "Let's give it a rest."

"Good idea," Diana said with an exasperated smile.

"Come on," Catherine said, and she bounded up the trail. Diana followed close behind. The trail sloped upward in a tree-lined zigzag. Diana's breath was heaving in and out by the time they reached the top. But it was worth the effort. Diana's eyes widened, taking it all in.

Up here, you could see miles and miles of Blackburn County. The view spanned out below the cliff like a CinemaScope picture, river winding through brown hills and forest, sky as big as forever.

The top of Ice Rock was flat and grassy. It was about twenty feet wide and twenty feet across, jutting into space. Diana and Catherine walked to the cliff edge. Diana, who feared heights, felt her heart suddenly slamming in her chest. She hesitated.

"You're perfectly safe," Catherine said.

Diana watched Catherine move along on her belly at the very edge of Ice Rock. Catherine leaned her head on her hands and peered over the edge. "Come on, it's beautiful," Catherine said. "Have a look-see."

Diana's heart pounded, but she went down to her knees, and then on all fours crawled to the cliff's edge. She could feel the coldness of the ground. Now they were side by side.

It was at least fifty feet to the rocky grass-covered plain below. A fall would be fatal. Diana looked out at the spectacular view of rolling countryside. She could see farms and strips of highway. Fat clouds lolled in the sky. It was beautiful.

The center of Ice Rock was clear of trees, but all along the edges there grew tall oaks and elms and hickory, and tall bushy green pines. Most trees up here were all but bare of leaves.

For a long time, they were quiet. They listened to the breeze moving over the hilltop, threading through the bare trees. Felt the sun warming their backs.

At last Diana felt calm.

"So pretty up here," Diana said.

"Yeah," Catherine said sleepily, eyes half-closed. "That's why it's so ironic."

"Why what's so ironic?"

Catherine smiled. "This is where the strangest of the Death Wish Traditions takes place, every year," she said.

"The what?" Diana said, feeling a pang of anxiety. "Do I want to hear this?"

"Now don't get nervous. It's just a bit of local color. Nothing that can hurt you."

Diana rested her face on her folded hands and gazed into the blue sky. "Okay, tell me about it."

Catherine sat up, making herself more comfortable.

"Okay, here goes. For decades, the locals, the really backward locals, descendants of the first Blackburn County settlers, have participated in a ritual unique to our area. Ice Rock got its name not only because it was formed by an icy glacier, but because after the first snow each winter the locals get drunk and tramp up here. This place looks like a big white iceberg. The old-time locals dance, daring one another to go closer and closer to the edge."

"You must be kidding! Don't the police stop it?"

"Of course not. It's a tradition, and the sort of mob scene a couple police officers could never control. Anyway, every few years some fool goes over the edge. Splat!"

"That's awful. I think falling would be a terrifying death."

Catherine just smiled again. "These people are insane, a whole community of village idiots. It's their idea of fun. Wait and see, the first snowfall, they'll all be up here."

Diana shook her head. "I hope I never see any such thing."

Catherine smiled. "I've seen it. I've even been tempted to dance right along with them. Do you ever meditate?" Catherine leaned back against the trunk of a young hickory. She pulled her knees up slightly. She looked out across the valley. "When I meditate, this is the place I visualize."

Diana was watching a squirrel. The squirrel was rummaging through a pile of fallen leaves. It darted beneath the surface, sending up a small explosion of churned leaves. Then it emerged again, nose flickering.

"I thought that in meditation you're supposed to clear your mind of everything," Diana said.

"You can do it that way, or you can visualize a peaceful place you want to see, a real place or even a fantasy place you make up or see in a movie."

"This place is beautiful," Diana said.

Study it.

"Why should I study it?" Diana asked, not even bothering to ask why Catherine telegraphed those words, rather than simply saying them aloud.

"I think it will help ease your dreams," Catherine said.

Diana stood up and brushed off her pants. "I seem to not be having dreams these days. Thank God for that."

Catherine rose and followed. "Don't forget this place. Remember every color, every tree and rock. If you take anything away from your time in Blackburn County, it should be this spectacular view."

Diana took a last glance around. It was as though a smaller version of the Rock of Gibraltar had formed here in the sylvan wilderness. And this gently sloping flat cliff had grown a skin of grass and bushes, where tall robust trees flourished. It was a strange and beautiful place, but hadn't Catherine called it the site of the Death Wish Traditions? Despite the beauty and dramatic scale of the place, Diana felt a slight chill, thinking of the bodies that must have fallen here. Of the people who died from some mysterious folly she couldn't begin to fathom.

They hiked down the steep trail, feet loosening dirt and gravel as they walked. Diana could feel the powerful strength of gravity pulling her back down to the valley. The world is full of such strange invisible forces, she thought.

The river trail passed through a dense wood. Diana found herself absorbed in the strange shadows that were cast upon the ground. When she turned and looked at Catherine, it appeared as if a webwork of shadow slid across her face as she walked. Catherine had pulled her long blond hair back and was tying it with a rubber band. She returned Diana's gaze, and she smiled.

Don't shut me out.

Diana had to stop. She reached out and held on to a low thin tree branch. She felt as though she'd just received a heavy blow to her stomach. Her heart raced and her breath came quickly.

It *hurt* to receive a transmission like that. A signal so clear and penetrating that it frightened her.

"I thought we were going to give it a rest," Diana said.

"Oops," Catherine said. She smiled, but her smile faded when she looked closely at Diana's hard expression. "Hey, we're friends, right?" Catherine said.

Diana swallowed hard. "It scares me."

Catherine leaned back against a tree, her hands behind her back. She looked up into her friend's dark eyes. "I don't think anyone else you know understands that quite as well as I do," she said.

Diana closed her eyes. When she opened them, she saw that Catherine's gaze had never left her. Catherine's eyes were so blue in this light. They gleamed.

"We don't have to . . ." Diana couldn't quite form the words. "We don't have to *use* it," she said.

Catherine shrugged. "What good is power if you're not going to use it?"

Here we go again, Diana thought.

"Use it for what?" Diana said.

"For fun, silly." Catherine stood up. She smiled. "I wish you wouldn't be afraid. I've never known anyone," she said, gazing intently, "like *me* before."

Diana smiled. "And I sure as hell have never known anyone quite like *you*, Catherine."

A cry came from the woods, a cry that wiped the smiles from their faces.

It was definitely human.

Diana turned to see what it could have been. Catherine caught Diana's arm, stopping her, nearly pulling her off balance.

"Don't go over there," Catherine said. A tremor in her voice.

There came another cry: "Help!"

"Someone's in trouble," Diana said.

"It might be a trick," Catherine said.

Diana looked at her. "A trick? It doesn't *feel* like a trick to me. Does it to you?"

"I don't know."

Diana said rather sharply, "Well, so much for controlling these powers. You can't even see into the bushes? Come on, let's see what it is with our own eyes."

They pushed farther on through the brush, and when they reached the banks of the muddy river, sunlight broke over a scene that chilled Diana's blood.

There, caught amid a thorny bramble, several feet off the grass trail, was an old woman. Thorns had scored her wrinkled, bony face and hands with thread-like red cuts. The woman's hair was silver-white and floated wildly about her head. Her golden eyes winced in pain.

"Oh," she cried. "I'm trapped in here!"

Diana looked at Catherine. Catherine shrugged. Quickly Diana moved to free the old woman, pulling the thorny vines from the woman's flowing skirts, and from what appeared to be some kind of hunting jacket she wore.

"Ouch!" Diana said, catching a thorn in the palm of her hand.

The old woman gasped, and began to fall. Catherine was able to support the old woman's weight.

"Ugh," Catherine grunted, pulling at the woman's leg.

"Hold on, you're almost out of there," Diana said. The woman was free of the tangle of vines everywhere but at her booted foot. How she got stuck in here, Diana couldn't have guessed. Diana stepped on the cord of tangled vine, and snapped much of it apart; most of the vine was dry and brown. But the tough vine held.

Diana stood up and looked around. She saw a flat rock with a sharp edge. She picked up the rock and came over to the vine, and bent down. It only took a few chops. The vine broke.

At last the old woman was free.

Diana looked at her hand, which was cut. She let the rock slip from her hand into the grass. The cut was not deep, but it stung the palm of her hand. A drop of blood stood at the entrance of the small puncture, grew, then turned into a thin streak of red.

"Oh, you've cut yourself," the old woman said. "Here, let me help you." She was breathing hard, but managed to pull, from one of the pockets of her coat, a white cloth. She pressed it into Diana's hand. "I've got to sit down," she said.

Catherine helped the old woman over to a wide tree stump, where she sat down to collect her breath.

"You're from around here, aren't you?" Catherine said, leaning back against a slim birch tree and wiping her brow with the back of her hand. "You're one of the old-time locals."

The woman looked at Catherine, assessing her. "And you are clearly one of our more recent arrivals," she said. "My name is Serilda, and, yes, I'm a local, an old-timer or whatever it is you fancy newcomers want to call us."

"I'm not really a newcomer," Catherine said. "I grew up here. My mother has lived here for a long, long time."

"Ain't nobody lived here long as the old-timers, child," Serilda said.

The word "old-timers," as Serilda said it, fairly echoed in Diana's ears.

Serilda now looked at Diana. "And what about you? You're not from around here."

"No," Diana said. She felt light-headed. It was all she could do to keep out the vibrations that seemed to be trying to get in. Diana imagined a kind of psychic thunderstorm brewing invisibly above their heads, between minds and hearts, connecting some spirit energy that resided in each of them. Diana felt it in her chest and stomach more than in her head.

Diana quickly changed the subject. "How did you get stuck in the bushes?" she asked.

"I was after some eggs. Some very rare eggs," Serilda said, her face stern.

Diana looked at her hand. The small cut had stopped bleeding. But it looked nasty.

"You'd better tend to that cut," Serilda said. "Clean it out good. Take care of it. Watch it closely."

Watch closely.

Diana started slightly. The voice was strange; it was not Catherine's voice.

Beware, child.

Serilda reached into her coat pocket. A moment later she withdrew her closed fist. Slowly, she opened her hand. At its center was a tiny gold bell. At the top of the bell was a small ring.

"I have something for you, a token of my appreciation. Who knows, I might have froze to death overnight in this bramble if you hadn't come along." She smiled, showing wide gaps between her teeth.

Diana looked at the bell, fascinated.

"This bell is very special," Serilda said. "It contains a kind of magic spell."

Diana and Catherine exchanged a glance.

"It can protect you if you possess it—or curse you if someone uses it against you. Heed this celestial admonition, children."

Catherine rolled her eyes. "Oh, really? Well, sure, if you say so," she said to the old woman.

Serilda's eyes narrowed. "I can sense in the two of you a strange power, unified but at opposites, like the two sides of a coin."

Diana felt anger now. Was this old woman playing a game? Or did she really sense the fledgling powers the two young women had only begun to realize? Diana tried to cast an invisible wave into the old woman's mind, but found her inscrutable. As so often, Diana's powers were as uncontrollable as her moods. One couldn't simply will a happy disposition on a day when you woke up feeling rotten. One could not necessarily will a magic eye into places, either. About the best she could do was wish and, if she were lucky, stand back and observe, as a dreamer observes her dreams.

If it were true that with Catherine's help the power seemed to clarify itself, to come under rein, however clumsily, then it was also true and evident now that Catherine could shut down the bond at will.

Diana could *feel* Catherine's unwillingness and hostility toward the old woman.

It was as if it were easier to will a *no* than a *yes*, to reject rather than to unify. Diana looked uneasily at her friend, and sensed her mood. Sure enough, an invisible icy barrier wall was palpable.

"Your power," Serilda said, "like this magic bell, can be used in the eternal struggle between good and evil, between light and dark." She shut her eyes tight. A spasm of pain seemed to visibly move through her body. Diana wondered if she'd been hurt worse than it appeared. "A warning," Serilda whispered. "The cold hand of death is ever near these cursed grounds. The Traditions shall be observed, and the dead shall be avenged. Use this as a charm against evil."

Serilda pinched the top of the bell and gave it several gentle shakes. The haunting tinkle of the bell sent a wave of gooseflesh-raising shivers over Diana's skin. This was the crystalline toll of her nightmares.

She held the bell toward Diana. Sunlight gleamed on its polished surface. Diana hesitated and Catherine reached over and snatched the bell, with a smile. She held it up to her eyes. Then she turned her gaze to Diana and shrugged. To Serilda she said, "Thanks."

Serilda smiled now, too. It was a strange smile, a knowing sort of smile, and she bowed her head.

Serilda stood up and brushed off the hem of her long dress. Diana noticed that Serilda's boots were caked with dried mud. A dark cloth bag hung at her side, and Diana saw the mouth of it hanging open. She could see the white raw tips of some strange kind of muddy root.

As if sensing Diana's curiosity, Serilda reached into the bag and withdrew three soft white eggs. They were tiny.

"Serpent eggs," Serilda said, holding them in a slightly trembling hand.

Diana wasn't at all certain if the eggs really were serpent eggs, she'd never seen any that she could recall. But she felt sure there was something else in the bag. Something still. Something dead. A feral animal, with a whiskered snout and small unseeing eyes. She saw its tiny black claws as Serilda slipped the eggs back inside the bag.

Diana reached out to a low-hanging tree branch, and took

hold of it, trying to brace herself. Her knees felt a little weak. The old woman frightened her. The bell frightened her. She wanted Catherine to get rid of it, just as soon as they were away from Serilda.

"Good-bye," Serilda said. "I must be on my way." She turned and stepped carefully away along the banks of the dark river. Catherine slid the bell into her pants pocket.

"A good deed for the day," Catherine said to Diana. "We saved an old loon. Now do you see what I mean about the Blackburn County old-timers?"

"Yes," Diana said quietly. "But what are we going to do with the bell? Why don't you just throw it in the river?"

"You really have the creeps about that silly bell, don't you?"

Diana shook her head as they walked along the trail, where blue spruces stood tall against the sky, and the dry husks of a plant called king's candle—they almost looked like big candles with wax dripping down their stalks— stood in the brown grass.

"It's just that she seemed to know about us," Diana said.

"The old-timers around here have been rumored to practice witchcraft. Yet you'll notice Serilda lacked the elementary powers to free herself from a tangle of thorny vines. Some magic, huh?"

Diana nodded.

"I think this bell is a worthless piece of dime-store junk," Catherine said. "But my mother will know for sure. She collects antiques and has quite a collection of dinner bells in our dining room. If it's worth anything, she'll want it, and she'll even pay for it. We can split the money fifty-fifty. But if it's junk I'm sure my mother will throw it where it belongs—in the trash."

"I don't want any part of that bell," Diana said.

"Suit yourself," Catherine replied, taking the bell out of her pocket and examining it closely.

The clinic loomed before them now, windows filled with blue sky reflection. Diana went up ahead, eager to get inside now. She was feeling chilly.

Catherine stopped for a moment. Frowning, she looked at the bell in the palm of her hand. She slowly closed her fingers around it, and held it tight.

Chapter Three

A few days later Diana took her first trip into town. Catherine arranged everything. Harriet Evans drove them into the village of Leonora, some ten miles southeast of the clinic, in her old green Buick. The fields were brown and dry, the country roads dusty. She let them off on Main Street, in front of the Royal Theater, a closed-down and boarded-up old movie palace. She promised to pick them back up at the same spot in exactly three hours.

Diana looked up at the old marquee. A few crooked letters spelled out FOR S LE. She pulled her white cashmere scarf a bit tighter to her neck, against the chill.

Leonora was a drab old place in November. The tall blighted elms that lined the streets were bare of leaves, and the bushes, too, were skeletal, so that as far as Diana could see there was nothing but gray. Gray upon gray, with black utility lines strewn overhead in all directions, like party streamers long, long after the party is over. And here, too, were the broken fences between yards piled with junk, rusted cars, the remains of swing sets. Beyond the block of businesses (low square brick boxes), most of them closed for good, were the sagging front porches of once-grand old homes, and lonely, dented cars parked along the crumbling curbsides. Where were the people?

Diana had no sooner wondered this when a gaggle of women, most of them old, emerged through the automatic door of the Save-U-Foods.

"The 'wives,'" Catherine murmured. "They're all old-timers,'' she said. By now Diana knew that the term ''old-timers'' did not necessarily mean old people; it was a disparaging term reserved for the poor descendants of Blackburn County's first rural settlers, a hardscrabble clan whose numbers were dwindling. They were mostly country dwellers.

The six wives dressed oddly, in drab old-fashioned winter coats. The scarves tied to their heads might have served double duty as dish rags, and their clunky boots would not have looked out of place on Frankenstein's monster. One of them wheeled behind her a small metal grocery cart. The others clutched plastic grocery bags.

Their faces, like Serilda's face, might have come straight out of a book of nineteenth century portraits. So harsh, yet in some cases starkly beautiful, Diana thought. Eyes that pierced through the roughness and bore a strange light. Diana had the unnerving impression of looking right through their faces to their skulls. Smiles revealed gaps where teeth were spaced far apart. One woman, who held her old black purse close to her body, had a bright blue straying eye. The other eye was milky gray.

Diana said, ''Hello,'' and even as she did so she felt Catherine's hand at her elbow, urging her on in the other direction, away from these ''wives.''

In Blackburn County, Catherine had explained, one encountered ''wives'' and ''old-timers,'' and, on occasion, a group called the ''the widows.'' The old-timers were a weirdly stratified society, isolated and sparse in number. Among the widows was a rarely seen subgroup, ''The war widows.'' Diana had been practically incredulous when Catherine had told her there was even a group called the ''orphans''—all grown men, most of them now in their fifties and sixties, who had never married, and who still considered themselves abandoned children! They were usually taken care of by their old-timer relatives, because they were not expected to work.

Diana had a hard time believing all this country lore— yet here was evidence of it, standing before her in broad daylight. These isolated Blackburn County wives were like no people she'd ever seen before.

A woman with white hair under a ragged tan scarf smiled at her. She was probably the oldest of the lot, whose ages ranged from about thirty-five to maybe sixty, Diana guessed.

"Hall-o," the old woman said. The others looked at Diana as they passed by. Despite the wives' rather grim appearances, they were clearly in a festive mood.

"You going to hear Nessie?" asked one of them, a younger woman with a ghost-pale complexion, a massive forehead and thatch of nerdy two-inch bangs.

"Nessie?" Diana asked.

"Nessie Jasper," the woman replied and nodded.

Diana felt an uneasiness in Catherine.

Catherine crossed her arms over her chest. She was wearing a finger-length black leather jacket today, and her shampooed blond hair hung down upon her shoulders. She stiffly flicked it back with a snap of her head. "Where is Nessie speaking?"

"Where else?" the woman said with a grin. "In front of the Great Northern Pub, where she's been since sunup, drinking and pulling her thoughts together." She laughed and the others twittered.

"Think she'll run against old Theda?" said the woman with the wandering eye.

"She says she's a-gonna," replied the older woman.

"She *says* a lot, and always has," answered a third, and the wives laughed again.

"Old Theda will have her hands full with Nessie!"

"Old Theda has her hands full with the devil's own, hasn't she?" the old woman said now, smiling wickedly. "But it's all her own doing, and I say she deserves what she gets—even if what she gets is Nessie!" She hooted at that, and the others bent to laugh and clutch at one another's arms.

Diana looked at Catherine. It was painfully obvious now the unwitting wives were talking about the woman who was planning to challenge her mother in a recall election. Catherine wasn't smiling. They hadn't recognized her.

"The pub's right over there," the older woman said now, pointing at a run-down brown brick structure, squeezed in between a boarded-up hotel and long-since abandoned bakery. The pub door opened and out staggered an old man. He was drunk, as anyone could see.

"Tsk," said the woman with the tan scarf. "Corky Marshall." The drunk put his cap on and when he saw the wives he waved and gave a toothless whiskery smile.

"We'd best get that old fool orphan boy something to eat, or he'll be passed out dead before the speech even begins," said the older woman.

"He's no doubt heard a dozen speeches already," said the younger woman with the bangs. "Nessie probably talked his ear off, abetting his thirst."

The older woman laughed richly at that. "This one needs no abetting, sister." She turned toward the young women now, and Diana felt her warning gaze. She looked from Diana to Catherine. "I recognize you now, Catherine Price," the woman said. The other wives were silent now. Grim expressions replaced festive ones. They looked sheepishly at Catherine.

Catherine cocked her head, pointing her chin at the old woman.

"You should have spoke up, child," the woman said to Catherine. "We didn't mean to be insulting the child of the mother."

"I'm not insulted," Catherine said. "It's a free country."

The woman smiled wryly. " 'Tis, 'tisn't it?" She held her grocery bag tight. Diana could have sworn the moist pink thing poking out near the top of the bag was a severed pig's snout. She shuddered. "We meant no harm to you, then," the old woman said. "All apologies to you." She smiled humbly and bowed her head.

The wives bid their good-byes, somewhat shamefaced now. And off they went after Corky Marshall.

Catherine looked really pissed off now.

"Are you really that concerned about what they think of your mother?" Diana asked, as the two young women walked past the Great Northern Pub, looking at its begrimed windows, where neon signs flickered pale against the daylight.

"No I'm not," Catherine answered. "But I hate hearing the name of Nessie Jasper. She's pure white trash and doesn't give a hoot who knows it. She's a damn fool, and if she thinks she's going to defeat my mother she's even more stupid than she looks. No fucking old-timer has ever finished grade school much less run for public office."

"Should we listen to her speech? We could spy for your mom!"

Something caught Catherine's eye. Diana looked up the street, where two lanky figures walked side by side. She could see from a distance the two boys, whom she guessed were around sixteen or seventeen.

Randy and Jon.

Diana could feel Catherine's excitement. These were the wild boys they had come to town to meet.

One of the boys, the taller of the two, waved at Catherine. He had long brown hair falling over one eye.

"That's Randy," Catherine said, smiling. "The other guy, the short one, is Jon Dover." Jon had thick red hair, parted on the side and shaggy, and some red whiskers forming an attempt at a goatee.

When Randy reached Catherine he put his arms around her waist and leaned in to kiss her. Laughing, she turned her head away and the kiss landed on her neck, tickling her.

"Shit, Catherine," Randy said, holding her tight. "You look good. And you smell good, too." His voice was deep, like he had a cold or something. He coughed and spat on the ground.

Jon grabbed Catherine from behind and lifted her up.

"Jon!" Catherine squealed. "Put me down. Come on!"

Diana noticed that Jon's hands were all over Catherine, that he seemed as familiar with her as was Randy. Were they lovers, all three of them? Diana wasn't sure. And Catherine wasn't letting on.

Jon smiled at Diana now. A wolfish grin. "Who's your friend?" he said.

Catherine introduced the boys to Diana, and they in turn shook her hand. Randy Curtis bent down on one knee and kissed her hand. He was sort of cute, if rough looking.

Square jaw and bright dark eyes. Jon Dover, the shorter one, had a rough but not unappealing animal look, accentuated by fierce green eyes. They were dressed in blue jeans and worn blue denim jackets, and they smelled of tobacco.

"You boys staying out of trouble?" Catherine asked. The four of them started back down the street, toward the Great Northern Pub, where a small crowd was gathering.

Randy slipped his arm around Catherine's waist. She turned and stepped out of his embrace, but he only smiled at her.

"Trouble? What kinda trouble do you mean?" Randy asked.

"You know," Catherine said. "Jail."

"Well, I never been in trouble *in* jail," Randy said.

Jon smiled, revealing a gold tooth. "I've never been in jail at all. Too smart." He shook a cigarette out of a crumpled pack and lit it. Then he offered one to Diana.

"No thank you," Diana said.

"What's going on over there?" Jon said, looking at the assembled crowd of about thirty people.

"Nessie Jasper, dipshit," Randy said. "Didn't you hear? She's giving one of her speeches."

"Why should I care what that pervert thinks?" Jon scoffed.

"Don't you care about politics, fool-boy?" Randy asked. "Nessie is gonna kick Catherine's mother outta office."

"You think so?" Catherine said, giving Randy a haughty look.

"You said yourself your old lady deserves to be out on her ass," Randy said to her.

Catherine looked sheepishly at Diana. But by now Diana was used to Catherine's contradictions wherever her mother was concerned.

"I was only kidding about that, of course," Catherine said. "But do you really think this *hick* Nessie Jasper could beat my mother?"

Diana caught a glimpse through the crowd of a short stocky woman in jeans standing up on a vegetable crate at the entryway of the Great Northern Pub. The woman had plain features, save for one striking attribute—her large dark eyes. Her dark brown hair was short and thick, cut in a functional but thoughtless style. About thirty-five people had gathered around her.

"What I have here in my hands today is a petition," Nessie said, loudly, in a melodious and pleasant voice. "It is a petition to recall Representative Theda Price from office."

A cheer went up in the crowd. Catherine frowned, but listened intently.

Nessie handed the petition to a gray-bearded man, who handed her a folded newspaper. Nessie unfolded it. She held it up. The headline said LOBBYING SCANDAL ROCKS CAPITOL. A subhead said PRICE IMPLICATED.

"We've known for a long time that old Theda has had interests in mind that didn't include the people of Blackburn County," Nessie said, angrily. Her breath steamed in the cold air. She rolled up the newspaper and whacked it hard against her hand. "It's time we let Theda know what we think of her. We're tired of her 'business as usual' politics—in her case 'business as usual' is graft, kickbacks, corruption, and votes sold to the highest bidder. It's all coming to light, folks. She'll deny it. She'll make her usual promises. But we cannot let ourselves be bought off with a new road project or a promise of jobs that never seem to materialize, unless they're minimum wage jobs attached to a business owned by none other than Theda Price."

The crowd booed.

"She has gotten rich over the years, while Blackburn County has sunk deeper into poverty," Nessie went on. "While our children go without health care and our schools are falling apart, Theda Price is wined and dined by the fat cat lobbyists in Madison, and in Washington."

Nessie opened up the newspaper to a full-page photograph of a lavish tropical resort, where swimming suit–clad people reclined on lounge chairs around a pool. "And in the Virgin Islands," Nessie said gravely, referring to a lobbyist-financed vacation Theda had allegedly taken in exchange for a vote—and for a share in a shady business deal.

Again the crowd booed and hissed.

"Lies," Catherine whispered, loud enough so that a couple of the wives turned and looked at her.

Diana felt embarrassed.

Nessie continued. "Now you all know as well as I do that any man or woman who goes up against Theda in an election is *marked*."

The crowd was very quiet now.

"Theda hurls the kind of mud that sticks. She doesn't much care if she tells the whole truth or nothing but lies with a grain of truth in them. She digs up your past and she paints the town red with it. I needn't mention any names, but I know some good men, and so do you, who were tainted by the Theda Price machine. I'm here to tell you today that I'm going up against that machine, and damn the consequences!"

The crowd roared its enthusiasm. Catherine and Diana remained motionless. But Jon and Randy both clapped, despite Catherine's proximity to them.

"I have had my share of scandalous affairs, I been fired from jobs, I've associated with nefarious individuals, not one of them a politician," Nessie said. "But my private affairs never cost you taxpayers a dime. I tell you that now. And I openly admit I like to have a drink, like any good old-timer does."

The crowd whooped.

"My house isn't pretty, and my kids aren't dressed in the finest clothes, and as many of you know, their fathers are no longer members of this community—which is a kind of civic improvement I can take full credit for."

The crowd laughed lightly, a bit uneasily, and was then silent.

"I tell you this now, in public, because it's the truth, and I know damn well that Theda Price will take the truth and twist it around and give it to you in a way that makes me look ashamed, or like some kind of liar. I am not a perfumed politician. I am just a woman who wants some justice. I want what the forefathers of America said we oughta have, and that's democratic representation, liberty, and at the very least, a real choice about who runs the government with our hard-earned money. And that's something Blackburn County hasn't had since Theda Price was elected. Join me, folks. Join me. Recall Theda Price. Send me to the state legislature in Madison. Give Blackburn County a real voice that represents the interests of the people and end the reign of that self-*coronated* queen of Blackburn County, Ms. Theda Price. Thank you.''

The crowd cheered and applauded, and a yellow-whiskered photographer from the weekly newspaper snapped a picture.

"Come on," Catherine said, pulling on Diana's arm.

When Jon and Randy noticed that Diana and Catherine were leaving, they followed them.

At Sammy's Lunch Counter, after the speech, Diana sipped a chocolate malt that tasted like pure bliss. She hadn't had one since she'd left Chicago. Luckily she'd scraped a few dollars together to be able to afford it. The boys were arguing with Catherine about Nessie.

Randy and Jon had been impressed with Nessie. Catherine kept interrupting them. And kept trashing Nessie with an ever-growing list of insults.

"Nessie is a ridiculous, retarded, old-timer cross-eyed country slut with a big mouth and a big can," Catherine said, dipping a french fry in ketchup and popping it into her mouth. She was wearing a bit of red lipstick today. As usual, she looked cool.

"Well, she did go to the Olympics," Randy pointed out. "You have to give her credit for that."

"The *Special* Olympics," Catherine said.

Jon laughed, and Diana tried to figure out what Catherine was really thinking, without a bit of success. The ice wall was up. And of course that made sense. Catherine was feeling threatened today, with her mother under siege. Diana wondered how much of Nessie's speech was true. Was Theda really a crooked politician?

"Before she volunteered for the Special Olympics she went to the real Olympics," Randy said. "You know that. She was an ice skater."

Diana tried to imagine Nessie in a tutu, and couldn't.

"She was a speed skater," Jon added. "But she didn't pick up a medal."

"So what?" Randy said. "At least she competed."

"A lot of good it did her," Catherine said. "She came back to Blackburn County and planted herself on a bar stool."

"Looks like she's about to do something now," Diana said. "Is your mom worried?"

Catherine wiped her mouth with a paper napkin. "I wish I could say no, but Mom lives for her job. She would absolutely die if she lost her seat in the state assembly. Everybody knows she's going to run for national office. Someday."

"Congress," Jon said. "That means she'll work in Washington, D.C. instead of at the State Capitol in Madison, and she'll be good'n'far away from you, Cat."

"Very good, Jon," Catherine said, "You get an 'A' in government."

He leered over at her. "Hope that's not my only reward."

"Dream on," Catherine replied.

The crowd at the diner was sparse this time of day. Diana finished her malt and felt full.

"Nessie doesn't hold a job?" Diana asked.

Catherine and the boys rolled their eyes.

"She's kind of an odd-job person," Catherine said. "The oddest job she had was—are you ready for this?— sex education teacher. She taught safe sex at all the high schools."

"They called her the *masturbation lady*," Randy said, and snorted. "And *condom-girl*!"

Diana smiled. "Really?"

"Of course she got herself fired from that job," Catherine said. "She was running around teaching all the kids about masturbation, about exploring your fantasies and what not."

Randy gave Jon an elbow in the ribs and they laughed.

Diana said, "So they fired her, huh?"

Catherine smiled. "The parents around here went ape shit," she said. "Said she was corrupting the youth with her permissive agenda. Theda came down hard on Nessie, and helped get her canned. So you see, the masturbation lady has a hidden agenda against my mom. She only wants revenge.''

Diana wondered about the charges against Theda, and about the ethics probe going on in Madison. No doubt a real battle was brewing here in Blackburn County; she'd arrived just in time to see it.

After they settled the bill, Randy and Jon went outside to smoke while Catherine and Diana went over to the dry goods section of Sammy's Lunch Counter, where a couple of aisles of shelves were stocked with toilet paper and soap and makeup. Diana had only four dollars left in her wallet.

Catherine held a tube of red lipstick in her hand. She looked at Diana.

The look said it all. She was going to steal it.

''I just don't have enough money,'' Catherine said. She shrugged.

And sure enough, Catherine turned her head, looking around, and simultaneously slipped the tube into her front pants pocket.

Diana tried to be cool. It made her uncomfortable to see this. But it wasn't like she hadn't shoplifted a couple of times before, herself. She could have sworn Catherine already knew that somehow. Catherine's arched eyebrow said as much.

It's easy.

Diana ran her fingers nervously through her hair. She walked toward the door, ahead of Catherine. She felt herself perspiring. Despite herself Diana was receiving telegraphed waves at such a speed it sounded as though the collected thoughts of every customer in the diner were swirling in her head:

. . . told Inez twice already I wasn't going to join her in making a mockery of Frederica, yet here she goes . . .

. . . and if it's cancer, well then there's not a thing I can do but sell the business to Teddy and . . .

. . . Mary Margaret said she would send her child to pick up the clothing left behind, but she will not know and will never know that her father had come to see her . . .

. . . That girl's one helluva sweet piece of ass, yes, sir . . .

When Diana reached the front door, her heart was pounding. Catherine was right behind her. The voice came from Sammy himself, the cafe proprietor—came loud and clear.

"Just hold on there, young ladies," he said sternly. "Come on back inside."

Diana recognized within herself the fever pitch of emotion that seemed to sweep away barriers between her mind and the minds of others. It struck her as a kind of nausea. Her skin felt raw, gooseflesh rose on her arms. She wasn't willing this to happen. It was as involuntary as an infection. Like a germ, it had the potential to multiply, to grow. She could feel it growing now.

"Come inside," Sammy said. Sammy had one of those comb-over hairstyles covering a large bald spot.

Catherine glanced at Diana and then faced Sammy.

"I'm afraid we're in an awful hurry, Sammy," Catherine said nervously.

His eyes narrowed. "Are you in such a hurry you can't deliver a package to your mom?" He held up a plain manilla envelope.

Catherine looked at the envelope. She smiled. "Oh, Sammy, why of course." She took the envelope he held out to her.

Diana felt her head cooling down.

"I barely recognized you, Catherine," Sammy said. "You're all grown up. Now when do you suppose that happened?"

Diana thought of the stolen lipstick in Catherine's pocket.

Catherine placed her hand over her thigh, as if the tube had suddenly pulsed with an icy coldness.

"What's in the envelope?" Catherine asked.

Sammy didn't flinch. "Your mother will know."

What's in the envelope?

Sammy blinked a couple of times, as though some dust had been blown into his eyes.

Diana concentrated on the envelope, too. She felt it now: being in tune with Catherine. A few minutes ago the swirling thoughts were like the discordant chaos of an orchestra warming up before a concert. Now, all thoughts were unifying, conducted through Catherine's and Diana's brains. *What's in the envelope?*

"It's sealed shut," Sammy said in a high thin voice. A strange voice that attracted the attention of the people at the lunch counter.

All at once every head at the lunch counter, old and young, turned and looked at the envelope in Catherine's hands. An envelope Catherine wouldn't dare open. One of her mother's secrets. Diana had a sensation of winter light, as when a cloud that has been blocking the sun clears off, and an intense brightness glitters over a snowy landscape. The disparate thoughts that had been swirling around only moments before evaporated. Catherine sensed it, too.

Minds were coming into focus. Coming under a *will*.

"What's in that envelope, Sammy?" asked a woman in a brown wig. The kid next to her, age six, said in a squeaky voice, "Yeah, what you got in there?"

Sammy sputtered for a moment.

Everyone was looking now. "What's in that envelope you're sending over to the state representative?" an old man said in a rough barking voice.

Sammy swallowed hard. But before he even said a word, Diana knew what was in the envelope. It was as clear as if he'd said it. Instantly Diana wondered just why Catherine wanted Sammy to say it in front of everyone at the lunch counter. Why wouldn't Catherine want to save her mother the embarrassment? Unless . . . Catherine wanted everyone to know the truth.

"Money," Sammy said. "Cash."

The woman in the brown wig clicked her tongue against the roof of her mouth. Whatever strange spell had befallen the diner vanished, like a blaring loudspeaker that is suddenly severed from its electrical source. Within the silence was an icy chill.

"Why did you tell me that?" the woman in the wig said now, annoyance in her voice. "I didn't want to know about that."

The little boy looked up at the woman. "But you asked, Grandma." The little boy looked at the other people in the diner. Most of them looked away, shamefaced.

"Money," muttered an old man, his face red as port wine. "Doesn't that figure?" He smacked his lips around the toothpick he was working between his blunted teeth.

Catherine didn't smile, but she flashed her teeth, which were white and straight, the product of years of agonizing orthodontic work.

"Why, thank you, Sammy. I'll be sure my mother gets *every dollar.*"

Diana and Catherine left the store, and met Randy and Jon. Randy was brushing his long dark hair, looking at his reflection in the window of a closed-up hardware store. He assessed himself in the mirror. Jon shoved him out of the way and mockingly ran his fingers through his much shorter red tangle of hair.

"I'm looking gorgeous today, don't you think?" he said, grinning.

"Fuck you," Randy said, and roughly shoved Jon into the glass, hard. The glass rippled but did not break.

"Dumb fuck," Jon cried. "You coulda killed me."

"Whoa, I'd miss you, man," Randy said.

Jon turned his attention to Catherine. He brushed off the front of his coat, dusty from the window glass. "What you got there?" he said, looking at the envelope Catherine was carrying.

"Nothing," Catherine said.

"What? C'mon."

"It's a letter to my mother, nosey."

The four walked down the decrepit Main Street.

"A letter asking her to resign?" Jon said.

"Very funny." Catherine picked up the pace a little bit. It was almost time to meet up with Harriet Evans. Diana noticed that the curbs were matted with leaves, presumably swept there and forgotten. The leaves had deteriorated and turned to an ugly brown web-like mass. Once, when she was a kid, Diana and some of her friends had walked home from school in the gutters, kicking up the beds of decomposing leaves, which had a pleasant autumn fragrance but also a mildewy basement smell, a damp odor. She remembered kicking something in the pile of leaves, something not hard but not soft. It was a dead crow, and a sizable one. She and her friends had run home, the smell of death in their nostrils, with a wariness of things hidden in piles of autumn leaves.

In front of the Royal Theater, Randy came up from behind Catherine and put his arms around her waist. He nuzzled the back of her neck.

"I'm really not in the mood for this," Catherine said, with a "tone" in her voice.

Diana frowned. Randy was being gross.

Randy lifted Catherine up and she dropped the envelope onto the tile sidewalk that led into the Royal Theater. The box office glass was smeared, and the doors were looped with heavy chains and padlocks. Leaves had blown into the recessed entryway, where the four of them now stood.

"Randy, don't be a dork," Catherine said. "Let me go."

Jon grinned at Diana. She was feeling a bit tired now. She ignored Jon. But she couldn't ignore Catherine, who was being held a little too roughly by Randy.

Put me down.

"Come on, Randy, let go," Diana said.

"First I want a little something," Randy said with a laugh. He cupped her breast in his hand and squeezed.

Diana concentrated. She felt angry. Catherine did, too. The next thought came as a bit of a jolt.

An invisible wave seemed to flow through Catherine and Diana, and bounce into Randy.

Diana felt a bit sick when she saw Randy's head snap back involuntarily, as if an invisible hand had clutched his hair and yanked on it.

Diana was surprised by the violence of it. Yet this violence was what Catherine wanted, it was what she was willing at this precise moment, and Diana seemed to be willing it, too. Some pain for Randy, an electric current of pain. A whiplash shock to the system.

Randy's arms went slack. Catherine didn't have to struggle away; she turned and watched Randy crumple. He fell down on his butt and leaned against the wall of the theater. He winced in pain.

"What the fuck's wrong with you, man?" Jon asked, running over to his friend.

Randy groaned. "My neck," he said, clasping his hand to it. "Oh, shit."

"You had a spasm, man."

Randy looked at Catherine. "What'd you do to me?"

Catherine rolled her eyes, stooping to pick up the envelope. Diana trembled and looked down at her shoes. What *had* they done to him? The sound of Harriet's tapping shoes on the sidewalk gave Diana a slight chill up her back.

Harriet looked at the four of them, and her eyes floated in the thick lenses of her glasses, ever wary.

Jon helped Randy up. Randy winced and limped out to the street. Jon followed him. But before leaving the theater entryway Jon stole a quick glance at Diana.

" 'Bye," he said. He smiled a little.

"So long," Diana said softly. She was glad to see them both leave.

Harriet looked nervous. "I went into Sammy's to pick up a delivery for Theda and Sammy said he gave it to you!"

Catherine held out the envelope. The envelope that contained the money.

"Now why did he give this to you?" Harriet asked, annoyed, taking the envelope. "I wish people would tell me when plans are changed. Why leave me in the dark? What purpose does that serve?" She turned and walked back to where her car was parked.

"It wasn't planned," Catherine said, following. "Sammy saw me and recognized me and gave me the envelope, that's all."

"Your mother won't like that."

"Well, tough shit," Catherine said, getting in the car.

Harriet turned around and pointed a finger at Catherine.

"Don't use that vulgar talk with me," Harriet said. "I'm telling you right now, Catherine Price. You know I'll tell your mother. You know I will." Harriet walked into the street, around to the driver's side of the car.

Catherine angrily got into the car and slammed the door hard.

Diana climbed inside quietly.

On the way out of town, Catherine wouldn't look at Diana. She just sat staring out the window. Harriet turned off the highway onto a curving drive where stately homes stood well off the road. Leaves were strewn over the broad lawns. At last Harriet pulled into the driveway of Theda's large white old wood frame house. A house that while not flashy exemplified wealthy conservative Americana and fastidious upkeep. Diana looked at the deep front porch, high lead-pane windows, a porch swing, and empty flower pots along the porch rail. Lights burned in the first-floor windows.

"You both wait here," Harriet said, opening her door. She had not only the envelope from Sammy's, but several more plain unmarked envelopes, and some folders.

"Doesn't your mom invite you in?" Diana said.

Catherine turned and looked at Diana with a kind of sadness in her eyes. For a moment Diana thought Catherine might cry. But whatever Catherine was really thinking was buried behind the ice wall she'd erected again.

"I don't want to see her," Catherine said softly. "And she doesn't want to see me. Not today, anyway."

"Your father . . ."

"Dead. Like yours." Catherine stole a quick glance at Diana before turning away again.

Diana sighed. "He died when you were small, just like my real dad did. Right?"

Catherine didn't respond.

"My real father died of cancer," Diana said, staring up at the gray sky.

"I don't," Catherine said firmly, "want to talk about my family."

Harriet returned to the car. In her arms, in place of the envelopes she'd entered with, were two brown expandable file folders. She dumped them on the empty seat beside her. Wordlessly, Harriet started up the car. She backed out of the long driveway.

Diana sat quietly, looking at that big all-American house. A house Catherine was apparently not welcome in, not without a special invitation.

✳   ✳   ✳

On the way back to the clinic, a black sedan with an older couple inside rode Harriet's bumper.

Catherine was an impatient passenger. Her mood worsened. Diana could only imagine what she'd be like as a driver.

"Harriet, let them pass," Catherine said flatly.

"I'm driving this car, Miss—not you."

"Just slow down and let them pass you," Catherine replied.

"Idiot drivers," Harriet said.

Diana looked behind her and saw the impassive faces of the old couple, he (driving) nearly bald and bespectacled, she with a tuft of thinning white hair. Harriet finally did slow down and the black sedan started to pass. But too slowly.

Faster.

Diana smiled, and she and Catherine exchanged a glance. They both started laughing, as covertly as they could ("snickering up your sleeve" was how Diana's stepfather, Jack Adams, would have described it).

"And what did I miss?" Harriet said, looking at them in the rearview mirror. "A private little joke?"

"Forget it, Harriet," Catherine said. "You miss everything."

"Smart," Harriet said. The old sedan was moving past them in the oncoming lane.

"Dumb," Catherine whispered, pointing at the back of Harriet's seat.

"I heard that."

"Congratulations, Harriet," Catherine said.

"Quiet while I'm driving," Harriet said. Harriet directed her attention to the black sedan, which, having successfully passed her, was now slowing down. It was Harriet's turn to ride the back bumper, which she hated doing. "Will you look at this?" Harriet said, exasperated.

"Blow the horn," Diana said. She hadn't intended to get involved, but felt she couldn't help it. She was feeling angry now, too. Dumb hick drivers. It was going to take forever to get back to the clinic.

"Ram them," Catherine said, and giggled.

"Get out of the way," Harriet called out, as if the old couple in the sedan could hear her. "You wanted to go fast, now get moving."

Get moving.

You wanted to go fast, now GO FAST.

Diana felt the wave building, zapping invisibly back and forth between her mind and Catherine's. She felt giddy, felt the wave bouncing up into the old black sedan on the road in front of them.

GO!

It was surprising that an old sedan like that could have the kind of pickup that would make it rocket forward as it did just then, so suddenly. It seemed to vibrate on its springs as it shot away from them. The old man must have just stomped on the gas pedal.

That's probably what made him lose control of the car.

Diana watched the whole accident occur as if it were in slow motion. The sedan surged forward and crossed the center line of the divided highway. There was no sound. Just a silent explosion of glass bits and plastic; a plume of instantly ground automobile as the sedan swiped the side of the beige economy car in the oncoming lane.

The economy car hobbled smoking to the side of the road ahead of Harriet's car. But the black sedan seemed to take to the air.

It spun around, and skirted the lip of the grassy ditch. Falling into the ditch it rolled over onto its top, and then rolled back onto its tires before coming to a rough stop.

Diana's mouth fell open.

"Did you see that?" Harriet said, and stepped down hard on the brake.

"Oh, my God," Diana said, putting her hand on the seatback in front of her, bracing herself.

Catherine just looked at the scene with awe. "Shhhhhhit," she whispered, astonished.

Harriet pulled her car to the side of the road and stopped. On the highway, bits of glass and fragments of plastic and debris were strewn everywhere. Red bits and white bits, glittering like the remains of a shattered jewel box.

A young blond couple and a small child in a red parka

scrambled out of the economy car. Diana bit her lip. She saw that the family was okay, if slightly shaken. But all on their feet.

Catherine opened her door.

"Stay right there, Catherine," Harriet ordered. But Catherine ignored her. Diana opened her car door now, too. She stood beside Harriet's car, looking at the black sedan standing motionless in the dry brown grass. White smoke curled upward from the hood. The dead engine knocked and clicked, the only sound that could be heard on this country road.

Catherine's hair blew in the cool breeze, which carried an odor of scorched rubber.

It was so quiet. The young mother was softly crying now. The passenger door of the black sedan opened slowly, and the old, old man climbed out. The young father, who had long yellow hair and a somewhat darker beard, ran across the highway to help him. Together, the bearded man and the old sedan driver opened up the passenger-side door. The elderly woman was helped out. Diana could see that she was standing, that she did not seem to be hurt. Yet her wrinkled face was as pale as bone.

"Let's get out of here," Harriet said.

"Is everybody really okay?" Diana said.

"It's a miracle," Harriet said, "but it looks like everyone is fine. We're getting out of here, now."

Catherine slowly climbed back inside the car, and Diana followed. Catherine pointed through the rear window at the old lady. Diana saw what Catherine pointed at; a red spot shone on the top of the woman's head, amid whitest hair.

"It might be a bow," Catherine said, as Harriet put the car in gear. It might have been blood, Diana thought. As Harriet pulled back onto the road, there came a sickening crunch of glass beneath the tires.

Diana looked at the people at the side of the road. And when Harriet sped past the economy car, Diana saw that the left front side was crumpled in, completely smashed. The wheel was bent in several directions. That car could never be driven away from the scene; it would have to be towed.

"What's the rush?" Catherine said to Harriet, annoyance in her voice.

"Everyone was fine, there's nothing we could do for them," Harriet said, also angry. "We don't need to get involved."

"But that woman might have been bleeding. Guess we'll never know," Catherine said. "Drive on, Good Samaritan!"

Catherine certainly was a cool one, considering what had just happened. Diana, for her part, felt her heart begin to race. The crash was an odd thing to witness. An even odder thing to have—caused? Had she? Had *they*?

Diana felt a sudden rush of guilt about the crash, and she didn't know if it was only her imagination making her feel that way.

She looked at Catherine.

"You're white as a sheet," Catherine whispered. Then she shrugged and smiled. Was this the "power" she'd talked about, the power they were going to have "fun" with? Was this Catherine's idea of fun?

Catherine started giggling.

"Honestly," Harriet said, "what could there possibly be to laugh about?"

Catherine shook with nervous laughter, turning her face to the window.

Catherine's giggles were infectious, despite Diana's best efforts to suppress her own nervous reaction. Catherine snorted and just let her laughter rip. Diana, trying to stifle her own giggles, laughed all the harder. Tears streamed from her eyes and her face began to ache, as did her sides.

Harriet remained as grim as ever. "Honestly. I don't see what's so funny."

Back at the clinic, Diana made herself some tea in the kitchen. It was early in the evening and she was alone. The cold wind blew against the windows. It got dark so early now. The tea warmed her.

She sat alone at the kitchen table and looked at the Monet prints someone had tastefully hung from the white walls. Steam rose from her teacup. She thought about the events of the day. Maybe she could look at them in a new way, as Catherine seemed to. Diana felt renewed sympathy for Catherine, who was obviously going through the same sorts of things she was. And worse. That cold mother of hers. Yet Catherine was tough. Maybe she *had* to be tough, just to survive.

How lucky Catherine was, to be brave and headstrong. Maybe it helped if you had a mother who provided a powerful example; a mother quite unlike Diana's. Evelyn had fallen apart completely when Diana's real dad had died, and she was an emotional basket case when Jack had married her. Now she drank too much and took too many pills. All she wanted was to escape into some warm cocoon, where people didn't die and daughters didn't suffer from nightmares and delusions.

Diana had no sooner had these thoughts when a young nurse, Sally, walked into the kitchen with a slim black cellular phone in her hand.

"Ah, here you are, Diana," Sally said. She wasn't wearing a white uniform this evening. Instead, Sally wore jeans and a ski sweater, upon which her name tag was pinned. She had curly black hair that might have been permed. It didn't look natural, but could have been, even so. She handed the portable phone to Diana, who remained seated at the round glass-top table.

"It's your mother," Sally said. "You just press this button right here."

Diana saw a little green light flashing. And she felt a chill skimming over her skin. If Catherine's relationship with her mother was weird, Diana's was no picture of normality, either. And it had gotten especially strained these past few months, when the nightmares had become unbearable. Diana swallowed hard and decided to try and be cool, like Catherine, to stuff down her rising emotions. It was weird; a minute ago she'd wanted her mother. Wanted to comfort and reassure her. Now that she had her on the phone, Diana felt angry and resentful. She pressed the button and held the phone to her ear.

"Hello," she said softly.

"Hi, Diana," came the voice, unmistakably Evelyn's.

"Jack, pick up the other line now," she said to Diana's stepfather. The phone clicked in Diana's ear.

"Hello?" came his familiar deep voice. She was filled with homesickness all of a sudden. But she fought it. Who, after all, had made the decision to bring her here, even if it was supposed to be for her own good?

Diana ran her fingers through her hair, still spiky sharp in the back, but longer and softer in the front. She felt renewed anger. And finally an appropriate target upon whom she could pour it all out.

"Yes," she said, softly. "Hello to you, Jack." She called him Dad sometimes. But she was allowed to call him Jack when she wanted to.

After a moment her mother asked, "How are you doing, Diana? We've thought of nothing but you, you know that, darling, don't you?"

"Didn't you talk with Dr. Sterling?" Diana said. "You speak with him regularly, don't you? Doesn't he report on my progress?"

"Is once a week often?" Evelyn asked. "It doesn't seem like enough. If I had my way I'd go right past Dr. Sterling and I'd call you up every day."

"Right," Diana said. "We'd all love that," she added, acidly.

Jack cleared his throat. "Rules are rules," he said. "We're not supposed to have a lot of contact with you at these early stages of treatment, not even by phone. You know that, Diana. And from what I hear, you're coming along beautifully."

"Don't you want to hear how Brenda is?" Evelyn said, referring to Diana's younger sister.

"Not really," Diana said. But she thought of Brenda anyway. Maybe it was sort of embarrassing for Brenda to have an older sister who had to be locked up.

"Diana, please," Evelyn said.

"Diana, we're only trying to do what's best for you," Jack said.

"Like cutting off my hair?" Diana asked.

Jack sighed through his nose, a scratchy sound over the phone. "I can see this is getting us nowhere," he grumbled.

"Diana, your hair was a . . . it was a loss, Diana," Evelyn said. "There were knots in it, tangles . . . and wildness, ugliness, so they had to—"

"Okay, let's drop the subject," Jack said, interrupting.

"Then you're *not* sorry about my hair," Diana said, angry tears in her eyes.

"We had to let them cut it!" Evelyn cried. "You were out of control!"

"You had to cut my hair because I was out of control?"

"Because you were sick—"

"Because I was sick, you had to *cut* my *hair*?"

"Hair—shmair!" Jack yelled. "It's only hair, it grows back!"

Diana was silent. She took a deep breath, but it didn't soothe her rage. She was pretty sure she really did, at bottom, hate them both. Not just because of her hair, or because they had brought her to this place. But because they were such failures. Because they kept trying to hang on to her in spite of everything. Hanging on to something they knew repelled them, in the hopes that Diana would change, would "get better." Would not, through some miracle cure, be Diana.

"Diana?" Evelyn said. "Diana, are you still there? This is long distance. Our calls to you are extremely restricted. Let's not waste them."

Jack coughed: "That's right. And let's not even get into the costs of this arrangement."

"Well, you just got into it, Jack," Evelyn said accusingly. She cleared her throat. "The point is whether or not Diana is getting better. Are you *feeling* better, dear? Dr. Sterling said the therapies are most promising, and that you're even getting a lot of exercise and good nutrition—"

"I have to go," Diana said. A hot tear rolled down her cheek. It was sad, but her parents just didn't understand her. And probably never would.

"Now, wait a minute," Jack said. "I'm paying for this call, and I—"

Diana looked at the small phone in her hand, a device that could pick up voices without wires. Modern magic. She strangled a tiny burst of laughter, and saw the little green light on the phone grow fuzzy through her tears. With a crooked smile she pressed the disconnect button.

Catherine was really the only other person in the world who knew what it was like to be here.

Diana set the phone down on the counter and pulled a paper towel from a roll hanging under the shelves. She wiped her eyes. But she still felt like crying. She wondered what David was doing. Was he outside, working on the cold clinic grounds at night, alone?

Then she saw, on the counter in a shadow, the strap of Harriet's purse.

Looking around, she made sure she was alone and unseen. Feeling mean, she picked up the black purse and opened it. Her heart pounded. Inside was a small leather wallet, the kind a kid makes from a leather-craft kit. HARRIET was impressed in block letters on one side, and a crude rendering of a horse's head was impressed on the other. The wallet was stitched up with some kind of thick brown plastic thread.

Inside was a twenty dollar bill and several singles. Forty-two dollars all together. Diana pulled out the twenty. It made a crisp little squeak. She put the money in her pocket and replaced the wallet in the purse, and put the purse back into the shadow on the countertop. No one saw her.

Feeling desperately lonely, Diana walked back to the room she shared with Catherine. Now at least she had a little money. Not a whole lot with which to start a new life. But more than she had when they brought her here, defenseless and broke—the way they wanted her to be.

The room glowed warmly in the lamplight. Catherine wore a pale blue nightgown under a thick green robe. She looked up from the book she was reading, "Fantastic Fables," by Ambrose Bierce. Diana closed the door hard and leaned back against it.

Catherine understood. Catherine *knew*.

Diana looked at herself in the mirror. Eyes puffy from crying.

"It's weird, isn't it?" Catherine said.

Diana looked at her. "What's weird?"

"Being us."

Diana said, "We could always just ignore it."

Catherine smiled. "Like your parents did for years? Like you've been pretending to?"

Diana changed into her pajamas. She thought, I don't have to do anything, think anything, feel anything. Yet she *did* feel something.

She felt *powerful*. She thought of Catherine, about what had happened earlier in the day, in town, and what they could do together—if they wanted to. The power they shared. Diana's stepfather had always told her to choose her friends carefully. Here, fate had intervened and given her a friendship that seemed inevitable. It didn't matter that Catherine was selfish and vain, and somewhat devious; she was more than that. Much more. Catherine was a tough ally.

When the lights were out, and they were in their respective beds, Catherine let out a long sigh.

"What do you think of Randy and Jon?" she asked.

"I'm really not the slightest bit interested in either one of them," Diana answered.

"Neither am I," said Catherine, "Except for Randy, on certain occasions."

"You mean . . . you guys are, like, lovers?"

"Would it seem like a big deal if I said yes?"

"Well, it's none of my business," Diana said, but even as she said this she knew that secrets between herself and Catherine were probably not possible any more.

"Jon had his eye on you today," Catherine said, a smile in her voice.

"Great. Just what I need," Diana said.

"Tell me about boys you know in Chicago. The kind you like."

Diana smiled, pulling the covers up to her chin. The cold November wind blew against the windows. She could hear the creaking trees. She thought about David again, and she felt her heart seeming to grow heavy and warm, filling up her chest.

"There was this French exchange student," Diana said. She let her head sink down into her smooth pillow. It had been a long time since she had thought about Luc. Now that, *that* had been a major crush. "My parents were out of town and my friend Luc came over. To make a long story short, we ended up smoking pot and fooling around. He slept over. God, my dad—I mean Jack—would freak if he knew about that."

"Tell me more," Catherine said.

"Well, we opened a bottle of good wine Jack had been saving in the basement. To this day he doesn't know it's missing. Luc said it was a very expensive, very fine wine. We opened it and we lit some candles on the coffee table. We sat on the floor, listening to music in the candlelight.

"What does he look like?"

Diana smiled. "Black hair, big dark eyes, curvy lips. He was more than cute. He was kissing me, sitting on the floor in front of me. It had gotten cold so he put on one of Jack's sweaters—a very expensive dark green wool thing Jack had picked up in Madrid. Luc had his back to the coffee table, where the candles were. And his sweater caught on fire."

"What? You're kidding!"

"No," Diana said, laughing. "He'd kiss me and lean back for a sip of wine, and what we didn't know was that when he leaned back, he was leaning against a small votive candle."

"God, what did you do?"

"He kissed me and said—his eyes all of a sudden kind of bugging out a bit—'am I on fire?' I thought I was, you know, having this effect on him."

Catherine laughed. "No! What did you do?"

"He turned, and sure enough, flames were growing on the back of Jack's big green sweater. So I started slapping the flames with my bare hand. It took a few good swats. But the fire went out and I knocked a lot of curly glowing scraps of wool to the carpet. There was stinky smoke all around us. He turned and asked if the sweater was okay. It had a big hole burned into the back, and the edges were burnt as black as the rim of a volcano. My hand was black with soot."

Catherine giggled.

"Oh, he was really humiliated," Diana said. "I guess he didn't think it was cool to have his clothes on fire."

"Or to have a girl put out the flames with her bare hand."

"He didn't even thank me, he just proceeded to get drunk."

"But you saved his life."

"I had to tell my parents I burned my hand on a pot on the stove. I threw Jack's favorite sweater in the trash. To this day he wants to sue the dry cleaners, whom he thinks my mother must have sent it to. They had the biggest fight over that stupid sweater. And he called up and chewed out the dry cleaner for like an hour. He still mourns that sweater. If they knew the truth—all of it, that I had a boy over and nearly burned the house down—God, I dread to think what would happen."

Diana heard Catherine laugh into her pillow.

"I have another confession," Diana said, impulsively. She felt a tremor of fear.

"Yes?" Catherine said.

"Do you know what it is?"

Catherine shifted in her bed. "No. I'm not reading you. It's hazy."

"I took twenty dollars from Harriet's purse," Diana whispered.

Catherine didn't reply at first. After a few moments of silence she said, "Nobody saw you?"

"Not a soul," Diana whispered, head up, neck straining.

"Why did you do it?"

Diana laid her head back down on the cool pillow. She felt sleepy, and oddly happy, despite the weird phone call from her parents. Telling these things to Catherine helped.

"I felt mean," Diana said. "And besides, we need money."

"Good, we can spend it together next time we go into town."

Diana smiled and yawned. The skylight windows let a shimmery blue light into the room. "Good night, Catherine."

"'Night," Catherine replied, voice thick with sleep.

Diana heard the rustle of blankets as Catherine turned over in her bed. Diana, exhausted now, felt herself drifting

off to sleep. Her mind was as still as the surface of a calm
sea, above shadowy depths.

Dreamland.

Diana could not have guessed the hour of the night, or
was it morning? But she "awoke" within her dream, as
she often had in the past.

It's only a dream, Diana.

Dr. Sterling had told her that when this happened she
should not try to force herself awake—truly awake—unless
it was absolutely necessary. Instead, she should watch the
dream like a movie. Now she felt she had no choice.

Here was a kind of smoky darkness. From this darkness
there emerged the small face of a little girl. Her hair was
red-brown, her expression bland and innocent. She came
fully out of the shadows now. And holding her hand was
another girl, a long-haired blond, who was unmistakably
Catherine.

Catherine at the age of seven.

The girls stood together in a child's room, a room strewn
with dolls and storybooks . . . and deep night shadows. A
room that sketched itself into being, like a filmy painting
illumined by a single shifting match-flame.

Diana felt a kind of creeping dread. She had the sensation
of being in a ghost-like body that seemed to float invisibly
above this room, near the ceiling like a moth hovering over
a lamp. Observing from some other place, as she had so
often observed herself in dreams.

It then occurred to her with the bracing cold shock of a
revelation: This was not *her* dream, it was Catherine's.

Catherine's *nightmare*.

A nightmare memory of childhood.

Diana had crossed over, in sleep, to this strange place.

All she could do was watch.

The two girls walked over the bare wood floor, their eyes
closed. A golden light barely illumined the scene. Into the
shadows went the sleepwalkers, and the shadows followed
them, shadows swimming and changing and swallowing up
the light. The golden room faded but retained a dull shim-
mer.

Now the shadows grew together and lengthened.

Diana felt her ghostly body descend. Her bare feet touched the cold floor.

From the black corner there came a scream, the scream of a child. And then blood seeped outward from the shadows, and flowed like a thick tide of poured syrup over the floor, until it reached Diana's bare white feet. Now Diana stood rigid and afraid upon the cold floor. Stood dreaming at the shadow-edge of someone's worst nightmare.

She'd slipped into Catherine's dreaming mind! She wanted to leave. Wanted to awaken—now. But how? It was as though she were trapped in this foreign place without a passport, without maps or guides, and with no recollection of how she had travelled here in the first place.

The blood was warm, almost hot, bright red and alive. It covered her toes. Diana cried out, but who could hear her? And the blood was rising above her feet now, to her ankles, and higher. . . .

Chapter Four

David scraped frost from the window of his blue Toyota. Still no snow on the ground, he noted. But it wouldn't be long now. He looked up at the sky, feeling the cold wind on his face. Sometimes there were blizzards as early as October 1st. Snow in September was not unknown. But no snow in November? Unheard of.

His breath puffed out in great smoky clouds. He used a small plastic scraper, and the frost flew in clotted white globs as he stabbed the windshield. The engine was running with the heater going full-blast inside.

He climbed into the car and drove from the grounds of the Albion Clinic. The car was sluggish in the cold. The steering wheel was like a piece of ice in his grasp. He needed to pick up some supplies in town for Micky, the chief maintenance guy, so the hardware store would be his first stop. If he found everything he needed—flat-head screws, lock washers, a couple bags of loose fill-insulation—he could run over to the drugstore afterward and look at the new compact discs, maybe even buy one.

Oh, yeah, he remembered now; he needed one other thing.

Ammunition.

David opened the glove compartment, crammed full of tapes and paper and dog-eared maps. A few old spent cartridges. He found the tape he wanted to hear, a piece by Prokofiev for ballet, called "Lieutenant Kije Suite."

He wanted to dance to it, though he really knew so little

about classical ballet, just what he'd seen on TV, mostly, and what he'd read in some star biographies. His true passion was for modern dance, he felt. But he also really liked the kind of things he saw on MTV, especially in Janet Jackson's videos. That kind of dancing blew him away.

Listening to the music he imagined what it would be like to be on a bare stage, before an audience, with the lights coming up. He would be dressed in black, and so would she—Diana. She had a lithe body that he could imagine in various aspects, flowing swan-like, or frozen, in an arabesque. And he could imagine how light she would feel in his arms.

The somber strains of "Lieutenant Kije" wove an almost magical spell. If he tried, he could easily see himself lifting Diana high over his head; see her touch the ground again with a reaching toe, then see her running, turning, a kind of black veil streaming behind her. How had these fantasies started?

He looked into his own dark eyes in the rearview mirror. The short black stubble on his chin looked coarse and scruffy. The mirror was so unforgiving in daylight. Every zit showed up in this mirror.

He wondered if he had the face of a dancer. He sort of doubted it. Too much of a regular guy, he thought. Not refined like, say, Nureyev's face. But maybe that didn't matter. What made for a dancer's face? If he became a dancer, then his face would be a dancer's face, simple as that.

He remembered now when it was he'd started thinking about dance.

At college, the gymnasium was shared by all of the athletes, including the dance majors. The jocks and the dancers rarely (if ever) crossed into each other's territory, despite the proximity of their training rooms. Even the way they dressed (or maybe especially the way they dressed) separated those who moved with skill—and sometimes with grace—in the spirit of competition, and those who exerted all their strength with a more poetic design.

Sometimes David would look through the door at the dance majors in their colorful tights, stretching at a wooden bar against the mirrored wall of their studio. He liked the clean look of the clean hardwood floor, so like a blank canvas. And he never forgot the music that swelled from the doors of these rehearsal studios, the belt of the Broadway show tunes and the lilt of the classical ballet suites. He started to admire the strength and agility of the dancers, the sweat they put into their craft.

Unfortunately, most of David's friends who majored in physical education disdained the dance majors. "Art, fart," his old pal Jamie would say. And when the jocks were required to take some dance classes, most of them rebelled. Some of the guys really prided themselves on their lack of dance ability. Others put forth so little effort, they might as well have been wooden soldiers rather than what they were; strong and fit young men, perhaps capable of stylized movement but too intimidated to show a flourish that might have come naturally.

David got into it though. He even went to the library and read up on dancers and choreographers. He found out about people like Martha Graham and George Balanchine, and he read the sometimes scandalous stories of young American dancers who had succeeded in an art form that was a dead-serious business, and an obsessive discipline.

He couldn't think of anything more beautiful, more moving, more *totally fucking cool.*

During breaks in his workouts at the gym, he would find himself gazing through the open studio doors. Gazing over a line he couldn't cross.

One day a dance instructor, a bearded guy named Professor Aberdeen, saw David looking in through the studio door and asked him to come inside and assist him with something. David was terrified—he'd been found out. And now he was being brought center stage, in front of Aberdeen's dance class.

Professor Aberdeen had danced in New York professionally. He was known to be very tough in his teaching style, extremely demanding. He was small and muscular, compact as any gym rat.

When he'd ordered David into the room, David had of course been reluctant to comply. Aberdeen was trying to make a point, at the expense of several of his male students. The dance class students were sweating and looking sullen. They watched David nervously enter the room.

Aberdeen asked David to lift a slim blond female dancer over his head. A simple move if done properly, he said. He placed David's hand on her stomach. She didn't flinch. Apparently the dance guys just weren't doing this in a way that pleased Professor Aberdeen.

"Anyone could do this better and more naturally than you people are doing it," Aberdeen barked at them. "'As I shall now demonstrate.''

He nodded at the girl, and she jumped in David's rising arms.

David lifted the girl, almost effortlessly. He had great strength in his arms. It felt absolutely sensational. The girl was light, and she held herself taut, arms outstretched. Balancing her above his head came easily. David turned, feeling pressure in his legs. The girl took a sharp breath and held herself still as a statue.

"There," Aberdeen said. "This is how it's done."

David lowered the girl. Standing beside him, she held his hand and bowed, laughing a little, pulling him down to bow with her. The others applauded.

Aberdeen shook David's hand.

"You should sign up for one of my classes immediately," Aberdeen said. "You're a natural."

David smiled. He looked at the girl he'd lifted above his head. She was beautiful, absolutely radiant. Her blond hair was tied back. Her face was calmly composed, with a kind of maturity uncommon among the girls he had known in college so far.

He'd been bitten by the bug. Had in fact in an instant found the passion and (he hoped, he *ached* with hope) the work of his life. He believed this was what great painters must feel when they know they are painters, or what great architects must sense when they begin to build the skyscrapers of their dreams. A profound and noble love.

How wonderful these feelings were to him. He said to the professor, "Thanks," and grinned in his self–conscious way.

Yet that semester his money had run out. His mother had faced the kind of economic problems neither of them could have foreseen. The possibility of homelessness became suddenly real. He would have to leave school for a while, return to Blackburn County and work—at least until he could earn some money. Not just for the continuation of his education, but for both of them. He would live and work with Shirley on the grounds of the Albion Clinic. Just until they were on their feet again.

There would be no more classes of any kind for him— not for a long time. And so his dream remained a secret. He never wanted it to be something he merely talked about. An intention. He wanted it to be real.

Yet sometimes he had dark moments when he told himself it was simply too late. And then he felt like such a damn fool. Here he was in Blackburn County, doing what? Sports therapy in a kind of loony bin, where his mother worked and had gotten him a job. And it wasn't even like the sports part was his main line at the clinic. He was an assistant handyman, a grunt, and that was his primary function.

Yet it was a job that paid decently, and in truth he was saving a little money. If only he had the nerve to really do what his heart was telling him he wanted. Run away and become a dancer. Run away anywhere, and learn the craft. Go to New York, Hollywood—even Las Vegas. Anywhere there was a promise of work. Other people had done it, he knew; he'd read their biographies. Took big risks and lived in attics and slept on cots in studios, and learned, found work, scrounged. Did anything to work!

For now, even a scary scenario like that seemed just another silly dream.

He thought about Diana again. Another unattainable, it seemed. Because she was as forbidden as anything else he wanted in his confused life. Loving her was completely and totally against every rule of the clinic. She wasn't well, they said. Getting involved with her in even the most casual way was tantamount to taking advantage of her. For all he knew there were even laws against it, and he could end up in jail.

He wondered bitterly, why was it that everything he really wanted was so damned hard to get?

Harriet walked into the kitchen. She saw her purse sitting on the countertop.

"Ah," she said, shaking her head. The purse was where she'd absentmindedly left it, of course.

She picked up the purse and started to leave the kitchen. She stopped suddenly. She opened the purse and felt for the wallet, squinting her eyes. Her fingers touched the leather surface. Her face relaxed.

Now she pulled the wallet out and opened it. She quickly counted up twenty-two dollars.

Counted it again. Then she looked up uncertainly, eyes fixed on nothing. She looked at the money and counted it again, shaking her head.

She couldn't remember how much was supposed to be there. Seemed like there should be more.

Diana dressed for a long run, wearing thermal underwear under her sweats. She tied her running shoes so tight she thought her feet might get numb. And then she put a dark knit cap on her head. She was all set to go, just needed to chart her course in her exercise log first.

She was obliged to keep careful records of everything she did here at the clinic, including keeping a list of the foods she ate. In the mornings, over breakfast in the sunny kitchen, she would write in her dream diary between bites of cold cereal and gulps of orange juice. Writing, she could avoid Richmond Garfield's small talk. She didn't really care to hear about his stock portfolio or his political opinions.

She kept up with her exercise log, too. Sterling was consumed with the relationship between hard physical labor and sleep patterns. The exercise diaries and the dream diaries his patients kept would prove great sources for his papers and the books he'd said he wanted to write—and a great source of information for future researchers.

Diana scribbled in her exercise log the route she would take this morning. First, she'd do some stretching exercises.

Then she'd take off down the driveway and run along the river path. She looked at her watch and noted the time. She was looking forward to being outside.

Catherine would have joined her for a run, but she was off with Dr. Sterling, having one of her therapy sessions. Diana would have her regular visit with the doctor later in the day. She hadn't decided yet whether she would tell him about the strange bloody dream. A dream that seemed to be about Catherine, albeit a very young Catherine.

A dream that *was* Catherine's.

Diana would have sworn to it. But how could she explain that to Dr. Sterling?

She needed one more thing before she went out: the portable CD player she could clip on the waistband of her sweat suit, and the earphones. Now Diana walked through the empty hallways of the modern building. Everything from the choice of colors on each wall (wheat and pale gray and off-white) to the built-in skylights to the sloping shapes of the ceilings, reflected order and calm. Perhaps to counteract the disorder of the patients' minds, Diana speculated.

She climbed the carpeted stairs two at a time. Ginger Montgomery, sitting at a chair near the second-floor bay window, peered out from behind her magazine. She smiled and Diana smiled back. Diana felt a pang of sympathy, seeing the large dark circles under the woman's eyes. She wondered about poor Ginger's nightmares and insomnia.

Diana walked into the small library and music room, glad to see that no one else was in there. The stereo was off. The room was quiet. Windows looked out over the bare treetops. A brown sectional sofa looked inviting and soft; someone had left a pair of stereo headphones sitting on the seat cushion. The earphones were not attached to the CD player, though. Diana went over to the shelves where the player was usually stowed, next to some CDs, mostly classical. The Snoop Doggy Dogg CD was there, where Catherine had left it, but no CD player.

It was too quiet here. Quiet enough to hear the soft shifting within the walls. That familiar and eerie sound: as if something alive was moving, creeping within the walls. It was possible squirrels had invaded. This was a new building, but squirrels were resourceful animals that sought warmth, and would find their way in.

The scratching sound frightened her.

It was nothing, she told herself. So why should she make something out of it?

Because you're scared, she told herself.

She closed her eyes, trying to fight off this feeling.

She opened her eyes and for a split second saw, in the darkest corner of the book-lined room, a small thin shadow withdrawing into a deeper shadow.

"Who's there?" she cried. No one answered.

She simply couldn't scream. It had been too fleeting to tell if what she saw had been real, or just another suggestion from her frightened imagination.

Diana fled the room, turned, and ran down the stairs, gasping for breath.

Outside, on the lawn, she felt the bracing chill of a November morning. It was bright and safe out here. The sky was gloriously real, and it actually felt good to shiver against the cold—against a *real*, bitter cold, the kind that almost burned.

Forget about the strange shadows, she told herself. Feel what you know is *real*.

All anyone talked about at the clinic these days was the lack of snow. It always snowed by this time of year, everyone said. Maybe they were just angry they couldn't have their weird drunken celebration at Ice Rock, Diana thought. Anyway, it sure felt like it would snow. Any day now.

Diana stepped off the paved walk and onto the frosted grass. It crunched beneath her feet. The hedge along the path held within its groomed, twisting labyrinth a frozen sheen of frost, so that it resembled something sculpted of gray-green glass. Very beautifully dark, Diana thought. Pretty as a funeral wreath. She bent over and touched her toes, stretching, then crouched down.

She started to run.

She ran past the track and the obstacle devices David had constructed. She hoped she'd see him down here. Even if he wouldn't be able to say much more than hello. But he wasn't out here today.

She saw her breath pumping out in great clouds. When she got to the river trail she felt a side ache coming on. She stopped and crouched down, hugging her knees, trying to deflate her chest, as David had instructed her to do.

The dark river rolled itself along, flowing quietly. The only way you could tell it was moving at all was to watch the bubbles and foam drawn across its surface. Tall pines were reflected on that dark surface, and they shimmered. The damp air was slightly colder here.

She thought about last night's dream. The shifting shadows.

Then she remembered, in a flash, the dream she'd been having since she'd arrived here. A dream that was distinctly hers.

A human skeleton stood at the top of a long flight of stairs. Shadowy, in deepest night. The skull turned and broke away from the neck bone and fell from the frame. It bounced and rolled down the stairs in slow motion. Bone by bone it fell apart, from the top down, rib by rib, also in a kind of sickening slow motion. Silently they rolled and crashed—ribs going end over end, scapula and delicate metacarpal bones bouncing down the stairs, femur and tibia sliding like felled trees down a chute in a pulp mill—complete chaos. But the chaos was replaced with an eerie order at the bottom of the stairs. As quickly as the skeleton had fallen apart, it came back together again, this time from the feet upward. Bones rose into place. Then the bones of the hands attached, as a final gesture, the skull to the neck, giving it a clockwise twist into position. It stood before Diana and grinned.

And this was one of her nicer dreams.

What the hell did it mean? Piecing bones together? Tearing a skeleton apart? What did a skeleton represent? Sterling would no doubt have some suggestions.

Maybe it didn't mean anything at all, that smiling skull that had pieced itself together before her. She shuddered. But at least now she'd have something to talk about with Sterling.

She stopped at a clearing off the river trail where someone had left a picnic table. The table had been painted a dull deep shade of green, but the paint was peeling and weathered. She sat down on top of it and looked at the dark river pulling itself heavily around a tree-lined bend.

She would return the twenty dollars to Harriet's purse, she decided. Maybe her dream was about guilt. She certainly felt guilty about stealing. She really didn't know why she took the money in the first place. Sure, she could have used it in town. But that didn't justify stealing from poor old Harriet, she figured, no matter how mean she'd been feeling.

She'd only done it to impress Catherine.

Alone out here, away from Catherine, she didn't feel the need to be as bad as her friend was—or tried to be. Catherine was full of bluff, that was obvious.

Diana took a bracing breath of November air. She wondered what her classmates at the Rawson School were doing today. Another pang of sorrow came, but it went away just as quickly. What if they were talking about her? About how she'd freaked out after Ted's death? On the other hand, she told herself, it was stupid to try to tune into what was happening in Chicago, hundreds of miles away. Let them think what they wanted.

She knew she wasn't crazy. Her dreams were confusing, but there were reasons for such dreams. She was here to find out about herself, and she'd already learned about the kind of power she and Catherine seemed to share. Catherine saw the power as a strange gift. If only Diana could really see it that way, too, she thought; really convince herself of it.

Here, after all, was a girl like her in so many ways. All the bitterness and anger that Diana had felt upon coming here had begun to fade at last. She was almost feeling her old self again. The Diana who used to have so much fun. Who really loved her family and all her friends. Who wanted nothing so much as to be with them all again, to take a walk down Michigan Avenue on a cold fall day, and look into all the shop windows. And not have bad dreams.

Some day she'd be back there. She was sure of it.

She would have the answers she needed to cope with the

way her mind worked. She trusted that her nightmares would stop. That she would gain control of her sleeping mind. These people were going to help her. Catherine was going to help her.

After her run, Diana showered and dressed and had a breakfast of two small tart apples, brought in from a local orchard. She kept an eye out for Harriet, but Harriet wasn't around the clinic today. She was at Theda Price's house. Poor Harriet was in such a dither over the mounting recall election. Curiously, the recall threat didn't seem to bother Catherine at all.

Diana, feeling only slightly apprehensive (as she always did before a therapy session), entered Dr. Sterling's dark windowless office. He was standing over a console, his back to her. She cleared her throat. He turned around abruptly.

His dark eyes widened as he took her in. "Diana, is it time already for our chat?" He ran his fingers through his tangled brush of salt-and-pepper hair. His white coat hung like a high priest's robe on his tall, ample frame. "Please, my dear, rest on the couch and I'll be right with you."

Diana reclined on the cool leather couch, and looked at the fish tanks that illumined the room. A shimmering blue fish with a large tail like silk moved slowly around a piece of bright pink coral, and came to the edge of the glass. It flicked its filmy silver tail. It seemed to look at Diana.

"Hello," she mouthed to the fish. A few bubbles came from its mouth. Its eyes said nothing, but she read wide-eyed alarm. Could he see her? Did he know he was a prisoner in a fish tank, she wondered, thousands of miles from a warm tropical home? Did he long to be free?

She didn't know if fish had emotions, like loss or love.

Sterling manipulated a keyboard and there came the mechanical inhalation of a laser printer coming to life, and the *slip slip* of printed pages sliding into a tray.

In other circumstances, Diana might have enjoyed this space-age gray room, with its dark curving secret places, and its mysterious technology. She nervously fingered a gold chain at her throat. Looking up, she gazed at the high ceiling with its galaxy painting and the starry bursts of white light that sent soft beams angling down to a desk top, and to a computer station.

The room was a perfect place for the study and perhaps even the creation of dreams. Yet hadn't she heard, just now, something beyond the technical hum of the machinery? Some stirring beyond the heavy plaster walls? Or was this just some paranoid aural hallucination? The room was, Sterling had explained, a blank canvas upon which the mind and all of the manifestations of consciousness, that folded bud, could be cast. So too were the wilds of Blackburn County, a place where dreams could be thrown into relief, away from the clutter of the city, and the clutter of elements that constitute and crowd a life.

Sterling sat down in his chair, the one with the wheels, so that he could scoot himself back and forth between his computers and the couch Diana lay upon. He opened his file folder. Clicked his pen into service.

"Tell me what you wrote in your dream diary this morning," he said to her, softly.

Diana told about the falling skeleton, about the way it had grinned at her from the bottom of the stairs.

"What do you suppose that means?" Diana asked.

Sterling smiled. "Consider the symbols. Such an event which you described could never happen, a skull cannot *see*, and bones cannot move of their own accord. So let's see the skeleton as symbolic. What do *you* think it symbolizes?"

"Death," Diana said, flatly.

"Yes, but death in action."

Diana smiled a little at that. "The skull really grinned at me when it put itself back together. I was standing at the top of the stairs."

"Do you think it could be telling you to put something together, to take the separate pieces and build a whole?"

"You mean, to solve a murder? Find out who killed the person who owned the skeleton?"

Sterling shifted in his chair. He laughed at that comment. "Diana, don't be so literal minded. How about a different kind of symbolism? Putting together the disparate aspects of your mind, a mind that is perhaps fragmented.''

''But aren't all minds sort of fragmented?'' she said. She hated being laughed at, and felt a burn beneath her face. Luckily it was too dark in the room for Sterling to see her redden.

''Let's say they are divided,'' Sterling said, leaning toward her. ''Let's then go beyond definitions and think about the process of dreaming itself. It's really a sort of child's play to interpret dreams, anyway. So what if the content of a dream suggests some repressed sexual desire, as is so often supposed? It's really much more interesting to examine the process of the dream, as far as I'm concerned. In your case, we want to give you back some of the control you've lost to these overpowering dreams.''

Diana smiled again. ''That's what I'm here for,'' she said.

He coughed into his bunched fist. ''Now,'' he said, ''Your dream. As usual you were both in the dream and outside of it, both a participant of the dream and somewhere just beyond it, observing yourself, weren't you?''

Diana nodded. ''Yes.''

''I want you to consider the way the mind sees. Do you know what peripheral vision is?''

''Yes.''

Sterling spread his arms and waved his fingers. ''Look me in the eye. Look close.'' He bent even closer to her now. ''You are seeing my eyes, you are focussed and directed upon my eyes. But do you see my hands? Don't turn your focus there, turn your *awareness* to my hands as you gaze into my eyes.''

Diana smiled.

''Count my fingers, one by one, as I wiggle them.'' Sterling wiggled his index fingers. ''You are not looking directly at my fingers, you are keeping your gaze steady upon my eyes.''

Diana found herself giggling.

''Yes, it is a bit odd, this other perception,'' he said. ''But did you know that many people have an acuity for things they see peripherally? They can almost see things more clearly and sharply that way than if they were looking directly at them."

"Is that what I'm doing in my dreams?" Diana asked, watching him lower his hands.

"I'd like you to consider something. I'd like you to consider that in your dreams and in your waking observations, your perceptions can contain more than one point of view, as it were. Which is to say, you can look at one thing but shift your *awareness* to another. Let's say you are here in this room, looking at me, but you are also thinking about a tree in the woods I describe to you, and you are also remembering a dream you had last night. You are simultaneously holding these separate images in your mind."

"Okay," she said, tentative.

"I'm merely suggesting that perhaps you might one day be able to pull into sharp focus aspects of the hidden mind, the subconscious, the creative mind—the direct consciousness and the peripheral consciousness at once . . . that's all. I want you to consider two senses of awareness, instead of the usual, which is only one point of view."

He rose suddenly and went to his cluttered work station, half hidden in shadows. He opened a cabinet and rifled through a shelf of papers and books. Then he withdrew a large picture book, which he returned with, and sat down. It was a book of paintings by Pablo Picasso. He rapidly turned the pages.

"Ah, here," he said, and he turned the book around and handed it to her. "What do you see in this portrait?"

Diana knew who Picasso was, and she'd seen some of his paintings at the Chicago Art Institute. Sterling turned the pages of color plates and stopped at one titled *Bather*. It was strange. In this full-body portrait of a nude woman, one seemed to see from every perspective, front and back, at once, all jumbled together. Here was a nose where an ear would normally be. The buttocks seemed to be swerving around to the front of the body.

"He created a new way of seeing, a kind of movement frozen in time, in which a single point of view is replaced with multiple points of view, unified into one image," Sterling said.

"But that isn't how people really see," Diana said.

Sterling drew her attention from the picture. "What is seeing? There is no fixed point of awareness. Blink and what's left but what you choose to imagine?"

Diana shrugged. "When you take a photograph, what you get is what's real, isn't it?"

"Sure, one slice of it. One angle, one aspect of reflected light. But what about what we see inside our heads when we try to grasp a thing in its ever changing totality, what about that sort of seeing? Think of your mother. Imagine her face. Do you see her straight on? Or in profile? And at what age? The present? Or the last time you saw her, or perhaps as a young woman before she became a mother? Or as the old woman she will become? Now put all these images together."

Diana smiled. "You mean, see my mom as a Picasso painting? I can't do that."

Sterling sighed. "What is seeing?" he asked again. "What are we seeing when we *remember*? When we imagine? What is dreaming—surely it is *not* seeing things with our eyes, yet we *see* in our dreams, do we not? My God, the brain is not a camera, it is a much more capable device! Why can't two or three or four or five aspects of perception be grasped at once?"

He seemed to be working himself up into a kind of frenzy.

"What is the process of dreaming if not the unconscious mind speaking in pictures and sensations to yet another mysterious fold within its labyrinth?" he asked.

Diana smiled. She liked it when Dr. Sterling got a little grand in his philosophizing.

Sterling said with a grin, "Imagine being in one place and perceiving another. Being two places at once!"

"That sounds to me like insanity," Diana said.

Sterling's arms fell to his sides. "We are here to talk of such things as dreams and perceptions, not of insanity. If you feared you were going insane, and I suppose that might be perfectly normal, considering the intensity of your nightmares, our approach would be different. Had you been mentally ill, certainly another course of action would have been taken, another kind of treatment. There is no shame in such things any more these days, thank goodness. Treatments are promising. But you are not insane. You possess a rare gift, which we have barely begun to explore."

Diana felt a chill of anxiety, like an influx of some hormone flooding her brain. She had never talked to Sterling about the strange powers. She'd always known instinctively that such things were never talked about. This was a *difference* in her that she guarded so closely she had barely admitted it even to herself. Only Catherine knew, but then that was inevitable because Catherine possessed the same weird abilities. Had Catherine told Sterling? That seemed impossible.

She looked away. "I wouldn't call having bad dreams a gift, Doctor." Now she looked again at Picasso's bather. She closed the book and handed it back to him.

He took the book from her. "Just for fun, just for a game," he said, "try to imagine multiple perceptions sliding through time and space, reaching in here and there in your dreams, seeing so much, seeing, even, through another person's perspective what you could never see on your own."

She was aware of his eyes upon her. His eyes fixed, penetrating as he spoke.

"Imagine piloting the flights of your dreams," he said, "and seeing as far as you want to see or becoming the proverbial fly on a wall. Imagine having a grasp on that power, and imagine what it would be like if you were steering the carriage of these quests."

"But they're only dreams," Diana said.

Sterling looked at his hands folded in his lap. His eyebrows furrowed down. "Yes," he muttered, like a man caught in an indulgence.

"That's enough for today," Sterling said, rolling his chair backwards and heavily rising to his feet. "But try to imagine yourself getting hold of the imagery in your next dream. When the voice says, 'it's only a dream,' find its source and see if you can take control of the you within the dream, and then the dream itself. And finally, the you that is observing yourself.''

The observer in the dream—the dreamer. Diana felt a bit overwhelmed by all of this talk. Yet it made a weird kind of sense to her. She sat up on the couch. She blinked her eyes, watching Sterling as he turned toward his computer. Even if she'd wanted to read what was going on in Sterling's head, she'd have been unable to. For now the anxiety that seemed to fuel her fuzzy, uncontrollable clairvoyance had gone away. Curiosity had replaced her fear, at least for now.

Catherine was pulling on a pair of pointy black boots when Diana returned to the bedroom.

''Ugh,'' she groaned. ''It's freezing in here.'' Catherine looked out the window and frowned.

Diana sat down at her desk and looked up through the skylight. The sky was gray and overcast. Not a sign of snow, though. Had the snow come, there would have been lots of new things to do, starting with cross country skiing. Maybe they could have even followed the local crazies to Ice Rock, to watch them dance at the edge. The thought gave Diana a chill. She was afraid of heights enough as it was without watching some crazy daredevils flirt with a fatal fall.

''Tell me about your session,'' Catherine said, her back to Diana now. Catherine sat in front of her mirror. She was wearing one of her expensive dark sweaters, looking every bit the young Miss America hopeful. Except where Miss Americas always seemed to have a glow of milk-fed innocence, Catherine's face already reflected a more mature beauty's mystery, with a dash of iciness. She ran a black brush through her hair.

Diana told Catherine about Sterling's weird theories. She told her about the multiple perspectives.

''He encourages me to think about those things, too,'' Catherine said. ''He tells me to imagine a movie with a split screen, two scenes going on at once. He says I'm the actors *and* the director.''

''He showed me a painting from a book about Pablo

Picasso," Diana said. "*Bather.*"

A strange electric charge seemed to bounce from the floor to the ceiling. A murky image flashed through Diana's mind. She blinked and ignored it, even though it had a human shape.

Catherine turned and smiled. "You didn't tell him about us, did you?"

"You mean . . ." Diana felt a tingle of anxiety. And at once she felt another presence in her mind. Perhaps even in her heart; it was that powerful.

Catherine was transporting a wave into Diana's mind. She was having a look around, as it were. Diana thought for a moment about trying to block her out. Catherine blinked her eyes rapidly, and she smiled, showing her white teeth.

"Why block me?" Catherine said. "I'm your friend, not your enemy. And anyway, I can tell you kept your mouth shut. You're a good girl, not some rat."

Diana willed a sense of calm over herself. She did it by laughing. That changed her perspective on the situation, too. And Catherine's wave faded out.

"Do you think Sterling would believe us if we told him what we can do?" Diana asked. "Or would he send us to a maximum security loony bin for sure?"

"Maybe," Catherine said. "But maybe he'd put a few interesting facts together."

"Such as?"

Catherine rose from the chair by the mirror and came over close. "Such as putting dream power to work," Catherine said in a whisper. "Have you ever heard of remote viewing?"

"What's that?"

"It's a secret government program. Sterling had something to do with some early experiments with it. The CIA or some sort of covert government agency was in charge of it, I guess. They used people they call remote viewers— people who can mentally observe what's going on in countries thousands of miles away, like in a military operation."

"Are you kidding me?"

"No, it's true. Sterling told me about it, a little. Anyway, maybe he thinks we could be remote viewers.''

"I don't want to think about that," Diana said.

"That's your trouble, Diana. You want to ignore your abilities. You've always tried to suppress them, face it. But what if you really are clairvoyant? If we really have the connection I think we do, there's no reason why we couldn't control it in the same way Sterling says we should take hold of our ... what does he call it? Oh, yeah, our dream narratives."

"Put ourselves in the driver's seat, huh? Sounds terrific, and absolutely crazy."

Catherine leaned in close. "I have an idea. An experiment. Let's find David."

Diana leaned back, up against the wall, her elbow on her pillow. "Nah, I'm tired. I don't want to go running around looking for David."

"Who said anything about running around?" Catherine gave a naughty smile. "Maybe we could find him without ever leaving this room. Anyway, you've been thinking about David off and on all day, shouldn't be too hard to find him with our radar."

"You've been eavesdropping on me?"

Catherine shrugged and smiled. "When you said the title of the painting, *Bather*, I felt something. And so did you."

Diana said nothing. But the image of the bather, dark and hazy, was at the corner of her mind's eye.

Catherine reached out her hand and placed two fingers lightly on Diana's closed eyelids. She held her fingers there for a moment, then took them away.

"You know we can find David and see him, right now, if we want to. If we put our powers together, Diana ..."

Catherine sat on the edge of Diana's bed, Diana kept her eyes closed. Her heart began to pound. She felt heat in her face, a warm glow that moved over the top of her head.

And just as Catherine had promised, a murky vision started to take shape in her mind.

It was as though the dark, half-remembered dreams and the fleeting memories of a lifetime collided here, in this fluid field of vision. There was a sound like the beating of wings. Diana felt afraid.

And now something even stranger happened.

Their merged consciousness entered upon a wave the mind of a tiny creature, a small black house spider, which sat in her web in a high corner of a distant room, where steam rose from a bathtub.

Diana gasped. "I can see . . . but through the eyes of . . ."

Catherine's mouth fell open. "Through *eight* eyes."

"Catherine, we're seeing through the eyes of a *spider*!"

It was true. Diana and Catherine had somehow taken possession of the spider's mind, and now held its tiny body still.

The strange patterns of light the spider received through the cells that formed eight simple eyes, six of which faced forward, two of which were set off on either side of the head, were channeled inward to make human sense. The spider moved a leg, securing its position on her web. She looked down at the dark human form in the bathtub.

"David," Catherine said aloud. "Oh, my God, this is . . . why it's almost a clear picture. I didn't think it was possible . . ."

Diana wished Catherine would shut up. It was too amazing just *being here* without her babbling on about God knows what. This was not a dream or an hallucination. It was real.

They were doing it together, unifying their strange power. Diana thought of the two sides of a coin Serilda had likened them to, the price of admission to the mind and senses of a living spider!

And there were other senses here, too; senses Diana had never experienced before. Every hair on the spider's body was sensitive to vibration, to movement and to sound waves. This sensing was especially acute at the leg joints, of all places. She also had the strangest sensation of smell—of soap and steamy bath water—picked up on the spider's feet.

Just a series of dark shapes at first, the images in the small room began to brighten.

David was sitting in a bathtub . . . in the bathroom of his mother's condominium on the clinic grounds. The mirrors were steamed up. David leaned his head back and closed his eyes. His shoulders were wet and shone in the light of the frosted-over window. Soapy water came up to the middle of his bare chest. Despite the grainy murkiness of the vision, Diana could now see swirls of steam rising from the hot bath water. It was strange, but she could *feel* the warmth of the bath, feel it moving in waves of steam over the hairs and spikes of the spider's body.

Diana opened one eye and looked at Catherine. Catherine, knowing Diana's thoughts intimately now, because she was sharing them, opened one eye as well. The young women grinned at each other.

This is cool.

"Yeah," Diana said aloud. The vision started to fade a bit. Then Diana felt another pang of anxiety. Was Catherine desirous of David? She tried not to have these thoughts, lest Catherine read them too clearly. She simply concentrated on what she was seeing. The image brightened again, this time coming in full color, like a movie.

Catherine thought

He's not bad.

Diana thought

Hands off he's mine all mine.

They both laughed at that.

Yet Catherine started projecting something—started transporting a new thought.

"What are you doing?" Diana asked aloud.

"I want to bounce our wave from the spider's brain over to David's."

"Wait a minute—"

"It won't hurt him. Come on, try."

Diana thought of David. Imagined sending him a signal. It was invisible, something that could only be felt.

"Let's get a good look at him," Catherine said. "We'll make him stand up."

"Are you kidding?"

"Come on, Diana, don't be so prudish. You know you want to get a good look at him. Here's our chance."

Stand.

Now this seemed like a total invasion of privacy. ''No, Catherine,'' Diana said. ''That's not fair.''

STAND!

''You have to help me, Diana,'' Catherine said.

Diana acknowledged that this was probably true, Catherine couldn't quite do it alone. And she found that she was as curious to find out if they could take control of David's mind as she was to see his naked body.

''If the situation were reversed,'' Catherine said, ''and a guy was looking in at you, and the guy had the power, he'd check you out, Diana. Of course he would!''

Catherine was obviously more powerful in this equation, if only because she was so persuasive.

Diana found herself giggling, eyes closed. She gave in to Catherine, as usual.

STANDSTANDSTANDSTANDSTAND!

Diana thought of the Shadow, who had the power to cloud men's minds. She thought of Spock and the Vulcan mind meld. She thought of the spider's tiny brain, its consciousness subsumed by two girls, and now entering David's brain.

STAND STAND STAND STAND STAND STAND STAND STAND STAND STAND!

David's eyelids fluttered open. He put his hands on the sides of the bathtub and gripped. His muscular forearms flexed and he pushed himself upward. Water cascaded down his body and he rose and stood bolt upright.

He turned and water ran down his back and over his white buttocks, where the lines of a summer tan were marked off like invisible swim trunks.

Now they were in the spider's mind—seeing—and in David's mind, manipulating him like a marionette. Two places at once!

Diana smiled, but the smile left her face and was replaced with another feeling. Poor David. If he only knew what was happening to him. She felt the chill he was feeling, standing wet and naked.

"That's enough," Diana said. And somehow the balance of power shifted. Whatever grip they'd had on David's mind was now released. He blinked and his knees started to buckle, and he slipped.

Diana cried out. The "wave" had bounced completely out of David and back to the spider. Apparently Diana could not just shut off this power. The wave retraced its path. From the spider's point of view she watched David slipping. She felt the spider rear back in its web. Water splashed high out of the bathtub.

David, falling, threw a leg out of the tub and onto the bathroom floor. He tumbled forward, slipping and sprawling out of view. Droplets of water splashed high and fell onto the spider's silken web, and beads ran along its connecting threads. Diana heard David crash on the white tile floor.

The scene in her mind started to short out, fading to black. But before it disappeared entirely Diana caught a glimpse of something in the corner of her mind's eye. Something she couldn't look at directly, only peripherally. Had it been there all along? Hovering in another upper corner like an angel was the faintest impression of a tiny frowning child. A girl with colorless long hair. As the vision faded to black the thing showed its teeth in a devilish—what? A grin? A rictus of extreme psychic pain seemed more like it. Aimed frighteningly at Diana. Had Catherine seen it?

That didn't seem likely, because now Catherine was laughing, gasping, her hand at her throat. It was just the two of them again, two real people sitting on a bed in a real bedroom.

Diana felt her brow, damp with sweat.

"Wow! I think we've learned the trick of a lifetime," Catherine said. "No more TV. We can watch *psychovision*, the 'Bathtub Channel.' " She rolled back on the bed, laughing at her joke.

Diana smiled, but felt a bit chilled. She hoped David hadn't been hurt too badly. People regularly broke bones slipping in bathtubs and showers; it could have been a serious accident. She was already feeling guilty about that,

an accident caused by their prurience. And by a new kind
of mischief she could barely imagine.

They looked at each other. Diana stood up, paced across
the room, and paced back. She looked at Catherine, and
Catherine smiled. They both broke up laughing again, Diana feeling giddy, confused, happy, and exhilarated—and
a bit frightened.

"Oh, Catherine," she said.

Catherine stood up and hugged her.

"Amazing, isn't it?" Catherine whispered. "What you
can do if you put your mind to it." She snickered.

Diana bit her lip.

"We're gonna have some fun," Catherine said. "You
and me!" She let go of Diana and twirled around the room.

Diana wished she could feel as good about this as Catherine did. She tried to. She smiled.

Catherine took Diana's hands, which were cold, and she
pulled and said excitedly, "Listen, guess what? We're getting out of here for a while tomorrow night. My mom is
going to meet us in town, and we're invited to have dinner
at our place. What do you say?"

Diana squeezed Catherine's hands and let go of them.
She sat down on her bed, and leaned back against the wall.

Get out of this place for a night? That sounded pretty
good to her. Her head seemed to spin.

"I say, let's do it," Diana replied. "Let's get out of
here."

Sure enough, David was limping when Diana saw him in
the basement workout room the next day. He didn't smile
at her when she came in, just walked over to the barbells
and did some curls. White light beamed in through the high
small square windows.

"What happened to you?" Diana asked, warily. She felt
terribly guilty. But it wasn't just guilt that made her want
to comfort him.

David took hold of the lower leg-band of his gray sweats.
He pulled it up, revealing a nasty black bruise on his shin.

"How did you do that?"

He thought for a moment. "I do stuff like this all the time. Clumsy, I guess."

Diana went over to the treadmill and programmed it, pressing the codes on the smooth grid. The machine started up and Diana trod along, watching David do his bench press. It was a little embarrassing to think about the way she'd seen him yesterday. On the other hand, Diana could not have put into words the wonder she felt at having this strange power. It wasn't fair that she could just look in on him, and she'd have certainly objected to anyone doing that to her. She resolved to never do anything like that to someone again. But the power to do it—it could be used in other ways. That excited her. So she couldn't say she regretted the "bathtub" experiment one hundred percent.

All her life she'd felt like such a weirdo. The strange fit she'd had at her cousin Jerry's birthday party, the sudden visions in school . . . eavesdropping on someone's private thoughts when you didn't want to, when you shouldn't. Sensing looming disasters. It felt like a curse.

Even her own parents' private thoughts about her were enough to make her turn from her own strange nature. Maybe she didn't want to be like everybody else, but she'd never wanted the weird quality that made her impossibly different. Not till now. Catherine was helping to change all that.

If only she had Catherine's self-confidence, and Catherine's boldness. It seemed as though Catherine could take on the whole world.

Now they were sharing a new game.

A potentially dangerous game, but one in which *they* were taking charge.

Diana stepped off the treadmill and wiped her forehead with a towel. She noticed that David was sweating as he bench-pressed. His short black hair was wet, and beads of sweat popped out on his forehead and ran down his face. His face was contorted in a pained-looking mask. Here they were, alone together in the exercise room. And he was ignoring her.

"I know you could lose your job if anyone finds out about us," Diana blurted. "On the other hand, you don't have to totally ignore me, either. We can be friends, right?''

He set the weight down with a clang.

''Friends, huh?'' he said, sitting up on the bench. ''You should choose your friends more carefully.''

''You don't even want to be friends?'' Diana asked, stung.

''I'm talking about your friend Catherine Price. You're pretty thick with her, aren't you? With a friend like that, who needs enemies?''

''What's that supposed to mean?''

''It means that even though I'm not supposed to talk about the patients here, I'm telling you I'd think twice before I became a good friend of hers.''

''Why?''

''Things don't always turn out real well with Catherine's friendships, is all.''

''Are you speaking from personal experience?'' It had occurred to her that maybe the hostility between David and Catherine might be based on their ''friendship''—or something more than a friendship—that hadn't ended well.

He snorted at that. ''Hardly,'' he said. ''Catherine and I have never been close, had barely spoken a word to one another until you came here. I was speaking of the Vaundra Austin case. But I've said too much.'' He wiped his face with a white towel. ''Anybody heard me say a thing about that ancient history, I'd be gone quicker than if I really did make a move on one of you girls.''

Diana was confused. ''Vaundra Austin?''

''Just never mention that name around here,'' he said. ''Especially not to Catherine. Though you can bet she wouldn't be here except for what happened ten years ago. Why, this place wouldn't even exist, except for that.''

She looked at him, astonished.

He whispered, ''They all claim she can't remember a thing about it—'bout what happened to little Catherine and Vaundra. And nobody is supposed to mention it. Ever. You just look out for yourself, understand?''

''But, David, I—''

''Hold on now.'' David wiped the sweat from his neck. ''Look, Diana. I'm your coach here. I'm the one who tells you what it is, got it? No more questions from you, and no more questions about *us*.''

She felt an awful pang of cold anxiety. To be talked to that way by someone she cared about. It hurt. And it made her angry to hear him whispering about Catherine this way. Was it possible that *he* was somehow jealous of Catherine? She thrust out her chin. She looked into his eyes. He looked back at her, rather nervously.

''I'm just another patient here, hmmm?''

He looked down, clenched and unclenched his fists.

''Don't be stupid,'' he said.

It was then that it occurred to her. The thought *arrived* in her mind, unbidden. It was almost funny. It was so unlikely. It's bizarre the secrets people hold onto like worry beads, she thought. His dream, held onto just below the thin surface of his every word and gesture and feeling.

She just plucked it like a ripe apple.

''If you can't be honest with me about this,'' she said, ''then you'll never be honest enough with yourself to do what you have to do to be a dancer.''

His jaw fell open. He might have stammered something back at her. She didn't hang around to listen. She flipped her towel over her shoulder and went out the door.

She was walking through the kitchen feeling a combination of anger and strength. People were such gossips around here, she thought. Everybody out to assassinate somebody's character. The hatreds . . . maybe that's what the weird nightmare had been about. A skeleton in every closet, waiting to be assembled by yours truly . . .

Diana stopped, seeing Harriet's purse on the countertop. Poor Harriet was so absent-minded about that purse. But it was a lucky thing, and provided Diana with her opportunity to return the stolen money.

She looked around. No one in sight. The bare black branches of a small tree waved in the window. Bread baking in the oven made a delicious smell. She pulled the twenty dollar bill out of her sock and quickly opened Harriet's purse, found the wallet, and stuffed the folded bill inside.

She felt the throb of a headache, and remembered what she'd written in her dream journal this morning.

Her nightmare of last night had been particularly brutal. But mysterious, unless maybe it represented the backbiting people of Blackburn County. It was about angry fighting dogs. These dogs had all their hair shaved off, even on their heads, so they looked like ugly space aliens. Pale blue skin with black stitches everywhere. They looked like they'd been zippered together by some mad surgeon.

She could hear their barking now, in her memory. See their teeth flashing. What was it they were fighting over, with lips snarling up over yellow fangs?

She only knew she had to escape from them. But how could she escape from them if she was made to recount nightmares in her journal, and remind herself of them all day long? Maybe it was best to simply forget a weird dream. Like the dark faceless things that had stalked her through so many nightmares, and which fell to their deaths again and again as she watched in horror.

She left the kitchen and headed for the stairs, went up them, and into the bedroom where she sat down and tore the fresh pages of her writing out of her dream journal.

She crumpled up the pages and threw them into the trash can.

Randy walked jerkily down the main street of Leonora, the neck brace making it tough to look from side to side. He had to turn his whole body this way and that just to see right and left. His dark hair blew in the breeze.

His neck would heal fully, the doctor had said, as long as he kept the neck brace on. But, boy, he thought, this neck brace is one pain in the ass. He laughed at his own thought. If a neck brace was a pain in the ass, what would an *ass brace* be?

He kind of cracked himself up sometimes like that. He'd never heard of an ass brace, but he had heard about people getting into trouble and claiming their ass would be in a sling. An ass sling.

His long dark hair streamed out behind him in the November wind. The town was as desolate as ever, a few cars parked in front of the taverns, but no people on the streets. People didn't exactly walk down the streets to sight-see and window shop and such, not in this town. He stood in front of the hardware store, where a bench with peeling green paint had been set out, but which was empty today on account of the nip in the air and the gray sky.

Signs in the window of the hardware store advertised paint and snow shovels. The door opened and a mass of warm air followed an older couple outdoors; air that smelled of sawdust and turpentine.

At last Jon came walking his hard-guy walk down the street toward him. Jon was still wearing his denim jacket, just as Randy always did, even though it was cold out today. But it wasn't winter yet, not quite. It had snowed in some parts of the northland, but not in Blackburn County. As far as Randy was concerned, winter didn't come until the first snow—a day he always looked forward to, because of the celebration on Ice Rock. He was feeling impatient.

Jon grinned and his sparse red whiskers spread on his face. He had an extremely bad fresh haircut, no doubt the work of his diabolical mother and her home barber kit. Randy had once gotten a good scalping from Jon's mom. He remembered that the electric shears had grown hot and a funny burning smell had filled the air. But that didn't stop Jon's mom from economizing on haircuts. And for some reason Jon, who was as uncontrollable as Randy, always gave in to his mother and let her cut his hair. He paid a price for this concession. His red hair was left ragged, so he looked like some kind of Eastern European refugee.

Jon spoke before Randy had a chance to razz him.

"You look like some kind of retard," Jon said, giving Randy a shove.

Randy winced in pain. "Ow!" He kicked Jon hard in the shin, and Jon let out a pained laugh as he hopped out of the way.

"You trying to cripple me, Jon? Don't fuck with me while I got this brace on."

Jon rubbed his leg. "You'll live, I'm sure."

"Yeah, I'll live better if you don't screw with my central nervous system."

"Afraid your dick is gonna get shorted out?"

"I'm afraid you don't have one."

Randy looked up the street in time to see Catherine and her new friend, the cute dark-haired girl. Diana. "Okay, time to shut up. Here comes sweetness times two. My double-decker love sandwich."

"You better go on a crash diet, loverboy. Diana is mine," Jon said. "And Catherine is about as sweet as a bucket of ammonia."

"Clamp your trap, Jon. Here they come."

Diana rounded the corner, following Catherine. Diana was trying to keep up with Catherine, who was walking fast and businesslike, with a purpose. The purpose was to meet Catherine's mother. Diana felt mildly apprehensive about that, but glad she was getting away from the clinic for the evening.

And she would at last meet the famed state representative who had built the Albion Clinic.

Catherine saw the boys. She stopped and adjusted the shoulder strap of her bag. She was wearing black jeans and a tight purple sweater under her brown leather jacket. She continued on toward the guys, a big smile on her lips. Diana saw the neck brace on Randy. She didn't say anything, just followed along feeling a bit weighed down. She had a backpack with her, a few books and her diaries inside. She wore the long dark raincoat she'd worn when she'd arrived at the clinic, over jeans and a white sweatshirt. She clenched her hands inside her green mittens.

Catherine smiled and walked confidently over to the guys, who stood waiting like cowboys in a movie, hands in their pants pockets. Whatever Catherine might have been thinking was blocked out completely.

"Hey, hey," Randy said. When Catherine got close he slipped his arm around her waist.

"My God, look at you," Catherine cried. She touched the neck brace.

Randy slid his hands over Catherine's rump and leaned

his face close to her. They shared a rather noisy wet kiss. Jon looked at Diana. Their eyes met for a second. Diana looked across the street, then up at the gray empty sky. Not a bird in sight.

"Does it hurt?" Catherine said, touching her fingernails lightly to the neck brace.

"Nah, not too much," Randy answered. But he kind of winced. "Freak accident," Randy said. "I can't blame anyone."

"Except yourself," Catherine said with a wicked smile.

Randy gave Catherine a funny, knowing kind of smile. Diana tried not to pay too much attention to whatever it was that was going on between them. A kind of antagonism, but one spiced with sexual attraction, too. She'd seen these kinds of relationships before.

Jon pressed in a little closer. "You wanna go over to the zoo?" he asked Diana. "It's the last day to get in, then they close it down for the winter."

Diana said, "I didn't know there was a zoo in Blackburn County."

"There isn't," Catherine said. "It's just a stupid farm with a few birds and goats locked up in cages."

"Oh, come on, Catherine," Jon said. "It's a lot better than that."

"Not much," she said. "And we haven't got a lot of time. We're meeting my mother."

Jon clicked his heels together and saluted. "Well, we wouldn't want to keep the führer waiting."

Catherine didn't look at Jon. Randy gave Jon a sharp punch in the arm.

"Ouch!" Jon cried. "It's a good thing you're in a neck brace. I'd thrash your ass."

"Not," Randy said.

Diana looked at her watch. Catherine looked at hers. They had about a half hour to spare.

"Okay, let's go to the goddamn zoo," Catherine said, running her fingers through her hair. "Just you two quit acting like a couple of junior apes."

Randy pushed Jon out of the way and put his arm around Catherine's waist, guiding her down the street.

Jon and Diana walked side-by-side behind them. He was about a half-inch shorter than she was.

"Mind if I hold your hand?" Jon said. He said it quietly. Catherine and Randy were several feet up ahead, laughing about something, and arguing a bit between giggles. Sometimes they'd put their foreheads together as they walked along. They would grin and kiss.

Diana looked at Jon's extended hand. A small, powerful, compact hand. The skin was red and chapped. A scab had formed over a cut on his knuckles. She didn't really want to touch him. But she didn't want to say no either. His eyes were pleading with her.

She stuck out her hand.

"You should take your mitten off," Jon said.

She took one mitten off and gave him her bare right hand. He enclosed it in his, tightly, lacing up their fingers. Despite the chill in the air, Jon's hand was warm and sweaty. Clammy. Diana felt a weird kind of recoiling in her stomach and her loins. Now he smiled at her.

She looked away.

"How are those bad dreams of yours?" he said.

"Same as ever," Diana said. "You sort of get used to them." That wasn't true at all. Why was she trying to dismiss her nightmares? She just didn't want to talk about such things with Jon.

"Do you miss being in school?"

"Yes," she answered. Feeling as uncomfortable as she did, she started to pick up a fizz of his thoughts. She didn't want to. He liked her, that was obvious. She tried to will a cold, unfeeling wall around herself. Amazingly, she shut off his thoughts, just like that. She couldn't do this with Catherine very easily. But she found now that she could with Jon. Maybe she really was getting a stronger grip on these weird powers. But then, so was Catherine.

"Don't you have a job?" he asked.

"Had one."

"Doing what?"

"Renting videos at the mall."

"Cool. Then you could see a lot of free videos, huh?"

"Yeah." They rounded an elm-lined corner during what

seemed like an interminable, awkward pause.

"I have a job," Jon said. "I work at the hospital, old Mercy General. I work there usually thirty hours a week, *and* I've got a solid 'B' average in school. Except for in gym, because the coach is a Nazi fuckhead who hates me."

Diana glanced over at him.

He reddened. Diana did find his job and grades sort of impressive. She would have guessed that Jon and Randy were not exactly the most employable guys, or the brightest. And here Jon was not only not flunking out of school, but doing rather well, by his own admission. His tough-guy dirtball routine was probably just an act.

"What kind of work do you have at the hospital?" she asked him. Catherine and Randy rounded another corner up ahead, passing by the local Historical Center, a red-brick mansion with dark windows, closed for the season.

Jon sighed. "It's dirty work. I clean up bed pans and even blood." He shook his head and smiled. "Why, I've smelled pus and slime that would make you cry."

Diana's hand in his felt as though a warm wet toad had just squirmed there, and started kicking its horrible, slimy, tickling legs against her bare skin. She felt that recoiling sensation again.

"Well," she said, and cleared her throat. "Someone's got to do it."

Turning off the main road through town, the couples continued on past a stand of blue spruce trees till they reached a narrow winding highway. A few badly deteriorated houses stood off the road, where old-fashioned mailboxes on posts were bent, as if from the wind. A home-made sign directed them: ZOO AHEAD.

Diana was surprised to see a yellow school bus parked just off the road, and slightly tilted toward the ditch. But once inside the gates of the zoo (gates made of wood and a chain-link fence) she saw groups of children in their winter coats, walking from cage to cage. The cages seemed to be empty.

Randy led the way to the badger cage, just a fenced-off little patch of dirt with a bucket of water and an old hollowed-out tree stump.

"So where's the badger?" Diana said.

"He's sleeping inside that tree stump," Jon answered. He pointed.

The tuft of black fur with the dirty gray stripe sticking out of the hole in the stump might have belonged to a real live badger; or it might have been a prop. It was either asleep or dead, or a fake—not terribly exciting to see. A sign said WISCONSIN MASCOT. Diana got a creeped-out feeling looking around, wondering if this zoo was regulated by any laws.

Next they went to the refreshment stand. A sign there said BLACKBURN COUNTY ZOO, A PUBLIC-PRIVATE PARTNER-SHIP, OPEN JUNE 1 TO FIRST SNOW. An extremely crabby looking lady sat behind the counter. She wore ear muffs and had a pile of permed blond hair. She wore the kind of gloves that had the finger ends clipped off. Kids in dirty parkas of all colors swarmed at the counter in front of her. No doubt this woman had expected the first snow of the season sometime back in September. She was selling cold popcorn to the kindergartners.

"Don't all yell at once," she said. The kids were jumping on tiptoe at the counter.

Catherine approached the counter and the woman behind it gave her a sneer. Then the sneer was replaced with an expression of blank surprise. A humble smile crept over the woman's mouth. She sniffed, and her nostrils flared and fluttered.

"Miss Price, why I didn't recognize you."

Catherine smiled. "Four hot chocolates."

"Coming right up," the woman said.

Catherine paid even though the woman said there was no charge. Sipping weak hot chocolate, Diana followed her friends along dirt paths between mounds of patchy dead grass. On the way to an exhibit called the "Monkey Bar-rel" Catherine explained to Diana that part of the money that kept the park going was donated personally by her mother, the state representative. Somehow Theda had also secured some public dollars for the little zoo.

The Monkey Barrel did not live up to its fun-promising name. It looked like a giant round cake, sealed off with more chain-link fencing. Inside, the monkeys shivered. Some of them looked sick, skin patchy, bellies bloated.

"These monkeys are so fuckin' gross," Randy said with disgust. "Look, that one has cancer." He pointed at a monkey with a large swollen neck, as though some kind of tumor had grown there.

"These are research monkeys," Catherine said.

"Do they really give them cancer?" Diana asked.

Catherine shrugged. Sipped her hot chocolate.

"You should see them fight and throw their shit at each other," Randy said and grinned. "And sometimes, when they're not picking on each other, you can actually see them screwing."

Diana said, "Gosh, that must be very interesting." She sipped her hot chocolate, staring blankly in the opposite direction of the monkey cage.

Randy leered, "Why, yes it is, as a matter of fact."

"Shut up," Catherine said, giving him a push.

"Ow!" he wailed, putting his hand on his neck.

Diana looked back into the cage. She felt depressed looking at these poor creatures. They looked out with faces that seemed to ask "Why? Why?" One of them in particular seemed to bore his small black eyes into her heart.

"Come on, let's get out of here," Diana said. She turned, not waiting for the others to respond. She walked to a landscaped fenced-in area that she could imagine looking almost pretty, had this been a summer afternoon in June, rather than a cold day in November.

The grass was brown, and the lawn was bare in places. But in the center was a fountain made of white marble. It didn't fit in, and that was all for the best. The fountain was not operating, and empty of water, but for a tiny frozen film of ice at the bottom. Leaves and a few squashed paper cups were held fast in the ice. At the far corner of the exhibit, huddled near a tall bamboo wall, were a dozen pink flamingos. Their pink feathers fluttered in the light breeze. Children pressed against the fence and called to them.

Diana sipped her hot chocolate and saw what some of the children were doing. They were picking up pebbles and hurling them at the birds. Their aim was bad, but occasionally a flamingo was struck. Pink feathers ruffled. Diana turned to look at the kids, whose stocky female supervisor was busy trying to figure out why the flash on her camera wasn't working.

"Piece a sh—" mumbled the blue parka–clad young woman, shaking the camera.

Diana stepped in front of a little girl in a navy blue knit cap who was about to throw a handful of sand and pebbles at the flamingos.

"That's not nice," Diana said.

The woman looked up at her for a moment, then looked back at her camera, held up to her nose. The camera flash went off, blinding the woman.

"Oh, for Christ's—" she said through clenched teeth.

"We want the flamingos to come over here," a little boy said. He wore a small black Raiders jacket.

"Throwing pebbles isn't the way to do it," Diana said.

Catherine leaned against the low fence. So did the little girl. The child wore big round plastic tortoise-shell glasses, and a knit pale blue cap that reminded Diana of a bonnet. She held her hand over the fence and opened her mitten. The pebbles and sand fell to the ground.

"What do you want to see those ugly things for, anyway?" Randy said to the kids.

"Leave the kids alone," Jon said. "Let 'em look at the birds if that's what they want."

Diana looked over and noticed that Catherine was smiling at her.

Birds . . .

"Bet the birds will come over here if we call them real nice," Catherine said to the kids.

Randy frowned. "I doubt it. Not unless you have some food on you that they like."

"I don't," Catherine said. "But what would you like to bet?"

"You'd lose," Randy said.

"So bet, dillbrain," Jon said.

"Ten bucks," Randy answered.

Diana smiled at Catherine. Then they both looked over at the forlorn birds.

Catherine reached out her hand and snapped her fingers.

"Oh, right," Jon said. "That will bring them over. Sure." He laughed.

A few of the kids called, "Come here," and one of them whistled.

The birds might as well have been stuffed, tucked into the basement of a museum. Diana tried to concentrate. But concentration was not the key, only a part of it.

"How long are we supposed to wait for the flamingos to come over?" Randy asked. "Till next June?"

Diana found herself feeling mildly irritated by this situation. And not just at Randy and Jon. It was presumptuous of Catherine to make this bet. The least she could have done was consult Diana before silently enlisting her secret powers.

The current of anxiety that swelled up in Diana did the trick. At once, every flamingo turned its head toward the crowd assembled at the fence. Little kids oohed and aahed. Some of them backed away from the fence. Others leaned over it and waved.

The flamingos stiffly lined up side by side. Diana was amazed. But she felt the wave penetrating each bird, up and down the line. The ones that were sitting down climbed to their feet. In seconds they stood side by side, long necks extended, heads turned toward the crowd. They were completely synchronized, mirror images of one another. *Sweep.*

Diana looked at Catherine, who winked at her.

"Mindsweep," Catherine said quietly, so that only Diana could hear.

Diana looked at the birds. She could feel them, feel those funny legs that bent backwards at the knee. Feel the cold ground through webbed feet.

She beckoned them, feeling Catherine's wave flowing through her, and through the minds of each of the flamingos.

They began to walk. They stepped forward, in sync, legs and feet rising and touching back down in the grass before them.

The bolder kids who had only moments ago been throwing pebbles reached out over the fence with glee. The woman with the camera stood with her mouth open, the camera momentarily forgotten.

"Shit," Randy said. Jon was silent.

The flamingos reached the fence line.

Stop.

The flamingos planted their webbed toes in the dirt at the edge of the fence and they simultaneously extended their necks. Hooked beaks reached over the fence. The children reached out to pet their heads. Diana watched in wonder. She felt fear in the birds' minds, and anger. And then something strange happened, something she hadn't planned on.

All at once, the beaks of the birds were flinging down, swiftly, on whipping pink necks, striking the heads of the children.

Diana gaped at a little girl being whapped on the head by an angry flamingo. There were screams. Flapping wings, pink feathers in the air. A flamingo brought its head down hard, butting against the forehead of a little boy. A red streak covered the child's terror-struck face. He screamed as the flamingo lashed at him.

It all happened so quickly. Catherine watched in awe, her lips parted.

"No!" Diana cried. She waved her arms at the birds. But they weren't backing off. Adults were rushing over to try to help.

Diana felt the wave break at last, bouncing out of the flamingos' brains and returning to its source, the minds of Catherine and Diana. Diana gasped, feeling the force of the invisible wave slamming into her body.

The flamingos scattered. Some fell to the ground, stunned. Others raced back to the far edge of the fenced-in exhibit. A few let out their plaintive cry. Diana looked at Catherine, and saw her try to suppress a smile. But Catherine couldn't contain her laughter. She doubled over, hand covering her mouth. And she turned so that the others couldn't see her.

"It's not funny," Diana said.

Catherine shook, trying to stifle giggles. "I know it

isn't,'' she said, looking at the crying mob of kids, some of them with bloody scrapes on their heads, some lying down on the ground and shaking with fear.

Catherine stepped over to where Randy stood, his face pale.

"Ten dollars," Catherine said, and snapped her fingers. She held out her open hand.

Randy took hold of Catherine's elbow. "Come on," he said, his voice weak, "let's get out of here."

"Wait a minute," Catherine said, pulling free. "Pay up." A man in a blaze orange hunting cap came running along with a short dark-haired woman in a brown uniform. He had a rifle. The teacher with the camera was screaming something at them. Something about a lawsuit. She was trying to comfort a little girl whose face was completely red, slick with blood. Diana couldn't make out every word. The poor teacher was hysterical. Her glasses were all fogged up. And it was hard to hear anything over the hysterical wailing of the children.

"Five bucks apiece," Catherine said, pointing at Randy and Jon.

"I haven't got it," Randy said.

"Neither do I," Jon said.

Diana wiped blood from a little boy's face with her scarf. She was bent over the boy, whose glasses' lenses had been cracked in the attack. He was crying softly. Diana gently took the glasses from his face. She saw that the cut on the boy's head was not deep. But facial cuts bled badly. The boy looked awful, like something out of a nightmare.

"Well, then, you shouldn't have made the bet," Catherine said, still arguing with Randy. "You still owe us, and you'd better pay up soon."

Diana held the crying child in her arms. She looked over at her friends, not quite believing Catherine's seemingly total indifference to the mayhem.

"Catherine," Diana cried. "Why?"

Catherine and Randy and Jon stopped talking and turned to look at Diana. Anger flashed in Catherine's blazing blue eyes. Then something else caught Catherine's attention.

Diana followed Catherine's gaze.

There, standing amid the crying children, in an expensive dark wool coat and hat, a stern and cold expression on her face, was a tight-lipped woman. Gloved hands tightly gripped a small black leather bag.

Catherine's mother, Representative Theda Price.

Diana knew without being told.

Chapter Five

Theda Price's house was even more impressive on the inside than it was on the outside, Diana thought. Rows of tall windows made the family room feel more like a posh screened-in porch than the remnants of an old farm house. Built in 1890 by a prosperous farmer, the home had been carefully restored by Theda. A lot of money had gone into it. But then, Theda was purported to have made a small fortune trading cattle. She was a cow merchant, a successful one. Even rock stars bought her cows. Presumably for investment purposes.

Diana had been deposited in this room and handed a tall glass of cola with ice and a wedge of lemon. Catherine and Theda disappeared, promising not to keep her waiting too long.

Catherine hadn't said a word in the car on the way over. Diana wondered if maybe the incident with the flamingos had freaked Catherine out, ultimately. She seemed to sulk, breathing out heavily through her nostrils a few times while glaring out the window at the drab country scenery.

Diana had been impressed by the faintly glamorous smell of the car's interior, by the smooth ride of a big American luxury sedan and the effortless way Theda drove it. Theda had blood on her white gloves. When Theda looked up at the rearview mirror, and caught Diana looking at her, she didn't smile, not at first. She looked very hard at her. Theda's thoughts were inscrutable. She was as tough and pretty as her red helmet of a hairdo. Her red lips were pressed together firmly. Her bosom fluttered with her inhalation of breath.

"Everything is going to be fine, girls," she said, and then she smiled. "Not to worry." She turned into the driveway, rather fast. Diana steadied herself by placing a hand on the seat. And Catherine held on to the door handle, which she opened the exact moment the car stopped.

Now Theda was on the telephone, under a large painting in the hallway. Diana peered out of the entryway of the family room and looked at Theda, who had her back turned. A long flight of stairs carpeted in red led upward to the dark second floor.

The man in the painting was young, wearing an open shirt. Not exactly handsome, but bearing an unmistakable resemblance to Catherine, especially in the eyes. Crystal blue and piercing. Hair wavy blond and relaxed. Diana knew instantly that this was Catherine's long-dead father.

"No," Theda said into the pale gray telephone receiver, "you've got it all backwards." She switched the receiver to her other ear and dragged on a cigarette. "Why quit a job on principle? You don't work at your job on principle, you work for money, like most people. You'd better reconsider your motives."

Catherine walked down the stairs, shoes off, fuzzy white socks on. She still seemed sullen.

She walked into the family room entryway and leaned against a wall, arms folded across her chest. "Give me a sip of that," she said, coming over and taking the soft drink from Diana.

"What was his name?" Diana said, gesturing at the painting.

Catherine looked at the portrait for a few silent moments. "Newall," she said. "Still wondering how he died?"

Diana shook her head, blushing. "I didn't mean to pry."

Catherine walked over to a stereo console, next to a window that looked out upon the spacious back lawn, where the vines of great weeping willows had turned golden, and where a tire-swing hung from a low branch. She flipped on the radio. Static and careering whistles swelled from the hidden speakers. At last, a news reporter's voice came in deep and clear:

"*. . . and police have told us that none of the children were seriously injured. By a stroke of pure coincidence, State Representative Theda Price was on the scene, picking up her daughter, when the violent melee broke out. Price was credited with assisting in the rescue.*"

The tape cut away to Theda's voice: "*I only did what any person would have done in the same circumstances.*"

Theda's voice was deep and melodious, as if her lines had been well rehearsed. "*I ruined a good coat. But that's not important. What's important is that the children are fine and this freak incident is behind us.*"

The reporter spoke again. "*Two children required stitches. Authorities have closed the zoo and are considering having the birds destroyed. No one knows what if anything provoked the bizarre attack, though witnesses say some of the children had been throwing rocks at the birds prior to the attack. Counselors will be available at grade schools on Monday to provide assistance to parents and children traumatized by the rare flamingo attack.*"

Catherine switched the dial around. On another channel, the familiar voice of Nessie Jasper came through loud and clear.

"*I disregard the notion that I'm running a negative campaign,*" Nessie said.

Catherine looked at Diana.

A male interviewer said, "*It's not as though you don't have a few of your own negatives, Nessie. You have a drunk-and-disorderly citation on your record.*"

Nessie laughed: "*Well who in Blackburn County doesn't?*"

The DJ's laughter, and the laughter of another male, could be heard.

"*Okay, Nessie, we'll give you that. But what about being fired by the school board? Can we even say on the radio why that happened?*"

"*Yes, we can use the 'M' word. Excuse me,*" she said. "*My throat's a little dry.*" She took a sip of something, and sighed. "*It's just water, folks, relax!*"

More laughter.

"*Sure I drink and I smoke, but so do a lot of people,*" Nessie said, serious now. "*I maintain that's my business, not yours, as long as I stay outta my car, which many drinking politicians can't seem to be able to do. But that's not what your question was about. Why was I fired by the school board? I was fired for what they called 'gross irresponsibility as a sex educator.' Only they don't call it sex educator in Blackburn County. They call it human growth educator. I haven't heard such a hilarious euphemism since I flunked out of nursing school.*"

Catherine looked at Diana and grinned.

Interviewer: "*Nessie, let's get to the root of this. Everybody in Blackburn County knows you were fired from Leonora High School for discussing . . . well, the 'M' word.*"

"*Masturbation.*"

Nervous laughter. "*Well, you can say that word on the radio,*" the DJ said. "*I can't say it. I'd probably lose my job. As you know, a lot of folks say that particular practice is self abuse, and a sin.*"

"*Are you telling me you never do it?*"

More nervous laughter.

"*Nessie, let's leave me out of this,*" the DJ said. "*We're here to talk about you. You're a candidate for public office. Now there are a lot of people, myself included, who think a woman who teaches teenagers about . . . masturbation, saying it's perfectly natural, and such . . . now, this person is not going to get elected to public office.*"

Nessie sighed. "*That's what some people would like it to come down to,*" she admitted.

Diana looked up and saw Theda, who was off the telephone now and listening intently. She had her arms folded across her chest, and she leaned in the doorway.

Nessie continued speaking. "*But what I'm going to talk about are real issues, like the lack of decent jobs in this community, and yes I'm going to talk about campaign contributions and about elected officials who are supposed to represent the people, yet sell their votes to the highest bidder, and I'm going to talk about—*"

Theda had crossed the room, and now she flicked the radio off.

"Hey!" Catherine cried. "What'd you do that for?"

Theda turned her back and walked toward the kitchen. "Come and give me a hand, Catherine," she said coolly.

"You're not even going to answer me, are you?" Catherine said. "I was listening to that program, which happened to be pretty goddamned informative."

Diana felt extremely uncomfortable now. As her stress level rose, so did the frequency of channeled thoughts coming into her mind; thoughts bouncing back and forth between mother and daughter. Not only were these two sparring verbally, they were shooting invisible poison darts at one another.

It was weird, because Diana had assumed Catherine worshipped her mother. But now, in her mother's presence, the antagonism was palpable.

Was there anything more embarrassing than witnessing someone else's family argument when you were a guest in their home?

Diana could sense that Catherine was trying very hard to get into her mother's head. A wave beamed from Catherine's brain, sucking, scooping, but now it was coming up blank. Somehow Theda was now blocking her thoughts and scrambling them. This astounded Diana. Did Theda know that Catherine was clairvoyant? Did she know how to freeze her out? Theda was as cool as a slab of ice.

Theda turned around and glared at her daughter.

"That's enough, Catherine. I'm warning you." They stood beneath the large portrait of Newall Price. Catherine looked away from Theda, and at the portrait. A stricken expression crossed over Theda's face.

"Daddy," Catherine whispered. "Make her stop."

"Catherine, that's *enough.* We have company," Theda said and looked at Diana, eyes suddenly pleading.

Catherine looked at Theda with open rage and a queer smile. She looked back up to the dark portrait of her father.

"Did you hear that, Daddy?" Catherine said to the painting. "Your wife is threatening me. Tell her to go to hell for me, just like she used to tell you to do," she said.

Diana was completely freaked out by this bizarre behavior. She was furious with Catherine for embarrassing her like this in front of her mother. She was almost glad to see Theda coming at her daughter with her hands raised, red claws out, face red with fury.

Theda clutched at Catherine's shoulders and spun her around.

Catherine screeched, "Let go of me!"

Theda shook her daughter. "I'm not having it, do you hear me?" Theda screamed.

The backhanded blow was swift but not particularly brutal. Just a light slap. It probably wouldn't have harmed Catherine much at all, but for the wedding ring Theda was wearing.

Catherine blinked and put her fingers to her cheek. She held her hand out before her eyes and looked at the drops of blood.

"Catherine, I . . ." Theda tried to speak, to come closer.

"I'm bleeding!" Catherine screamed. Diana, clutching at her elbows, her heart slamming in her chest, could see the small nick on Catherine's chin. Theda reached out, arms extended, but Catherine darted back.

"Oh, Catherine," Theda said, tears coming into her eyes.

"Don't *touch* me!" Catherine wailed.

Catherine ran stomping up the wide stairs and across a second-story hallway. Her footsteps caused the chandelier in the foyer to vibrate. An upstairs door was slammed shut and locked.

Theda remained frozen beneath the painting, holding her hand, touching the ring on her finger, like some alien thing.

"I . . . I," Theda said to Diana. Tears stood in her eyes.

Diana couldn't speak. She was really appalled, but felt pity for both mother and daughter. And she couldn't help but see a parallel between their relationship and that of herself and her own mother. It couldn't have been easy to have a daughter like Catherine, or one like Diana. And Theda didn't even have a husband to help her.

"I'm so sorry you had to see that," Theda said. "I didn't mean to hurt Catherine. It's just that, well, you saw her talking to . . .'' she looked sadly at the portrait of her dead husband. She lowered her eyes.

At once an image of flames came into Diana's mind. Flames crossing over Newall Price's face, over his closed eyes. She saw the fiery car crash that consumed him one night. The empty booze bottles in the car. His face slack as it blackened.

Diana trembled.

"Oh, Diana," Theda said. "This is not good. Not good at all. Please go to Catherine. See if she's all right." Theda turned, covering her face with her hand. She quickly strode from the room. A door closed slowly behind her.

Diana stood there alone now in the glow of the copper pendant lights. She widened her eyes and sipped the last of the soda through a straw. It made a loud obnoxious sound. She stared blankly ahead. Wondering at it all.

"It's not a bad cut," Diana said a while later, sitting at the edge of the big pink bathtub in Catherine's private bathroom, off her large bedroom. The bedroom had gloriously big bay windows, and through them Diana could see the bare branches of cedar trees, which seemed to lower themselves like a ladder at the very edges of the window panes. Sheer curtains on black forged iron rods were pulled from the windows. The room was almost a fantasy stage set, like in some movie with a young Elizabeth Taylor.

Catherine looked at the nick on her face in the paneled mirror, surrounded by small golden squares of lighted glass.

"Well, now you know what kind of mother Theda Price really is," she said.

"You were expecting a peck on the cheek from her? You told her to go to hell. Why?"

Diana silently counted all the bottles of expensive bath oil and shampoos and perfume lined up on the edge of the sink. Catherine was, like so many unhappy rich girls, pampered and spoiled with material things.

"She *is* going to hell!" Catherine said with a tremor in her voice. "She keeps me locked up like some . . ." she choked on her words. "She'd even have them give me a lobotomy, to shut me up."

"Shut you up?"

"I know all her little secrets—and a few big ones."

Diana nodded.

There came a soft rap on the door.

"Catherine," Theda called, through the closed door. "Diana, too, come on downstairs now and have some dinner."

"Go *away*, Mother," Catherine bellowed.

The door knob turned. The door was still locked. Theda rapped loudly on the door now.

"Catherine, unlock the door this instant. I want to apologize."

Catherine ran out the bathroom and through the bedroom to the door. She slipped on the bare wood floor, but recovered her balance. She leaned against the door. Diana rose slowly from the edge of the tub and walked into the bedroom, observing this bizarre scene. She felt herself perspiring.

Here we go again, she thought.

"What if I called up the radio reporter?" Catherine said, a bitter sing-songy tone in her voice. "I could show him the cut on my face. I could tell him a few other stories, too!"

Catherine, grinning and putting a hand over her mouth, looked over at Diana. Diana did not smile.

Theda didn't answer for what felt like a long time. "I'm sorry I lost my temper with you, Catherine. And the cut was an accident, as you well understand."

"An accident!" Catherine said. She turned the lock and flung open the door. Theda stepped back, her eyes wide. She wore a white apron with navy pinstripes. Catherine raised her arms and lunged out into the hallway at her mother with fists flying. But Theda caught Catherine by the wrists.

She held her daughter tight.

They did a strange struggling kind of dance, staring fiercely into one another's eyes. Catherine seemed to growl, and shook her blond hair wildly.

Diana had really seen enough. She felt disgusted. This dysfunctional family made hers seem like the Brady Bunch.

"Catherine," Theda whispered, "*Catherine . . .*"

Mother and daughter stood frozen together, like two rams with locked horns.

But then all of the psychic rage that had been swirling madly about the room evaporated. Just disappeared.

And Catherine melted, trembling and crying into her mother's arms. As Theda caressed her daughter's gleaming blond hair and whispered, "There, there now," the door slowly closed, leaving Diana alone and bewildered yet again.

When dinner was served on the big dining room table, Catherine hardly said a word. And Theda calmly read a thick report, incomprehensible with figures and charts.

Occasionally, between bites of a delicious lamb stew, Theda asked Diana about her family, and about Chicago. Diana answered politely. As if the violent row had never happened.

Catherine picked over her food, a relaxed and vacant look on her face. But at last she spoke. She looked at Diana.

"Guess you think we're pretty nuts, huh?" Catherine said, and took a bite of mashed potatoes. She smiled. The cut on her chin had dried into a small hair-thin dark line, less than a quarter-inch long.

Theda laughed, quietly.

"Well, *every* family . . ." Theda started to say.

"No, I asked *Diana*, mother," Catherine said, very lightly, not at all combative.

"Oops, well, I'll just shut up, then," Theda said, and cut a chunk of lamb in half.

"Yeah, wouldja please do that?" Catherine said and smiled at her mom. Theda smiled back. Catherine and Theda both looked at Diana now.

Diana opened her mouth. "Uh, well, it's really none of my business. I'm not judging you."

But of course she was. And she tried to be cool, to keep Catherine from knowing what she was really thinking.

After supper, Catherine and Diana watched a video about a girl who goes west after her parents die and becomes an outlaw until a handsome lawman tames her and wins her heart.

Then Theda drove them back through the night highways to the shelter, the radio softly playing Frank Sinatra.

Lying in the dark, in her bed at the clinic, Diana tried to read Catherine's thoughts. Catherine turned and looked at her. Minds were impenetrable tonight, but then, so much had already been said.

"Do you hate your parents?" Catherine asked.

Diana didn't answer for a moment. "No," Diana said. "I don't hate them. Do you hate your mother?"

Catherine turned over in her bed, and faced the wall. Moonlight made a shadow of the window on the wall. The shadows of the heavy branches of the trees swayed silently.

"We have always fought," Catherine said. "And it's because . . . because . . ." she let her voice trail off.

Diana lifted her head from the pillow. "Because?"

"She is going to destroy me," Catherine said and sniffed loudly.

"Destroy you? How? Why?"

"She knows about . . . reading thoughts and things."

"That's no reason—"

"She knows I know certain things. About her political career, for one thing."

"So what? Isn't that private between the two of you?"

Catherine turned and looked at Diana. Diana saw the tears streaming down her face. Catherine clutched at her pillow and let out a sob. "I have to tell you . . ." Catherine began. But stopped.

"What?" Diana said. Though she wasn't sure she wanted to hear.

Could it have been something Catherine discovered in a dream? Diana speculated. She tried to delve inside that troubled mind of Catherine's. But she found a wall of ice, a translucent screen, like frost building up on a window pane.

"No," Catherine said. She laid her head down. Whatever tiny spark of a revelation she might have had about herself, about the two of *them*, was gone now. Her breathing was even and soft.

"You're not going to tell me any more?" Diana asked. "No family scandal, no secret you could die for?" She smiled. Really, how bad could it be? People tended to ex-aggerate the myths and secrets in their families, as Dr. Lin-den had explained to her. Then the fact of keeping the secret became bigger than whatever it was—some minor infraction or another—that was being kept hidden.

"There's nothing to tell, not really," Catherine said in a flat monotone voice. "Theda's secrets are spilling out in the daily newspapers. She's in the race of her life. I love her. I hate her. Ever feel that way about someone?"

"She's your mother," Diana said, firmly. "You're a grown woman, almost. She's your past, not your future. You'll be gone from here, soon enough. It only seems like a big deal right now, but it won't once you're on your own."

Catherine held her breath. She closed her eyes tightly.

"On my own . . ." Catherine whispered. Then, in a clear voice, she said, "Have you ever wanted to kill someone?"

Diana didn't answer. She felt a chill creep up her spine.

"I mean *really* kill someone?"

"That's mad, Catherine."

"Being held prisoner is mad. Is wanting to escape as mad as all that?"

"You're angry and upset," Diana said, trying to calm herself every bit as much as she was trying to calm Cath-erine.

Catherine was silent for a long time. But then, just as Diana was about to fall asleep, she heard Catherine whis-per, "It would be so easy."

A center for dream research, even one with as obscure (and shady) a reputation as the Albion Clinic, must abide by certain standards. Even if your wealthy (or aspiring to be wealthy) parents want you locked up somewhere—a mental institution, a boarding school, a hospital for the damned—society has the right upon occasion to cast an eye toward your corner.

The Albion Clinic, because it occasionally housed juve-niles, and because it received, through labyrinthine chan-nels, some government (but mostly private) funds, faced occasional scrutiny. Politicians, grant administrators, educators and child advocates had each in turn taken their breakfast tours through the sunny modern building. And the curriculum of the dream center was also a point of interest to certain authority figures. Along with therapy and exercise, diet control and the odd chemical cocktail, the Albion Clinic kept its few patients busy with the standard, approved practices that typified, even bettered, the modern human warehouse.

Diana was almost pleased to be back "home" at the clinic after the bizarre visit to Catherine's. Despite having shared a room with Catherine these many weeks, the evening at Theda's house had proven that even the best of friends (as it seemed they were becoming) shouldn't spend every waking moment together. Diana, seated in a sunny bay window in an out-of-the-way attic hallway, noted in her diary the irony of her new desire for a little more privacy. Here, it seemed that even her private thoughts were not exactly her own.

Diana scribbled down her feelings about Catherine, about Catherine's mother, and about her strained relationship with her own parents, and took sips of herbal tea. The bay window was like a small bed, padded and cozy. She moved her feet, in new warm wool socks, over the pillows and gazed out the frosty window, down through the high bare tree branches, to the rolling grounds. Still not a flake of snow, and it was almost Thanksgiving.

Yes, she thought to herself; how ironic to think you could distance yourself from a girl who shared your room, who felt as you did, who was really more like you than any other person in the whole world. Who, truth be told, shared your thoughts. Your dreams. Your nightmares, too. She wrote this down in her diary.

Catherine's relationship with Theda was the worst Diana had ever seen between a mother and daughter. Certainly the most violent. Far too close and suffocating. And while Diana didn't take Catherine's comment about killing Theda seriously (Catherine had been, after all, very upset at the time) it was chilling to ponder.

Diana looked up from her diary. Then she closed her eyes. She had been sleeping again, more or less regularly, so in a way her parents had been in the right, sending her here, despite the persistence of the confusing nightmares. What was more, the exercise was making her stronger. She could feel the strength in her legs and arms. She liked it.

Yet she couldn't help but resent the secrecy involved in her institutionalization. She remembered how her mother had promised no one would know where she was going, that some lies would be told on her behalf. It was like when a girl got pregnant in the old days, and was shipped off to a place run by nuns until she delivered the baby. Everyone in her own community would be told that the girl had some exotic disease, and required mountain air, or a seaside retreat. Or maybe they would say she was off tending to a sick relative. When the baby was born it would be taken from her and put up for adoption, and the girl would return home as if nothing had happened.

Secrets.

In Diana's case, the secret was that she had been shipped off to a kind of loony bin, a rehabilitation center. Some of the kids she went to school with had been sent away to such places, and they seldom returned to school.

Diana remembered her mother saying most emphatically, "You are *not* going to an insane asylum. You are *not* insane. This is a respected clinic."

Her mother was very ashamed of mental illness in the family. Yet Diana now thought with a smile that it was her parents themselves who were crazy, paying a fortune to this cozy dream clinic, where all Diana really had to do all day was dwell on herself, talk about herself, do a few minor chores, and exercise.

She was feeling quite strong today. Yet she had what she might have called (at Dr. Sterling's suggestion) a divided mind. She wanted to get rid of her nightmares. Yet she also wanted to delve into them. Take them on—head on. She knew they were leading her somewhere, and to something. But where, and to what?

A sound shook her from her introspection. She heard Catherine's voice; it was coming from the front stairs.

"Have you seen Diana?" Catherine asked someone.

"I thought I saw her go up that way," came another

voice, an older woman's. One of the Montgomery sisters.

Then the sensation, the pressure around her ears and her head. Catherine searching her out. Diana tried to freeze out this reaching, questing energy Catherine sent soaring through the house, to find her.

Diana swung her legs to the floor, and on tiptoes ran in the direction of the back flight of so-called servant stairs. She was escaping Catherine, and it made her smile. At last a clear intention! It wasn't that she disliked Catherine. She just felt a bit antisocial just now. She didn't notice that she'd left the diary behind, sitting in the bay window in a square of sunlight.

Diana escaped down to the kitchen, where Shirley, dressed in her white cook's uniform, selected a heavy black iron skillet from a rack of several pots and pans hanging from the ceiling. She did not smile at Diana. Through the window, Diana saw David sitting on the back porch of the clinic. He was wearing an orange hunting vest and a hat with flaps over the ears, and he held a rifle in his hands. She looked back over at Shirley, who was frowning now, pouring olive oil from a tin over the bottom of the skillet. A blue flame rippled against the pan's underside, and the smell of heating olive oil drifted through the kitchen.

Shirley's son. The rules of the house. Diana wanted to say something to Shirley, remind her that David was a grown man now, and she herself was nearly of voting age. Rules or not, parents needed to let go of their kids. Yet Diana realized that a desire to explain things to somebody's mother was not exactly an impulse of adulthood, if adulthood meant freedom to make your own decisions.

Diana tapped on the glass and David looked up at her. She opened the door and stepped outside, not bothering to put a jacket on. It was cold. The ground was gray and hard. A streamer of fog hung in the bare treetops.

David looked away from her and continued cleaning his rifle.

Diana crossed her arms over her chest and held onto herself, against the cold. At last he looked up at her.

"Yeah?" he said. Not friendly. Still sore at her. Because

she'd guessed about him wanting to be a dancer, she supposed. But why would that make anyone sore? What was so bad about it?

It was a secret, that's what.

"Yeah, nothing," Diana said. "I saw you out here, so I thought I'd say hi. Did you know the treadmill is broken?"

"Repairwoman is supposed to come next week. Meanwhile you can walk around the house, run up and down the stairs and such—but stay outta the woods unless you want to be mistaken for a deer."

"You're going hunting?"

"'Course," he said with a snort. "Always have."

"I'm sorry about the way I mentioned your being a dancer," Diana said. "I suppose I should have been more discreet, if it's really something you don't want people to know about."

He gave her a low scowling glance. "Who told you about that? Has someone been spying on me? Was Catherine?" He had some kind of wire inserted into the barrel of the weapon. "I don't talk about being a dancer with anyone. But somebody must have seen me practicing or found one of my books. Someone spied on me, or heard the music I like to play." He gestured to his small stereo cassette player, sitting next to him.

"What are you listening to?" she said, not really caring now if she was annoying him or not.

"Doubt you'd be interested."

"Try me."

"You know who Prokofiev was?" He looked at her, challenging.

"A composer," Diana said. She wasn't reading his mind. Didn't have to, and certainly didn't want to. "You listen to Prokofiev when you hunt?"

"Not while I'm stalking," he said. "But when I stop and light up a cigar, then I like to slip the headphones on and listen to a few measures." He smiled now, seeming to warm up a bit. "It's, like, the best thing in the world. Looking through the woods, maybe seeing a big buck. Being in nature. And the majesty of that music. I wonder if you could even imagine it."

Diana bristled. "Well, I've never hunted before," she said.

"I doubt you'd enjoy it. It's dangerous. Even if you don't get shot, people have been lost in these woods. Ask your pal Catherine about that."

Diana frowned. Maybe she felt guilty about ditching Catherine herself, but she didn't like other people making fun of her.

"What do you mean by that? Stop dropping hints and explain what you really mean, David Hauser."

"I'm talking about Vaundra," David said, pulling the wire from the rifle barrel. "Catherine didn't tell you about Vaundra, did she? Well, she wouldn't. Even when we were kids back in school, the subject of Vaundra Austin was not to be mentioned."

"Vaundra . . ."

"Most everybody has forgotten about Vaundra. And everybody protects poor delicate Catherine, like she'd spaz if anyone ever mentioned it. Catherine is said to have amnesia on the whole subject. But I remember Vaundra. She was a real quiet kid. She and Catherine were thick as thieves, best friends. Then one day they went for a walk in the woods," he glared at her now, liquid brown eyes gleaming. "And Catherine came back alone."

Diana blinked her eyes. Didn't quite believe what he was saying. She leaned against a chair. "What happened?"

"Well, no one knows for sure. They got lost. And then they got separated. Ten years ago. That's the official story, you see. Catherine's mom sent out search parties. But they didn't find even a trace of Vaundra. It made news statewide. And as for Catherine, well, she had one of her famous fits. She couldn't speak. People thought that maybe some pervert got hold of them."

David looked through the sight of his rifle, squinting an eye. Then he lowered the rifle and wiped the barrel with an old rag. "Anyway, Vaundra was never found."

Diana closed her eyes.

"You don't think Catherine did something to Vaundra, do you?" Diana couldn't imagine such a thing. But then hadn't Catherine, in one of her black moods, talked about murdering her own mother?

"No one ever suspected it," David said. "But people do find Catherine creepy. *Mental case* is what everybody says. Still, no way a little kid could have disposed of a body, even if Catherine was a killer. And no body was ever found. See, it happened in the winter when the ground was frozen, so there would be no way to bury the body." David grinned. " 'Course, maybe Catherine *ate* little Vaundra, winter coat and boots and all."

"Stop it," Diana said. "You aren't making all of this up about Vaundra, are you?"

David stood up. "You can look it up in the old newspapers if you don't believe me." He looked past her. The back door opened. Diana's heart nearly stopped.

Catherine stepped outside now, too. She had something hidden behind her back.

"So here you are," she said to Diana, slightly out of breath. Her breath steamed. She handed Diana her diary. "You left this out where anybody could read it," she said. She smiled and bit her lip.

Diana took the diary, feeling a cold rush of anxiety.

Where anybody could read it . . .

Diana reddened.

"Catherine, did you read it?"

Catherine laughed. "Did I? By gosh, by golly," she batted her eyelashes. "If you're going to hide every little thing from me I guess I'll just have to read all about it in that pretty little handwriting script those nuns taught you back in Chicago."

"Hide everything from you?" Diana said. "Catherine, we're going to have to have a talk. You *did* read my diary, didn't you?"

David was collecting his things, oily rags and a handful of shells.

Catherine didn't respond. She looked at David. Her face fell and she groaned. "Oh, my God, David, you're not going out to *slaughter* deer are you?"

He didn't answer.

"You are!" Catherine said. "How barbaric."

"Oh, shut up, Catherine," David said. "You know all the men in Blackburn County hunt deer."

"Well, Dr. Sterling doesn't hunt deer. He doesn't even eat meat. Did you know he's a vegetarian?"

"Big deal, so was Hitler," David said.

"He was?" Catherine said. "Well, that still doesn't make it right to kill defenseless animals."

"Fuck 'em," David said. He stood up.

"Oh, you really are just like every other heathen in these woods."

David pushed past them. "I'll bring back the heart for you, fair damsel," David said to Diana.

"Wait!" Diana cried. "Let me go and get my coat. I want to come with you."

David turned and shook his head. "Forget it, Diana. You don't have a license, and you don't have a blaze orange coat. You might as well be wearing an antler hat. You just wouldn't last five minutes."

He turned and off he went, down the sloping trail toward the woods.

"You know something, Diana, he's not worth chasing after," Catherine said. She was shivering now. "He's a loser. He'll spend the rest of his life here, living with his mother and running after deer in the woods."

Diana turned and started toward the door. It was cold out here. "What makes you so superior?" Diana said, as she walked away from her friend.

Catherine let out a yip of a laugh. "I might ask what's gotten into you?" she said.

Diana turned around.

"In a word, *you*."

Catherine smiled that creepy smile again. She started to sing "I've Got You Under My Skin." When she saw Diana turn around again she followed after her, into the warm kitchen. The rich smell of seared beef made Diana's stomach growl with hunger.

Shirley wasn't in the kitchen at the moment. A heavy iron pot simmered on the stove top. The seal of the lid was cracked slightly where a plume of steam blew ceiling-ward.

"So I peeked at your diary, big deal," Catherine said.

"It's not like I had time to read it. I'm not a speed reader. I just glanced at it. And besides, why should we have secrets?"

Diana stopped again. She rolled her eyes. "Catherine, there are some things I don't want anyone to know about, and there are some things that you don't need to know about."

"Like your crush on that loser, David?"

"Uncalled for," Diana said. She turned and started toward the door. But she stopped abruptly and turned and faced Catherine, feeling really angry now.

"I'm just trying to warn you about him," Catherine cried, before Diana could speak. "If I were you I'd steer way clear of that drippy little—"

"You are not me!" Diana shouted. She looked into Catherine's serene face, a face almost feline in its arrogance. It infuriated her that Catherine at least *seemed* to be so self-assured.

"For the last time, I'm not asking you, Catherine," Diana said, "I'm *telling* you. Back off."

Diana turned and left the room. She heard Catherine snickering.

"Back off?" Catherine said to herself. "She tells *me* to back off."

On the stairs Diana could hear Catherine talking to herself. Catherine spoke in a mean tone of voice. Diana was almost at the top of the stairs when she heard Catherine arrive at the bottom and yell up at her, "You just try and find a place I don't know about! You just try it, missy!"

It might have been a bluff. It might have been a desperate threat. Whatever it was, Diana now knew (goosebumps crawling up her back) that she'd crossed a line with Catherine.

Under the big glass dome, walking past the potted palms, Diana wondered if she hadn't just made a big mistake. Why bring things to the breaking point like this? It was a foolish thing to do when you had to face someone every day, had to live with them. Had to share a room with them.

Diana went into that room now and closed the door behind her. She went to her bed. Catherine didn't follow this time. And for once a trail of thoughts didn't trace up the stairs after her like rippling fog. Catherine projected nothing over the airwaves that linked them. Whatever Catherine was doing or thinking just now, Diana simply could not know.

Randy looked into the barrel of the shotgun, squinting an eye.

"Don't do that, dumbshit," Jon said. "It might be loaded."

They'd come to a clearing in the woods. The ground was leaf-strewn. Randy had a blaze orange jacket on, and his neck brace, which made his movements stiff and jerky. He lowered the shotgun.

"It's not loaded," Randy said, the glowing butt of a cigarette hanging on his lip.

Jon sat on a tree stump. He wore an orange cap with an orange bill, and two days' worth of red beard growth. He shook his head.

"Famous last words," Jon said.

Randy held the shotgun by the barrel. He let the butt swing to the ground, where it struck a rock. The weapon fired instantaneously, straight upward. A cascade of smaller tree branches showered down upon Randy and Jon.

Jon covered his head with his arms.

The two boys looked at one another.

"You are an amazingly lame piece of dookie, man," Jon said in a whisper.

Randy looked pale. "I could have sworn . . . I coulda been k-k—"

"Mmm-hmm," Jon said, and he grinned now. He pulled from his coat pocket a wineskin, and unscrewed the cap. He stood and walked to his shaking friend. "Open up," he said.

Randy opened his mouth and Jon aimed a stream of red wine at his friend's tonsils. When Randy's mouth overflowed with wine, and it slopped out over his chin, Jon redirected the wine into his own mouth. He swallowed and sighed and recapped the wineskin.

"Come on," Jon said. He picked up his rifle and started

toward a new path, his boots crunching loudly in the leaves and twigs and pine cones that covered the forest floor.

In another Blackburn County wood, David drew in on a long cheap cigar. His rifle was leaned up against a tree. He felt good today. He let out a long stream of smoke, savoring the peppery bite of tobacco. When the smoke cleared there stood before him, about twenty feet away, the biggest buck he'd ever seen: a magnificent animal with a huge rack of antlers.

At once, David's heart began to hammer in his chest. The buck turned its head as though surveying the area. Its brown eyes gleamed beautifully. Jets of steam shot from its nostrils. It had been running and now it was at rest, seemingly unaware that David stood so close.

The cigar fell from David's mouth and landed on the frosty ground with a hiss. Still the buck didn't move. As slowly and quietly as he could manage, David took hold of his rifle and brought the sight up to his eye. He was trembling badly. Buck fever, it was called. The thrill-terror before the kill.

He looked through the scope and saw the buck's massive neck. He aimed at a spot just behind the animal's right shoulder. The lines of the crosshairs veered wildly.

Hold still, he told himself. His finger touched lightly on the trigger. It was as though he hadn't the strength to squeeze. Yet now the gun steadied. Calmness swept over him. The great buck stood like a statue against the gray woods. David pulled the trigger.

Click.

The buck turned its great crowned head and looked at him now, ears erect. It thrust its head downward and pitched its weight to its side, legs flailing over the ground. Soon it was bounding noisily through the woods, away from David, who felt his own legs weakening.

The gun hadn't gone off. It wasn't loaded. He sank down to a squatting position, then fell backwards, landing hard on his butt. Breathing rapidly, he lay down flat and looked up through the tree branches at the November sky.

*   *   *

Sterling had just finished a session with Diana, and he was looking over his notes. Diana, who had slipped her shoes off, now sat at the edge of the black couch and laced the shoes up.

She wondered if he was angry with her, because although she'd been cooperative, as usual, she was not forthcoming about her nightmares—or about the way things had been going with Catherine of late. She'd been less talkative, more eager to wrap things up and leave the dream chamber. At last he'd said, "That's enough for today's session. You're free to go."

She stood up now to leave. "'Bye," she said.

He didn't turn around.

"Mmm," he said absently.

Diana left the dark chamber, closing the door behind her. When she was gone, a figure emerged from the shadows. Theda.

She wore one of her eye-popping blazers, this one blood-red over a white blouse and black skirt. Her face was grim.

"She's getting stronger, isn't she?" Theda said flatly.

Sterling remained expressionless. "In every way," he said. "She's practically off the charts."

Theda turned her back now. "I'm . . . a little frightened."

Sterling had to suppress a laugh. "You? Frightened?"

She crossed the room, stood before a black console. "If only because . . . because I can't fully believe in this . . . *experiment*," she said.

He rolled up beside her now on his little wheeled stool.

"These girls make the government's remote viewers I've known look like four-eyed, buck-tooth seeing eye dogs," he said. "Trust me."

"No," she said, referring to his hand, which now travelled up beneath her skirt. She *did* trust him. Had for ten years. But what he proposed, the way in which he wanted to harness the powers of Catherine and Diana . . . it frightened her now. In a way it never had before.

She turned around to face him, feeling the elastic of her panties crawling downward in his fist.

She leaned over him. He kissed her mouth deeply.

"We're very close to our goal, Theda, and success turns me on," he said, licking his lips. "Almost as much as it does you."

"Someone might come in here," Theda whispered, looking around behind her.

"So what? We could hear them in plenty of time."

"Catherine will know," she said. "If we do it here again."

He let his lab coat fall to the floor and unfastened the buckle on his belt.

"Not to worry. Leave everything to me."

Theda felt her knees weakening. She was falling off the console she was pressed up against.

"I'm slipping," Theda said, eyes pressed closed. She fell astride him, her sharp-nailed hands gently holding him by his hot ears.

"I have you," he said, and poked his warm, wet tongue into the hollow of her neck.

Driving through the twilight, Randy shivered. The car's heater didn't work well. Jon, beside him, rubbed his sleeve against the windshield.

"Shit, it's freezing in here," Jon complained.

Randy didn't respond. No snow on the ground, yet the country roads were slick with a layer of frost. The sky was patchy with high, thin clouds. Between them, a few stars twinkled dimly over Blackburn County.

"Winter's coming," Jon said.

"I know winter's coming, numbnuts."

Jon closed his eyes. "Don't get pissed at me," he said. "Ain't my fault you didn't get a deer."

"Did I say it was your fault? I'll get one tomorrow. Maybe it'll snow. Easier tracking."

"Weatherman says no snow."

"What does he know?"

Jon screamed. He saw the deer dart out in front of the car before Randy did. Its eyes shone in the headlights. A doe, Randy saw, right before the awful impact.

He struck the deer with the right side of his vehicle. He heard the headlight shatter. *Felt* it pop. Saw the deer's neck jerk back, head swinging. Its eyes seemed to beckon toward the black night sky. Then the car went into a skid.

"Fuck!" Randy wailed, slamming his foot down on the brakes. The car slid to the side of the road. The front end nosed down toward the ditch, and the car stopped.

Jon jumped out of the car and ran to the center of the road, where the deer lay dead, its tongue protruding from its mouth. Jon heard Randy swear, examining the crushed right front end of his mother's Plymouth.

"Looks like you got your deer," Jon said gravely. He looked up at his friend, who was shaking.

Randy came over to look at the deer, the neck brace as usual making his movements jerky and awkward. He didn't smile. He registered no expression at all. He just walked back to the car and leaned against the door. He sniffed loudly. Tears ran down his face.

After a long moment Jon walked over and leaned beside the car next to him. He pulled a white handkerchief from his inside jacket pocket. Handed it to Randy.

Randy accepted it and dabbed his eyes.

"Shit, man," Randy whispered. "I didn't mean for that to happen . . . I didn't . . ." his voice trailed off, catching in his throat.

Jon took in a deep breath. "I know, man. I know."

Randy wiped his running nose. He gave the bunched up wet handkerchief back to Jon, and Jon stuffed it into his jacket pocket.

"S'pose we should tag her and haul her in," Jon said. "Might as well."

Diana managed to avoid Catherine for the rest of the evening. She stayed a step ahead of her. Catherine could sometimes read Diana's thoughts clearly when they were in the same room together, especially if Diana was nervous or stressed out. But Catherine couldn't search Diana out as easily if Diana remained calm, and kept her emotions in check. Together, they had this tremendous strength. Apart, they were weaker.

When Diana finally went to the darkened bedroom, Catherine was already asleep (or pretended to be) in her bed.

Catherine lay on her side, back to the room, blond hair protruding from an opening in the blanket. Diana quietly changed into her nightshirt and brushed her teeth. She washed her face and dried it with a thick blue towel. Turned off the bathroom light. In the dark she found her way to her bed, illumined under the shadow-bars of the skylight.

Catherine was so still. Diana tried to breathe quietly. To ease her head down upon her pillow without causing a ripple of disturbance.

She did not sleep. She forced herself to stay awake. For hours she held herself as still as an ice statue. Yet when the first rays of the morning sun glowed upon the panes of the overhead skylight, she drifted off.

She dreamed of that blank-faced child, Vaundra. Vaundra's face pressed up against the inside glass of one of the aquariums in Sterling's lab, peering out with outraged eyes. Hair swirled slowly about her head in dark water.

A dead, floating thing.

Later that morning, Diana awoke, before Catherine. She showered and dressed quietly before Catherine even had a chance to look up from her bed and say hello. It seemed sort of mean, Diana thought to herself, to be sneaking around like this. But Catherine had practically asked for this cold treatment.

Downstairs, Diana was taking a few grapes from the bowl on the kitchen table when she saw, through the kitchen window, Harriet getting into her car.

Diana ran through the hallway to the cloakroom, threw open the door, and rifled for her coat. In seconds she was flying out the front door, waving her arms at Harriet, who was about to turn down the front drive. The red brake-lights went on and the car came to an abrupt halt. Diana ran to it, her coat half on, sliding her arm through the other sleeve.

Harriet rolled down her window.

"Are you going into town?" Diana asked.

"Yes, to Leonora."

"Oh, great," Diana said, opening the back door and piling in.

"Excuse me, miss, but does Dr. Sterling know you're coming with me?"

"He suggested it!" Diana lied. "Wants me to look up some materials at the library. How boring. But doctor's orders."

"Mmm," Harriet said, suspiciously. "I'm not staying there all morning. We'll be back by noon."

"Perfect," Diana said.

A great stroke of luck.

As the car pulled out the long drive, Diana took a wary glance back at the clinic. The windows shone black against the gray morning sky.

The public library was a small building, a large red-brick house on Main Street willed to the town by an illustrious widow many years ago.

Inside, Diana smelled the closed-up musty scent of a public building in winter.

In the basement was a room where bound newspapers were kept, some dating back to the mid–nineteenth century. A morgue for dead stories. You needed to fill out a little card, and a helper (in this case an asthmatic gray-haired man) brought you the dated bound volumes you wanted to see. Wheeled them in on a squeaky cart.

This room was windowless, lighted by a single naked bulb hanging from the ceiling on a green wire. Diana sat down at a table with a worn waxy-yellow Formica top. The chair was wood and the varnish was peeling in amber flakes. It had a smell that reminded Diana of school rooms, of pencil shavings and eraser dust, and sweat.

A look through an index file under Vaundra Austin's name yielded several days' worth of entries. She paged through the first volume. The disappearance had chilled the county through to its core. Police and local politicians expressed shock and anger, and finally exasperation.

Diana gasped when she saw the school photo of Vaundra.

It was the little girl from her dreams. Long hair the newspaper described as "reddish brown," face composed in a modest smile. A face of innocence. It was shocking to see the features of this small, pretty, childish face—features that had been blurred in Diana's dreams.

And now, just as she had in her nightmares, Diana thought she could hear the distant tiny crystal toll of a small bell. And then, more real, the feeling of terrible hot breath on her neck. A hand that reached out behind her and touched her shoulder.

"Oh!" Diana cried, and turned around quickly. A wave of gooseflesh whirled upon her skin, crawling upward, to her scalp. Her hair felt as if it were rising like the feathery crown of a distressed bird.

But it was only the asthmatic old assistant. He grinned sheepishly. Breath like tobacco and peppermint. Skin colored copper (some disorder of the liver, Diana speculated vaguely). Glasses that reflected back to her a frightened face—her own.

"You scared me," Diana said. Then angrily, "Why'd you sneak up on me like that?"

"I saw you looking at the girl's face and I wondered, is all," he said. "Wondered why you were looking at Vaundra."

Diana felt afraid. She knew about creepy old guys who kidnapped little girls. They existed in small towns, didn't they? Pedophiles. But then, Vaundra had never been found. There was no evidence to suggest she'd been abducted by a perverted sex killer.

And maybe the old coot standing in front of her wasn't a sex killer either, all appearances to one side.

"You remember the Vaundra Austin case?" Diana asked firmly. "Can you tell me about her?"

"She was so pretty," the old man whispered.

Diana felt her guts lurch a bit.

"Real, *real* pretty . . ." he said again.

Here was a certified freak, she thought.

"I think about Vaundra a lot," the old man said. "I guess I think about her nearly every day."

Diana almost didn't dare ask what she wanted to ask next. "Did you . . . do you know what happened to her?"

He shook his head. "No one does. 'Cept maybe God.

You see," he said quietly, "Vaundra is my little grand-daughter."

Diana was speechless. Here she'd been thinking . . .

"I'm very sorry," Diana said at last.

"Vaundra is with—well, I *hope*, anyway—that she's with God. That's where her mommy is."

"Her mother is dead?" Diana asked.

"She got real sick, you see. Drank herself crazy from the fear," the old man said. "My only daughter. Vaundra was all she had. No man around, don't you see. I don't mind telling you, seeing as how everybody else knows. And it's obvious you're interested, looking it up in the old papers. Are you an FBI agent or something? Or a reporter? Are you gonna solve this case?" he asked hopefully.

"I'm . . . new to the area," Diana said. "And I'm doing some research . . . for a paper. I don't mean to pry."

He nodded. "You might as well know my daughter turned to the bottle when she lost Vaundra. Being drunk was about all she could stand, I guess."

"She died of alcoholism?" Diana asked, voice soft.

"In a way, yes. What happened was I guess what happens to drunk drivers who don't kill somebody else first. She crashed into a big tree and killed herself, kinda by accident on purpose, I reckon. Anyway, when I saw you looking at the picture of Vaundra, well, I had to come over. But I come quiet, because, well, it *makes you quiet*, thinking 'bout Vaundra."

Diana lowered her eyes. She couldn't look at the poor man. But she had to look at the school portrait of Vaundra, run on the front page of the *Express Bugle*. She turned a few pages. More photos. Vaundra and her birthday cake. Vaundra sitting on the floor in front of a skinny Christmas tree, holding up a new doll, wrapping paper strewn upon the floor beside her.

What had happened to her?

What happened to Catherine?

"I'll leave you alone now," the old man said. "Name's Milt if you need me." He smiled shyly.

Diana nodded her head. "Thank you, Milt," she said. As he was turning to go she tried to say something, but found her throat too dry to speak. She cleared her throat. He turned around at the dim end of the hallway. He looked at her, sadly.

"You don't have to say anything," Milt said.

Diana said, "I only wanted to say again that I'm truly sorry."

He whispered, "Thank you." He walked away into the shadows, his worn old black shoes tapping softly on the concrete floor.

Diana read about the frantic search for Vaundra. Even the attorney general of the state was involved. Politicians jumped in everywhere, promising swift justice, and severe punishment for the perpetrator. Rewards were offered.

The widowed State Representative Theda Price offered $25,000 for the capture and conviction of Vaundra's abductor or abductors, even though her daughter could not provide a description of any kind. It was said that Catherine Price could not speak at all.

Another article revealed that Catherine Price had not returned to school, that she was still suffering from amnesia and terrible nightmares many months later. Theda thanked, in print, all those who had sent cards and flowers. But now she begged for privacy.

Diana turned the pages and found an article about the groundbreaking of the Albion Clinic, being built by Representative Price to "help those like my dear daughter recover from the traumas brought on by sleep disorders," Theda was quoted as having said.

Still no sign of Vaundra. And the press complied with Theda's request for privacy. Not another word was printed about Catherine. If people suspected the worst of Catherine (and as many people defended her as thought ill of her), they only whispered it, Diana knew, from her conversation with David. Because there was no evidence. No body. And no memories of what had happened in the mind of the sole survivor.

The last article Diana found on the subject was headlined ONE-YEAR ANNIVERSARY OF VAUNDRA'S DISAPPEARANCE. Below that: NO LEADS IN CASE THAT FRUSTRATES LOCAL DA, FAMILIES.

Diana looked at her watch. In a half hour she would have to meet Harriet and catch a ride back to the clinic. But she wanted to read about something else. Something called the Death Wish Traditions. That weird phrase played through her mind the whole time she read about Vaundra. She could ask Milt for more volumes.

She looked again at the newspaper portrait of little Vaundra.

She couldn't really sense anything beyond the photograph. Couldn't feel any waves, or see deeper into Vaundra's mystery. Of course, photographs and painted portraits are not human, and only provide human likenesses. And while some clairvoyant people were said to be able to receive messages from inanimate objects—such as old keys and even houses—the picture of Vaundra yielded nothing. Nothing but haunting questions.

Diana skipped back through the photos of Vaundra printed under the heading *Remembering Our Little Vaundra.* She felt her throat closing as she looked again at Vaundra holding up that doll in the Christmas photo. The doll had a fat plastic face, long dark hair, the kind of eyelids that opened and closed, sharp brush-like eyelashes on them. And a strange little bell around its neck.

Diana's pulse quickened. The bell was blurry. She had to blink her eyes. It was weird, but Diana would have almost sworn that the bell around the doll's neck was identical to the strange little charm Serilda had given Catherine in the woods that day they'd helped free her from the thorns.

Milt wheeled in another stack of bound old *Express Bugle*s. She'd asked him for items under the heading "Ice Rock." Even though the townspeople rarely referred to the place called Ice Rock (Sometimes called Lovers' Leap in the spring and summer months, when it was usually fenced off with barbed wire—wire that was always torn down in the fall), the newspapers had reported various disasters associated with the first snowfall ritual.

1877. Two Men Killed in Reckless Tragedy.
1918. Six Dead in Plunge off Local Cliff.

1925. Woman Falls to Her Death.

The stories were accompanied by photos of the astonished onlookers. The most recent accident at Ice Rock
occurred in 1987.

Diana flipped back to the 1925 photograph.

At first Diana didn't quite believe what she saw. She had
to blink. There, in the frozen crowd, was an oddly familiar
old woman.

The old woman she and Catherine had freed from thorny
vines in the woods that day.

Serilda.

But how, Diana thought, was it possible? Surely the old
woman in the photo would be dead by now. Unless it was
some relative of Serilda's; a relative bearing an uncanny
resemblance.

"Milt," she called out now. He came into the room
again.

"Do you recognize this old woman?"

He squinted at the photo. "Why should I recognize
her?"

"Do you know of an old woman who lives in the countryside out beyond Old River Road?" Diana asked. "And
who looks exactly like this woman in the old photograph?"

He slowly shook his head. The frail plump woman
seemed to glare out of the grainy photo at him. The woman's wiry hair was the same as Serilda's, Diana remembered.

"Don't know her. Anyway, she'd be dead by now. Long
dead. Why she looks as old as Methuselah already in . . ."
he scanned the date. "Why, in 1925!"

It was a relief to get out of the old library basement. Upstairs, Diana checked her watch. Almost time to meet Harriet. If she'd come here seeking answers, she'd only
succeeded in raising more questions. She walked past the
card catalogue, and past a table where new computers sat
in boxes, waiting to be installed.

The checkout table was near the front door. Diana saw
a woman standing at the counter with two small children,
a boy and a girl. The little girl, in her purple winter coat

with the hood pulled up, had seven or eight small books in her tiny arms. The books were slipping.

The mother was Nessie Jasper; Diana recognized her now. The familiar short-cropped dark hair, sturdy body, intense dark eyes. Diana had never seen her up close before. Nessie had an intelligent, friendly face. A face Diana instantly liked, despite herself. Out of loyalty to Catherine, Diana felt she had to dislike Nessie a little. Who did this upstart think she was, challenging a woman like Theda Price, who had obviously done so much for Blackburn County?

The little girl cried out when one of the books fell from her arms to the floor with a slap. Then all the books started to slide from the child's arms.

"Mom!" she cried. The books spilled noisily to the floor.

Diana knelt down and picked up one of the books that had fallen at her feet. A colorful volume about dinosaurs.

She stood up and Nessie reached out to her, smiling, and took the book.

"Thanks," Nessie said with a laugh, piling the books on the countertop now. The little boy held on tight to his single book and looked at Diana, unsmiling. He wore thick glasses with one of those bands that holds them to the head. He had a white patch over his left eye.

"Say thank you to the nice young lady, Julia," Nessie said.

"Thank you," Julia said in a small flat voice.

Diana smiled. "Sure," she said. "No problem." Turning to leave now, she saw Nessie hoisting up the little boy so that he could put his storybook on the checkout counter. He turned his smiling face to his mother and she gave him a kiss on the lips. Then she set him back down next to Julia, who gently took his hand.

Diana felt an overwhelming need, all of a sudden, to call her mother on the phone. She turned and all but ran through the door. She wanted her mother's help. She wanted to go home.

Outside, standing on the concrete library steps, Diana saw Harriet's car parked beside a tree across the street.

Realizing she was late now, Diana ran down the library stairs and across the street to the car.

Through Harriet's car window, the Blackburn County landscape looked spooky, although it was only early afternoon. Still, the darkness of the overcast day added to the barrenness of the dying little town and its shabby outskirts. The old teetering power line poles along the highway reminded Diana of crucifixions, miles and miles of them, a surreal image out of a nightmare. The black wires sagged between the poles, measuring the distances between dead cornfields and seedy roadside taverns. Diana was silent all the way back to the clinic.

As soon as she was inside she went to the phone in the white marble foyer and punched in the personal code she'd been given by Sterling to make outside calls. She shrugged off her dark coat. A recorded voice said in her ear, "Sorry, this access code is no longer valid."

That was odd. Diana frowned and tried the number again. Even as she pushed the buttons, she had a sinking feeling.

The same voice repeated, denying access.

Trembling, Diana put the receiver down. She wanted to ask her parents to come and take her home. She was frightened.

"Diana," came another voice.

Catherine's.

Catherine stood behind her, on the stairs. Blond hair pulled back and tied in a pony tail. A dark green sweater and black jeans making her look like a Gap model coming down a runway.

Diana slowly turned to face Catherine. And she thought of bolting out the door, running away right this instant. Maybe she could hitchhike. It might take a long time to walk to Leonora. But once there, where would she go? To a pay telephone. Or a bus station. But she didn't have any money. Panicky thoughts raced through her mind. Maybe she was overreacting, she thought. Stay cool, she reminded herself. But it wasn't going to be easy. She looked out through one of the high windows.

It would be cold out tonight, so cold you would almost

be able to see it in the obsidian blackness. The clouds had cleared off. Darkness was only a few hours away. Icy wind moved through the creaking trees.

"I've been looking all over for you," Catherine said in a mock teasing tone.

Diana said sternly, "You knew I was away from the clinic. You knew without being told."

Catherine smiled. "Diana, don't get upset. As soon as you do, you lose all control of yourself. Your thoughts come spilling through like gum balls out of a shattered penny machine." She grinned.

Diana tried to brace herself. Tried to put up that wall of cold ice, Catherine's trick. But she couldn't quite manage it. How could she take her fear and turn it into something else, something like courage?

Catherine held out her hand. "Come on, I want to talk to you."

Diana did not accept her hand.

"Oh, *come on*," Catherine said, stamping her foot. "I'm not gonna bite you."

"Catherine, please . . . I think I want to be alone right now. I asked you to back off a little."

Catherine giggled. She closed her eyes and held her hand over her mouth. She snorted and sat down on the stairs.

"What," Diana said, annoyed.

Catherine shook her head, really laughing now. She looked up, blue eyes watering with tears of mirth. "When I tell you, you're gonna kill me," Catherine said.

Diana looked at her, gravely.

"You'll want to kill me at first, but then you'll thank me," Catherine said.

"Catherine, what in the hell are you talking about?"

"Well," she answered, catching her breath. "I've been trying to tell you. But when you said, 'Back off a little,' I had to laugh, forgive me. It's so funny because I just sent a letter to your parents today, saying exactly the same thing. That was before Sterling changed the access code on the phone."

Diana shook her head in disbelief. "Wait a minute, slow

down. Why would my parents want a letter from you, they don't even know you.''

"Okay, that's the funny part, Diana. Are you ready? The letter is not from *me*, it's from *you*! I signed your name to it.''

Catherine widened her eyes. Again that smile crept over her teeth. Her blue eyes sparkled with mischief.

"I told them they wouldn't be hearing from you for a while,'' Catherine said. "And not to worry—it's all a part of growing up, becoming independent, blah, blah . . . nice touch, huh?''

Diana felt like she might get sick. "You *what*? How in the—''

"I copied your signature. You know I'm a good artist! And you signed your name all over your diaries, so I had lots of practice copying it. I mailed out the letter today. The outgoing mailbox has a key, and well, I happen to know where it's hidden.''

"Catherine,'' Diana whispered. She felt faint. "You're pulling my leg, right?''

Catherine grinned and shook her pretty head.

"I saved the letter on the computer so you could see it. It's not like I wasn't going to tell you.''

Diana wanted to see the letter. She ran past Catherine, and up the stairs to the bedroom. Catherine followed behind her.

"You'll thank me some day,'' Catherine said, coming into the room.

Diana went straight to the computer, atop the desk cluttered with Catherine's papers and a few of her books. The letter was still "up'' on screen. Diana read it quickly, seeing that it said everything Catherine had said it did. Maturely, calmly, forthrightly asking her parents not to contact her until further notice—real progress was being made, and she "hoped they would some day forgive her for all the trouble'' she'd caused them. The letter ended with the words, "I just need a little time to grow up.''

Tears blurred in Diana's eyes.

"You can't do this,'' Diana said. "This is crazy. I'll tell

Sterling. I could call the police over this ... this ... *fraud*!''

''Diana,'' Catherine said sternly, ''I *am* doing you a favor. You know you hate your parents, it's all over your diary.''

Diana's mind reeled. She took a deep breath, feeling utterly speechless.

Yes, she hated her parents.

Yes, she loved them.

It wasn't their fault she was the way she was. Yet every good intention, every move they made on her behalf—especially sending her here!—was the *wrong* move.

But that wasn't the point, Diana furiously told herself. The point was this was none of Catherine's business.

''You had no right to do this!'' Diana screamed. ''You have no right to interfere with anything in my life. What do you think Sterling will do when I tell him?''

Catherine sat down on the bed. Damn her, she was cool; she had this all figured out. Almost disbelieving, Diana watched Catherine smile again, and look askance.

''You're not going to tell him,'' Catherine said flatly.

After a long moment Diana said, ''The hell I'm not going to tell—''

''I've got the goods on you, Diana. The twenty dollars you stole from Harriet, for example. Your little thing with David, which will get him fired immediately.''

Diana felt her knees weakening.

Catherine wasn't smiling now. ''Tell Sterling one word of this and I'll send another note to your parents,'' Catherine said. ''Oh, I don't want to, but I will, for your own good. And this note will be all about that boy you had over at your house, the fire you almost started, the times you lied through your teeth to those dear parents of yours. Oh, and another thing! I took a few pages out of your diary, and I'll enclose them so your mother can see in your own words what you think of her.''

Diana couldn't believe what she was hearing. ''How could you? How ...''

''Imagine how your poor frail mother would like to read those names you called her. I read them, Diana. Awful things. They might send your mommy dearest to the nearest bottle of sleeping pills. How sharper than the serpent's tooth—''

"But that was not meant to be read by anyone!" Diana whispered. She covered her eyes with her hand. Her head throbbed. "And those secrets I told you . . ."

"Will remain secrets—*if* you have the sense to trust me."

"Trust a blackmailer? Because that's what this is. It's blackmail."

"I'm not asking for money. Can't you see that?"

"You sent my parents a lie—''

"For your own good."

"And what about the telephone access code? Why can't I call out of here?"

Catherine lay back on her bed and stared at the ceiling. "I had a talk with Sterling. About the *real* Diana. So let's just say that he agreed to the new arrangement."

"Let's just say you're a psychopath." Diana turned toward the wall and leaned against it. She buried her face against her arms, anxiety and guilt gnawing at her belly. What had Catherine really told Sterling? It could have been any number of things, from minor infractions, to outright theft. Of course he'd believe her. Her mother was his boss!

No sooner had Diana thought of this than Catherine flew from her bed and whirled Diana around. She screamed in her face, "You're the one who crossed me, Diana! What did you expect?"

Diana looked at her, horrified. "Crossed you? I only want to get away from you. And I will. I'm leaving! I don't care if I have to walk."

"You'd freeze to death out there. And as of tonight, you're forbidden to leave the grounds. No more secret trips into town. Sterling's orders."

Diana, enraged now, turned and raised her fist. Oh, how she wanted to smash it into that spoiled rotten pretty face. But Catherine caught Diana's hand. She squeezed Diana's wrist painfully. Then grinned as if she'd just gotten exactly what she wanted.

"Now, now," Catherine whispered. "Don't kill the messenger. As I said, you will thank me some day." The grin faded. "Why, Diana, can't you see that I'm a better friend to you than you are to yourself?"

Tears of anger and frustration came into Diana's eyes now. Diana pulled her hand free. Her wrist ached. She stumbled to the door and turned the knob. The door was somehow locked now—from the outside?

Diana cried out and pounded on the door.

"Stop that," Catherine said. "Shut up, for God's sake, no one can hear you. You could make things so much easier for both of us if you just get with the program. And so much worse for yourself if you don't."

Diana slowly turned around. She looked at Catherine, who was moving a stray strand of limp blond hair from her face. Tucking it behind her ear. She was breathing hard and deep, and her breast moved, heaving up and down.

"When you go to bed tonight, Diana, I hope you sleep well. And try to remember that you made things tougher on yourself than they needed to be. You. It's *your* fault. Not mine."

"I trusted you," Diana said, softly. She was too angry now to try and bargain logically with this insane girl. Tears streamed down her face.

"Past tense—*trusted.* Maybe when you wake up in the morning you'll trust me again. Maybe then you'll see that I'm the only one who can really help you. I think you'd better try to understand that. Because you're not leaving this place any time soon."

Diana collapsed onto her bed and cried silently and mournfully into her pillow. Catherine, humming eerily and jingling some keys, turned off the bedroom light, unlocked and opened the bedroom door, and stepped out of the room. The door closed. There came the sound of a lock turning.

Diana jumped up from her bed and ran in darkness to the door. Tried the knob, and found that the door was indeed locked again. Diana pounded with her fist.

"Catherine!" she cried. "Someone! Can anyone hear me?"

She listened. No one came to answer her cries. She leaned her head against the door and sobbed. Not only could she not hear a thing outside this bedroom, she couldn't sense another being in this house. Distant, muddy, and garbled channels flashed dimly in her mind, like a storm at the edge of a city.

Diana felt horrible. She felt guilty and stupid, desperately confused and betrayed. Not only by Catherine, but by herself, by her own words and the feelings, as confused as they were, written in her diary.

And she felt afraid. From across a dark chasm she could now feel the cold anger that emanated from Catherine's mind, wherever she was. A feeling like sharp splinters of ice in her chest and stomach.

It occurred to Diana that in Catherine's view, it was Catherine who had been betrayed, snubbed by a friend who was growing ever distant.

Catherine really did feel that *she* was the one being tortured. She was making this painfully clear.

Sobbing, sniffling, Diana went to the window, and looked out to the cold twilight-blue grounds of the clinic. She thought longingly of David, and yet it frustrated her so much to think of him. Why couldn't David understand? Why couldn't he help her?

Because she was just another patient here, that's why. And he didn't love her. Not in the way that she loved him. He saw her the same way he saw Catherine, as a kind of *freak.*

Oh, God, she thought, it was awful to see yourself the way other people must see you when you're sick, when you're desperately trying to be like *them*, and the more you try, the more you struggle, the sicker you get, the uglier . . . until everyone can see it on you, everyone can see you trying to hide what cannot be hidden anymore.

There wasn't anyone—not a soul—who could help her.

And then she had the most awful sensation of all. What if Catherine was right? What if Catherine really was isolating her here for her own good?

What if this is all my fault? Diana thought bitterly. Trying to be someone I'm not, trying to be something I could never be.

David would never love a freak like me, she thought. Nobody would.

No one else understood her the way Catherine did. It was true. And maybe Catherine was the only one who could really help her. Diana trembled, laying her head down on the cool pillow.

"Catherine," she said, eyes closed tight. Trying to project. To transport a wave through space. She sniffed, and wiped her eyes. "Catherine, come back here and unlock the door . . . Catherine, *please*!"

Chapter Six

It was always a little eerie to be in Sterling's dark lab in the middle of bright day. The days were getting short enough as it was without adding these extra sunless hours of night blackness. But Diana didn't have much of a choice; she had to be here.

She closed her eyes, listened to the whir of the aquariums.

This—this therapy, or whatever they wanted to call it—was supposed to help her, she reminded herself. Help her get over her nightmares, perhaps even explain them. Help her get out of this place. It was getting more and more difficult for her to believe this.

So play along, she told herself.

Play along, play along.

Lying on her back on the cool leather surface of the couch, she tried to calm herself. She wanted to tell Sterling her fears, and about how scary Catherine had become. But she couldn't. Catherine was what Diana's stepfather would have called a "loose cannon." Capable of the most unpredictable kind of destruction. Would, Diana thought, I be able to convince everyone—parents, doctors—that Catherine was more than a little unhinged?

She could just hear them all saying, "Well, that's no surprise, Diana. Not when you consider the place you're in. You're bound to meet a few odd ducks."

In the meantime Catherine could do a lot of damage if she wanted to. It would be Catherine's word against Diana's. There had to be a better way to handle it.

Sterling leaned over her now. "Diana, I'm afraid we have to talk about something that will not be pleasant for either of us."

Fear again. It came on like a submersion into icy water. Diana swallowed hard. "Okay," she said.

"Did you take twenty dollars from Harriet Evans's purse?"

Catherine *had* ratted on her. But Diana had tried to *undo* what she'd done, too, by putting the money back.

"You already know the answer to that," Diana said. "The money was returned."

He cleared his throat. "The fact remains, you did it, didn't you?"

She smiled, feeling her face flush, and whistled. "Boy," she said bitterly. "You guys have flat out got me up against the wall."

"Diana, stop this behavior at once," he said sternly. "Why can't you own up to what you did? Don't you see that your primary trouble in life is your duplicity? You are truly your own worst enemy at times." He sighed, exasperated.

Yeah, she knew what he meant. Maybe she wouldn't torture herself with nightmares, or fight with her parents, or steal, or lie, or hide things—like secrets about boys—if she really had . . . well, if she had a mind of her own.

A mind of her own. She could have almost—almost—laughed, thinking this. Catherine, Sterling, her parents and teachers and shrinks had all laid claim to a piece of that mind, in different ways.

Yet Diana really didn't blame anybody but herself at this moment.

Sterling was on his little stool, the one with the rollers. Diana noticed they were more squeaky than usual today.

"You are in many ways a typical teenager, not sure which *you* you are today," Sterling said. "But then again you wouldn't be here in our care if there wasn't quite a bit more to it than that."

She felt her heart sinking. Yes, there was so much more to it! She was going crazy! Tears stood in her eyes now.

If only he knew all she was going through, and had gone through, all her life just because she could . . . perceive things and *feel* things in ways most other people could not.

She wanted to tell him to fuck off. She hated him just now. He waited a long time before he spoke again. She listened to his labored breathing, coming in and out of his nose.

"Very well," he said at last. "Your privilege of coming and going from this place as you please is revoked for a month."

A month! Would she be here a month from now?

I'll run away, she thought.

Run away where? Into the cold, where I'll freeze to death?

Tears rolled down her cheeks. It was all a bit too much. Sterling put his hand on her shoulder.

"There," he whispered softly. "Please try and understand. We cannot simply look the other way."

After a while she stopped crying. Her eyes were red and her nose ran. He handed her a box of Kleenex.

"Okay," she said, and coughed. "Okay . . . I stole the money . . . and . . ."

"Yes, Diana."

"And I want to get better. I want your help. But I'm begging you for one little thing. Please. Just one thing."

She reached out her trembling hand to Sterling. He grasped it.

"I want to get out of that room. I'll sleep anywhere else in the clinic. But I have to get away from Catherine. It's really gone sour between us."

She saw the look on his face.

"Did Catherine make this trouble for you?" he said tenderly. "Or is Catherine your friend who is trying to help you?"

Diana felt so deflated, how could she possibly address these questions? Once again, in this mad-house of a room, she felt as though she couldn't tell the floor from the ceiling. She felt, trembling now, almost as awful as she had the night she'd come here.

What about all her so-called progress? It seemed to be sinking like the Titanic.

"Separate rooms are really out of the question, Diana," he said. "Catherine's progress depends on you, and yours upon her. Catherine needs her best friend now more than ever. Can't you see that you need her, as well?"

"Why do you think I need her?"

"Diana, we are building trust here. Close peer relationships are critical to my methods."

"Aren't there any other peers you could place us with?"

"Because of a momentary fissure in your friendship?" Sterling rolled back on his stool slightly. The wheels squeaked under his weight. "Diana, I can't allow you to do this to either one of you. You must change your thinking on this. Just as we are working to help you get a handle on your dreams, you must learn to control your own emotions. Ask yourself, what kind of person would you be if you abandoned Catherine now?"

Diana felt confused, and felt the dark sensation of guilt gnawing at her stomach.

Sterling said, "Catherine is as a shattered mirror that holds your reflection in a thousand pieces. You've got to help put those pieces back together, for both of you."

Diana nodded. She had no idea whether Sterling's insistence on this friendship-as-therapy was orthodox. But then, her parents had sent her here precisely *because* of Sterling's unorthodox approach, a controversial one, indeed; but also one that was believed by some to be successful in radical cases.

Diana was a radical case.

And what was more, at the Albion Clinic everything would be handled very hush-hush.

Diana sighed heavily. Nothing was normal here. Nothing was what it was expected to be. Everything was inverted, distorted, as crazy as one of her nightmares.

Yet one truth could not be denied. She'd stolen the twenty dollars. The consequences of that were like the closing of a prison cell door.

She knew which side of that door she now faced.

* * *

It was already mid-afternoon by the time Senator Hobbs and his ubiquitous staff person, a tall lanky man with an elfin face, arrived at Theda's house. The others—Representatives Brown and Norse, and Harriet Evans—were already seated around the dining room table, drinking coffee.

"Theda," Senator Hobbs said, kissing her cheek in the doorway of her home. "I can only stay a few minutes."

"Of course," Theda said. She knew that none of them would stay long. They had a lot of politicking to do around the state today. There were seats in the Senate to be gained—or lost—in the spring elections.

In Theda's case, her assembly seat was very close to being lost in her upcoming recall election, if she wasn't careful. The muck had gathered itself so high around Theda lately, none of the other politicians particularly wanted it known they were paying a social call today at her home in Blackburn County.

Hobbs brought the cold in with him, upon his coat and hat. Outside, the silvery trees and the gray light signalled winter, and the high bare branches seemed to beckon snow that wouldn't, for some strange reason, fall from the low stone sky.

Theda showed him in to the dining room, where he shook hands with the others while Harriet poured coffee for him, adding a generous splash of whisky.

Old friends, Theda thought, cynically. Not that they would stand by you in public. No, that was far too expensive. What mattered to them was her vulnerable seat in the state assembly. She couldn't, mustn't, lose it. That was the primary objective today, making certain that she didn't.

Theda watched Hobbs seat himself in the frail dining room chair. The chair creaked under his weight. The tiny chair legs seemed to tremble beneath him. He took a draft of hot coffee and whisky. He put on his horn-rimmed glasses and touched his fingers to his black hair, hair too black for a man in his late sixties. Hobbs's aide dug through a briefcase, then passed around a photocopied page.

"I won't bullshit you, Theda," Hobbs said. "You're in trouble, and everybody knows it."

Theda, seated now, leaned forward to pick up one of the

pages being passed around. Representative Norse, whose lantern jaw hung slack over his grizzled scarlet neck, grinned, reading the page. His thick mass of silver hair looked unusually natural today. That must have cost plenty.

Representative Brown, who was as deeply bland-mannered as he was tall and slim, squinted at the document in his hands. It gave him no pleasure to be here today.

"I know I'm in for a tough battle," Theda said.

"The ethics panel is about to wring *my* neck, Theda," Hobbs said. "It's not only here in Blackburn County that you're in trouble. If this thing goes down, it might not just be you and those six lobbyists who are going off to the gray-bar hotel."

"Senator, you exaggerate," Theda said softly.

"You've got to beat this recall thing, one way or another." He looked down at his pudgy, hairy hands. "Theda," he said, "we go back many years, and we'd hate to see you thrown out of office, much less sitting in the can. But Blackburn County is considered a swing district all of a sudden."

"But I've had it locked up for years."

"That's just it, Theda. When it sours for a pro like you, the shock waves are felt in Madison. We *need* to hold onto this seat." He might have added, *and to you, Theda.* But he didn't. She frowned.

"But my opponent is an absolute . . . malcontent," Theda said. "Not credible. You know that as well as I do."

Brown cleared his throat. Norse and Brown refused to look at Theda. Hobbs's voice was phlegmy. "She's trouble, Theda," he said, and swallowed. "Our people tell us the tide has turned up here—turned against *you.* And this Nessie Jasper has won a lot of sympathy. A lot of folks feel she was done wrong, publicly humiliated for no good reason. They might remember her as that kid they sent off to the Olympics a long time ago. Don't you be surprised if in the privacy of the ballot booth, they vote to avenge her while at the same time, well, decide to screw old Theda Price." He smiled.

Theda remained frozen in her chair. The light from the French windows made the varnished pine table gleam.

"That's why we had this special *shit sheet* drafted in Madison," Hobbs said now.

A "shit sheet," Theda knew too well, was a cheaply produced flyer, either mailed or hand-delivered, usually sporting an unflattering or mocking photo or drawing of one's political opponent. But most important, the shit sheet listed in the most inflammatory ways possible every political fault and liability one's opponent had or might have had, said, or done. Theda had used them before, whenever it was necessary.

Hobbs had shit-sheeted Nessie Jasper, focussing primarily on her firing as a sex educator, because she talked about "immoral and unhealthy perversions." Her drinking was also recounted, along with a few of her more inflammatory quotes.

The photo was of her leaving the Great Northern Pub. Her face was blurry in the shot. Somehow, the eyes in the photo looked as though they were crossed, giving the impression of inebriation.

Theda found herself laughing, reading the sheet. She caught herself and looked up into the glare of Senator Hobbs.

"It's not going to be easy, Theda," he said. He pulled a yellow envelope from his pocket. The envelope was fat and worn, dog-eared.

He tipped the envelope upside down and a fat roll of bills fell out. The bills were bound with a dirty red rubber band.

"If you can buy your way out of it, do it," Hobbs said.

Brown smiled. "Well, that goes without saying."

Theda trembled inwardly. Here were the most corrupt officials in the state, sitting at her table. Outwardly, they projected respectability, virtue, and morality. But in Madison people whispered about them. And here they were, trying to help her.

"I don't think this Nessie Jasper would be too difficult to destroy if you weren't up to your eyeballs in misconduct, Theda," Representative Norse said, picking up a pear from the blue ceramic bowl that was the centerpiece of the table. He bit into it. With a mouth full of pear and juice upon his lips, heading toward his big chin, he said, "You got sloppy, sis. That's tough turds for you, but it's also tough for us. You aren't gonna bring us down with you. 'Cause blow this one and there won't be no next time."

Theda took in a deep, pained breath.

Hobbs held up his hand. "What Norse means is, we're counting on you to pull through this one, Theda. But if you don't, we are not gonna cry at your funeral. Hell," he said with a deep laugh, "we might not even attend."

Her funeral. She didn't care for metaphors like that. They meant her political funeral, she reminded herself. But of course she knew that if the likes of Nessie Jasper could bring her down, she might as well be dead. She would not, she simply couldn't, go to jail. What would become of Catherine?

Catherine. Her *real* salvation.

She thought of Sterling, and she also thought about the money that was at stake.

These con men, sitting here at her table, drinking coffee, plotting strategy—they knew nothing about the business deal she and Sterling had cooked up with a Japanese consortium. It was a multi-million-dollar agri-science deal, and Theda and Sterling stood to make a fortune. If she were suddenly to lose her assembly seat, the deal would die. If the deal failed, she and Sterling would lose their shirts, she knew.

Simply put, if she didn't remain in office, the deal—half-legitimate, half-crooked—would fail. Theda would lose everything.

She'd even lose the dream clinic. That was unthinkable. The tiniest smile played on her lips. If Hobbs only knew. . . . Theda was just a few steps away from not only taking care of Nessie, once and for all, but would in time have him wrapped around her little finger, too! He'd bark like a trained seal for a piece of the Japanese action.

This knowledge braced her. She swept the dollars into a paper bag. She looked at Hobbs, and her eyes twinkled. He didn't return her smile. He didn't flinch.

She smiled politely, thinking, *bastard.*

✳   ✳   ✳

In the clinic's workout room Diana pushed the bar that moved the steel weight upward. She was flat on her back, in gray shorts and a white T-shirt, sweating, her arms trembling.

The bench press was a great way to work out your aggression, she acknowledged, gritting her teeth.

She pushed again, then let the weight come down with a crash.

"You wanna be a little more careful, please?" David called to her, from another room.

She'd thought she was alone. Panting, she sat up and wiped the sweat from her eyes with a small white towel. A door was cracked open at one corner of the exercise room. She had assumed it led to a closet. Light gleamed from the doorway. Diana had awakened this morning with a promise to herself to remain calm, to not let anything affect her mood. She wanted to be cool, rock solid. But here was David, melting her again.

She walked over past the high window and looked inside this adjacent room. There he was, clad in black sweats and a black T-shirt. The room was very small. One wall was entirely covered with a mirror—or on closer inspection, mirrored tiles. In front of the mirror was mounted a kind of horizontal wood railing. He had a leg up and a foot upon the rail, and had bowed his head down, almost touching his knee. Above, pipes had been painted white against a white ceiling.

"What are you doing?"

He looked up at her. He was sweating, too.

"Barre exercises," he said. He said it sort of defiantly. In the corner was a boom box, silent.

She leaned against the wall. Of all the wealthy girls she'd known going to private schools in suburban Chicago, she was perhaps the only one who had had no interest whatsoever in ballet lessons.

"It's for my knee," he said. "An old sports injury. This helps."

"You don't have to explain it," Diana said. He looked kind of cute in his dancer's gear. His feet were bare. She smiled at him.

With that he spun around and leapt into the air. He landed and reached out an arm, pointing a finger, and extending his leg.

"Arabesque," he explained. Then he smiled and leaned against the concrete wall, hands behind his back.

"You really know how to jump," Diana said, impressed. He grinned at her.

He picked up the single chair in the room and spun it on his hand and smacked it down on the floor in front of her.

"Have a seat," he said.

She wiped her forehead and sat down. She realized she must have looked like a slob. ·

"So what brings you down here today?" he asked. "Shouldn't you and Catherine be in town, causing trouble?"

"I'm not allowed to leave the building," Diana said, glumly. She wanted to say more. But she didn't want to get David into trouble. And he'd probably not believe her anyway.

David pressed the button on the boom box. Music swelled.

"Prokofiev," David said. He held out his hand to her. She took his hand. It was warm. He pulled her up out of the chair. She laughed as he spun her around. Together they did a sort of dance, a kind of mock ballet. He put his hands around her waist. Laughing, she held her head up high, like a ballerina, and she danced around him as he swooped about the room.

Then he held her from behind. Held her arm out in a dancer's pose. Spun her around to face him. They looked into each other's eyes. A moment later they collapsed into one another's arms, laughing.

"Oh, God," Diana said. "I've got nothing to laugh about." She let go of him and stepped back, turning her face from his.

"What's the trouble?"

"Well, for starters, I'm a prisoner here."

"Pampered little debutante is more like it," David scoffed. "Do you think that if your daddy wasn't spending a fortune to keep you here you wouldn't be somewhere a lot worse?''

"Like a state mental hospital?" Diana asked. "I'm not crazy.''

He didn't reply. She turned away from him, and walked to the mirror.

"Okay, you're not crazy,'' he said at last. "But if someone wasn't paying a lot of dough, you'd be home sifting through your nightmares without a fancy doctor to explain it all to you.''

"He explains very little, actually.''

"You're in touchy-feely land, Diana. Me, the rest of the staff, we're just here to cater to your needs while you get in touch with yourself.''

She lowered her head. "Okay, you've made your point.''

He took hold of her hand again. She tried to pull away, but he held her close.

"Anyway, you'll get out of here soon enough,'' he said.

She looked into his eyes. It was crazy, foolish, maybe even hopeless, but she wanted him to kiss her. Willed him to kiss her, if it was possible. She knew he wanted to.

He kissed her mouth. Just once. She closed her eyes, like they did in the movies. His lips felt warm and soft.

It was a feeling like no other. Unmistakable. She looked up into his dark eyes.

"No one will know,'' he said softly. "And no one *can* ever know about this.''

He closed his eyes. His face reddened. He held her tight.

"Catherine will know,'' Diana whispered.

"Not if you don't tell her,'' David said, and kissed her again.

Diana thought, *tell* her? Telling was not necessary. She turned her head, away from his lips.

"What's the matter?'' he whispered.

"I'm tired of secrets,'' Diana answered, eyes closed.

He grinned. "Why? Everybody's got secrets.'' He went to his black backpack and withdrew a white envelope. He handed it to her.

"What's this?'' she asked.

"My secret ticket out.''

She took the letter out of the envelope. It was an application of some sort. In bold letters were the words CYPRESS MODERN DANCE COMPANY, MILWAUKEE, WISCONSIN.

"I'm applying," David said. "They have a little performance company, but what I'm really interested in is their classes. It's a school, you see."

Diana smiled. "That's wonderful, David! When do you leave?"

"Well, I haven't been accepted yet," he said. "But I could leave soon if I get some financial aid. Move to Milwaukee and maybe find a part-time job, too, waiting tables, or maybe working in a gym as a trainer. That way I could still send some money home to my mom." He rolled his eyes. "I haven't told her about it yet. She'll hate it, think it's absolutely crazy and wildly impractical." He grinned. "But I've already made up my mind."

"Take me with you," she said, smiling. "Let's leave tonight. I'm serious."

He seemed not to hear her, so lost was he in his revery. "What I'd like to do is work with dancers. Help them with strength training. And then learn the biz from the inside, you see. Learn to choreograph by working with real professionals."

"That's great," Diana said. She put her hand on the back of his neck and caressed his hair. His enthusiasm was infectious.

"I could work in New York or in Hollywood or Vegas." His eyes glittered. "Or maybe I could start a little company of my own, right here in Wisconsin."

"I'm glad you're finally making a move."

"I have to send them a personal essay, and a videotape of myself. You know, showing a few moves. It's all described in the brochure. I'm going to borrow a video camera. Will you help me? Just aim the camera is all you have to do."

"Of course," Diana said.

He grabbed her again and kissed her. Suddenly she felt very desperate.

"David, listen to me. Have you heard anything I've been trying to tell you? I'm frightened of this place, and of Catherine. They won't let me use the phones, won't let me leave the grounds anymore without permission. I want to run away from here. I want to get out of here as soon as possible. I need a car. Do you understand? Are you going to help me or not?''

David looked at her, smiling, teeth apart.

He took a breath. ''Diana,'' he said, a trace of exasperation in his voice. ''Wow, Diana, you're serious.''

''Of course I'm serious,'' she said, pulling away from his embrace. He held her hands tight in his. Now he frowned. He exhaled through his nostrils, looking gravely at her.

''Diana, you're asking me to break the law, do you know that? My leaving here is one thing, but taking a patient with me—'' He gave a low whistle. ''Hoo boy, you're asking a lot.''

Diana pulled her hands free of his. ''Then you won't take me out of here?''

''Everything takes time, Diana,'' he said, bending to pick up his towel. ''We can't just run away to Milwaukee in the night because you're afraid of Catherine.''

''But I don't have time, don't you understand?'' Diana said, heading for the door.

She crossed through the weight room. He called out for her.

''Diana . . . just be patient,'' he said. ''Can't you just be fake friends with Catherine for a while?''

Play along, play along. She wondered, how long could you play along?

She was out the door. But she heard him calling for her, from down the basement hallway.

''I want to be with you, Diana,'' he called out, ''when you're well.''

She stopped for a moment.

When you're well.

It rang in her ears as she climbed the steps, two at a time.

Catherine touched Randy's bare neck where the brace had been. She traced a finger down his back. He rolled off of her and pulled the condom off with a snap. The bed bounced and the mattress springs squeaked as he extended his arm from beneath the sheets and tossed the condom to the floor.

He leaned over her again and his long dark hair fell across her chest. His kiss landed on her cheek, as she turned her head. She saw the glowing lights of the clock.

"Shit, your mother is going to be home in a half hour," she said.

"That gives us plenty of time," Randy said, kissing her neck and straining his head downward. She pushed his head away.

"Ow!" he yelled. "Be careful." He rubbed his neck.

"Sorry," she said. All of a sudden she felt a bit uncomfortable here in Randy's bunk bed (his little brother, at school this afternoon, had the upper bunk). Even though she'd changed the sheets before they'd climbed in, Catherine felt the grubbiness of the unkempt room closing in on her.

The floor was strewn with clothes and with Randy's little brother's cars and toys. On the walls were posters of rock stars and athletes, a big photo of the Red Hot Chili Peppers and another of Courtney Love.

Randy didn't mind cutting class this afternoon. Especially not for this. It seemed he was back in Catherine's good graces. So they'd come here and smoked pot and the next thing they knew, they were in bed again, naked.

Catherine climbed out of bed and put on her big sweater. She pulled her long blond hair out of the neck opening.

"God, this place is a pig sty," she said.

He grinned at her. "So clean it. That's a woman's job, isn't it?"

She threw the nearest thing, a heavy yellow toy dump truck. It glanced off the wall between the bunks, leaving black tire prints, then bounced off the bed to the floor. Randy scrambled out of the way. The noisy bedsprings squeaked.

"Ouch!" Randy cried. "I told you not to make me move my neck." He clamped a hand over his neck and rubbed.

Catherine finished dressing. "I'm outta here," she said.

And muttered, "Don't know why I came here in the first place."

Randy whistled and said, "Well, I know why." He lifted up the covers and looked down at himself. "Next time bring your friend, Diana."

Catherine turned and looked at him, feeling really angry now. The look must have registered on her face, because Randy was gazing back at her with a quizzical expression, eyebrows arched.

"What's the matter now?" Randy said.

"Not a thing," Catherine replied, picking up her purse. "I'll let myself out, don't bother to get up."

"I've no intention," Randy said, laying his head back on his rumpled white pillow. He was flicking a disposable lighter, the stub of a joint between his lips.

Catherine didn't want to think about Diana just now. It was too painful. Letting herself out into the cold gray afternoon, she shivered.

She took a few deep calming breaths before getting into Harriet's car.

Leonora High School was an old dark brown brick building, four stories high (though its stories were nearly double those of more modern buildings). Upon the pitched slate roof were stacks of chimneys, which on this cold dark afternoon trailed smoke into the late November sky.

A new section had been built onto the back portion of the school, adding an Olympic-size swimming pool and commons area, a music facility and a new boys' lockerroom. The new section had been added in the 1970s, with Theda Price's assistance. The pool had actually been named after her late husband, Newall: The Newall Price Natatorium. The new section of the school was connected to the older part by a concrete corridor and a long flight of stairs.

On the second floor, banks of drab dark lockers lined the wide hallway, where doors to classrooms were open, and the sounds of lecturing teachers mingled together.

In one classroom, the lights were off and the blinds pulled down over the windows, and a black-and-white film about agriculture flickered as students rested heads upon their arms, folded on their desks.

A white porcelain water fountain at the end of the tiled hallway was kept running at all times. The water was as cold as the frigid underground pipes which drew forth the arcing stream, humming and splashing musically in the basin.

An air of ennui permeated the school in the last darkening hours of the school day. Especially in Mr. Gordon's history class.

Jon could usually catch himself before he fell completely asleep in U.S. History. Not today, though. He'd been drifting off ever since Mr. Gordon had begun his lecture on the industrial revolution.

"Jon, wake up!" Mr. Gordon screamed, about an inch from Jon's face.

Jon jolted awake, blinking his eyes. He'd been dreaming. He had an erection. Everyone was looking at him now. He closed his knees together and hoped nobody noticed the bulge. Shreds of his dream dissolved under the ugly fluorescent lights of the classroom. A dream about Diana.

"Jon, how late were you up last night?" Mr. Gordon asked. His greasy hair seemed to be one with his plastic-framed black glasses. He was a man gone to seed at the age of thirty, thickset and bitter.

Jon looked warily around the room at the bored faces of his classmates, some staring, some looking away.

"I had to work last night," Jon said. He wiped his red hair out of his eyes. A flame of red stubbornly fell back over his left eye. He scratched his chin. Red itchy beard growth. He must have looked a mess, he figured.

"We all know you had to work last night," Mr. Gordon sneered.

"At the hospital," Jon said, quietly.

"Of course. You had to work at the hospital and now you're sleeping through your education."

Jon said, "Not my education. Just your boring class."

His classmates laughed.

Mr. Gordon swooped around and faced them, bringing them to silence. He slowly turned back to Jon.

"Boring, eh? If you want to sleep, you'll do it somewhere else, not in my class."

Wordlessly, Jon picked up his history textbook and stood. Thank God the boner was gone, he thought. When he reached the door, Gordon spoke again.

"Wait a minute, Jon," he said, sourly, holding a stack of papers, the tests he'd promised to hand back at the end of class. "You might be interested in this, before you go."

All eyes fell on Jon again. He felt a bit ill.

Gordon mumbled something, finding Jon's test and essay, and crossed the room to hand it to him. A red letter had been marked at the top of the page. It was a 'B'.

Jon took the paper and folded it; stuck it in the back pocket of his jeans.

Gordon stood there looking at him. "Imagine what you might have achieved if you'd actually tried," he said, then added sadly, "Close the door behind you."

Jon closed the door as ordered and listened for a second as Mr. Gordon started droning on again. He unfolded the test and looked at his grade again.

Now he was wide awake.

Konrad Sterling was having one of his spells of depression. Rising anger, and the cold anxiety of hopelessness. Centered in his chest.

He listened to the soothing sounds of the aquarium and sipped his bourbon. His fourth, he acknowledged, in the space of an hour.

A blue fish moved dreamily close to the pane of glass, the silvery membrane of its tail flowing delicately around its gleaming body. Mouth working. Sterling, ever noting, ever compiling data, ticked off in his mind the parts that comprised a fish's mouth: the premaxilla, the mandible, the maxilla, all working in harmony. The fish scooped a mouthful of tiny pink gravel from the bottom of the tank, then spewed it back out again.

Sterling sipped his bourbon, watching with dull fascination. He was in pain. Considering the anatomy of a fish was as benign a distraction as he could manage.

Operculum, pectoral fin.

He attributed his anxiety to the usual sources and circumstances—Theda's increasing political problems, and her rock-steady lack of love for him.

Why did he, an eminent scientist, have to put up with so much bullshit? He poured more bourbon. Nodded to his reflection in the glass, and watched his little fish lazing about in its warm artificial environment.

Soft ray. Spiny ray.

An eminent scientist? he mused. He spilled some bourbon on the console.

"Damn," he whispered, and found a paper towel to mop up the spill.

A fortune in technology in this lab, and he was having his usual self doubts. Of course he was regarded in the scientific community as a kind of charlatan or quack. But didn't Einstein himself once say something about great minds having ever to fight against the mediocrities?

The bourbon burned pleasantly in his throat. He bared his teeth in an angry flash of a grin, thinking, if you bastards knew what I've got right here under this roof you wouldn't mock me!

He thought of the the remote viewing experiments. The dream and sleep research community that had quietly, unceremoniously disowned him.

Child's play, compared to what he now had within his grasp.

The state-of-the-art lab, the elaborate funding process that kept this obscure place running in the black year after year—these were minor trifles next to the mysterious and ancient forces at work in his two prize patients.

Powers he knew they drew up from the very ground upon which this clinic had been built.

He shuddered and smiled.

Crude magic, dark and mysterious. And he was the one to rein it in, if . . . if only . . .

You're a nut, Sterling.

That's what they'd called him, that and worse. Well, wouldn't they be surprised if they could read his files on Catherine and Diana? Of course, no one would see the files.

Not for many years. Not until he had a power so refined no one could stop him.

He winced now, and took another long sip of bourbon, draining his glass. It was all still so uncertain. As though resting in the palm of his hand, but so slippery that the slightest pressure would cause these forces to slip away.

They'd put him in prison if they knew. Maybe someplace worse.

Sterling laughed, a low rumbling in his throat. He filled his glass yet again. What strange thoughts clamored around in his brain.

"Theda," he said, thinking of his lover. "Oh, Theda, what we'll have together." He closed his eyes, relishing the thought. Then you'll love me unconditionally, he thought.

He didn't mind having to prove his love to win hers, ultimately. It made him feel strong and virile. He'd risk his very life. That made him feel rather, what was the word? Macho? No, that sounded too crude. A winner. A champion!

He looked at the uncomprehending fish in the tank.

He'd given up his life for Theda long ago. His thoughts seemed to slur around in his head, tempering the fears and the mountainous bitterness.

The only thing left, then, was his work.

The blue fish blurred, turned fuzzy. And slipped away behind a white stone castle.

Later that evening Diana returned to the bedroom she shared with Catherine.

The room was warm, the lighting soft. She put the book of Rilke poems she'd been reading on the table beside her bed and rubbed her eyes.

Catherine didn't look up from her sketch pad when Diana entered the room. She was sitting cross-legged on her bed, drawing, her wooden box of pencils and glue and tools beside her. A scented candle burned on a table beneath a window thick with a whorled pattern of frost. Diana smelled sandalwood. She flopped down on her bed.

She was so tired of fighting.

Just be cool, she told herself. It was as though she felt herself on the edge of a great black chasm of hatred. If she fell into it, Catherine would know her every thought. The emotions would surface everywhere.

Diana knew that if she could let go of the rage, she'd have more power. It took energy to hate somebody, and why waste the energy?

Maybe she could even pity Catherine a little.

Poor Catherine.

Diana looked at Catherine, quietly drawing. She's harmless, Diana told herself. She's a pathetic creature. She only had as much power as one gave her, and no more. She looked tiny in her white bathrobe, her long golden hair, brushed to a perfect sheen, gleaming in the light.

Now Catherine looked over, into Diana's eyes. That mischievous smile appeared. Candle flame reflected in her blue eyes. She looked down again at her sketch. Touched her pencil point to the paper, blackening a line.

"I'm a real bitch, huh?" Catherine said softly.

"Mmm-hmm," Diana answered. She lay flat on her bed, looking at Catherine.

Catherine smiled again and Diana did, too. Diana truly wasn't a hater. She was touched by Catherine's self-effacement, even if she didn't trust her for a second.

"Do you forgive me?" Catherine said.

Diana climbed off her bed. The springs creaked. She came over and leaned against the desk next to Catherine, and she looked at the drawing, a portrait of a frowning, muscled god.

"No," Diana said. She grinned at Catherine now. "I don't forgive you. You've fixed me good."

Catherine sighed. "I had a shrink once who told me I hated myself," Catherine said. "He said I worked overtime to make the people I love feel the same way about me." She smiled at Diana. "I had him fired."

Diana looked down at the floor.

"I don't hate you, Catherine," she said, looking up again. "But the fact remains, thanks to you I can't leave this place, I can't make phone calls. I can't even call my parents."

"I'm truly sorry about all that, except for the parents part."

Diana rolled her eyes upward.

"No, wait a minute, listen," Catherine said. "You *will* thank me for that, someday. I promise! Keeping your parents away is a blessing. Wish I could get *my* parent off my back for a while. Wish I knew how."

"Oh, you'll think of something," Diana said with a nasty grin. The picture caught Diana's eye again. "What are you drawing?"

Catherine held up the portrait. "Morpheus," Catherine said. "The son of sleep and god of dreams."

Diana nodded, admiring the drawing. Atop a muscled neck was the strong head of a god, wide-set eyes blazing out at her. Catherine had talent. Not the least of her talents was her conniving charm. She was awful, a liar, a cheat . . . a basket case. But somehow, on some tiny level, you had to love her, Diana thought. Catherine could no more stop being Catherine than a beautiful lioness could stop from sinking its fangs into the soft throat of an innocent lamb—to survive!

"Listen, how would you like to spend Thanksgiving with me at my mom's place, overnight?" Catherine said.

Diana froze a little. Be calm, she told herself. Be an ice cube. This could be the ticket out. Don't just reject the offer out of hand. Think about it.

Play along, play along.

"I suppose that will be all right," Diana answered, nonchalant. Yet her mind fairly whirled with the possibility of escape.

Catherine put her arms around Diana and kissed her on the cheek. "Great!" She leaned back, her hands tight on Diana's shoulders. "Just tell me one thing."

"Yes?" Stay calm, she told herself. Keep that icy, emotionless wall up.

"It's really important. Tell me you forgive me."

Diana smiled. "But I don't forgive you."

Catherine's mouth fell open. Diana smiled coolly.

"Then you have to do something to me, something equally awful," Catherine said. "Something mean."

Diana smiled. "Like what? Do I get to take a free kick at you?" She laughed.

"You can get me in trouble, you can . . ."

"Catherine, *nothing* can hurt you."

Nothing, and no one but yourself, Diana wanted to add. But didn't.

"We have to be even," Catherine said.

"We'll never be even," Diana said, "Unless . . ." Something in the box at Catherine's side caught her eye. Reflected candlelight flickered on metal.

Diana picked up the scissors. As Catherine gasped, Diana reached over and took up a length of golden hair. She put Catherine's hair, at about ear level, between the blades, and started to close the scissors.

Catherine closed her eyes. "Oh, God, not my hair!"

Diana stopped. Not one hair had been severed. She withdrew the scissors.

Catherine's eyes popped open. Diana laughed.

"I'm not really going to do it," Diana said. "I only wanted to scare you."

"It worked," Catherine whispered.

Diana shrugged. "Okay, we're even." She put the scissors down in the wooden box.

Catherine looked at the scissors. She shook her head.

"We're not even yet," she said.

Without a word or change in her expression, Catherine took the scissors and placed the same length of her hair between the blades.

Diana opened her mouth, surprised. The scissors closed.

Catherine clipped off a thick mass of hair. Diana's heart lurched in her chest. Golden hair fell, scattering on the bed.

"Catherine," Diana whispered.

Catherine sheared off as much hair as she could, until all that was left was a ragged fringe that fell at the longest point to her chin.

"Now we have the same lovely hairdo," Catherine said. She giggled and hopped up off the bed. She went to the mirror.

"Catherine, my God," Diana said.

Catherine turned her head this way and that, smiling. In

her fist she clutched a length of her severed blond hair.

Diana didn't want to feel what she was feeling. But Catherine was signalling her, wordlessly. A message glowed from her forehead, passing through the walls of Diana's skull, illuminating and warming. Saying . . .

Now we're even.
Now everything is going to be okay.

That night, Diana dreamed of scissors, of hair falling, of heads tumbling from bodies.

And of a dark faceless figure that fell backwards, falling from darkness to darkness.

The clinic was empty early the next morning. Diana put on her heavy wool jacket, peering through the dim, cold rooms.

Thanksgiving Day.

From the top of the stairs came Catherine's voice. She was speaking to someone. Diana closed her eyes. She wondered if it was really such a great idea to go to Catherine's mother's house. But it was too late to back out now.

She opened her eyes and looked through the translucent gray curtains in the front parlor. She pulled the curtains aside. Frost like an ornate Victorian glasswork had grown jagged in the corners of the window pane. In her mind, Diana heard the soft tinkle of a small bell. She shook her head, trying to clear it of the strange sound. Outside, the hills were a faded, dead shade of brown. She was tired, had forced herself to stay awake all night. She knew she couldn't risk having a dream that might have given away her plan to Catherine.

The sky overhead was heavy, pressing down, a cold stone-like gray.

The stairs creaked.

David followed Catherine down the stairs. He wore a blue ski jacket, and carried a large sack filled with linen to be laundered.

Catherine smiled, a fuzzy moss-green beret on her head, hiding her hair.

"It'll be good to get out of this place for a couple days,"

Catherine said in a cheery voice. David remained expressionless.

Diana looked at him, but he didn't return her glance.

"The car's here," Catherine said, looking out the front window. She looked at Diana and David, who seemed to be avoiding each other.

"I'll wait outside," Catherine said with a wink. She picked up her overnight bag and went out the door.

"Well, have a happy Thanksgiving," David said to Diana. "I'll be here with my mother and a few of the other staff members who don't have any place else to go."

"At least you *have* a mother to be with today," Diana said.

He looked away.

She came over close to him. Stood before him, arms at her sides.

She put her hand on his arm.

"You'll get out of here," she said. "You'll make it. And so will I." She didn't tell him that if her plan worked she wouldn't be coming back here. That with luck this trip to Catherine's would provide an escape for her.

He kissed her. He smiled at her. She wanted desperately to tell him. She had the awful feeling she might never see him again. Yet she could not implicate him in her scheme.

"Better get going," he said. "Catherine and the state representative are waiting."

Yes, Diana thought. And in a matter of hours, she would be able to make a phone call. Not to the police, they would simply return the "sick" girl to the institution from which she was naturally trying to escape. No, she would call her parents, and she would put all her trust in them.

She would find a way to make that phone call, even if she had to wait deep into the night, until everyone at Catherine's house was sound asleep.

Theda's house smelled richly of roasting turkey, an aroma that made Diana happy almost despite herself. The table was set and wine glasses gleamed with firelight.

In the kitchen, Theda's ever-helpful assistant, Harriet Evans, helped prepare the gravy. Everyone was dressed up for the occasion. Harriet wore a dark navy dress and green jacket. A snowman broach that looked like an old Christmas cookie was pinned to her chest. Maybe it *was* an old cookie, Diana thought.

Theda wore one of her blazing red suits, and a white silk shirt that was lacy at the neck. Catherine wore clean faded blue jeans and a peach-color sweater. And that fuzzy green beret.

"Aren't you going to take that hat off?" Theda said to Catherine.

"It's part of the outfit, Mother," Catherine replied, aiming the turkey baster filled with hot grease at her. Of course Theda's back was turned; only Diana saw, and had to stifle a giggle. Catherine smiled and squirted grease over the stuffed bird.

Theda muttered, "I don't care for it." She continued stirring the pureed squash, and Harriet kept up her babble about how it had apparently snowed everywhere in the state except for Blackburn County. "Most unusual," she said. She licked butter from a knife.

Diana wore pressed black jeans and a not particularly dressy wool sweater, gray and white with a snowflake pattern. She consoled herself that her freshly shampooed hair had finally grown out enough to look presentable, and she liked the way it fell over to one side now without having to use too much gel.

Diana sliced the bread and brought it to the table. The others were all busy in the kitchen. She was alone now. Her heart pounded. This was her chance—now!—and she knew she'd better take it.

When she was sure no one was looking, she sneaked up the wide, red-carpeted stairs. If anyone asked, she'd say she was going to the second-floor bathroom. Why not use the one on the first floor? Well, it wasn't as pretty, she'd explain if she had to. Nor was it close to a phone and some privacy.

But no one was looking. No one asked. No one saw her.

The upstairs corridor was carpeted in pale green. A small round wood table stood before a frosted window. On the table was a tall black vase filled with fresh daisies. The corridor was long, and tidy. Bedroom doors were kept open, and dull light cast gloomy daytime shadows. The bathroom was at the end of the hall, and the bathroom door was wide open. She was entirely alone up here.

With a backward glance, she entered Theda's stately bedroom. The flowery print drapes were pulled from the windows, but the sheer curtains that remained over the panes obscured most of the light. It was cold in here. Of course it would be; the temperature outside registered below zero. The wind-chill factor made it even colder. It was deadly out there.

The telephone was an old-fashioned plastic rotary model from the 1960s. Despite its age, it was clean and shined like new.

Trembling now, Diana lifted the receiver. If anyone downstairs became suspicious, or picked up the phone themselves, Diana would be caught red-handed.

She listened and heard the dial tone, a deep chilly drone. She dialed, the rotary phone clicking and whirring. She wished it could be quieter.

A chilling thought was ever-present in her mind. Wouldn't Catherine be monitoring her today? And now that Diana was frightened, would Catherine sense it, even all the way downstairs? Catherine was potentially always just a wavelength away.

Diana dialed the last few numbers quickly. If Catherine wanted to catch her, she'd catch her—if Diana didn't stay cool, she reminded herself. Freeze up the wavelength. Remain calm. Diana saw her own reflection in the vanity mirror as the call went through its connection process, clicking and phasing into another area code: Chicago.

Her face, she saw, was grim.

At last, the ringing began. Two rings. Then a third. They had to be home! It was Thanksgiving.

After the fourth ring, the familiar sound of an answering machine engaging itself started in her ear. Tape wound with a hiss. Then came the recorded message: Steel drums, pounding out a tropical tune. Then her mother's voice came on the tape.

''Hello, you've reached Evelyn and Jack. Happy holidays—but don't you wish you were us? While you're enjoying the arctic blast of winter, we're on holiday in Grand Cayman with the girls, barefoot in the sand . . . oops—just dropped the sun-screen. It's gonna be hot, hot, *hot* today. Oh, and if you're a burglar feel free to try out our new security system. All others, leave a message. But don't expect to hear back from us anytime soon. Tah—''

Diana's mind reeled. In Grand Cayman with the girls?

The beep came at last.

"Diana?'' came a voice from the bottom of the stairs. Harriet's voice. Diana looked at the phone.

She waited a moment and hung up.

She quickly and quietly ran out of Theda's room and into the bathroom. She closed the door quietly, then called out, "In the bathroom, Harriet. Be right down.''

Diana leaned against the bathroom sink. Her parents had told everybody they'd taken her with them on vacation, when in fact they had probably only taken her sister Brenda. To hide the truth.

The truth about where Diana *really* was.

Tears stood in her eyes. She sniffed and blinked away the tears. Then she flushed the toilet and ran water in the sink.

Trembling, she opened the bathroom door. Were they getting suspicious downstairs? She was so shocked she almost didn't care.

Play along, Diana, she told herself. You have got to stay calm.

When she returned to the kitchen, Catherine looked over at her from the counter, where she was arranging some parsley on top of a mound of steaming mashed potatoes. The potatoes were so white and so perfect. In a cavity at the top, butter melted and ran in a greasy golden stream.

If Catherine knew about the phone call, she wasn't letting on. She carried the potatoes to the dining room. Diana sighed heavily. She had not been caught. But *now* what?

Theda rang a small dinner bell. Diana felt the chiming toll as if it were an electric charge, crawling up her back, under her skin. She tried to smile, and just knew it must have looked like some sort of sick grimace. She joined

Theda and Harriet and Catherine around the table.

Catherine was last to pull up her chair. The turkey was set in front of Theda. It looked like something in a Norman Rockwell painting.

Diana had this weird feeling like her face was some kind of plastic mask, misshapen, numb.

"Now, let's bow our heads for a moment and thank the Lord for this heavenly feast. A lot of people around the world are not as fortunate as we are, and will not be sitting down to such a delicious meal."

"A lot of people in Blackburn County, too," Catherine added, interrupting.

Theda shot a sidelong scowl at her daughter. But she rapidly recovered her serenity.

"And let us pray that our children, all over the world, and especially in Blackburn County, will understand just how lucky they are, and will be thankful to God, and to their parents, for all the sacrifices made on their behalf. Amen." Theda looked over at Catherine. "Now are you going to take that silly hat off?"

Catherine smiled, not looking at her mother. She speared a slice of white meat and put it on her plate.

"Nope."

Diana felt her heart thumping in her chest. It was already dark outside. Cold and forbidding. Her parents were on a sunny tropical beach with her little sister Brenda. Here she was, with somebody else's dysfunctional family.

Harriet ate her meal quietly. Luckily Theda seemed to forget about the hat for a while. She talked genially through dinner. Mostly about various ways she'd cooked Thanksgiving turkey over the years, and how Catherine had always wanted the wishbone when she was little, reminiscences of that sort. She didn't talk about the recall election. That wasn't too surprising.

After the meal, when Diana carried her plate to the kitchen sink, she saw today's newspaper in the red plastic mesh trash can. The headline was: MORE TROUBLE FOR THEDA PRICE. Diana scraped the remains of some cranberries and squash over the newspaper.

Coffee was brewing, smelling delicious. There was an

oily sheen on the surface of the pumpkin pie.

Catherine stood at the sink, running hot water over some dishes. Steam rose around her. She didn't see Theda sneaking up behind her, a smile on her face. But Diana did. *Watch out!*

Catherine turned around, astonished, just as Theda pulled the beret from her head.

"Mother!"

Theda's jaw clenched. "Jesus..." she whispered. "What in the *fuck* have you done to your hair, you little ... *tramp*!"

Catherine fumed, "Out of my way, Mother!"

Theda threw the beret to the floor. Her hands flew to Catherine's neck. Diana thought of the praying hands of a statue; that's what Theda's hands looked like, steel or marble, crushing Catherine's pale neck.

Harriet stood in the doorway with the remains of a casserole, which slushed dangerously till she tilted the pan upright.

Catherine kicked at her mother, her red face pinched in rage.

"You stupid old bitch!" Catherine cried. "You goddamn cow!"

"How could you *do* such a thing to your hair!" Theda screeched. Diana backed into the doorway, and she caught a glimpse of Harriet hurrying around the table, collecting silverware. Harriet gave a desperate shrug that almost made Diana laugh. How many of these ugly scenes had Harriet witnessed over the years?

Theda turned to Diana. "Who did this? Did you help her?" Theda shouted.

Catherine broke free of her mother's grasp. "She had nothing to do with it," Catherine said, gasping.

"Now you both have the same ridiculous chopped hair style," Theda said. "Is this some kind of bizarre new fashion?"

Catherine smiled bitterly through her tears. "It's *not* a new fashion, Mother, you fucking idiot."

Diana looked away, but heard the smack as Theda's hand struck Catherine's petulant face.

"Upstairs!" Theda cried. She turned and looked at Diana. "And you . . . you get out of my sight!"

Me? Me?

Diana felt as though she would cry now, too. She wanted to say something, but couldn't find the voice with which to say it. She turned and ran up the stairs after Catherine.

She found Catherine face down on her bed in that lovely spacious room of hers, crying. She sat down next to her and put her hand on Catherine's shoulder.

Catherine turned her head, and Diana saw her puffy eyes and red running nose.

"I hate her," Catherine said. "I hate her and I'd like to kill her."

Diana squeezed Catherine's shoulder. "Shhhh," she said, hoping it sounded soothing.

Catherine suddenly pressed her open palm on Diana's forehead.

"Look," she said.

A strange sort of flash rippled through Diana's mind's eye.

Diana felt the force of it, a wave moving in like a heavy blow.

Sitting in this darkened bedroom, they could both see Theda now, coming into focus. Could see her downstairs in her pink rubber gloves and fancy suit jacket, furiously scrubbing a pot at the kitchen sink. They were seeing her through Harriet's slightly blurred vision, Diana realized.

Harriet went a bit stiff in the kitchen just then, quite unaware of a presence inside her head peering out. She put a hand on the kitchen table to steady herself. How dreamy it felt, rather narcotic. She wondered if it was the red wine doing this.

Yet upstairs, the source of this penetrating wave was far from being calm and relaxed.

"We could ram her head down into the sink and drown her," Catherine whispered. "We wouldn't have to lift a finger. Or we could make her fall down the stairs."

Diana shook her head. She stood up and took a couple of deep breaths. She felt herself cooling down, and she blinked away the vision.

Theda faded from her mind's eye.

Diana went to the window. She looked down at the street, to the closest house, a good distance away. Yet she could see light in all the windows. Did they all fear Theda Price, these people who dwelled in her neighborhood, in her town, in *her* county? Could she turn to them for help? The street was dark, a kind of winter blue.

The bare tree branches reached to the empty sky. She longed suddenly for the comfort of snow, of rich blanketing, quieting snow.

But now she saw something that scared her even more than the vision of Theda, and the horrible row, and the threats in this troubled house.

As she looked at the window, a thread of frost drew itself across the pane.

It grew. It startled her, but was too amazing to look away from. From this thread grew veins of crystal, as fine and delicate as the veins in an eyeball. And from these veins grew a tissue of frost, whirling and growing, shaping a feathery pattern.

Growing like a dream.

Her breath made a patch of fog on the window. And now that, too, frosted over, diamond-encrusted. In the pattern grew two icy eyes. An old woman's stern, admonishing eyes.

The eyes of the old woman they had freed from a bramble, piercing through the darkness.

Serilda.

The ice eyes seemed to move, to look around and blink. Diana held her breath. Clamped her hand over her mouth. Thought, am I going insane?

The eyes gazed at her, beckoning. Sad. Pleading!

A crystal tear emerged from a frostwork eye, and ran from the pane to the window sill. Diana braced herself. It splashed onto her hand, so cold it hurt.

Diana watched as the eyes closed and then disappeared in a heavy new film of spreading frost. The strange impression of a landscape emerged. A cliff. Covered in snow.

Finally, Diana had to look away.

Catherine was sleeping.

* * *

Diana had been so tired, it had taken only moments to fall asleep. Whatever the hour, wherever she was, it didn't matter now; she recognized that she was dreaming, and perhaps had been dreaming for hours.

As she had so many times before, she was able to stand apart and observe her own dream, even observe herself in it.

It's only a dream, she told herself.

It was so peculiar a dream, she wondered if she wasn't possibly having another of Catherine's nightmares again, or—because this strange place she found herself in the dream was clearly Catherine's mother's house—maybe this was some dark corner of Catherine's memory.

Diana felt her dream self floating like an angel through the very house she slept in. She saw, in this dream, her shadow sliding along the wall next to her, though the light was faint. She saw the table and the vase filled with daisies. Starry light shimmered upon the walls, and every surface seemed glazed with glassy frost.

"Catherine," she heard herself calling, as if from some greater distance.

Don't go in there.

Another faraway voice!

Her dream self floated before the closed door of Theda's bedroom. She looked at the door, where a scary impression of trees, of a primeval forest, was cast in the dark wood grain. From a window behind her, moonlight gleamed through frost.

It was like the entire hallway was the inside of an icebox, coated with glittering frost. Cold smoke drifted over every surface. It was so cold here, so frigid.

It's only a dream, she told herself again.

Stay away.

She could probably wake herself if she would only try, she guessed . . . yet some part of her wanted to see. Even though she was afraid.

The door faded away to blackness, and in the distance she saw the dark figure standing over Theda's bed with the butcher knife pointed downward. And in the blackness she saw the drop of blood that grew at the tip of the gleaming blade. Grew and quivered and fell upon the bed sheet.

Diana wanted to scream. She saw herself, mouth open . . . but she could not make a sound. She saw that the white sheet was pulled tight over the head of the still body in Theda's bed. Like a corpse in its shroud. Moonlight crept over the bed. Everything twinkled with that cold pale blue-gray sheen of frost.

The figure with the knife turned. Catherine's hair had grown back, long, and seemed to flow around her face like a mermaid's hair in an underwater film. Blood seeped through the sheet at the head, until the shrouded head was dark and wet and dripping. Rivulets of blood ran down the folds of the sheet. Catherine buried the knife in at the neck, turning it and driving it in deep, so that a black fountain of blood fanned out over her hand. She was trying to take the head off—hack it off through the sheet.

Wake up, Diana.

No, Diana mouthed, No!

Her heart pounded with fury. And in a moment that seemed like the final struggle of a drowning woman to reach the surface of the ocean—to break through the surface into the life-giving air—Diana awoke.

She awoke in Catherine's dark bedroom with a gasp. She was safe in bed, feeling gooseflesh rise upon her skin. There was a terrible chill in the room. Her face was awash in sweat.

It was only a dream, she knew. And she drew in a long deep breath. But before she exhaled, she froze.

Slowly she turned her head to look for Catherine.

But Catherine wasn't in her bed. The covers were pulled down, rumpled, white in the frost-muted moonlight.

Catherine was not in the room.

Chapter Seven

Diana sat up in bed, awake. "Catherine," she whispered. "Catherine, where are you?" She looked around the dark gloomy room. Moon shadows were cast against the wall above Catherine's empty bed; the crooked, reaching limbs of a tree, with its grasping bony fingers.

"Catherine," she called again in a high frantic voice. She clutched the wool blanket to her throat.

She was all alone in the room. Silvery blue light shimmered behind the sheer curtains of the big bay windows.

The bed creaked as she touched her bare feet to the floor. The wood possessed a coldness that surprised her. It felt like a smooth sheet of ice. She pulled a thin robe over her nightshirt. She didn't dare turn on a light. She called, through her mind
Catherine . . .

The bedroom door was closed tight.

She opened it. It moved silently toward her. The brass knob felt like a jewel of ice in her hand. In her mouth was the metallic taste of fear.

A sleeping house held so many terrors for her. Out here in the narrow hallway, strange shadows were cast like webs over the walls, from the carpeted floor and the high ceiling. Daisies in a vase looked evil, petals turned inward as if composed into the lips of small snarling, sneering mouths.

The moonlight through the frosted-over windows at either end of the hallway cast a blue filmy glow over the scene, and the walls themselves seemed as though they sparkled with a crystal sheen of frost. Just as they had in her nightmare.

Diana held her freezing fingers to her lips and blew on them. Her feet felt numb. She took slow, wary steps.

At the end of the hall was Theda's bedroom, the door closed but for a tiny crack. A shadow swam across the cracked opening, and Diana felt her heart lurch and her throat close.

No.

She walked toward the door.

No.

She reached out her hand to push the door open.

NO!

Her eyes adjusted to the deepening darkness of the room. Tall heavy curtains had been pulled over the windows. Theda was sound asleep in her bed, still, her breathing shallow. And Catherine, standing, was poised above Theda, the heavy butcher knife rising in both hands high above her head. Her dark face was fixed upon its target.

Catherine, no!

Catherine turned her head and looked at Diana. In this faint light, all that was visible were the whites of Catherine's eyes. Diana noticed that Theda was on her back, her nose pointed upward, nostrils exhaling breath. A black mask over her eyes. Odd thing to notice at a time like this, Diana thought.

"Stop," Diana whispered.

Catherine held the knife a bit higher. Diana took a step closer, terrified that Theda would awaken. That if she screamed and tried to warn her, Catherine would strike.

Give me the knife.

Catherine pointed the knife at Diana now. She bit her lower lip and drew out a strange smile, until her teeth shone in the faint light.

Diana stood next to her now, and put a hand on her wrist.

Catherine violently jerked her hand away. The knife caught on a piece of fabric that covered the window. Diana pulled Catherine's arm, and Catherine twisted the knife violently in the curtain, trying to free it.

Theda slept. It amazed Diana, who expected Theda would wake up at any second, hearing this, sensing this violence like the beating of wings all around her.

But it was still so quiet in the room, all Diana could hear was Theda's labored breathing. And her own heartbeat.

Sweat dotted Diana's brow now. She heard the sound of the knife, muffled in the fabric. A great piece of fabric, cut away, fell silently, flopping like an elephant's ear over Catherine's face. Catherine fought it aside, and freed the knife, but lost her grip on it.

The knife flew out of her hand. It turned over in the air. It landed like a javelin in the pillow an inch from Theda's masked eye. A plume of tiny white feathers coursed— *pffffff*—up into the air from the hole in the firm pillow.

Theda took a sleeping breath. Her lips parted. She swallowed. But she did not awaken. Diana watched, breathless.

Silently, the feathers fell around Theda's face. One feather landed on Theda's lips. Her mouth twitched and she unwittingly blew the feather aloft. Catherine reached for the knife, but Diana was quicker. Diana withdrew the knife from the pillow, like a knight pulling a sword from a stone. On tiptoes Diana ran from the room. In the hallway, Catherine chased after her. Beyond the frosted-over windows there pulsed the first faint light of morning. Catherine pushed Diana into her bedroom.

"Why did you stop me?" Catherine whispered in a frantic cry. "What gives you the right?" Catherine's chopped-up hair was wet with perspiration, and her eyes flashed with a kind of madness.

Diana opened the closet door and threw the knife as far as she could to the back of a high shelf. It made a thud against a cardboard box. But it was gone now.

"You idiot," Catherine said. "You vile little fool!"

Diana pushed her aside. She pulled off her robe and dressed quickly, pulling jeans and a sweatshirt on over her nightshirt while Catherine muttered and cursed.

"You don't know what you're doing!" Catherine said. "You should have let me kill her! You've never understood what any of this is about."

Diana quickly and with difficulty pulled her shoes on, her hands shaking.

Catherine put her hand over her eye, as though she had a headache, some deep flash of pain. She shook her head. By the time she opened her eyes to look, Diana was fully dressed and pulling on her coat.

"What in the hell are you doing?" Catherine said. "Where do you think you're going?"

Diana reached for the door knob, not answering. Catherine grabbed hold of Diana's arm with one hand and her hair with the other, and pulled her back.

Scalp burning like fire now, Diana was spun around with tremendous force. She looked at Catherine's face. At her parted lips. Felt the cold breath that heaved in and out of her. Catherine's eyes gleamed with tears.

With all her strength, Diana pushed Catherine backwards. Catherine sprawled noisily to her bed, careering off it to the floor. The crash was the first really loud sound among all the frightful, violent events that had transpired, and it shook the house.

Diana knew she didn't have time to fight. She had to act now. She turned and pulled the door open, ready to bound out of it—to where, she didn't know; and it didn't matter. Outside. Away.

She hadn't counted on Theda being there, standing like a rock in the doorway, blocking her.

Diana stopped dead, a thousand cold pinpricks seeming to burst outward through her skin.

That morning, David carried the last plastic bag of garbage out to the trash heap. His breath steamed up to the treetops, it was so cold. Too cold to snow, he thought. Yet the overcast sky seemed heavy, pregnant with snow.

He wore earphones and listened to the community college radio station. It was time for the *News Minute*. A young woman with a droning voice read the weather forecast—more cold, chance of snow unlikely. David snapped the plastic lid onto the garbage can. He saw Harriet Evans's old green Buick pulling up the drive.

The newscaster continued her report.

*"Nessie Jasper held a Thanksgiving Day press confer-
ence outside the chained doors of the old Leonora Tool
Manufacturers factory, closed down since the 1980s,"* the
newscaster read.

David turned the volume up a notch, and heard the voice
of Nessie Jasper.

*"Factories like this one sit empty, and more and more
people have less and less to be thankful for,"* Nessie said
in a booming voice. *"Isn't it time we elected a representative who will fight for the common working person? Isn't
it time for a real change? In fact, isn't a big change way
past due here in Blackburn County?"*

David nodded, and glanced over at Diana and Catherine.
They climbed out of the car, their overnight bags at their
sides. He waited for Diana to look over at him. She didn't.
With her head down and her angry eyes fixed on the stone
path, she followed Catherine into the clinic. Harriet Evans
followed close behind, like an old sheep dog.

The newscaster said, *"Local experts are now saying that
the controversial one-time sex educator has a fifty-fifty
chance of defeating the embattled incumbent, Representative Theda Price, in the upcoming recall election. We tel-
ephoned Representative Price for her reaction, but she did
not return our calls. Next, sports. The Woodchucks went
down in a blaze of—"*

David switched off the radio. Fuck the Woodchucks, he
thought. He watched the door close behind old Ms. Evans.
What was going on with Diana and Catherine now? God,
he hated this place.

Still, even if Diana was disturbed, he had feelings for
her. Strong ones. Lately he couldn't seem to get her out of
his mind. But wasn't that the way with him? He shook his
head, feeling miserable. He only wanted things he wasn't
supposed to have. He wondered when he was going to get
his act together. Or if he ever would.

He switched the radio dial around until he was able to
tune in a distant classical music station he'd been listening
to lately. He recognized a piece by Samuel Barber, *Adagio
for Strings*, which suited his mood.

Smiling sadly, he looked up and saw his mother staring

out the window at him. Shirley had her dark hair tied back around her unsmiling face. Her arms were crossed in the window. Had she seen him looking at the girls? Looking at Diana? Her disapproval was palpable.

Frowning now, and embarrassed, he looked away from his mother. Then, suddenly, he was overcome with an exhilarating kind of anger.

He turned up the volume on his radio. He extended his arms and took several slow dancing strides, feeling the music building to its aching crescendo. He leapt into the air, striding over the cold ground. He spun around on one foot, hand raised to the window. Took a deep bow.

But when he looked up again, his mother was gone.

Diana bounded up the stairs. Catherine followed.

"Now hold on a minute," Catherine said. Supremely confident. Like she hadn't tried to stab her mother last night. Like this was just a normal life they were leading, and last night had been just a typical sleepover.

Diana quickened her stride and slipped into a hallway bathroom. She closed the door and locked it. She felt Catherine's weight pressing up against the other side of the door.

"Go away, Catherine," Diana said.

"But nothing happened," Catherine whispered.

Theda had miraculously slept through the murder attempt. She simply had not woken up. Not until she heard the fight in Catherine's room. Then she'd angrily marched the girls downstairs. She made them sit in silence while they waited for Harriet Evans to come and pick them up and drive them back to the Albion Clinic.

Whatever sort of childish prank it was that had been going on, Theda wasn't having any of it. She smoked five or six cigarettes waiting for Harriet to come. She exhaled smoke angrily, until Diana could barely see Catherine through the thick haze, even though Catherine was seated just a few feet away from her. No one had spoken a word. *Come out, come out, wherever you are.*

"Catherine," Diana said now, her voice a tiny screech. "Get the hell out of my head!"

Too late.

Diana tried to compose herself, but a chill swept over her. She was actually shaking now. She braced herself against the red enamel sink.

"Too late, baby," Catherine whispered wickedly. "I'm here. You're with me now. We've grown together, you see. We're like Siamese twins of the mind." She giggled.

"Catherine, you've got to stop this." Diana sank to the cold tile floor.

"You're connected to me with scar tissue, Diana. I can take you anywhere now. Any place I go. Your scarred up little soul is in my grasp."

"You're not funny, Catherine," Diana screamed. "Not in the slightest."

Diana looked over at the tall narrow window. She scrambled to it, feet sliding on the polished bathroom floor.

Catherine said, "Come on out of there and let's talk this over like adults, then. If that's what you want." She rapped on the door with her knuckles.

Diana said, "You want to be a killer, Catherine?" She unlocked the window, and thrust it open. A window just wide enough for a body to pass through. A wave of bitter cold air blasted inside, blowing her hair and chilling her to her scalp. Diana put her arms on the window frame and leaned her head outside. The air was frigid . . .

Down below was a drop of more than two stories. At the bottom were gnarled leafless trees, miniature fruit trees with hard, heavy, stunted limbs, raised like deadly spears.

"I can see them," Catherine said, quietly, behind the locked door. "Daggers," she said. "You'd probably die fast if one of them went through your heart. But that's not what you want. Not what *we* want."

Diana looked down and swallowed hard. Yes, this was a way out. A way to end her fears. She felt dizzy now, terrified as always of these heights. Of falling. She held the window frame tight in her hands, which were numb from the cold. She closed her eyes and felt dizzy.

Diana screamed out . . . but she knew the other patients had all gone away for the Thanksgiving holiday. No one here but the staff. Staff who considered her a thief, an insomniac—a nutcase. No one was outside today. No one around for miles. Tears were freezing on her face, which felt raw in this cold wind. She imagined that this was what it must feel like to stick your head out the window of a 747 at thirty thousand feet.

She heard Catherine sigh deeply.

"Okay," Catherine said. "Don't do something stupid. I'll leave you alone. I'll go."

For now.

Diana closed her eyes. Her lips were numb. The tears had frozen at the ends of her lashes.

"For now," Diana whispered to herself. She slammed the window shut.

She felt Catherine leaving, fading from her mind. Quieting their unified mind.

Diana went to the blood-red porcelain toilet, opened the lid, and slid to the floor. She leaned over the clear water of the toilet. Felt that horrible chill, sweat blooming on her brow, limbs weakening. She spat into the bowl. How she hated it, couldn't bear this feeling of nausea.

She vomited into the toilet, feeling the pain of her stomach convulsing her small body, all the way down through her crotch and seizing upward. Her stomach seeming to wring itself out completely, to the last drop, choking off her breath like a strangler. Her body seemed to have a violent will of its own.

She gasped. Then another convulsive thrust came, but there was nothing left in her stomach to come forth.

At last she could breathe again. That vile, sour, unspeakable taste was in her mouth and her nose, burning there. Yet she felt a little better, felt the sweat on her forehead, and a sudden calm in her body.

She flushed the toilet and ran cold water in the sink, and rinsed her mouth over and over. Took a cool drink from her cupped hands.

She looked at her pale white face in the mirror.

Diana went to the bathtub. She pushed aside the clear, red-striped shower curtain and sat down, fully clothed at the end of the dry, cold tub. She drew her knees to her chest. Lowered her head.

She tried to erase consciousness, every thought racing through her mind. To suppress all emotion. Just empty your head, she told herself; then there's nothing left for Catherine or anybody else to hold onto. No more dreams. No more nightmares. No more brain sampling, telegraphing, mindsweeping . . .

She shook her head and pressed her forehead hard into her knees, almost till it hurt. Until she felt she could have split her own skull open with the pressure.

As the thoughts cleared from her head, she heard the faint ringing of a bell. From a distance, beyond the walls of the bathroom. A servant's bell. Or a dinner bell.

Or perhaps a child's toy.

Diana awoke in the night, her face pressed against the cold porcelain of the bathtub. The bathroom was dark, but for blue moonlight filtered through the frostwork of the high window.

She raised her head, neck stiff and aching. Trembling and perspiring, she clawed her way up out of the bathtub and onto her feet. She quietly opened the bathroom door and saw that the shelter was dark and quiet. A digital clock on the teak side table flashed 3:07 A.M.

She ran down the stairs as quietly as she could, looking back to make sure no one saw her. The shadows of the tall potted plants that lined the walls were streaked across the stairwell.

In the marble-plated foyer she picked up a heavy coat. It didn't matter to her who it belonged to. Dark wool, hopefully it would be warm enough. She buttoned it up, and found a black cotton scarf in one of the pockets. She wrapped it around her head and tied a knot at her throat. Found some gloves in the pockets, too big for her, but they'd do. They would have to.

She twisted open the locks on the heavy front door, and with a wary backward glance pulled the door open to the chill night air. No doubt the opening of a door in the clinic would trigger some secret night alarm. She had to hurry. For all she knew, Catherine was monitoring her every step. Yet she couldn't feel Catherine's cold presence in her head.

Remain calm, she told herself. Be a cold fish, inscrutable.

The cold air massed at the doorway. Diana stepped outside. It is so dark out here, she thought. So cold. She closed the door tightly, and then she ran down the path, trying not to slip on the patches of ice built up from the freezing morning dew.

The cars were all locked up in the garage, of course. Even if she'd been able to find a key, she wasn't sure she was in any state to drive. No time. They'd catch her. The only thing she wanted now was to escape. That was *all* she was thinking of. It didn't matter to her now that it was insane to be out on a night like this—a night of bitter cold.

She ran in the direction of the river, following the exercise trails David had cleared. Pine needles and grass snapped beneath her feet. She reached the unlocked tool shed, and ran past it. Then she stopped. Hurrying, she yanked the door open. The first thing she found was an axe with a short handle. It might come in handy. She picked it up, gloved fingers tight around the handle. It was heavy. She took it and ran.

The frosted ground crunched beneath her feet. She couldn't see much more than a few feet up ahead. A light, low vine smacked her coldly in the face, but she kept running. But to where?

Was she really insane now? she wondered. She should have tried to find David. But he didn't believe her, and wouldn't—couldn't—help her. He would probably be sent to jail for helping a minor run away. So, she wondered, What right did she have to get him into this mess? He had his own problems.

Yet she wanted him now, wished he could be beside her. She'd never been more alone.

At last she came to the place where the trail met the narrow part of the river. She stopped, heart racing, breath heaving in great smokey plumes. Here the path widened, and the low moon, behind a scrim of cloud, shone down upon a scene of crystal-blue pine forest.

Where was the river?

As if in answer to her question, the cloud bank parted and revealed the huge white half-moon. Diana looked down at her feet. She stood at the edge of a mounded, massive sheet of white glass, which seemed to her to be like the still, flowing robes of a marble statue.

The river. The river had frozen here. She stood upon it.

She heard something. Something stirring. She listened closely. It was the roar of the river, coursing under a shell of ice. It flowed beneath her. Beneath her weight.

She heard the cracking, shattering sound before she felt the first shifting of the hard ice upon which she stood. It echoed and boomed all around her. She slipped on the great moving shaft of ice, and fell on the axe she'd been holding. Luckily the blade had bitten into the ice and not into her. She spat ice from her mouth.

Her head throbbed.

Damn them! she thought. Thinking of Sterling and Catherine and even that awful mother of Catherine's, Theda Price.

She felt the cold air on her bared teeth. She was losing her grip, and could hear the sound of water bubbling up around her, seeping up.

Damn them! She was more angry than she was frightened.

She hoisted up the axe, high above her head. She brought it down with a crash. Splinters of ice exploded into the air, flashing in the moonlight. With the axe buried in the ice, she pulled herself a little closer to the shoreline. She pulled the axe out, checked her grip, and brought the axe down again, smashing through this time.

The icy water of the river surged through the hole in the ice before her as she pulled herself up on her knees.

She listened to the cold geyser of water spraying up over the slabs of breaking ice. The spout grew wider as the force of the stream increased through the break. A massive chunk of ice broke free, and river water coursed through a hole the size of a car.

She heard the ice cracking. It was breaking up massively all around her, booming like cannon fire, sending sprays of ground white ice to the air. She felt the masses of ice rumbling and tipping now, ramming into one another with seismic force. Within seconds, water had sprung up between the new cracks, and sheets of ice upended and crashed together. A slab of ice, ten feet tall, wedged between two others, and then upended, like a vertical sail, water running down its side. The racing river wind screamed around it. The ice wall towered over her, blocking out the moon, which shimmered like a white nucleus through the dense frozen mass.

Diana scrambled over the slick white ice, and saw the roots of a huge black tree that stood at the shore up at the bend. She was coming closer to it, on her raft of ice.

The ice wall above her rippled like a pane of glass in a high wind. All at once it shattered.

The sound was thunderous. Particles of airborne ice, like snow, were caught by the wind and blew over Diana. The heaviest pieces cascaded down into the deeper part of the river, splashing up great pillars of icewater. She held the axe tightly. The ice slab she was on began to rush forward as the river raced around a bend. She was still on her knees. And coming closer to the gnarled roots of the tree at the river bank. Now she put one foot on the slippery surface, and with all her strength pushed off, diving for the roots of the massive tree.

She raised the axe as she fell and chopped down hard, the blade biting into a heavy black root. Now she was up to her waist in the coldest water she had ever touched, water that pulled with a tremendous undertow.

Holding on to the axe with both hands she hoisted herself onto the dry riverbank, and lay on her back, gasping for breath.

Within seconds the icy walls were swept away on the smooth, open black water. She listened as the mighty upended pieces banged together downriver, the sound slowly fading.

Then there was only the quiet of the black flowing river, a rippling reflection of the white moon gleaming on its calm surface.

At last the moon went behind a cloud, casting the scene back into darkness. Diana wearily picked herself up again, feeling heavy. She was soaking wet. Her clothes were freezing, becoming stiff.

She ran along the side of the river.

She kept running, and after a time the river was no longer beside her. Her eyes were bleary with tears that rose against the bitter cold. The woods grew deeper. She had to stop, to turn around. But which way to turn?

If she turned back around, would she end up closer to the clinic? Indeed, which way was "back around"? She was lost, utterly. And now she knew, wearily, that maybe this had been her plan all along. To run away to the deepest woods, to disappear.

She ran crazily, her lungs as cold and aching as if they were filled with blood. Her feet were entirely numb, her face slick with freezing tears.

No, she told herself. No, she would run, she would always run. She would never stop. She did not want to disappear. She was running with all the fight she had within her. Running to save herself.

No one could stop her. If she were to die out here, her soul would keep soaring. She knew it now.

She let out a cry that scared her, an unearthly, wolf-like scream.

She felt that her spirit kept running even as her exhausted and broken body fell and tumbled over the cold, frosty ground. She cried out, and rolled to a stop. Pines towered overhead, branches rustling softly. Surely she would freeze to death, she thought. A part of her would die here. No one would find her. Animals would eat her corpse. But she felt that her spirit would keep moving swiftly over the moonlit trail.

With her head upon the cold ground she slipped into a deep black sleep, and dreamed she was free, running, and then flying over the treetops in the moonlight.

Had hours passed, or only minutes?

Out of the gray-blackness of morning, hands fell upon Diana. Two hands that reached out and touched her face, stroked her hair, felt for her pulse in her neck. She heard a young man's voice, but couldn't see his face. It was too dark in these woods, and she hadn't even the strength to open her eyes. She felt herself being lifted by him. Up into his strong arms. She was so tired. So weary. Someone was carrying her.

She was too weak to do anything but be saved.

Sterling blew on his hands and rubbed them together. He looked out over the horizon through binoculars. His breath clouded the view of the fog-shrouded forest in dim morning light. David stood at his side. Catherine, bundled up, stood behind him, a blue scarf covering her mouth.

He was angry with these children. The morning was cold, and he feared the worst. Somehow, everyone had let him down, as usual. He couldn't even bring himself to look at Catherine.

"David, you take the river path," he said sternly. "Catherine, you come with me."

"But, Doctor, shouldn't we call the police?" David said.

Sterling turned and looked at the young man, who had never before questioned him. For as long as Sterling had known him, David had always been a kind of unthinking foot soldier, a squared-away young man who was the picture of sobriety and unquestioning duty.

Or was he?

"We haven't time," Sterling muttered. "Get moving."

David took a step back. "But the police could bring their dogs, and we could trace her more easily if—"

"Go!" Sterling shouted, and David's eyes turned downward. He winced as if from a blow to the head. David was as obedient and loyal as a German Shepherd, when properly disciplined.

"Blow your whistle if—when—you find her!" Sterling called out. David gave the whistle a single high piercing report as he ran.

Sterling turned now to Catherine. She had her white knit cap pulled down nearly to her eyes. The morning was more than a bit nippy, it was damned cold out. He could feel the coldness of the ground seeping through the bottom of his rubber, thermal-lined boots.

He didn't need sniffing dogs to find Diana. He had a far more sophisticated tracking device.

"Is she alive?" Sterling said to Catherine.

Catherine was chewing bubble gum. "I already told you she was," Catherine said. She put on a pair of dark sunglasses.

"Come on, Catherine," he said, a warning growl in his voice. "Cooperate with me."

"I *am* cooperating," Catherine said, angrily, as she brushed past him and started to walk along the trail.

Sterling sighed inwardly. Why was it that Catherine was on your side one day and hating you the next? She, who was the true focal point of his existence, his research—his everything. Now was it all going to be blown because of Catherine's recalcitrance?

This was all her fault. It was over, wasn't it? If Diana were dead, he'd have to start over again, from scratch. An unbearable thought.

He didn't even want to think about what this would mean for Theda. The whole goddamned plan was crashing down around his ears. It hurt like hell, and as usual he felt it in his bowels, a hot wire twisting and churning in there.

He stopped himself thinking such thoughts. He didn't want Catherine to get any more upset and cranky than she already was. Catherine would have picked up on his rage easily. And she would use it to her advantage.

Yet he'd never been angrier than he was this morning. He'd saved Catherine's life, after all, spared her who knew what kind of dreadful fate. He was on the verge of helping her realize her greatest powers. And she was thanking him by behaving like a snotty little bitch.

As if she'd read that thought in his mind, she turned and smiled at him. She walked backwards a few steps, chewing her gum. Silently laughing at him, she was.

Christ, everything was such a *game* to her!

Sterling turned his eyes from her. He tasted something sour rising at the back of his throat. Remorse. Regret. The sudden sense that the colleagues who'd thrown him out of the scientific community, who had laughed at him and mocked him, had been right. He was a loser.

No, don't think this way, he told himself. Control your thoughts, rein in your emotions. How easy it was to tell his patients that, he mused. How difficult it was to practice. To step aside from a thought as a dreamer steps aside in a dream, and observes. Self-control in action was one thing. But in thought, quite beyond him at this moment.

His love for Theda might have been the only thing that would keep him going through this ordeal.

That, or the promise of Theda's wrath if the girl wasn't found . . . or was found dead.

"Damn it, we've got to find Diana," he said, voice choked.

Catherine looked at him now with mild annoyance. "We'll find her, relax."

"Relax! Where is she?"

Catherine kept walking, deeper into the woods.

"Catherine, *think*. Where is she?"

"I'm thinking, I'm thinking. Will you please shut the fuck up?"

Diana blinked her eyes and strained her neck to touch her lips to the cup. Hot tea steamed delicately about her face. The tea was strong and hot, a taste of jasmine and mint. She looked up into the old, warm eyes of Serilda. Next to her was Jon, his smile framed by a stubby growth of red beard. Jon held the hot cup of tea before her.

"Jon," Diana said, shivering. Her voice was so hoarse, a feeble croaking. "Did . . . did *you* carry me here?"

Here. Where was here? She looked around. She was in a warm rustic cottage, lying on a sofa with a dark quilt and several other blankets over her, and pillows beneath her head.

"I found you in the woods," Jon said. "I was hunting pheasant, and I nearly stumbled right over you."

He leaned back on his chair. She saw the rifle leaned up against the wall beside him. He wore a blue flannel shirt, faded jeans, and a knit black cap. His heavy leather boots were unlaced. He absently pulled off the cap and a hank of his red hair flopped over an eye. He scratched the sparse red whiskers that had sprouted on his chin, and he smiled, his eyes watering.

"I'm glad you're okay," he whispered.

He held the cup to her mouth again, and she took another

little sip. She felt hot, feverish. She could barely speak.

The cabin was small but packed like a queer doll house with strange items. Over the frosted windows hung charms from string: crystals and feathers, and, Diana saw now, the tiny claws of a bird. The walls were made of raw wood, gray and weathered, and on them were hung more of the oddest charms. Pieces of bone and antler bound with dark string or thread. Bundled herbs and dried flowers were hanging everywhere, even from the beams of the low ceiling. The place had a smell of lavender, of incense, and of burning tobacco.

Serilda drew on her corncob pipe. She smiled. She exhaled and smoke shot from her nostrils.

"You might have froze to death, if he hadn't found you," she said.

Around Serilda's neck, as on the wall, were small bags of muslin tied with black thread, and black beads, and a necklace made of tiny shells. Serilda saw Diana looking at a small dried vine she was wearing.

"Moonseed," Serilda said, touching the herbal necklace with the tips of her fingers.

She was dressed in layers of ragged clothes. Beneath her dark skirts were stout legs clad in the red leggings of a pioneer, and worn old dark boots. She rose and brought a small pot of hot water to Diana's cup, and poured. Steam curled upwards. Serilda's body was plump, but her hands were thin and frail, freckled with age. She wore a ring on her index finger, just a small silver band. Diana wondered about Serilda's true age. She remembered the old newspaper photo.

Now Serilda smiled and her golden eyes gleamed. A log burning in an iron stove in the center of the room popped, and a shower of sparks rose up through the pipe chimney.

Diana tried again to speak, but found she was too weak. At last she was able to ask, "Do you have a telephone?"

Serilda shook her head. "No, I do not, and never will. The invention of the devil." She shook her head. She saw Diana straining to speak. "Save your energy, child," Serilda admonished.

Jon smiled. He was trying to roll a handmade cigarette, without much luck. He licked the gummed edge of the cigarette paper.

"What were you doing out there, sleeping in the woods?" Jon asked. "You lose your mind?"

Diana almost laughed into her tea cup. Lost her mind. Yeah, you could say that. She opened her mouth to speak, and again words failed to come out. She felt a feverish wave of heat flush through her face. She started to lose the tea cup; luckily Serilda saw, and let the cup rest in the palm of her hand as Diana took another drink.

"You'd better get some rest," Serilda said. "Jon can take you back to that retreat house or whatever that place is you been living at."

"Not a retreat house, Serilda," Jon said. "A kind of clinic."

"A *sanitorium*, then," Serilda said hopefully.

"Okay," Jon said, smiling at Serilda. "Call it whatever you want."

"The Dovers haven't changed," Serilda said with a laugh, looking him over. "I can clearly recall your grandfather and his father, too. He had red hair like yours. He was a book-learned man."

Diana tried to cry out, shaking her head, which felt too heavy. She let it fall back on the soft pillow. Sweat beaded on her forehead. She swallowed, and the burn of a raw sore throat brought tears to her eyes.

"You don't want to go back there?" Jon said. "Maybe I should take you to the hospital with me. You don't look well."

Diana felt herself on the verge of fainting. She remembered the tiny chime of a bell Serilda gave to Catherine that day in the woods.

"The . . . bell . . ." she croaked to Serilda, who now stood at her kitchen sink shredding cabbage into a pail.

"The bell I gave you," Serilda said. "A charm against evil."

"Wha . . ." Diana could barely speak.

Jon rolled his eyes.

"It's old-timer magic again," Jon said. He stroked the

barrel of his rifle with a white rag. He looked at Serilda. "You gave her a bell?"

Serilda hesitated a moment before telling Jon what had happened. As if she needed to try hard to fire her memory.

"I got myself caught in a bramble of thorns, out there in the woods," Serilda said. "This girl and her friend helped me get loose, so I gave them a little bell. To reward them."

Jon smiled and said suspiciously, "What kind of bell?"

Serilda looked away. "Just an old antique bell."

"The kind you collect?"

"*Used* to collect. I don't have any more of *those* bells. People knew I'd had such things they'd burn this little cottage with me in it." She raised her hand, oath-like. "That was the last one." She poured cold water over the shredded cabbage. Then she relit her pipe, and the smell of burning tobacco filled the little cottage again.

Jon looked at Diana. "You know what those bells were for?" he said with a grin. "They used to bury people with 'em."

Serilda's eyes narrowed. "That's not what this bell was for, I told you. This was a bell I found in the woods. Someone had thrown it away."

He paid her no attention.

"You know what a premature burial is?" Jon asked Diana. "In the old days, before embalming, sometimes living people were buried accidentally, thought to be dead, you see. Folks used to be buried with a bell here in Blackburn County. If you woke up in your coffin, you were supposed to ring that bell like the devil, hoping some lonely passerby, going through the graveyard, would hear you through six feet of earth."

Diana swallowed again.

"*Ting, ting, ting*," Jon said. " 'I'm alive down here! Help me!' " He laughed.

"That's quite enough, Mr. Dover," Serilda said. "You trying to scare her?"

Jon shrugged. He lit up a home-rolled cigarette and took a draw. "What about that bell you gave her? Got some kind of curse on it?"

Diana wanted to say, *But I don't have it! Catherine has it!*

Serilda said, smoke coming from her mouth, "That bell is a charm *against* evil. It's the opposite of what you think it is, Jon."

Jon smiled. "What do you mean?"

The expression on her face was almost a smile. She pressed her old hands together, then held them still at her sides.

"The old-timers used to give their children bells," Serilda said softly.

"Quaint tradition," Jon said, trying to sound sophisticated. He looked longingly at Diana. She listened raptly to Serilda.

"Of course it was a lovely tradition on the surface," Serilda said, her voice quiet. "It had a deeper significance. You see, the influenza swept through these parts nigh a century and more ago. The reaper didn't spare children. All the prayers a mother had seemed to go unheard in Heaven. So the old-time people went to a Blackburn County witch, who placed a spell on the bells. Each newborn was given a bell. But if the child died at the hands of the reaper, their mothers could, if they so dared, ring the bells and wake their children from the black sleep."

Diana's head pounded.

Jon smiled, "So some of our ancestors woke from the black sleep, huh?" he said. "They cheated death?"

Serilda slowly nodded her head. "Married to death, they were, these innocent children whom death had unjustly snatched away from their mothers. And it was believed that only a witch could take the waking dead back across, back to the eternal resting place. Whence they came."

"You suppose that might have happened to my great grandpappy?" Jon said.

Serilda regarded Jon with a faint smile. A knowing smile. After a moment she said, "The people were terrified of what happened when the children did indeed seem to wake in their coffins, and so the elders put a stop to the bells, at least publicly. Though as you well know, Jon, our people never did give up the romance with the dark side, and with our incomparable Death Wish Traditions. And some families continued to give the bells to their newborn babies, in secret.''

Diana croaked, ''That bell you gave us,'' she swallowed hard. ''You found it in the woods . . . it belonged to someone . . .''

''Every lost and found thing belonged to *some*-one,'' Serilda said. ''Every object that changes hands leaves behind something of its previous owner.''

There came a loud rapping at the door.

Diana gasped.

Jon held his rifle. Diana watched him now, this boy who had saved her life. Serilda rose warily from her chair.

''I never get visitors out here in the winter, and now I seem to be having a houseful.'' A wiry orange cat rubbed up against her ankles, seeming to block her way to the door. The rapping came again, harder.

The door opened.

It was Sterling, bundled up in a parka and scarf, glasses fogging against the warm air of the cottage.

Diana cried out.

''Say,'' Serilda protested, glaring at Sterling. ''No one opens my door but me.''

Sterling brushed by her. Jon stood up.

''Diana, my God, you're all right!'' Sterling said, kneeling down at the sofa. He touched her hand. He felt as cold as death. She closed her eyes, the lids hot and feverish.

She tried to cry out, ''No!'' But her voice wouldn't come. She was too weak.

Catherine stood in the door now, too. A hat pulled down low. Blue eyes watering. She entered, looking warily around the strange house, sunglasses in her gloved hand. She didn't smile when she saw Diana.

Diana closed her eyes. Catherine had found her. Had traced her here as no one else could have.

Last to tramp in was David. He pulled off his gloves and rubbed his hands together. He looked around, frowning at what he saw in the strange little room. Jon frowned back at him.

Sterling put his cold hand over Diana's feverish brow.

"She's burning up," he said. "We've got to get her back to the clinic as soon as possible."

"You should thank Jon," Serilda said. "He found her and saved her. She would have froze to death without him. Why on earth was she out in the cold?"

Diana saw Sterling squinting his eyes at the peculiar old woman, as if trying to recognize her. He looked away, seeming to dismiss her. Just another old-timer, he probably thought.

Jon nodded. "She needs to go to the hospital, not back with you," he said defiantly.

But no one was paying attention to him. David helped as Sterling lifted Diana up into his arms. Catherine regarded Serilda warily, pulling her scarf up to cover her face.

"Thank you for rescuing Diana, but she's in my charge, and she's coming with us," Sterling said gravely.

Diana felt her consciousness fading away. She couldn't look at Catherine.

She looked at Jon's pleading, angry eyes, aimed at Sterling. And she passed out.

Hours later, Diana woke to find herself in her own bed in her room at the clinic. The glass in the skylight held a dim gray gleam. With a shudder she realized that she'd been transported right back to where she'd started.

A dark form stood before her bed, twisting something in its hand, a small bottle with fiery liquid contents that glowed.

Diana strained to cry out. Sterling was preparing some kind of mixture, which he poured into a small paper cup. He put his hand on her forehead again. Fingers dry as paper.

"Don't try to speak," he said. "You're feverish."

"Catherine tried to . . . kill . . . her mother," Diana croaked.

Sterling frowned. "Try to get some sleep, Diana."

"No, no . . . it's true." Diana raised her head, feeling the muscles in her neck straining. Her hair was soaked with sweat. "She tried to stab her in her sleep," Diana said.

He took a breath, seeming to try to keep control of himself.

He touched her arm. She *felt* it shaking there. Would that she could go inside his head just now. Feel *his* fear. But whatever it was that made him quake remained a mystery. She was too weak to read his thoughts or even to manage her own.

"Drink this," he said. "It will bring the fever down." He put the cup to her lips. She resisted, trying to turn her face away.

He roughly took hold of her chin, forcing the liquid into her mouth.

"I'm losing my patience with you," he said thickly.

She parted her lips and the strange coppery-tasting liquid swam through her teeth. She swallowed.

"That's better," he said, withdrawing the cup. The liquid coated her throat with a kind of warm bitterness. She felt herself drifting off again.

She slept.

Sometime in the night, Diana woke, and looked over across the dim room to Catherine's bed. Faint light glowed in the windows. The light might have come from a moonset, or even the first glow of winter dawn. A spasm of fear went through Diana when she saw Catherine, her head on her pillow, and eyes open. Gazing across the room at her.

Blue eyes that bored through the gloom.

Diana coughed. She cleared her throat, trying to speak.

"What time is it?" she asked, voice strained.

Catherine turned her head and looked at the clock. Its display was illumined in a shade of glowing aqua. But Diana couldn't see the numbers.

"It's almost seven in the morning," Catherine answered. "It'll be light soon."

"Mmm," Diana said. She felt her forehead. It felt cool and dry now.

"The door is locked, from the outside," Catherine said evenly. "So don't get any more dumb ideas."

Diana closed her eyes. It felt warm under the blankets. But her hands felt cold.

"I'd find you again. I'll always find you, Diana."

Diana coughed. "You're wrong about that," Diana said. "I'll find a way to fight you."

"The wavelength between us has grown so much stronger." Catherine smiled crookedly. "It has a life of its own. It's stronger than both of us."

Diana looked away. The patterns of frost on the window were so intricate now. Like magical engravings, deep and mysterious.

Catherine grinned and, looking askance, said to Diana, "Penny for your thoughts." She giggled and snorted.

Diana sighed. "Some day you *will* pay for them," she said.

"Ha, that *is* funny. I've been shoplifting your thoughts and dreams for so long, they have practically no value for me anymore. It's like . . . *junk-picking.*"

"You're insane, Catherine," Diana said flatly. She closed her eyes.

"Maybe," Catherine said. "Or maybe you're just paranoid."

"You could use these powers for something good, Catherine. Instead, you're a manipulative little—"

"What sorts of good deeds do you propose?" Catherine said. "What makes you so righteous?"

I stopped you from killing your mother, for starters.

Diana hadn't necessarily meant to transport that message.

Diana cleared her throat.

After a long moment Catherine spoke.

"I love my mother," Catherine whispered.

"Must be what they call 'tough love' then, isn't it, Catherine?" Diana smiled bitterly.

"Very funny," Catherine turned her head away.

Diana sat up, feeling a tiny bit of strength. She pushed the covers off, came over to Catherine's bed. She stood over her, shaking.

"I stopped you, Catherine. From committing *murder!*" she whispered. "Murder, Catherine. Do you know what that means? Do you understand what you were trying to do?"

Catherine pulled her knees up to her chest. She buried her face in her hands.

"I'm a sleepwalker . . . I didn't know what I was doing."

Diana took hold of Catherine's wrists. She pulled them down from Catherine's face. It wasn't easy. Catherine was strong. Her arms shook.

"Look at me," Diana said.

"No," Catherine said.

"Look at me." Diana put her hand on Catherine's chin. Catherine slowly raised her face. A tear streaked down Catherine's cheek. And for a second she resembled the child she must have been. Blue eyes set in an angelic face, a face that now took on an aspect of feline beauty and mystery. Morning light now filled the room with a perfect smoky whiteness. Catherine seemed to glow in it.

"We could leave here," Diana whispered at last. "Together."

Catherine shook her head free of Diana's hand. She looked away, and she laughed softly. Wickedly.

"No," Catherine said. "We can't leave here. Not ever."

Diana sat down on the bed, unable to stand any longer. Her mouth felt dry. She tried to swallow, and couldn't.

"Your coming here was no accident, Diana," Catherine said at last. "Not really."

Diana said nothing.

"I suppose I can tell you this now," Catherine said. "There's nothing you or I or anyone can do about it now, anyway. Well, especially you. You're not going to fool me or anybody else. You're stuck."

"What," Diana said, "do you mean?"

"I mean that you're like me. You're the other half of me—the *counterpart*. Mother and Sterling have been looking for you for years . . . and maybe I have, too. But as usual, it's a disappointment."

Diana took a deep breath. "I'm not the friend you'd hoped for?" Diana almost laughed.

Catherine laughed haughtily. "What do you think all those experiments were about? They're about mind control. About taking control of the brains and the will of this little county."

Diana cocked her head. She was hearing what Catherine was saying, but she couldn't be sure if it was the truth, or just another game.

"Telegraphing, mindsweeps, brain sampling, eavesdropping—whatever it is we want to call it, it's about power, Diana. Political power. And it's getting more and more refined. In fact, I'll let you in on a little secret. We can cause accidents. Bad accidents. Don't look so surprised. We've done it before, but not on the grand scale Sterling is planning for us."

"I won't do it," Diana protested.

"Just like you won't have bad dreams, and you won't have me eavesdropping in your head?" Catherine asked. "You'll do it, Diana. You will. You see, we're going to arrange a little accident for someone. Nessie Jasper."

"Your mother's opponent . . ." Diana said.

"Same. And we'll do it from right here. We won't even lift a finger."

"But your mother, how can she participate in something so . . . so *evil*?"

Catherine rolled those sparkling blue eyes.

"How could she not? She's going to lose her election if some people don't die, don't you get it? In an accident, mind you. They will die in an accident, or so it will seem. And everything Mother has ever worked for will remain *whole*."

Catherine yawned and it turned into a gasp. She shook her head and smiled. Smiled like a kid who has just won a game of Go Fish, knowing that she cheated. She raised her arms and ran her fingers through her short blond hair.

"We are not going to fail," Catherine said.

Diana took in a deep breath.

"Theda knows all about us," Catherine said. "She knows all about you. Of course she's known about me and my *gift* for years. Since I was a baby. Since I was a kid. Why do you think she brought Sterling here in the first place? Why do you think she poured so much money into building this research facility? Because *she wants to use the power she has at hand*! 'Course now she has to, she has no choice.''

Catherine yawned again, leaned her head back dreamily. "She read about Sterling in the newspapers, years ago," Catherine said. "She knew that she had something powerful in me. What she didn't know was that it takes two to tango, or to direct these powers. Sterling figured all that out. He's really a genius, you know. Knows all about mixing the forces of light and dark, and piecing together what he calls a unified wave. You see, Diana, we needed you. Your parents fell for the bait. Understood they had someone they needed to get rid of."

"That's not true!" Diana cried.

Catherine's face crumpled into an ugly frown. "Yes, yes, yes, it is true, don't be daft. They had money and they could afford us. They matched your symptoms with Sterling's less-than-orthodox methods in our non-stigmatizing, oh-so-out-of-the-way little clinic. So they found us, made arrangements, and they brought you here, to have your dreams analyzed and your head shrunk, all quite off the record, all here in the remote, discreet splendor of Blackburn County. Where we were waiting. Waiting, Diana, for so many years."

Diana shook her head. Closed her eyes tight.

"And you arrived, right on time, to help us with our meddlesome old-timers," Catherine said. She took hold of Diana's wrists. "Can't you just see it?" Catherine said. "Can't you see them all going over the edge at Ice Rock? Fifty of them. A hundred! An accident. And Nessie Jasper with them."

Diana sputtered, "No . . . how could we possibly—"

"Any day now. The first snowfall. The town drunks, dancing at the edge of their favorite local cliff—Nessie, too. And off they go. We put little ideas in their heads. They become lemmings, racing toward death with a purpose."

"No," Diana whispered.

"If you can dream it, you can do it," Catherine said with a leer.

"I couldn't," Diana said. "Commit murder? Push people over the edge of Ice Rock?"

"Oh, yes you could. All it takes is a little creative visualization."

"I won't!" Diana cried.

Catherine closed her eyes.

As if you had a choice!

Diana stood up now. She ran to the door. She turned the handle, but of course the door was locked. She pounded on the door.

"Knock it off," Catherine said. "You're gonna wake the dead."

Diana turned to hear Catherine giggling beneath her bed-covers.

Diana ran to the bed and pulled the covers off Catherine. She grabbed her by the hair and pulled. Catherine screamed.

"I'm not going along with this!" Diana said. "I'm not helping you! You fool—don't you realize you're falling for your mother's trick? You don't have to go along with it! We could both escape from Blackburn County, from this . . . this *nightmare*!"

Diana was too weak now to fight, and Catherine was angry.

"As if I could trust you," Catherine hissed, scratching Diana's arm with her nails.

Diana felt a hot burn and then sticky wetness. The scratch was deep. Catherine broke free of Diana's grasp, and fell on the floor at the foot of her bed.

"You're confused," Diana screamed at Catherine. "You don't know who to trust. One moment you want your mother's love and approval, and the next you want her dead."

"Maybe I want *you* dead," Catherine said. She thrust her hand beneath the bed. Out came the wooden box where she kept her art supplies. She fumbled the lid open and withdrew the scissors.

She waved them in front of Diana.

Diana fell backwards against the bed. "No!" she cried. She screamed.

"You're never getting out of here," Catherine screamed. "You've touched down in an evil place, Diana. Blackburn County, a place where you finally fit in, finally! Only you're not becoming a part of it—it's becoming a part of you!''

Catherine lunged at Diana with the shining scissors, and the point of the blades snagged into Diana's nightshirt.

Diana screamed again.

The blade tore through the fabric, and into the air as Diana fell backwards.

There came some jiggling at the bedroom door handle. Keys jangled.

''Help!'' Diana screamed, though she realized, pulling at the rags of her nightshirt, that she'd not been cut.

The bedroom door flew open. Sterling, a black bag in his left hand, caught hold of Catherine's raised arm. He saw the scissors in Catherine's hands. His eyes bulged out.

''Catherine!'' he shouted, violently yanking her arm.

Catherine dropped the scissors. She turned her back to Sterling and ran over to the window, chest heaving.

''Now do you believe me?'' Diana pleaded to Sterling.

''You'd better do something about her,'' Catherine said tersely to Sterling, not looking at him.

He was already withdrawing a syringe and a small amber vial from his black bag.

''You never learn, do you Catherine?'' he muttered, taking Diana's arm.

Diana screamed, and fell back weakly upon her bed. She had barely a drop of fight left in her. She quaked now, thinking of the scissors, and seeing the needle he was preparing for her.

''Why?'' she said, her voice a trembling whisper. He swabbed her arm with an alcohol-soaked cotton ball. He didn't answer her. His hand on her arm was crushing. She tried to squirm across the bed, but he actually put his knee into her stomach, and pressed her against the wall with it, never once really looking in her eyes.

She felt the prick of the needle. The tranquilizer flowing into her bloodstream worked instantaneously. He released her, and she slunk down on the bed, her eyelids already drooping. She was paralyzed, drifting to sleep, the room whirling about her.

Sterling lifted his leg off her and turned to Catherine, enraged.

"You haven't learned a thing!" he shouted. "Think you can get away with it again, do you!"

Diana, sinking fast, hung on his words.

"Sometimes I wish your mother had never contacted me and begged for my help, aroused my curiosity," Sterling raged at her. "Kill this one, Catherine, and there will be no easy hiding place for another dead best friend. Moreover, the entire project would collapse! Can't you understand that?"

Catherine angrily tried to push past him, but he grabbed her by the arm and flung her around.

She stood directly over Diana now. With her face a mask of rage, Catherine lifted her foot and brought it down hard on the bed next to Diana. The bedsprings squeaked.

Slowly they squeaked, slowly and heavily. As Diana drifted off to sleep, the springs sounded to her like great metal jaws, like the screams of dying birds. It was as if she was on a slow-motion sea, on a raft, the waves carrying her up and down, up and down, until her vision blurred and the room faded.

Diana could barely hear, just beyond the room, from somewhere not quite real, the crystal tinkle of a tiny bell.

Chapter Eight

Randy turned the radio dial, trying to tune in a weather report between all the fuzz and static and country twang. Sure looked nasty today, he thought, looking through the dirty windshield. His bare hands felt cold on the steering wheel. Lost his gloves again. At last a voice came in clear over the radio speakers mounted in the back window ledge. The reporter confirmed Randy's suspicions about the gathering darkness. It was a little past noon, and you could feel the heaviness of the cold clouds pressing down.

"Looks like we are finally gonna get some snow, and what a snowstorm, folks. A doozy of a blizzard has been predicted by the National Weather Service," the radio announcer said. *"Travel advisories are out, schools are closing early. Get yourselves home and keep it tuned to W—"*

Randy flicked off the dial. In the back seat of the car were two loaded rifles. Nothing unusual about that. Only thing unusual was he didn't have his regular hunting partner. He took the exit off the highway where the blue hospital sign was posted, as he always did when skipping school. The storm would keep him from hunting today. What a drag, he thought. But if it really did snow tonight, tomorrow there would be one hell of a celebration. Up at Ice Rock. At least for the old-timer people of Blackburn County. And after the celebration, he and Jon could hunt pheasants. If they sobered up enough.

Damn that old Jon, Randy thought. Ever since he got in trouble for sleeping in class he'd refused to play hooky and hunt with him on school days. He was turning into a regular goody-goody. Studying and working, working and studying. What a life.

Then again, Randy might have expected as much from a boy like Jon, who came from such a weird, eccentric family. Eccentric even by Blackburn County standards.

He supposed it was only a matter of time till Jon weirded out completely.

Randy passed by the old four-story hospital, Mercy General, a grimy sprawling place where Jon worked most nights. He turned left by the big brown brick church with its dilapidated transept spire and clock that had stopped working years ago, and he turned up Main Street. He noticed the big sign that read RECALL THEDA PRICE. He didn't see Corky Marshall. Not until he was almost bearing down on him.

Randy slammed on the brakes. The old town drunk looked up through the windshield and into Randy's eyes. The car was skidding on dry concrete now, tires smoking to a screeching halt. The car rocked on its suspension system, and was still.

Corky stood there in front of the car, eyes bloodshot. He blinked, pulled off his black knit cap and ran his hand through white wisps of hair. He put his hand on the trunk of the car and braced himself up, seeming to mutter to himself. Randy hadn't seen the old drunk up close in a while. And now he was so close he could count the veins on Corky's swollen red nose.

With his heart racing, Randy rolled down his window.

"You stupid old sonofabitch," Randy cried. "Why don't you look where you're goin'?"

Corky swallowed sheepishly. "Well . . . I . . ."

"You coulda been killed, old-timer," Randy said. He threw the car into reverse. Turning his head to watch over his shoulder, he stomped on the gas pedal and lurched backwards.

Corky lost his balance and fell forward. Fell first to his knees and then down and smacked his face on the pavement. Randy squealed by him, leaving a cloud of brown exhaust hanging over the street, where Corky lay.

Two of the older "wives" stood on the corner. They'd seen the whole thing. "Tsk," one of them remarked. They held their purses tight and peered out from their shabby wool scarves, until Randy was gone.

Then they ran into the street to help Corky. He was on all fours, his face black with soot from the street, eyes blinking.

"Yuh must be more careful, Mr. Marshall," said the one with the taped-together glasses, her hand on his arm. She looked up at the darkening sky.

"Aye," Corky said, and coughed. "This town ain't safe no more."

The wives helped him to his feet, and brushed off his dirty clothes and they walked him to the curb.

"I thank you," he said primly. "Thank you most kindly." And he turned toward the direction of the Great Northern Pub. His nose was bleeding.

"You'd best be gettin' home, Mr. Marshall," said the stouter woman. "Gonna snow. Fierce weather tonight."

But he paid them no mind. He turned his back to them and looked up at the sky now, feeling his heart lighten almost at once. Snow, he thought, and smiled, showing a few brown teeth. At last it will snow. Only right and proper to raise a glass, to the snow.

He pushed open the door to the pub and the sound of the jingling bells made him happy.

The wives shook their heads in dismay.

Theda, dressed in one of her red blazers and skirts, a black-and-green paisley scarf over her shoulders, walked out of the North Hearing Room at the State Capitol in Madison. Heels sounding on marble. Lobbyists in dark suits leaned against the pale yellow marble walls and spoke into cell phones. Theda was eager to get on the road. The hearing on food pantries for the poor was over. She'd already instructed one of her aides to cancel her late afternoon meetings.

"Theda," someone called, a man. She turned and saw Brice Fenton, a reporter for *The Milwaukee Listener*. More an institution than a mere reporter, he was known as the "toothless lion" around the Capitol. His paper had been rumored for years to be on its last legs. "Do you have five minutes?" he asked, pen in hand. He shambled toward her.

Brice was about sixty and thickset. His editors had transferred him from Milwaukee to Madison after his divorce, back in the eighties. Now he covered the legislature, in a rather half-hearted way. His social life was his job, and his job seemed to consist mainly of friendly after-hours drinks with just about anybody who felt like talking, liberal, conservative, raving lunatic—all stripes welcome. Most politicians were only too happy to sit down and talk with Brice because he went easy on everybody, even "embattled" politicians like Theda. His days of stirring up trouble were over, it seemed.

"Hurry up, Brice," Theda said with a smile, "I want to get on the road. We're expecting a hell of snowstorm up in Blackburn County, and I want to beat it home."

"I heard," Brice said, smiling, showing his dentures. "Statewide radio news network is reporting lightning and thunder up there in the north. Lightning and thunder in a *winter* storm. Now that's rare."

Cut the polite bullshit, Theda wanted to say. She had a very uneasy feeling around reporters, especially these days. Even a laid-back old cat like Brice Fenton might show his claws. She had to be careful.

"Yes, very rare," she said, stopping at the rail that looked out over the rotunda. A few people milled around under the twenty-story-high dome. A huge Christmas tree was surrounded by a scaffold. Voices echoed through the ornate galleries.

"I wanted to talk to you for a moment about the recall election," Brice said.

Just as she had suspected. "Speaking of storms," Theda said with a smile. "And speaking off the record, of course."

Brice smiled, sort of sadly. "Okay, but I want to get some quotes from you that are *on* the record. But before we do that, I gotta tell you, Theda, it looks like you're in trouble. Not only is the recall election a go, you're facing some angry stares around this place.''

"The Ethics Board hasn't ruled yet, Brice. Ever hear the expression 'innocent until proven guilty'?''

"Some people say that your opponent, Nessie Jasper, is creating a populist wave that she's gonna ride right into your job.''

Theda smiled harshly. "The voters will decide, Brice, not political pundits in Madison.''

"They say your people have been trying to smear her as some kind of sex pervert.''

"Now that's false. Don't print that, don't say 'sex pervert,' Brice. I don't go in for that kind of cheap mudslinging.''

Expressionless, he flipped a page in his reporter's notebook.

"What about her firing from the public schools? Can you comment on that?'' he asked.

"I've never been the slightest bit interested in Nessie's history, or the way she was fired as a public school sex education teacher,'' Theda said. "That was a matter the school board decided, well within its rights. Not my jurisdiction, you see. On the other hand, Ms. Jasper has a past and she has to reconcile that with her wish to become a public servant, just as you or I would. The people have a right to know the facts, and to make up their own minds.''

"With a little help from your campaign committee?''

"If you print that I might have to sue the *Listener* for everything it's worth, which I hear isn't much. Maybe it's time someone put that tired old dog to sleep,'' Theda said with a smile.

"Yes, so they say,'' Brice said, grinning. "But some old dogs just have a way of hanging on and on.''

"Is that a vote of confidence for me?'' Theda said with a grin. Still smiling, Brice looked down at his worn-out brown shoes.

"Thanks for your time, Theda. Now you go beat that storm.''

He walked toward the stairs, fishing a cigarette from his breast pocket. She was pretty sure he hated her politics, always had and always would. Yet she had the distinct impression that he liked *her*, that he wasn't faking it. She was sentimental about such things. It helped take the edge off her bad mood for a few minutes.

She hurried to her West Wing office, to call Sterling. Her heart raced. Yes, it was going to snow at last. Plans were in motion.

Her office was in a recently remodelled wing of the Capitol, up on the fourth floor. She whisked past her staff, Doris and Hank, and went into to the smaller inner office where her desk was, and closed the door. Two small windows looked down over the grounds of the Capitol Square. She didn't turn on the brass light atop her neat desk.

She sat down on the large comfortable black chair.

The time of reckoning was drawing near.

She folded her hands together and closed her eyes.

She had the power now, she had to remind herself, though she took no pleasure in it. Hadn't really enjoyed her success in years, hadn't really cared about much else but preparing for this day, a day of atonement for those *bastards* who had always tried to put her down, to shove her out of the way.

She had a string of enemies who continually played through her mind, over and over, like worry beads rubbed smooth, except these feelings were never smooth, never easy. It always hurt to think about the people who didn't support her, didn't love her, were ungrateful to her. Who as much as said aloud she was a conniving loser.

Because of where she'd come from, and how she'd been raised, in rural poverty.

Oh, don't do this to yourself again, Theda, she thought. She tried to talk herself out of reviving these bitter scenarios. But they always tramped in like uninvited guests, one after the other. So used to getting their own way. The humiliations and defeats of a lifetime seemed to crowd around her.

She squeezed her hands together, feeling the pain.

She thought of her mother, now dead, and their dreadful farm that wasn't a farm at all, just a country shack . . . her father's madness, his ravings, Bible in hand . . .

"Stop this," she whispered to herself. But of course she

couldn't stop it, and as always when she was on a down-ward spiral like this she thought of her late husband Newall, the smiling young Blackburn County Board candidate who rescued her from that bitter life when she was only seventeen, and taught her about politics. Taught her about *power*.

As Theda Price saw it, Nessie Jasper was the main obstacle standing between her and the United States Congress.

Or prison.

Theda stood up and collected her papers, putting them into the alligator bag and snapping it shut. Her staff would be delighted to see her leaving, she knew, and she hated to give them the satisfaction.

But the storm was coming. She had to get out of Madison. She pressed the intercom button on her phone.

"Yes, Theda?" Doris answered.

"Have a page bring my car around," Theda said. And disconnected. On the desktop was a portrait of Newall. An informal shot that had been used in one of his campaign brochures, years ago. Open collar. Almost a smile. Not a good-looking man, by anyone's standards, certainly not Theda's.

Sometimes she couldn't bear to look at that photo.

Before she put on her coat and left the office, she turned the photo face down on her desk.

Night fell over Blackburn County at about three in the afternoon that day. It came in the form of dense clouds, towering into the sky, blocking out light, and it came with winds ripping down from beyond Canada, from the top of the world.

Now the clouds roiled together overhead in the gathering darkness. Thunder in wintertime was rare, but the atmosphere rumbled with it. Lightning flashed. More clouds were packed in, and the pressure grew.

Everything changed. All the elements in the atmosphere seemed pressed more tightly together. A farmer, walking from his barn to his house could hear his wife's voice, inside, on the telephone, as clear as if she had been standing next to him. In town, the streets emptied. The Great

Northern Pub closed early, a home-made sign saying CLOSED DUE TO WEATHER was taped onto the glass in the front door. The old school-bus driver dropped off the last kids on his rural route, and chugged home.

At about five P.M. the snow started to fall. Great flakes, wet and soft, fell down from the sky with a dense unceasing force. A sound like fragile, feather-light glass Christmas ornaments rustling together seemed to fill the valley. Children gazed with fascination out the windows of their darkened homes to watch the snow.

In minutes, the first layer of accumulation had covered the county, and every tree was frosted in white. Now the darkness contained a glow that shone over the miles.

Serilda stood at her open doorway, her orange cat in her arms. She stroked the big cat's head and watched the snow falling. The "Death Wish Traditions" would soon be underway again.

The cat yawned. Serilda closed the door, and felt a chill. A chill that she knew could only have come up out of the ground from these lands. Lands that spoke to her.

She was reminded of the bell, the bell she'd found in the woods so many years ago. *A charm against evil.*

It wasn't mere fate that brought the girls to her that day she'd been tangled in a thorny vine. No, that had not been left to chance, she decided.

Someone had discarded that bell, thrown it deep into the woods years ago, hoping it would never be found again.

The bell sought its owner. The forest had led the way.

Serilda sat down on an old soft chair, the cat purring in her lap. Above her head hung the strange bundles of herbs and dried flowers.

The dead were calling, howling from beneath layers of snow and earth. Staring into space, she stroked the cat's soft fur. Felt its purring rumble beneath layers of fur and skin and bone.

In Blackburn County, the dead had a way of returning.

Serilda closed her eyes, and she saw a river. Not the bucolic river of the Wisconsin countryside. A dark river, flaming beneath its black glassy surface as if reflecting a sunset. Yet this familiar river was far beneath the earth, in the blackest of caves; a primal river of antiquity. The river between life and death, a crossing that awaited every person.

Serilda listened to the snow.

The snow fell steadily into the night.

Theda, home now after a long, long drive and dressed in a green workout suit, sat at her kitchen table before the telephone. She was sweating from a workout on her exercise bike. Her legs felt stiff, but she was so full of nervous energy there was nothing to do but try to burn off some of it. She picked up the receiver, taking a draw on a cigarette. Konrad Sterling answered.

"Yes?" he said nervously.

"It's me," Theda said.

"Good, good . . ." There was a tremor in his voice she didn't like.

"What's wrong, Kon? We're all set, aren't we?"

"*Nothing* is wrong," he growled. "I'm having a mild case of nerves. So what? You know very well that success is not . . . guaranteed completely."

"If I know that already, then why remind me?" she said crossly. She looked out the window. Black night, endless snowfall. Roads were out for miles. The entire county was shut down, and would be all the next day. Most of the phone lines were dead, too; she was lucky to have reached Sterling, though she was not appreciating him very much at this moment.

"Diana is sleeping," Sterling said. "I had to sedate her."

Theda closed her eyes. "And Catherine? Is Catherine sleeping?"

"She's with Diana, keeping an eye on her."

Theda said nothing.

Sterling cleared his throat. "My darling, we must have faith. Even if the plan doesn't work, the beauty of it is there will be no fingerprints, no evidence, no witnesses. That is the glory of the transported mind." She heard the barely controlled excitement in his voice.

"Don't congratulate yourself just yet," Theda said.

He breathed into the phone, a desperate sigh. "I'm sorry, Theda . . ."

"Just make sure Diana wakes up on time tomorrow. Make sure she's up to the *task*."

"Ah, but Catherine has already succeeded in winning her over."

"So why is Diana sleeping under sedation then?"

Sterling cleared his throat. "Of course, she is a very disturbed child. Isn't sure what she wants or where her allegiances lie. But Catherine has the upper hand."

"Have you thought about what we're going to do with Diana when this is over?"

Sterling bit down on his lip. He bit hard. He thought if he bit any harder, blood would spurt out and spray across his face.

"It will never be over," he whispered. "If this works, darling, this is the beginning. Do you see? This is where it *all* starts."

"But if she causes trouble . . ."

"If she's too much trouble . . . we can dispose of her, but at a tremendous cost to my research and my life's—"

"That's all I wanted to know," Theda said.

She hung up the phone.

David lay in bed, the covers halfway up his naked chest, and paged through a magazine. He looked at a near-naked model, whom he guessed must have been about nineteen. She was Polynesian, the caption said, posing with some kind of suntan lotion in her hand. On a warm island halfway around the world from Blackburn County. He turned the page gently. His nipples hardened from the cool air fanned by the turning page.

His room was dark but for the pool of light from the reading lamp on the table next to his bed. He felt sleepy, his eyelids drooping. He turned a few more pages and yawned. Then he dropped the magazine on the floor and turned off the light. Pulled the covers up over his shoulders and turned onto his side.

He thought of Diana.

He knew that if he didn't stop thinking about Diana this

way it wouldn't be long before he would start doing anything she wanted. He might even start believing her.

If only . . .

What would it be like, he wondered, getting lost in a pleasant revery, to escape this cold place and go somewhere warm and tropical . . . with Diana at his side? To a beach with royal palm trees and white sand, and aqua-blue water shimmering with sunlight, like the kind he'd seen in magazine ads and in the movies. A place for just him and Diana.

He threw off the blanket and writhed upon the bed.

What was real was only a dark cold room in his mother's condominium, and the frigid air moving over his warm skin, now filmy with sweat. Outside his window there came the sound of the howling wind, heavy with falling snow.

He closed his eyes and whispered her name.

"Diana . . ."

Nights at Mercy General Hospital were usually quiet, but this night was *too* quiet, Jon thought. He closed the utility closet door, the pine scent of a disinfectant lingering in his nose. His hands were wet and he didn't have a paper towel, so he wiped them on the white coat he wore over his street clothes.

He walked down the hallway to a waiting room that always smelled faintly of burnt coffee. At this hour the room was empty, and all the visitors had gone home. That's where he would have liked to have been, too: home.

Looking out the big second-story picture window, he saw a sight that cheered him, a devastating, town-stopping blizzard. His face was reflected ghostlike in the window. He picked up the magazines that were strewn over the big low tables, and stacked them neatly. Then he turned off the light and went back to the window.

He looked down at the street. What a lonely town. Cars were blanketed in snow now. Even the streetlight was snow-shrouded, its white beam muted. And in the beam he could see the hard and steady snowfall that covered every roof and chimney. Smoke curled from the chimneys across the street, where yellow light glowed in the windows like a promise of safety and warmth. But not for him; for other people.

Jon didn't feel like a hero, even though Serilda had told him emphatically that if he hadn't found Diana she would have frozen to death. But it was all more or less a matter of luck, he decided. Of course he'd been by the old cottage in the woods before and knew that the old woman lived there. Yet what if he hadn't found the cabin that morning? Diana would have died. He couldn't bear to think how close a call it had really been.

He sighed, thinking of Diana, and of the way she was hustled back to that strange clinic in the woods. What would become of her now? Would she run away again? And what was she running from?

He and Randy had had too many bad experiences with cops around Blackburn County for him to call them for help. And even if he called them, what would he say? That a patient had run away from the clinic? Maybe such a call would get Diana into even deeper trouble.

Wearily he turned the lamp back on before leaving the room.

He knew he'd feel better in the morning. He thought of Ice Rock, and his heart lifted. Still, he felt a pang of longing and regret. Going to Ice Rock would certainly be a lot more fun if he could take Diana with him. That just didn't seem very likely, though. She had some kind of bad cold, he knew. And no doubt that creepy doctor would be keeping an eye on her.

And so would Catherine.

He silently cursed himself for not running away with her in the first place.

It didn't matter where. He'd have taken her anywhere she wanted to go.

Thousands of miles away, a hot tropical breeze carried the scent of hibiscus through the cabana. Evelyn Adams looked out over the patio table strewn with empty glasses at the night sea. She wore her sleek black one-piece bathing suit, her sunglasses still perched above her hairline even though it was night. She was a little drunk. Had been all day.

Jack came out of the bathroom, a robe on now. His gray, full head of hair was drying with the marks of a comb, and his nose was red with sunburn. He carried with him out to the patio a sweet, sharp smell of soap and shampoo. He sat his big frame down on the chair next to hers. She looked at his bare feet, red from the hot shower. He had a habit of placing the toes of one foot over those of the other, and fidgeting.

"Ah," he said. "Don't you love the sound of the surf? The smell of it." He breathed deeply. He was in good shape. And of course she'd been starving herself for him for years, so she was as slim and agile as he was.

She didn't say anything. They silently read each other's moods.

"Where's Brenda?" He put his hand high on her bare thigh, which was a bit greasy from the white sunblock she'd smeared on a couple of hours ago.

"She's at the disco, Jack. I told you that before you went in the shower."

"Things can change in an hour," he said. "I had the radio on in the shower. Did you know the Midwest is having a blizzard dumped on it right now, as we speak?" He grinned. He had a deep nasal voice, a heavy smoker's voice, even though he'd quit smoking. He slipped his glasses on.

She exhaled through her nostrils.

"I keep thinking about Diana," Evelyn said.

He rubbed her shoulder. "Of course you do."

She didn't care for that remark. Even though he'd probably meant it to sound comforting. It wasn't.

"Shouldn't we at least try to call her?" Evelyn asked.

His turn to sigh. "You've got more guts than I do," he said. "Frankly, I think it would ruin my vacation to be called a son-of-a-bitch over long distance by my own step-daughter. But if you feel like a fresh tongue-lashing, be my guest."

"She doesn't mean those things. That's not Diana talking. It's somebody else."

"Yes," he said, standing. "Exactly right. That's why we don't call her. That somebody else is taking a break and getting her head together—I hope to Christ—and I'll be happy to talk to the *real* Diana when she calls and apologizes.''

"If she's sick, why does she need to apologize?" Evelyn looked at her husband. Gray chest hair curled up out of the robe at his neck.

"Honey, you're here to relax, not to think about *her*. And you're ruining my surprise."

"What surprise?"

"I called Charlie. We're staying another five days."

Evelyn gasped and smiled, despite herself. She'd been dreading going home to Chicago. "Oh, Jack! Really? Oh, but what about Brenda, she's got school—"

"That's the good part," Jack said. "She's flying back home day after tomorrow. We'll be all alone."

Evelyn said, "She's not going to like that."

Jack frowned and hissed, "Well isn't that just too bad? Frankly, I'm a little tired of worrying about the sensitive feelings of those two spoiled brats."

She turned her face away. She didn't know if she wanted another stiff drink, or maybe one of her pills. She felt him nuzzle the back of her neck. He kissed her.

"Tomorrow we're going shopping," he said. "You can pick up that cute little emerald you've had your eye on."

She put her hand on his. What a cold bastard he was. He always made up with money and gifts the fact that he couldn't stand any of them—"you girls" he called them, casually dismissing them on his way out the door on a business trip, or to a mistress, the evidence of which was so overwhelming Evelyn herself had had to conspire not to notice what was going on. "You girls be good while I'm away," he'd say.

Sometimes Evelyn wondered who really deserved to be locked up in the bin—her daughter, with her bizarre nightmares, or herself.

Evelyn now took in a defiant breath through her nostrils and thought what a bore life was without emeralds. Emeralds were exciting things, with the kind of hard brilliance that seemed to blind her to the vicissitudes of fate. Emeralds helped wipe out memories of a hardscrabble Southern Illinois childhood, and of present-moment pain that was getting harder and harder to cushion with pills and expensive booze.

"That will be wonderful, darling," she said. She would take the drink *and* the pills, even though she wasn't supposed to. The combination hadn't killed her yet, though the kinds of drug combinations she'd been taking lately would have sent a normal woman into a coma, or worse.

"That's my baby," he said, kissing the top of her head. "I'm gonna run over to the disco and talk to Brenda," he said. "Don't worry. I'll bribe her." He winked and stepped into his sandals, then was off into the warm night.

She looked out at the black surf and felt a strange sensation. It occurred to her suddenly that she was actually becoming the poison she'd taken for so long.

Konrad Sterling felt like he was on the edge of a straight razor. Oddly enough, it was an exciting feeling for him. He sat at the computer console in his windowless laboratory, and in the dim blue light of the monitor he sipped bourbon and ice, and went over his notes. Papers were scattered atop the console and spilled onto the floor.

In here, without windows, the snowstorm that raged outside could not be seen or felt. Yet Sterling chuckled now, because he *thought* he could feel the snow. Thought he could sense the silence of the snow, and feel its racing cold freshness. Maybe he had a gift, too, he thought, smiling.

No such luck, he told himself. He was no more clairvoyant than a lion tamer is a lion, he told himself.

He set his drink down carelessly upon the console top and a bit of amber-colored liquid sloshed over the side of the glass.

The small round table where the young women would produce their unified mindfield was strewn with wires. He would carefully measure brain wave activity during the *event*. He would compile all of the data and add it to the several volumes of handwritten notes he'd kept over the years. This event would of course be his pièce de résistance and a major scientific discovery. Not that he expected his report to be published in the *Scientific American* or in any present-day scientific journal. But there were future generations to consider. They would know of his glory, even if in his lifetime only he would understand the full impact of his experiment.

Theda would be all the reward he could ever want, or a substantial portion thereof. He thought grandly of the old saying about the woman behind every great man.

Of course there would be those who would hate him, bleeding heart types who hated anybody with the tenacity to grasp and exploit real power. Yet couldn't these people (whoever they were) see that a greater good could be accomplished through a little evil? No matter, for he held the view that whoever wrote the history books would decide who would be cast as the good guy and who as the bad.

His work would continue, that was the main thing, and Theda would continue to champion his efforts.

He smiled, slapping his hand on his chin. And besides, he thought, who cares about public opinion? He was about to harness a force beyond morality. This was a matter of pure science, not one of politics or perceptions.

It involved the kind of risks most scientists didn't have the balls to take, Sterling thought; not if they knew what they were getting into. He had an inkling of what he was dealing with here, and it very nearly frightened him.

Here he was stirring up the hidden forces that existed within the very clay of Blackburn County, forces only he had the guts to exploit.

He had calculated that the region contained a field of energy that would enable unlimited experiments in extrasensory mind travel. It would be from here, someday, perhaps as little as a few years from now, that mankind would shed his space-bound, time-bound physical body and travel into the universe at a speed beyond light. The weightless astral body would seek and explore realms heretofore never imagined.

His mind reeled with the possibilities of it all. Mankind's space travel would not be bound by the need even for oxygen. The astral body wouldn't need air any more than one of his prized fish in its tank needed air! It could inhabit any form, travel any distance, it knew no limits. Its secrets resided in the manner of its control.

And finding the answers to these secrets begins here and now, Sterling thought, nearly giddy with anticipation. Barely able to contain his excitement, he poured out another glass of bourbon. His hands trembled badly.

"Just a little more," he said, looking at one of his tropical fish. "To steady the nerves." He reached out and tapped his finger on the aquarium glass.

The blue fish swished its tail and darted behind a heavy piece of bright purple coral.

In the blackness of night the snow fell. The massed clouds churned the snow down, blanketing the countryside. The old country churches looked like frosted Christmas confections, and the highways disappeared into the rolling white landscape.

In the dark, quiet room, Diana and Catherine slept in their respective beds, dreaming.

Diana had that odd sensation again of becoming aware that she was dreaming. Where was she? Floating in a black field. It was so strange, because she could see herself and now she could see something else. Serilda's enormous eyes, blazing in the dark.

Look!

Diana surmised she was in a kind of slipstream of consciousness, at the borderlands between dreams and memory. Moving toward a secret place that belonged to Catherine. As she crossed over into Catherine's sleeping mind, the whirling pictures that surrounded her now were oddly familiar—the flotsam of childhood, birthday cakes and dollhouses . . . and childhood friends.

Catherine's.

Out of the fuzziness of a kind of Super 8 movie-memory came a clear scene . . . a shard of memory? Or just the haunted illusion and symbolic imagery of dreams? Diana felt afraid.

Serilda's golden eyes narrowed.

It's only a dream, Diana told herself.

No, Diana.

Serilda's voice!

What a strange place, Diana thought as she moved deeper inside. This was a dark place, like some Biblical garden at night, stars overhead in a clear onyx sky. A long-ago spring night.

Now faint light pulsed over the scene and she could see palm fronds moving aside, and smell something like fresh flowers. She wasn't outside at all, but in a bedroom. A child's bedroom.

She was frightened and tried to turn away from what she was seeing: the twin beds pushed up against opposite walls of the room. On the walls were Muppet posters. A huge open toy box was stuffed with dolls and storybooks.

She knew this room. It was Catherine's bedroom, just as it must have looked ten years ago. The large bay windows, the door to the private bath—she recognized this place.

Diana felt her heart racing with terror as she saw the blond-haired little girl standing over her sleeping friend, a huge knife in her tiny hand. Frozen there like a figure in a wax museum chamber of horrors, eyes closed.

Catherine . . .

"Catherine!" Diana cried, "Don't do it! No!"

She tried to disturb this scene, to stop Catherine and save the sleeping child, Vaundra Austin, whom Diana recognized from the old newspaper articles.

But of course the young Catherine couldn't hear her—how could she? She wasn't real. These children were the figments of a dream, were they not?

Or something real, frozen forever in a terrible memory.

Diana wanted very much to stir herself awake, to flee this nightmare. But she couldn't.

Diana shouted again to Catherine: "Stop! Before it's too late!"

But the children couldn't hear her voice. Diana was no more than an invisible kind of ghost in this place.

She could not wake the child, whose round sleeping face was composed in an expression of consternation. She breathed in and out, lips parting slightly, small hands gripping the tops of the covers. Her hair lay across the white pillow, just as it always would. For, Diana now understood, this memory was etched vividly not in stone but in something almost as permanent, and could never change.

What happened was here forever, locked vault-like in Catherine's skull, a frozen possession.

This was not a flight of fancy or an abstraction, Diana knew. No more than the newspapers she'd read in the basement of the public library were abstractions. She had once again found what she'd come looking for. Her powers were indeed stronger now, just as Catherine had promised. Like a computer hacker, she'd "accessed" a hidden file from Catherine's memory. She was sure of it. And it seemed Serilda was helping her make these discoveries.

Yet now Diana couldn't bear to watch what her mind grasped and turned over and over, like a strange stone in her hand: another person's most private horror.

The knife rose in timeless darkness.

Why, Catherine? Why?

And now Diana could not watch. Could not bear to see. But how can you stop a memory of murder? It could not be erased, ever. It played out again and again, over and over.

The knife came down in the darkness.

How many times have you replayed this memory, Catherine? *For this is the hell only a killer could know.*

Diana screamed, yet it came out as soundless as a shadow.

She wondered, do killers bury these memories in ways ordinary people never could? Memories ordinary people would probably be driven insane by?

It sickened Diana to witness this crime in its shadow version, a burnished and darkened memory, careworn through endless repetition. Something dark and buried, but endlessly returning like a monster that refuses to die. And now the images were themselves frozen, and glowed like a series of lantern slides. Theda, younger, rushing into the dark, dreamy room. The light coming on, flashing the room to ugly brightness like the sudden appearance of a white leering skull. The bed, the wall, splattered red.

Theda's scream.

Then blackness.

And then it started over again. Catherine standing before

the bed again. Vaundra's last moments alive, sleeping. The vision sped by this time in fast motion.

"No!" Diana cried out. "Make it stop!"

Diana felt as though suddenly buoyant on a wave of pure memory, shuttling forward. She seemed to float away from the room—or were the images sliding away from her? She could only hang onto herself, like a skydiver waiting and hoping for a parachute to open, to gently return her to earth.

Blackness again, and then she was swooping over tree-tops, coming at last to a stop above a hill, over which she seemed to float. She saw herself hovering there, hair floating about her face like a swimmer's.

Below her was the Albion Clinic, half-built and skeletal. It rose from a wooden shell as workmen spun around it like ants. Nights and days passed like a strobe light flickering. In seconds, the structure was nearly complete.

Night again. Stars in a spring sky.

Diana saw Theda and Sterling, as they were ten years ago, emerging from a car, where Catherine sat, face expressionless. They carried something under cover of night into the empty clinic. Something wrapped in blankets. It took the two of them to carry it. Construction rubble lay all about the muddy grounds.

What they carried looked in the dark like a small, rolled-up carpet. But it was not a carpet. The sound of a small bell rang delicately as Diana felt herself swimming upward to consciousness.

"Vaundra," she whispered, her face turned skyward. She kicked and swam toward the stars—

—and broke through the dark surface—

Abruptly, the connection to Catherine's memory was severed—the picture went blank, like an unplugged TV. White light flooded in.

Diana awoke with a start, blinking. The room seemed to shift into focus all at once. She turned her head to see Catherine coming awake, rubbing her eyes.

Catherine raised her head and looked over at Diana. Her blue eyes were sunken, and the whites of her eyes gleamed. Her face was composed in a zombie-like mask.

Diana lurched in her bed, pressing herself up against the wall.

Catherine yawned and her eyes seemed to clear and come into focus. Diana pulled the covers up to her throat. The room was so bright, it hurt Diana's eyes. It was morning.

"It snowed last night," Catherine said, pushing off her covers and swinging her feet around to the floor. "Come on, time to get up."

Catherine's voice was deep, as if it were somehow slowed down. Her eyes still looked sunken. Something was wrong.

Diana swallowed hard. Did Catherine know Diana had been eavesdropping on her? Surfing through her darkest memories? Catherine just stood there with this blank expression on her face.

The memory of the murder was buried in there, behind those gleaming blue eyes and beyond that fresh smile she was showing now, teeth bared.

"Didn't you hear me?" Catherine said. She kind of winced. "It *snowed* last night." Catherine turned and stretched, staring out the window. "And you know what that means."

Diana felt herself shaking. It meant the Death Wish Traditions at Ice Rock. It meant an "accident." It meant mass murder.

"I know about Vaundra," Diana blurted. "I know about it, all of it."

Catherine slowly turned her head. She forced a bitter smile, which fell almost as quickly, and she said in a droning voice, "Crawling around inside my head, were you?" She grinned. The blue of her eyes rolled up, so that only the whites were showing again. She grinned madly. "That's a lie, Diana," she said.

"You killed her," Diana said softly, climbing out of her bed, enraged. "I know all about it. You murdered Vaundra, and now you want to make a killer out of me!"

Diana lunged at Catherine. Catherine fell back with a heavy thud against the wall beside her bed. A lampshade on the table next to her tipped down like a spy's hat. Diana pinned Catherine to the wall, holding on tight to her wrists.

"Ouch!" Catherine wailed. "You're cutting into me with your nails." Now her voice was its usual tone again, agitated and bossy.

"This is our last chance to get out of here!" Diana screamed. "Don't you understand that? We could use our powers against Sterling and your mother, instead of *for* them! We could get help for you, don't you realize that?"

Catherine's blue irises rolled down. She looked at Diana and she said, mockingly. "You're too much, you know that?"

Diana let go of Catherine's wrists. She moved away from the bed. Catherine rubbed her arms.

"Look, just go along with me, just this once," Catherine said. "Be a friend instead of a fucking traitor."

"A traitor?" Diana said. "A traitor against *what*?"

"I thought you were different," Catherine said. "I thought you were my friend. But you're not, you're just like everybody else."

"If only that were true," Diana said, and ran to the window and looked outside. The view was dazzling, a bright white scene of winter splendor. The gently sloping hills were covered in white, and the tall pines were thickly frosted with perfect, fluffy fresh snow. It was like a dream.

"Come on," Catherine said. "It's time to give it up. You're beaten."

Diana remembered something else. The bell! It entered her mind in a flash of anger, but she quickly took a breath and counted to ten. It was critical that she remain cool and calm if she was really going to defeat Catherine. And she wanted to now, more than anything. She took another deep breath. Her mind raced.

The bell is a charm against evil, she reminded herself. Had Catherine given it to her mother? Did she understand its significance?

Catherine pulled a white fuzzy sweater over her head and went into the bathroom. Diana pulled her jeans on and rushed over to Catherine's dresser, and quietly opened the drawer.

It had to be in the room somewhere. She pushed socks and underwear aside and found nothing but lipsticks and a few coins, a pack of peppermint gum and a box of matches.

Diana closed the dresser drawer. Catherine was humming in the bathroom, the door slightly ajar.

"If you're looking for the key to the door, save your energy," Catherine called from the bathroom. "I have it in here."

Diana gulped. "Of course you do," Diana answered.

She looked at Catherine's bed. With a wary glance at the bathroom door, she went quickly to the bed and slipped her hand beneath the covers. Came up empty-handed.

If Catherine had tried to discern the power of the bell, and found it useless, would she have thrown it away? Or would she have kept it somewhere, for safekeeping? Diana did not discount the possibility that Catherine had recognized the bell as a possession of Vaundra's, even though it had been ten years since the murder. Yet hadn't Catherine famously repressed all her memories of Vaundra? Hidden them in that secret, locked room in her mind?

Diana slipped her hand between the mattresses. Fished frantically. An old gum wrapper fell to the floor.

"You know, I never should have cut my hair," Catherine called from the bathroom. "I can't do a bloody thing with it. You weren't worth it, Diana." Catherine sighed and giggled. Diana heard the spritz of hairspray.

Diana had her whole arm, up to her shoulder, between the heavy mattresses. Still, she felt nothing there. She hoped Catherine wouldn't come out of the bathroom and catch her. She withdrew her hand and sighed with frustration.

She looked up at the stack of books on the desk. There, at the bottom of the stack, was the thick old edition of the *Complete Works of William Shakespeare*. Where Catherine had hidden the leaf that blew into the room that first day when she and Diana had really started to get to know one another.

Diana had the funniest feeling about that book. But how could you hide a bell in a book?

She stood up and glanced at Catherine, still fussing with her hair in the mirror. The tangy perfume of the hairspray wafted into the bedroom.

Diana pulled the heavy book from the bottom of the stack. The top book slipped, and almost fell to the floor; she caught it in her left hand. Looking at the bathroom door, she set the slim volume on the desk and lifted the heavier Shakespeare collection. She opened the book. Turned a few pages. And found, in the hollowed-out recess, the shining gold bell.

Its gold surface gleamed in the snowy light of the window. Picking it up, Diana was careful not to let Catherine hear it ringing. She put her finger up into the hollow of the bell. There must be some way to silence it at least until Catherine unlocked the door, she thought. She saw the gum wrapper on the floor. She bent down and picked up the paper. She quickly wadded it up and stuck it into the hollow of the bell.

"Oh, look out the window!" Catherine called from the bathroom, which had a window of its own. "Cars—heading up to Ice Rock!"

Diana shuddered, slipping the bell into the front left pocket of her baggy jeans. She hoped the bell wouldn't be noticeable. She wasn't sure how to use it, but she knew she needed it. She almost smiled, thinking of Serilda. Would have smiled if her heart wasn't pounding in her throat. Then she went again to the window. Sure enough, a caravan of cars was heading slowly up the snowbound highway in the direction of Ice Rock.

"We're going to Ice Rock, too," Catherine said, flicking off the bathroom light and coming back into the room. "But in a different way, a way you can barely imagine— Oh—"

Diana spun around. Standing in the doorway was Sterling. He had opened the bedroom door without a sound. When? How long had he been standing there watching?

"What did you just put in your pocket?" he asked Diana, eyes small and red.

Catherine cocked her head, looking suspiciously at Diana.

"Nothing," Diana said glumly.

He held out his hand.

"Give it to me, now," he said, coming closer.

With a sinking heart, Diana reached into her pocket. She was going to pull the bell out. She'd ring it now—ring it for all she was worth; maybe this would be her only chance.

Before she could get the bell out of her pocket Sterling put his hand on her wrist. Slowly he withdrew her hand from the pocket. When he saw the bell emerge his eyes widened.

"What is this nonsense about?" he demanded, looking at the small bell. He snatched it from her hand and shook it. Not a sound came forth, the paper inside held tight.

"Hey!" Catherine said. "That's mine!"

"Never mind," Sterling said, putting the bell into his lab coat pocket.

"You goddamn little thief!" Catherine said. "I might have known."

David walked in just at that moment, a large wicker laundry basket in his arms. Diana was sure he'd seen the bell go into Sterling's pocket. He looked into Diana's eyes.

"I was just here to collect . . ."

"Get out of here!" Sterling bellowed at David, completely unnerved by the sudden presence of someone behind him. David, in a baggy sweatshirt and jeans, looked back at Diana.

David turned and started out of the room. Diana tried to cry out. Sterling roughly put his hand over her mouth.

"Keep going, David," Sterling shouted. "This is none of your affair—don't turn around, just leave here at once."

David hurried out of the room. Sterling kicked the door shut. He removed his hand from Diana's mouth and shoved her onto her bed.

Diana cried out.

"Not a word!" he screamed at her. Catherine stood with her arms crossed over her chest.

Sterling looked hard at Diana. She felt her palms sweating. A throb in her temples.

"You like David, don't you Diana?" Sterling said. She didn't answer. "Now you're going to do exactly as I say, or David is going to have an accident. A very painful accident, from which he will never fully recover. Do you understand? He would never be able to walk again—much less dance." He leered at her.

Trembling, Diana nodded.

"Good!" he shouted in her face. "Now come with me!"

He stalked out of the room, leaving the door open.

Catherine gestured to the door with her hand, palm up-turned.

"It's *time*, Diana. Let's go."

Chapter Nine

They tramped through the snow, just as they had for generations. Men and women, young and old, tramping to Ice Rock just as their parents had, and their grandparents before them.

Old Corky Marshall was helped along by the "wives" and their husbands, children, too, through deep drifts and over roads buried in snow. Elders and young people, left their cars by the roadside and took to the country trails.

Though their numbers were fewer now, the old-timers pressed on. They sang like soldiers, made merry by the sight of fields and pastures that blazed white with snow, and by the majesty of the snow-covered pines and evergreens, and by whisky and ale.

They laughed and jostled one another, but even the youngest among them felt a kind of exhilarating fear, for each citizen was afraid of something dark beneath the snow, and something darker inside themselves, something that called them to Ice Rock.

This nervousness helped to push them on, up the steep trail, and when a man hooted and howled in exultation, the country people laughed and smiled. Yet even the oldest and the deafest among them could hear the slight edge of desperation in such a scream.

Jon put the mouth of the open whisky bottle to his lips and threw back his head. The snow had stopped coming down, and the sky was as white as the rolling fields and the sloping grade that led to Ice Rock. In the top of a tall pine he now stood under he saw the small, fat winter birds, perched on snow-covered boughs. Clusters of pine cones were frosted white. Men passed by him, singing. Randy slapped his back, making him cough on the whisky.

"Come on, Jon!" Randy cried. "Let's not be the last ones up there!"

Jon handed the bottle to his friend. Both were bundled in heavy winter parkas. Randy wore a multi-colored Guatemalan knit cap that came to a high peak, with large ear flaps that dangled on either side of his head. His long dark hair fell across his face as he laughed. With gloved hands, he pushed his hair aside, and drank.

Some Blackburn County "wives" tramped past them, giggling.

"You'd better hurry," one of them said, and smiled, revealing several gaps where teeth had once been. Jon pulled his small black knit cap down over his ears, which he imagined must have been as red as Randy's nose was. It was cold out here, but not bitter cold. Instead, the cold was fresh and bracing. A feeling that thrilled him as much as it thrilled all the others.

"To the Death Wish Traditions!" Corky roared, stumbling by. He wore a furry brown cap made of some kind of animal.

"I'll drink to that," Randy said, and took another long swig, toasting the old man he'd nearly run over in the street.

Jon put his hands into the pockets of his parka and tramped along. He had the kind of gloves on that had openings at the second knuckle. Randy handed him the bottle and he shook his head.

"Come on," Jon said, "let's get up that hill."

They came to a wood with a clearing, and a steep grade. Pines heavy with snow stood like sentries on either side of the path, upon which the Blackburn County old-timers began their giddy climb. People were laughing and falling down, and a young tall Nordic-looking guy, with short blond hair, strummed a guitar, while another fellow, a fat, short red-faced young man, squeezed a tune out of an accordion. It was not clear to Jon whether the two were playing the same song. He didn't recognize the words or the tune.

"Come on!" shouted the stout man with the accordion, his black moustache slick with melted snow. "To Ice Rock!"

Up the grade they climbed, Jon and Randy following along, feeling a rush of excitement.

At the end of the trail, a lone woman followed at a distance. Theda would not be recognized with the hood of her old gray wool coat pulled up high, and the wide red scarf pulled around her face just above her nose. Only her eyes remained unveiled, and they gleamed intensely in the white radiance. The snow-light seemed to stir liquid energy into those green crystal eyes of hers, like dawn pulsing through cathedral glasswork.

She would see with these eyes what others would never be able to believe second-hand. She could not resist the temptation.

Theda put her gloved hand to her throat. She could feel her heartbeat in her neck, and almost sense the blood rising into her face.

Slowly she climbed, boot-clad feet sinking in snow, sometimes to her knees; yet she kept a safe distance behind the others. Sparrows lighted in the bare, snowy branches, that were as fine and sharp as a cluster of thorns. The birds sang in their high voices.

At last she reached the base of the snowy plateau, where the Blackburn County old-timers massed noisily. She saw, at the head of the crowd, in her drab dark coat, Nessie Jasper. Nessie drank from a can of beer, and her bright smile shone across the nearly blinding white cliff-top. But she did not notice Theda, nor did any of the others.

Theda placed her gloved hands on the trunk of a wide black elm tree, and peered around it. From here she would be able to secretly observe everything.

David put his leather jacket on and looked outside the clinic's kitchen window. The grounds were deep in snow, with drifts up to six feet high. He absently rubbed his two days' growth of beard stubble. He knew that his mother had al-

ready joined some of the old-timer "wives" on their trek
to Ice Rock. She'd asked him to join her, of course. But
he'd told her he had a few more chores to attend to. He'd
catch up with her later, he'd explained.

He looked around warily. At last Sterling crossed
through the kitchen, Harriet following close behind him,
seeming to rattle off a list of grievances. He wore his long
white lab coat, the pocket of which contained the small bell,
David knew.

Sterling looked up at David and stopped.

"Still here?" he asked, somewhat irritated. "I thought
you'd be out at Ice Rock with your fellows by this time."

"Yes, sir," David said, feeling his heart seeming to buck
in his chest. "I needed to finish loading the garbage bags
onto the truck. I'm heading up to Ice Rock now."

"That truck's not going anywhere in this snow,"
Sterling said. "Probably won't be able to budge for a few
days. Don't worry about it. Have a good time up on that
rock," he said, and turned to leave.

"Thank you, sir," David said and opened the back door.
He stepped outside and closed the door behind him. Then
peered through the window into the kitchen. The cold wind
on the back of his neck raised gooseflesh.

When he was sure Sterling and Harriet were gone, he
quietly opened the kitchen door and stepped softly back
inside.

At the top of Ice Rock was a sheer plateau, flat as an ice-
skating rink. And completely snow-covered, open, and
lined with black elms, except at the cliff's edge, where the
ground rose slightly. Jon carefully knelt down there and
smiled broadly, looking out over the cliff's edge. The white
valley and distant white hills looked like something out of
a fantastic painting. A vast, soft, rolling whiteness, dotted
with tiny farms and trees. In the distance, the gray spire of
a country church pierced the overcast white sky.

Randy pushed him from behind, and Jon fell forward in
the soft snow, just a few feet from the drop. He turned on
his back just as Randy lunged on him, laughing. They wres-
tled in the snow, far enough away from the edge so as not

to truly endanger themselves. Yet Jon felt a little bit frightened. The sky and the valley whirled around him.

Now they rolled closer to the edge, and Jon felt his heart pounding. A fall would be certain death. He was able to get hold of a handful of snow, and now he tossed it in Randy's face, and Randy, still laughing, released him.

Some of the men were singing now. Jon saw someone trying to get through the thick crowd.

"Let me by," said a woman in a bold, deep voice. Nessie Jasper.

"Let her through," called a man in red-and-black checks. "It's Nessie, our next great member of the state assembly!"

"With any luck!" Nessie cried, and laughed. Nessie came close to the cliff's edge, and gazed out, eyes taking in with wonder the spectacular valley view.

"Yes," he said, beaming, "and then it's on to the governor's office!"

"Hear, hear," cried some others.

Jon peered over the edge of the cliff. Randy breathed heavily next to him. A bit of snow spilled over the side and fell like an old dish towel, turning and disappearing, never quite landing; being blown away, high over the jagged, snow covered rocks far below.

Jon looked up and saw the winter birds. Fifty or more. Flying over the assembly of revelers. Then he saw a flash of red in the white branches of an old elm. A lone male cardinal sat perched high above, seeming to take in all the madness below him. For now, some of the men, about seven of them, had linked arms. Together they kicked their legs into the air, then bowed. They came squatting down together, and again slowly rose, each time moving ever closer to the edge, as the watchers urged them on.

"Hiiiii-eeeiii!" cried an old man, and he threw his head back, an amber bottle draining into his mouth. Jon recognized the old town drunk, Corky Marshall. A streak of clear fluid ran from the old man's puckered lips down his jaw to his neck.

Jon watched the dancers with fascination. He wondered

if he'd ever have the courage—or the madness—to join
them.

"Crazy fuckers," he said with a grin.

Randy, whose eyes were already glassy with drink, nodded. "Yesssss," Randy slurred. "To the Death Wish
Traditions!" He drank and handed Jon the bottle. Jon
smiled and drank ravenously, letting the whisky burn his
throat. Some of the women had linked arms and were whirling themselves around, "crack-the-whip" style, and laughing hysterically. And singing

> *We are pioneers*
> *Brave pioneers*
> *Men and women*
> *Young and old*
> *Fearless and bold*
> *And we'll go to our graves*
> *Unafraid*
> *Not afraid*

Jon saw the little boy hurl the snowball at him, but not
in time to duck out of the way.

The snow splattered off his face with a wet shocking
chill. He heard Randy laughing, and started to laugh himself, the bitter-tasting slushy snow running into his mouth.
Jon swallowed and coughed, and before he knew it, he was
being pulled off his feet into the rough throng of singing,
shouting old-timers.

> *We who never sleep*
> *We who never die*

The sleek laboratory was as dark as usual, and as far removed from the bright world just beyond its walls as it
could possibly be.

The blue squares of the banks of computer monitors
shone like cloudless summer sky. The big aquariums
glowed in the gloom. And a thin white beam from the artificial galaxy-strewn ceiling shone down upon the simple
round black table.

Diana was seated next to Catherine. Catherine wouldn't look at her.

That was okay. It helped Diana stay calm not to have those angry blue eyes of Catherine's fixed upon her.

Be cold, Diana told herself. Stop all feeling . . . Catherine mustn't know a thing . . .

If it were possible to cease to exist at that moment, Diana would have. No memories, no feelings. No fear.

But even thinking this, she felt her palms beginning to sweat. Catherine, in her faded gray sweater, now looked over at Diana. The slightest smile appeared on her lips. She was trying to get inside.

Diana felt anger rising in her. A hot rage. The computer monitors started fading from blue to lava orange, to red. Sterling stopped what he was doing, a length of yellow wire in his hand, and looked at the monitors.

Diana took a deep breath and folded her hands on her lap and closed her eyes as Sterling affixed the last of the small electrodes to her forehead with a special kind of glue that had a funny smell, an odor rather like lilacs. After a few moments, several spaghetti-size primary-color wires streamed from her head, fell to the floor, and traced their way to the monitoring devices and computerized machines.

Diana opened her eyes and traced along the gray carpet, which moved in a clean line to the walls, painted a matte dark gray. In a corner was the couch she'd been on so many times these past many weeks, recounting her dreams to this . . . this *madman*.

He smiled at her now.

"Good," he said. "Let your anger flow. Open up completely."

"Do you think you'll really get away with this?" Diana asked in a thin high voice. She put her chin out, trying to look defiant. Trying to feel defiant, even as she heard Catherine humming, twisting the slim gold chain that hung loose around her neck.

"Please, Diana," Sterling said. "This is all a matter of perspective, isn't it? I am, as you see it, *trying to get away with something*, and you're the innocent victim. But that's your scenario.'' He went to his work station and readjusted the lights.

"And what's your scenario?" Diana asked, looking up at the indentations in the ceiling, which housed more lights, the white-golden beams of which crossed as they swept across the floor and became still. She felt too warm, and fingered the top button of her blue denim shirt.

"Ah, in my scenario, you're an ungrateful little monster who could just as easily be languishing in the filth of a mental institution, or in the basement of some crack house. Let's face it, Diana. That's where your sanity was taking you."

Diana shook her head. "You're wrong," Diana said. She glanced at Catherine, who closed her eyes, as if bored by this defiant confrontation.

Sterling frowned.

"Don't be foolish, Diana," he said. "I'm giving you a chance to strike back at the society that will never be able to understand you, that in fact *hates* you, Diana. Fears you. And what do you do? You sit there playing prisoner."

"No!" Diana shouted. "I don't want to get back at anybody, I just want to go home!" she started to rise from her chair. He stepped over and pushed her back down into it.

"Be still!" he shouted. "Make another move and I promise you, your friend David will pay for it." He squeezed her shoulder in his large grip. "You have a task ahead of you. A big task. How well you perform will determine your fate. And the fate of those you love, I might add."

Diana, despite herself, felt tears filling her eyes. They stood in her eyes, then burst and ran hotly down her cheeks.

She didn't see what choice she had but to follow him into this madness. All of her defenses seemed to be coming down now, and she felt a familiar wave building inside her head.

"And now it's time to gaze into the crystal ball, as it were," Sterling said.

Diana watched him, and saw the mad gleam in his eye, and the way he looked at Catherine, who kept her eyes closed, the slightest play of a smile on her lips.

What a cool one she was, Diana thought. And that bit

about a crystal ball. There was no crystal ball to gaze into. The crystal ball was the connection made between Catherine's mind and her own.

"Catherine, don't do this," Diana whispered.

Catherine cleared her throat. She looked at Sterling. "Ready when you are," she said to him in a sing-song voice. Then she looked at Diana and smiled wickedly.

"You don't know what you're doing," Diana said.

Catherine said angrily, "Will you pul-*lease* get over it, Diana?" She closed her eyes. "There's nothing you can do. You're as much a weakling now as you ever were. I can't believe we were actually *friends*."

"Catherine, stop. I'm begging you to stop."

Catherine said, in the voice of a ten-year-old, "Why don't you try and *make me*?"

Diana felt sweat building on her brow. She couldn't freeze Catherine out. It was impossible. And within seconds she felt Catherine's superior power, sensed a deep pressure in the top of her skull, and the presence of another mind mingling with her own.

"To Ice Rock," Sterling whispered, and his voice seemed to echo off the curving walls of the windowless room, a room like the bottom of an aquarium, liquid, shuddering, and vastly cold.

Blue watery shadows moved across the walls, and soon Diana was aware of a sort of vision, a picture coming into view. Yes, she could see actual light—a fuzzy whiteness.

"Send your eyes," he said. "Transport your senses."

Diana could feel it happening. It was as though her mind and Catherine's mind were two eyes in the same head, unifying, focussing one clear field of vision.

A whiteness, cold and clear, came to her. Other senses followed. She could hear singing, and raucous laughter. Feel the wet winter coldness. She could smell the whisky and the fresh winter scent of pine.

And in a matter of seconds, it was as though she was actually there, on Ice Rock, seeing through the eyes of the people assembled there, sensing everything they sensed.

Despite herself, Diana opened her mouth and gaped with wonder. The wave had penetrated into this army of revelers.

Looking up to the sky, she could see that a light snow had started to fall again, so that the scene before her resembled nothing so much as something from those Currier and Ives picture books her mother used to set around the house at Christmastime. A nineteenth century engraving come to life.

It was a truly dazzling sight, a scene of flowing whiteness, yet muted, as clouds closed in and yet another winter storm commenced. Catherine started to speak to her.

It's beautiful.

"Yes," Diana answered in her real voice, the voice attached to the body, miles away, in a dark room—not here, here in this brilliant snowswept present moment, as clear as no other she'd ever before dreamt of or imagined.

The people were singing. "Look," cried an old woman, "It's started to snow again!"

"Don't shove," someone cried.

"Billy, you're getting a bit close to the edge, dear. Come along back to your mother."

A man of about sixty nodded. "Yes'm," he mumbled, and strode through the crowd, which was now packed shoulder to shoulder. Most of the people had their arms linked together with their neighbors'.

The old town drunk, Corky Marshall, stood near the edge of the cliff. He tipped his bottle and let a length of amber booze spill over the sides.

"To the dearly departed!" he cried. And a hush fell over the crowd.

"Hear, hear!" cried another. A cheer broke out.

How strange, Diana thought.

Together, she and Catherine could move about the crowd, in and out of multiple sets of eyes at once, just as quickly as a fly darting from a table to a window. The vision of so many unified senses was focussed as one all-seeing sort of swooping camera. Diana felt it was like seeing a movie in which the camera is hung on a great overhead moving crane, except in this movie you could smell the bracing air and feel the snow beneath your feet— even feel the collective buzz brought on by the alcohol.

"Do you see her?" Sterling said, his voice close to them,

close to those human shells that sat in the windowless room at the clinic. "Come on!" he said. "Do you see Nessie Jasper?"

And in seconds they found her. She appeared before them, smile bright, chest heaving as she laughed, steam rising from her open mouth.

She tramped close to the edge, taking in the view.

"We can see her," Catherine said. "It's perfect. She's standing at the edge."

Sterling clapped his hands and rubbed them together. Diana's heart seemed to skip a few beats.

"It's time for the *mindsweep*," Sterling said. "Line them all up now, just as you did with the flamingos at the zoo."

As soon as he said it, it started to happen. Against her will, Diana could feel the glow of energy flowing into the minds of the throng upon Ice Rock. A hush fell over the crowd.

Just as the flamingos had done, a group of men on Ice Rock stood side by side, shoulder to shoulder. Diana recognized some of the women who stood near them. The "wives." The women smiled. They thought the men were about do some kind of dance. But now, with a pulse of thought from Catherine, the men pushed through the crowd, knocking several of the children down. An old woman in a black coat sprawled upon the ground, too. She cried out. Diana wanted to stop them, but she couldn't. Catherine had the upper hand. And the more Diana tried to fight it, it seemed, the greater hold Catherine had on the wave they both produced.

Children were crying. Other old-timers turned their heads to see what was the matter.

Now the possessed, blank-eyed men were rushing toward the edge. Sweeping some of the old-timers along with them.

"Hey!" Randy cried, angrily. They pushed to the edge where Nessie Jasper stood with Corky Marshall.

"*No!*" Diana cried out. She tried to leave this place, this suddenly hellish view of Ice Rock. Tried to disrupt the flow of what was happening. But she couldn't.

Nessie screamed. "Be careful, you drunken fools!"

A throng pushed toward the edge, and a quantity of powdery snow slipped over the side, raining down to the jagged rocks.

Both Diana and Catherine flinched, eyes closed. A flash registered on one of Sterling's video monitors.

Diana screamed. With every bit of strength she had she fought against what was happening. She tried to imagine the invisible wave splitting apart, and rushing about the minds of the women and children.

Catherine gasped.

Diana clenched her teeth. She told herself it didn't matter if she didn't know her own mind, or whether she could control or not control what she felt, or the kinds of thoughts that came endlessly into it. What mattered to her now was what she was going to *do*, perhaps even in defiance of her own strange nature. A nature that had for so long been a kind of enemy.

What she found, then, was a kind of whip. An angry whip she recognized as her own will. It was there. It had been growing stronger all this time, without her even knowing it.

She took hold of the wavelength and twisted with all her might.

The marching men, so close to the edge now, were suddenly met by yet another force—men, women, and children who tried to hold them back. Tried with the sudden help of Diana.

It was as though the people on Ice Rock had become at that moment warring zombies, their minds conflicted, their limbs entwined, forcing against one another. They were literally tied in a knot. In a tug-of-war with human bodies.

Diana, with eyes closed, could see the scene at Ice Rock just as clearly as if she were there herself. She could feel every straining muscle. Some of the people were close to the edge. A woman's green knit hat had fallen off her head, and it fell, spiralling to the rocks below. The woman, whose ears and nose were red, cried out, and tears streamed down her cheeks. She was pressed between two men, like a person trapped in a burning theater.

"I can't breathe!" she cried.

Diana knew now that her mind was almost one with

Catherine's, but that that double-mind was now in violent conflict with itself. Diana was using the power to turn inward, to reverse the impulse. Sweat poured down her face. Her eyes were closed, but all of a sudden she felt something burn into her wrist.

She opened her eyes and looked directly into Catherine's snarling face. Catherine's nails were digging into Diana's arms. Her white face shook, and beads of sweat flew from her nose and chin.

Catherine tried to speak, but all that came forth was a deep angry growl. She was fighting back, pushing the men closer and closer to the edge of Ice Rock.

Like the dreamer suddenly "awake" within the dream, Diana felt herself simultaneously in two places at once, with two perspectives. The mindsweep on Ice Rock held fast, in this frozen knot, pushing harder and harder against itself, nearly crushing those old-timers unlucky enough to be squeezed into the middle.

Diana felt Catherine digging her fingernails into her arm. She fought her arm free.

Sterling jumped up from his chair and picked up a long white towel. He stood behind Diana and pulled the towel around her arms, holding her fast.

"No!" he screamed. "You must concentrate! Complete the exercise."

The *exercise*! Diana felt a surge of strength, almost laughing at Sterling's euphemism. She struggled against the towel he bound her with.

"Catherine," Diana screamed hoarsely, "I know you killed the little girl. You stabbed Vaundra Austin to death, ten years ago!"

Diana could feel Catherine's rising fear.

Sterling sputtered, "Catherine, what have you told her?"

Catherine shook her head, confused, trying to hang on to her grasp at Ice Rock.

"Sterling told me your mind is like a shattered mirror, Catherine," Diana said. "And now you've let me in, among the shards of memory. You didn't expect me to go looking around in those dark places you've been afraid of all these years, did you?"

Catherine shuddered. "You haven't any right to look at my life!" Catherine said weakly.

"But I can't leave," Diana said. "You brought me here. I'm in your head right now! I can look anywhere I choose." Diana smiled and sweat rolled into her eyes, burning them. She didn't care. "You've never been more open and vulnerable than you are right now, Catherine!"

Catherine closed her eyes. Ice Rock did not leave their minds. It remained vividly before them. They hovered over the scene. People were screaming and crying, crushing together.

"Doctor!" Catherine screamed.

Sterling stepped back against the console. The computer screens were blinking now. His experiment had taken an unexpected turn.

"Catherine," he stammered. "Just concentrate. Don't let anything interfere with the wave!"

Diana saw the helpless faces of the people on Ice Rock. Within seconds they could go tumbling over the edge. She had to do something to stop it. She had to defeat Catherine.

It was then that Diana saw something . . . just the tiniest spark of a dim memory, long suppressed, now rising to the surface. Rising with Catherine's anguish.

Catherine felt it, too. Something deeply buried was stirring to life.

"No!" Catherine screamed.

But Diana had access to these memories now, too, like a cyber-thief who had broken into a harddrive of a vast computer, from miles away. And now she could rifle through the files.

One "file" in particular.

The darkest and most forbidding.

The act that had shattered the "mirror" of Catherine's young mind.

Sterling cursed, "What the fuck is going on?"

But he couldn't see into their minds. No one could. They were alone, together. And now Diana knew what she had to do.

Follow me, Catherine.

No! I can't! You have no right to look in there!

Look, Catherine! Open that dark door, and see!

The effect on their minds was like a split screen in a movie. Memory, with its sensory guide posts, almost overwhelmed the psychic present, the blinding whiteness of Ice Rock.

Here was light, the bright white daylight of Ice Rock, and here, too, was the deepest and blackest of nights, swimming beside it.

A dark night, long ago, long before the night of Vaundra's murder, but inextricably linked to it.

A dark bedroom. Clouds drifting over the moon.

A child old enough to stand in her crib . . . a baby . . . *Catherine.* The baby Catherine waving her sticky wet pacifier. Blue eyes watching, fear in them.

Theda, younger and slimmer, her perfume suffusing the room, so strong now that Diana could actually smell it.

Theda bending over the bed. Over her sleeping husband, Representative Newall Price. The man in the painting at Theda's house. The smell of liquor on his sleeping breath.

Catherine's father.

Theda withdrew the knife from her dark coat, the long blade reflecting moonlight. In a single furious motion she pulled it across Newall Price's white throat as he slept.

His eyes opened for just a single moment, bulged in terror, and then closed forever.

Diana's lips quivered, seeing this dim memory. She could barely watch, as memory spooled, clear as a video.

Catherine cried, pulling the electrodes from her head. Diana smelled smoke.

The dark memory was fading—fading to white, to the snow and the crisis at Ice Rock. But before the memory blipped away completely, Diana saw the child standing in her crib, watching her mother, eyes wide. Saw the red arc that gushed forcefully from Newall Price's neck. The stream of blood coursed into the crib, and into the eyes and mouth of the suddenly squalling child.

Smoke and the smell of electronic circuits frying filled the small laboratory. Diana looked at Catherine now. Catherine's face was pale, zombie-like. Tears traced down her cheeks. Her lips moved, but no words came out of her mouth.

"Stop this at once!" Sterling said, and he shook Catherine from behind.

He turned and slapped Diana's face, putting all of his weight into it. The blow snapped her head back, but she barely felt it. Felt only numbness. She tasted blood.

"Focus on the mindsweep! Push those peasant bastards off the fucking cliff! Push them all off if you have to, but get that Nessie Jasper, and do it now!"

Catherine trembled, and Diana could "see" why.

Back on Ice Rock, a new wave of panic had erupted.

Catherine cried out, as if seeing this disaster for the first time.

Diana could barely sense the cries of the townspeople over Catherine's sudden wailing in her ear. And if this wasn't enough, Diana now saw a strange woman come bounding onto Ice Rock, her face veiled in red. Beyond the circle of the mindsweep, she had not been affected by its trance-like power. The veiled woman moved freely about the crowd. In fact, she seemed to angrily stalk through the snow.

Who was this veiled woman? Diana wondered.

The crowd was still locked in a weird battle with itself, and the veiled woman looked as if she was trying to free them. She pushed and tried to unlock arms that were linked and smashed together in a kind of frozen death-lock.

"Help us!" a boy cried.

"I'm trying to," the woman said, her voice strangely familiar.

The woman wasn't successful. The people were packed together too closely. She moved close to the edge. Closer to Nessie Jasper.

Nessie was only a few feet from the edge. The veiled woman recklessly took hold of the man next to her, old Corky Marshall, and pulled his leg free. If she was really trying to help him, she was being extremely rough about it. She gave him a hard shove out of the way that might have been accidental.

Diana screamed. Corky was slipping to the side of the cliff. He cried out, sliding over the edge.

He dragged his hands through the snow, and at the very last second grasped a protruding root, and hung there, legs swinging. Clumps of snow fell off his wildly kicking boots and fell to the jagged rocks below.

Now all the people on Ice Rock were screaming. They were standing, half falling into one another, legs wrenched in pain. In a mass, they slipped a few inches toward the edge, like a car on a roller coaster, crawling toward the big plunge.

A collective gasp rose up from Ice Rock, over the snow-covered valley and rolling hills. The birds in the trees took flight.

One false move would send them all tumbling over the edge.

The root the old drunk hung on to cracked.

"Oh, my God, help me!" Corky shrieked.

Then the root cracked again and broke free. With a blood-curdling scream, the old man fell.

"You pushed him!" Nessie yelled at the veiled woman.

Nessie reached out and snatched the veil from the woman's face.

Everyone gasped.

"Theda!" Nessie cried.

They had all seen exactly what she had just done. The old-timers all recognized Theda.

Diana and Catherine recognized her now, too.

Theda's eyes widened. She took a deep breath and tried to push Nessie, and the people in the crowd screamed again.

At that moment, the door to the dark laboratory banged open. David ran inside, his rifle pointed at Sterling. He glanced at the crying, shaking young women, and gaped at them.

On Ice Rock, Theda, panicking, broke free from Nessie's grasp and started to run toward the tree-lined path.

No! Catherine screamed in her mind.

YOU CAN'T RUN ANYMORE!

Sterling raised his hands. "David," he said, trying to sound calm, but failing. "What is the meaning of this?"

''The meaning of it is, put your hands up in the air before I blow you away, Sterling,'' he shouted.

Catherine let go of her grip on the mindsweep, that fatal push toward the edge. Diana felt the release instantaneously. The tangled throng on Ice Rock fell to the ground on their backs, close to the cliff's edge, but not over it.

Diana felt Catherine redirecting the paralyzing power toward Theda, and Diana let her own thoughts swim in sync. *Stop!* Catherine commanded. Diana thought,
Stop, Theda!

And with that, Theda's feet froze to the ground, and she halted, kicking up snow in a sudden skid. She twisted her head around to look at the crowd, picking itself up. In seconds the entire population of old-timers was on its feet. Theda screamed, unable to move as the people came at her, fists raised, an angry collective cry roaring up out of them. They saw what she'd done to Corky, and what she had tried to do to Nessie. Fear of what had happened to them on Ice Rock today mingled with rage against Theda.

They pounced on Theda, pulling her hair, their fists flying, pounding on her head.

''Catherine!'' Theda cried out.

They were dragging her to the cliff's edge. The mindsweep was fading out . . . the wave was leaving Ice Rock.

In seconds, the vision disappeared entirely from Diana's mind.

''The bell!'' Diana cried.

Sterling darted toward the door. David fired his rifle.

The sound of the rifle made Diana's ears ring. The shot missed Sterling, and the bullet fired into the plaster wall, sending a large fissure racing up to the ceiling. White dust fell upon the black table.

Sterling pounced on David, pushing the rifle aside. The rifle fell to the floor, and David fell on top of it. Sterling dove on top of him, fighting for the weapon.

David felt Sterling's big fists pummelling his head. But he managed to break away, tearing at the lab coat Sterling always wore. The bell spilled out onto the floor and rolled. David lunged for it, tasting blood in his mouth.

Just as he clasped the bell in his hand, a shot rang out.

David felt a burn rip through what felt like bone in his chest. He stood upright, dazed.

Diana screamed. Sterling had the rifle in his hands, still aimed at David. Smoke curled out of the barrel.

David fell to the floor, shot, bleeding from the side. The bell fell from his open hand and rolled to Diana's foot. It didn't make a sound. The paper was still wadded up inside it.

Diana dove for the bell, electrodes popping from her head. When she had it in her hand she remembered that she had stuffed the piece of paper up inside the hollow of the bell. She put her finger inside the bell and tried to scrape the paper free.

The bell is a charm against evil. She remembered Serilda's words. But as she struggled with the bell she felt cold fingers closing around her neck. And a bite upon her back that hurt so bad she knew it was drawing blood.

She wrenched her body free of Catherine's grasping arms, and saw with horror that Catherine's eyes were like the mad eyes of a rabid animal.

"Give me that!" Catherine screamed. Diana kicked at her, and heard the boom of gunfire. Sterling had shot at her and missed, firing a hand-size hole into the outer wall. White winter light streamed through the gun-blasted hole. A few snowflakes alighted over Diana and Catherine.

"This is Vaundra's bell!" Diana gasped. "Do you recognize it? Did she have it with her the night you murdered her?"

Catherine leapt at Diana, struggling for the bell.

At last Diana freed the paper from the bell. Winter light swam across its polished brass surface. Catherine's nails dug into Diana's neck.

"No!" Catherine screamed. "It belonged to Vaundra! I remember it now! My mother took it into the woods and threw it away, where no one would ever find it! I remember! I remember it all now!" Now Catherine's hand closed around Diana's wrist, inches from the bell. Diana struggled to free her hand, which was being shaken violently.

The tiny bell rang out.

Its chime sounded small, crystalline. But it resonated

through time and space. A wave of pure energy seemed to pulse through the room. White light flashed. Catherine had at last arrived at her reckoning.

Miles away, Theda had been driven by the mob to the very cliff-edge of Ice Rock, her back to the resplendent white valley.

The mob came closer to her, Nessie out in front, eyes angry.

"No, you don't understand!" Theda cried. She took another step back.

"Killer!" someone cried.

Slowly, so slowly, arms flailing like a dancer's, Theda felt herself slipping backwards off the edge.

"No!" she cried, trying to recover her balance and her footing.

Nessie screamed, seeing what was happening.

Theda's jaw gaped open, and her eyes were like white suns, wide with terror.

She screamed, and fell backwards over the cliff into the frozen sunlight.

Back at the clinic, the walls of the small dark laboratory began to quake.

Diana looked up. The dark ceiling swayed, and the floor undulated. The glass in the aquariums trembled and cracked. Water, fish, colored sand, and breaking glass burst out and pooled on the floor.

Catherine, who still had her fingers wrapped tightly around Diana's neck, looked up, too. Catherine's blue eyes bulged with terror. Her lips parted and she grimaced, showing teeth. Her short blond hair was massed wildly about her face, and her hairline was traced with beads of sweat.

"No," Catherine whispered, and she winced.

"Catherine!" Sterling screamed, aiming the gun at the two of them. Catherine gave Diana a vicious shove, releasing her. Diana clutched at her burning neck and crashed into one of the computer consoles. A video monitor shattered at her back. Diana felt the tiny shards of glass spilling down the back of her shirt as she fell to the floor. Her hands were cut. She dropped the bell, which rolled away into the shadows. She looked up to see Sterling taking aim at her with the rifle.

"No!" Diana screamed. She held up her trembling, bleeding hands.

His finger began to close on the trigger.

But before he could fire the rifle, Catherine stepped in front of Diana. In the line of fire, Catherine spread her arms before Sterling. She was shaking her head, Diana saw, from behind.

"Get out of my way!" Sterling shouted at Catherine, and lowered the rifle barrel. "I'm going to kill her! She has ruined everything! Don't make me kill you both!"

Catherine reached out her hand. Sterling was only a few feet away from her.

"You're not going to shoot me," Catherine whispered. She laughed, her voice catching on her tears, and took a few more steps toward him.

"Stop!" Sterling screamed. He closed an eye to take aim again, raising the rifle. He aimed at her heart.

She closed in on him.

"Give me the rifle," Catherine said. Diana, still cowering on the floor amid pieces of broken glass, pulled her knees up to her chest, trying to make herself small. Catherine completely blocked her in shadow as she took slow, steady steps toward Sterling. The machinery all around Diana whined in distress.

"I'll kill you!" Sterling cried. "Stop, Catherine! Don't come any closer. I'm warning you." His hands trembled.

Now Catherine stood directly in front of the rifle. She walked right into it, bumping the barrel against her stomach.

She reached out and took hold of the barrel of the rifle, pushing it aside, but not releasing her grip on it. Diana could barely watch. Her heart pounded wildly. Sterling tried to wrench the rifle away. Catherine grasped it tightly, and now she pulled on it violently. They struggled over the weapon, both of them grasping, Catherine kicking at Sterling. Catherine moved tight inside.

The rifle went off. The blast was deafening. Diana held her hands over her ears.

The rifle had been pointing straight up. Now a shower of plaster and dust rained down from the blasted ceiling. Diana covered her head with her hands. She felt the cool dust spilling over her. Sterling, startled by the blast, lost his grip on the rifle. Catherine wrenched it away. Now Catherine pointed the weapon at Sterling, who fell backwards against the black inside wall.

"Get over there," she yelled, pointing with her chin at the dark black column in the center of the gloomy dream chamber. Hands in the air, he scrambled over there, keeping his back to the wall.

"Catherine, please," Sterling said.

"Shut up!" Catherine cried.

Catherine aimed the rifle at Diana.

Diana opened her mouth to scream, but couldn't. She raised up her hands, and she tried to turn her face away. But she had to look. Had to look into those fire-blue eyes again, perhaps for the last time.

Catherine put her finger on the trigger. Squinted, taking aim. Catherine's eyes were blue flames, pulsing, feeding on the mayhem.

Catherine abruptly turned, aiming away from Diana and at one of the long low banks of computerized instrumentation. She fired the rifle. In an explosive roar metal and circuitry were blasted flaming out of the wall. Gaping holes let in winter light.

Diana scrambled on her hands and knees to David, who lay on the floor near the entryway. Sparks and pieces of burning debris fell all around her in the gloom. David's hand was over his side, fingers red with his own blood. But he was breathing. He was alive.

Sterling saw Catherine aiming at one of the aquariums.

"No!" he cried. But before he could finish screaming, Catherine blasted the aquarium to white shards, spilling water and colored sand and gasping tropical fish over the floor.

Catherine started shooting wildly. She shot great holes into the outer wall with deafening blasts. Shafts of white light beamed through the holes, snowflakes drifting in them like shooting stars. Catherine shot up the expensive high-tech equipment as Sterling screamed and shook, his hands in his hair. A ceiling panel broke open and a mass of tangled, flaming red wires fell like a giant curtain, hanging near Diana and David and blocking the laboratory entryway with fire and smoke. Sterling ran frantically to a smoking black console near the shattered outer wall.

"My laboratory!" he shrieked. He tried to put out flames with his bare hands. He didn't see the expanding puddle of water from the aquariums. Water ran across the floor like a silent black wave to his feet.

Diana saw it all.

He must have been touching a live bare wire. The puddle engulfed his left foot. His right leg jolted upward in a kind of spastic fit, and shook. His hair crackled and stood on end. Electricity surged through him, green bolts shooting from the console into his fingers, and up from the floor through his smoldering wet oxford shoes. He screamed, his mouth gaping, as thick black smoke rolled out of his open lab coat.

Sterling crashed backwards into the melting black console. The hissing console exploded in a blinding shower-burst of white sparks, opening up more huge holes in the outer wall. Catherine fell to the floor in the blast, and at last let go of the rifle. Sterling lay dead, burning upon the floor, engulfed head to foot in flames.

Tiny gleaming fish flopped among shards of glass in puddles of water on the floor. Diana could see all their colors now, as full white daylight and a chill wind gusted in from the human-size gaping holes in the walls.

Diana coughed. Heavy black smoke was filling the lab, and the flames from the blasted electric circuit panels were roaring. A stench of burning acrylic fiber filled the air.

She pulled at David. She was certain they had only seconds to escape the spreading fire. It was hard to see through the smoke. Where was Catherine?

"We've got to get out of here!" Diana cried out. "Catherine, help me!"

Diana stood over David. Her eyes burned. Through rippling curtains of black smoke she saw Catherine, standing at a shattered inner wall, pulling at the plaster, trying to smash through, it seemed.

"Catherine," Diana cried. "We've got to get out of here! Catherine!"

Catherine seemed not to hear her. She was reaching into a large hole in the inner wall, her back to Diana.

There was no time to argue. Diana bent down behind David. She pushed him upward at the shoulders, and he groaned in pain. It didn't matter. She had to get him out of here. Stooping behind him, she leaned her chest hard up against his back and put her arms through his, grasping at his bloody chest. If only she could drag him across the floor and through the gaping hole in the outer wall, then she could pull him outside into the snow, to safety. It was getting darker inside the burning dream chamber. It was so hot Diana was drenched in sweat.

David was heavy, but she was stronger now. She had to use every new muscle. He would be proud of her. Walking backwards through broken glass and debris, hands locked together across David's chest, she dragged him across the floor toward the shattered outer wall. As they got closer to the outer wall, snowflakes fell on David's face and closed eyelids. So did drops of her sweat. Snow drifted and blew into this black burning room at the bombed-out outer wall. Only a few more feet, and they'd make it.

"Catherine!" Diana cried, breathless as she pulled David. The small of her back burned, her arms felt numb. The heat nearly seared her throat.

Catherine was still breaking off pieces of the inner wall, struggling. Her face was smudged black. She seemed not to hear Diana's cries.

David moaned.

Diana pulled him through the opening in the wall and out into the snow, which had drifted nearly waist-deep. Sinking deep into the snow, Diana pulled David clear of the building. She had to squint her eyes, it was so bright out here. And so very cold. She leaned over him, and touched his face. He opened his eyes. He looked at her, and he tried to smile. It was cold out here, but at last they could breathe. He coughed. She knelt down beside him in the snow and cradled his head in her lap.

From within the dream chamber there came another loud explosion. Diana had to turn her face away. She could feel the heat of fire on her face. Now she stood up and ran, sinking into the snow, slipping and climbing desperately to the entrance, where a veil of fire made it impossible to enter.

"Catherine!" Diana screamed. And through the flames she saw Catherine—saw in a kind of hazy heat-mirage, Catherine pulling something from a hole in the wall, some large, limp, rag-like human form. Through the flames the thing in Catherine's arms looked like a doll, very old, in ruinous disrepair.

"Catherine! Run!" Diana cried.

But Catherine could not hear her. Catherine looked only at the doll.

Diana realized with horror that the thing in Catherine's arms, which she cradled and held close to her now, as she sank to the floor, was not a doll. It was the corpse of Vaundra Austin, entombed these many years inside the walls of the clinic.

There was nothing Diana could do. The roar of the flames pounded in her ears. She could not get back inside to rescue Catherine. In a moment the room would be an incinerator. Diana cried out, seeing only two blood-red figures in the bloom of a raging fire. Catherine cradled the dead child in her arms, caressing it, stroking its ragged hair, speaking to it, and even, it appeared to Diana, singing softly to it.

They glowed red, like lava, like shapes of molten steel in a room of fire. The walls, floor, and ceiling rolled with roaring flames. Diana had to step back from the intense heat. She couldn't watch Catherine and Vaundra fusing together in this furnace. She couldn't listen to Catherine's screams of pain—screams that seemed to exist only in Diana's mind. For no voices could be heard above the din of the blaze. Diana's face felt so hot. She turned and bent over the snow, and she filled her hands. She held the cold snow to her face. She filled her mouth with it.

She rushed back to David, wading through the cold dead weight of the snow.

Crying now, Diana leaned over David, trying to shelter him as best she could from the cold. His eyes were closed again. She tried to listen to his breathing, put her ear up to his warm lips. She felt now that she would faint.

She lay her head down upon David's heaving chest. He was alive. He would live. She closed her eyes and felt herself slipping away.

At Ice Rock, most of the people had already fled from the cliff-top. But a few stood near the edge, silently looking over it. Jon stood next to Randy. Nessie Jasper looked over the edge, too, and she wearily shook her head.

It was very quiet here now. Snow was falling lightly from a stone-gray sky.

It wasn't easy to look, but Jon found he just couldn't look away. Far below them, sprawled upon her back, not too far from the facedown body of Corky Marshall, was the corpse of Theda Price.

Her red veil flapped silently about her face in the breeze. Snow had already collected in her hair. Her dead eyes stared upward at them, blank and unseeing.

Chapter Ten

The hospital room was like most others she'd seen. Sterile and white, bland blue curtains parted over the dark window, and the sound of the soft, steady pulse of a heart monitor.

David appeared to be sleeping, but when she approached the bed, he opened his eyes and smiled. His shoulders were bare and the army green blanket had fallen to reveal the white bandage that had been wrapped and rewrapped many times around his chest. A tiny hose was attached to his arm, and another had been inserted through his nose. She handed him the flowers, six white roses and some fern leaves and baby's breath in white tissue paper. Outside the window, night had just fallen over the snowbound town.

"When we get outta here . . ." he said, smelling the flowers. His voice was weak.

"Shhhhh," she said, putting her fingers over his lips. She unbuttoned the top of her borrowed dark rain coat and sat down gently at the end of the bed.

"Diana," he said, "don't you want to come with me?"

"My stepfather is coming to take me home tonight," she said. "The police notified my parents, and he's flying in." She looked at him sadly.

"But you don't want to go with him," David said. He closed his eyes, wincing from the pain. "If only I could . . ."

"You need to get better," she said softly.

"We could really run away together, you and me . . . go

wherever we wanted to.'' He looked at her earnestly now. ''I want us to be together. I want that more than I want anything. I love you, Diana.''

She put her hand on his warm arm. ''You're going to be a great dancer some day. But not unless you give yourself time to heal. I wish I could stay and take care of you until you're back on your feet, but don't you see, I can't. I'm going home to Chicago. In just a few hours.''

Tears filled his eyes.

''But, Diana,'' he said, his voice cracking, ''when will I see you, when will be together?''

She looked at the window, at the flowers. Anywhere but at him.

''Maybe someday.''

He wiped his eyes with his fingers.

''No more somedays, Diana,'' he said. ''Let's do what we want to do right now. The doctor said I could be out of here in a week.''

''I have to leave. . . . Now,'' she said, standing. And saying it, she felt it. Felt the urgency wash over her. She looked at her watch. Then she gently bent toward him. She could see he wanted to say more, but what was there he could possibly say now? She kissed his mouth.

She turned to go. She walked to the door.

''Diana,'' he called. But she didn't turn back around. The door closed slowly on its hinge behind her, and she could still hear him calling out for her.

''Diana!'' he cried.

Standing in front of the closed door, she looked askance, and took a deep breath.

She saw the policewoman who'd brought her here. A stocky woman of about fifty, with short brown permed hair and a bulky blue cop's uniform and winter jacket, standard issue. Seated in a folding chair and looking at a magazine.

''I have to use the bathroom,'' she said to her.

The cop looked up from her magazine, then at her watch.

''Try and hurry a little,'' the cop said. ''We have a hell of a lotta paper work to do before we turn you back over to your father.''

''*Step*father,'' she said.

"Yeah, yeah . . . let's move it."

She nodded, sniffing a little. The cop shifted on her chair. "The bathroom's over there," the cop said, and pointed. Then looked back down at the magazine article she'd been reading in the *National Geographic*. An illustrated story about sharks.

She walked to the bathroom door. She pushed the door open and stopped. Then she looked over her shoulder. The cop did not look up from her magazine.

As she rounded the corner toward the exit stairs, the bathroom door slowly closed, a soft, gentle *sssss*, followed by a wooden thud.

She opened the exit door quietly, unseen. Jon, black cap pulled down to his eyebrows, grinned at her, standing near the bottom step.

"Car's running," he said. He pulled off his white jacket. Beneath it was his winter coat. He let the white jacket fall to the floor.

"Then let's hurry," she whispered, coming down the stairs to him.

He reached out with his gloved hands and pulled her close. He kissed her mouth. She kissed him back, hard, straining against him. Then she looked into his eyes.

He could take her anywhere she needed to go. Far from that miserable stepfather, who even now was speeding north in a private airplane, crossing over the moon.

"We'll never see this place again," Jon said. He smiled, red whiskers spreading on his mouth. "I emptied out my savings account, just like you said."

He turned, holding her hand, leading her down to the exit and into the night, where the warm idling car was waiting.

Any place at all—any place she wanted to go.

"I love you," he whispered, and beamed brightly at her. She shuddered.

No, she would never see this place again with her own eyes. But she trembled, following Jon, holding his hand, feeling the deep cold of the night and the snow. Because she knew, even as she was escaping, that every moment she had spent in this shadowy place resided quietly in a black chamber within her. And she knew what waited for her in her dreams, and in her nightmares, in the dark. Catherine was already there.

Joanna Carr awakens in a hospital after six months in a catatonic state, only to be told that her beloved husband, David, has been brutally murdered, and police are still searching for the killer. Grief-stricken and confused, she flees to the safety of the country home they once shared to try to piece together the crime—and her life. But Joanna knows that something is dreadfully wrong—and that the nightmare is just beginning...

MEG O'BRIEN

I'LL LOVE YOU TILL I DIE

A WOMAN'S DESPERATE SEARCH FOR THE TRUTH PLUNGES HER INTO A WEB OF DECEPTION, DESIRE, AND DANGEROUS OBSESSION.

I'LL LOVE YOU TILL I DIE
Meg O'Brien
_____95586-3 $4.99 U.S./$5.99 Can.

Seventeen-year-old Emily Jordan ran with the wrong crowd in San Francisco—and got into trouble with the law. Now she's been banished to tiny Blackburn County, Wisconsin to perform community service at the Hamilton Home for the Aged.

But Emily is desperately afraid. Something is dreadfully wrong at the Hamilton Home and something sinister hangs over Blackburn County. The elderly residents whisper they are being held prisoner, and there are horrifying tales of young girls vanishing without a trace. Are these just the ramblings of old people...or the seeds of a chilling conspiracy?

Soon, Emily will come to know the strange powers that are her gift—powers that will draw her deeper into the wicked web of destruction that has haunted Blackburn County for centuries...and bring her face-to-face with the most terrifying kind of evil.

BRIAN RIESELMAN
WHERE DARKNESS SLEEPS